Somebody Wants to
Kill Me

Also by Richard Rees

The Illuminati Conspiracy

The Reikel Conspiracy

Twice Upon A Thanksgiving

Dear Abigail

Somebody Wants to Kill Me

RICHARD REES

ISBN: 978-1-0912194-2-7

Front cover design: Paul Simpson, www.artychoke.com

Cover illustration: Elfyn Jones RCA

Book design: Dean Fetzer, www.gunboss.com

To Elfyn, my brother and pal, who illustrated this book's cover.

-one-

-1-

A gray day in northern Wisconsin. Karen Archer was driving to see her mother and father. She loved her mother. Hated her father.

Her silver BMW coupe emerged from the darkness of the forest, tall white pines bordering a narrow twisting country road, and the familiar tall black-rusting ironwork gates came into view, padlocked as always, and past them the driveway, a wide dirt track winding through overgrown shrubbery.

She parked in front of the gates, swung her legs out, changed out of flat shoes into stilettos and stood up. Slim, about five six tall, attractive rather than pretty, shoulder length tawny hair, wearing what was clearly a new, ermine collared, white designer coat to knee length, the equally new stilettos accentuated her shapely legs. She took a spray of flowers from the BMW, locked it, and headed along the stony track for the gate, but teetered on her heels. In a pique, she aimed the key at the BMW, replaced the stilettos with the flats, hurled the heels into the car, and relocked it.

Pocketing the keys, she creaked open a side-gate set into the main gates. Perched on it was a solitary raven with coal-black feathers – the size of a red-tailed hawk. It croaked, flapped its wings in protest, then took flight. Still croaking, it circled as though to attack her before making for a ring of trees that visibly encircled a large clearing hidden from view.

She headed down the dirt track, winterberry and reed canary grass tendrils impeding her and whipping back at her as she brushed her way through them, as if stretching out to entangle her in their grip, the branches of rampant birches and willows forming an intertwined vault above her head, nature gone wild, creating a choked wilderness, until finally she emerged on to the weedy and untended grassy edge of the clearing.

She paused and surveyed the cemetery.

Centuries old, formed in a shallow hollow encircled by a natural embankment crested by trees, white oak predominating, it was dotted with rough wooden crosses rotting with age, and ancient headstones, granite gray in keeping with the dark sky above, some plain, others surmounted by angels with outstretched wings, and gargoyles with twisted faces and protruding eyes, most of the stones tilted at perilous angles to the black earth below them, holed and cracked as if the fossilized skeletons buried beneath it were slowly but surely digging their way to the surface.

She shivered and pulled her fur collar higher around her neck.

In the center of the cemetery an oak tree, dead and stripped of its bark, was silhouetted stark against the dark sky, black ravens perched on its white branches, strangely, ominously silent, with only an occasional croak breaking the silence. A thick branch, stretched out low and parallel to the ground, had given the tree its name, "The Hanging Tree", dated to when, centuries back in time, French Jesuit missionary priests had drugged five Ojibwas braves and hung them by the wrists from the branch in retribution for their local tribe refusing to convert to Christianity. Their backs then scourged to the bone, they were left there dangling, their red, raw flesh eaten by scavenging birds while they were still alive, until, with no sinews to hold them together, their skeletons fell to the ground and were buried by their tribe in a circle around the tree. Cursed by their shaman, from that day on the tree had slowly died, and ravens, revered by the tribe as their spiritual bird, had since perched on it, guardians of the burial ground, driving away the smaller crows.

In retaliation, the priests were buried alive, standing up to their necks in the same earth then scalped and left to die. It was summer, the sun was hot on their bleeding heads stripped of skin and hair, and the Ojibwas sat cross-legged in front of them and impassively watched them fry to death.

The braves and the priests were the first to be buried in the hollow, but from then on, others were interred there over the centuries, serving the nearby outpost of Ravensburg and the sparsely populated country for forty miles and more in all directions – fur trappers, early settlers, and plain good-for-nothing miscreants lynched from the same branch, whose spirits, it was said, roamed the burial ground from midnight to dawn, crying out for vengeance. Neglected for years now, the only time to visit the graveyard was at midday when the light was at its best, before creeping shadows began to once more enfold the silent hollow in their dark embrace.

Karen shivered again and pulled her fur collar higher.

Hurrying between the ever-spreading brambles and the graves, only a few with flowers and all withered, telling it was months since anyone had last visited here, she reached a black marble headstone that stood out among the other granite stones and crosses surrounding it. Its earth had not long past been dug up and was still mounded, not yet sunk.

The headstone's gold lettering read:

ELIZABETH RYAN

AGED 37

WILLIAM RYAN

AGED 53

Placing the flowers on the black marble base below the headstone, Karen caressed the name "Elizabeth Ryan", gold letters faded now after fifteen years of weather-beating.

'I miss you Mom. I'll bring Paul with me next time I come.' She affected an air of casualness. '*Paul?* He's my new husband.' Exhilaration replaced it. 'Yes, big surprise, Mom, I'm married now – *Mrs.* Karen *Archer* – and want you to meet him.'

Her gaze shifted to "William Ryan". His gold letters were recent. 'And for you to meet him, too, Father.' Her tone was now bitter. 'Knowing how much you'd hate the thought of me having a man, someone who lets me be my own person, for the very first time in my life.'

She addressed her mother again, as if sharing a confidence with her. 'Fate, Mom, it couldn't have come at a better time. He was going to change his will – leave most of his money to Madison University, where he wouldn't even let me attend, making me stay at home and do my art course online. What's more, scholarships in his name, would you believe: The William Ryan Memorial Fund in economics, just because he was lucky enough with his stock market gambles to think he was an ace at finance, leaving me only a fraction of his money.'

She scooped up some mud in her left hand and rubbed it in William Ryan's gold engraved name. 'But death intervened…didn't it, Daddy dear? And it all came to me anyway.'

She paused, as if letting her father dwell on it, thinking this was the way Shylock must have felt when his daughter Jessica – her favorite heroine, in *Merchant of Venice*, her favorite play in high school – had finally defied his domination over her and eloped with Lorenzo, particularly loving the part when Jessica threw her father's casket of jewels down to her lover waiting below her window, and stuffing her pockets with Shylock's gold.

Jessica sort of mirrored herself in a way. True, it had necessitated her father dying for her to get his money, nor had she flown off with Paul to Positano until months later, but now she was here at his graveside, twisting the proverbial knife into him, it amounted to the same thing, surely. And getting great satisfaction out of it, despite him being earth cold.

Scraping the mud remaining on her left hand across his lettering again, she knelt, arranged the flowers in a brass-gold rose, then stood and gave a half-twirl for her mother to admire her new clothes. 'This is the new me, Mom. The coat's Italian. A Gucci. Paul chose it. It's how he likes me to dress. Chic, classy, in the very latest styles…

'I'm no longer your little girl, Daddy, all dowdy. After years of the shoes you made me wear, I wear stilettos. How you would have hated that.'

She returned to her mother. 'But to tell you how I met Paul, Mom. I was taking Sue with me on a vacation, to start making up to her for what Father did to Uncle John. We looked online – sorry, I should have explained this when telling you about my art course, it's jargon for searching things on a computer, not just at home but worldwide – and decided on Positano, Italy, on the Amalfi coast, where the film stars go – it's beautiful there, Mom, the very opposite of here, you'd love it – stopping in Chicago to take in some shows before flying out. We stayed at the Thompson Hotel–'

She broke off, spoke witheringly to William Ryan. 'The best hotel in Chicago, Father, where you never stayed, not willing to pay more than your cheap three star prices.'

She let this sink in, then continued talking to her mother. 'On our very first day there, Mom, Sue took me to a beauty parlor to be hair-styled, and manicured, and made-up – eyebrows, eye-shadow, lip-gloss, the lot – and shown how to do it myself. And in the afternoon, she took me shopping for new clothes for my very first show that same evening, at the Cadillac Palace Theatre – only to find myself sitting next to Paul. Fate again. To use an old cliché, it was love at first sight.

'Did you hear that Daddy?' she drew out her words, stressing each one '…and married but three days later.' She glanced at her new Cartier gold watch. 'I only wish I had the time to tell you just how wonderful Paul is, but I promised I'd be back to him soon.'

A black truck, black windows, it looks like an old Jeep, tops the eastern rim of the embankment and stops hidden in the trees. The driver cuts the engine. In the resulting silence, he looks down on Karen as she rearranges the flowers.

A butterfly settles on the driver's tinted window. Orange wings ringed with black and spotted white, it's clearly a Monarch, king of butterflies. Even more, with a wing span that looks as if it exceeds four inches, this is a king amongst kings, extraordinarily beautiful, taking a rest before continuing its late migratory flight south before the winter.

The driver eases down his window. The Monarch flies in, seeking the warmth inside the cab, and settles on the dashboard. A black dashboard, pristinely clean and tidy, not the minutest speck of dust or a scrap of paper. Removing a tight black leather glove, the driver places the first finger of his other gloved hand on the Monarch's body, pinning it down, pulls off its four wings, slowly, one by one, then its four legs, its two antennae, enjoying inflicting pain on the butterfly, then lifts off his first finger and watches its body writhe as it slowly dies.

Karen caressed her mother's name. 'But to finish off what I was saying, Mom, Susan insisted on Paul taking her place, and straight after the wedding she drove back home. But we'd need a car for when we got back, so I bought Paul a new Lexus SUV as a wedding present before we flew out, and left it at O'Hare to pick up when we got back.'

Finding a rock she scraped it across William Ryan's muddied gold inscription, leaving gouge marks in the shiny black marble underneath. 'It was fifty…thousand…dollars, *Daddy,* from that Bank of America savings account you'd never touch. How does that make you feel down there?'

She returned to her mother. 'I wanted to stay in Italy, Mom. Now I've got my diploma, I want to paint, and the light on the Amalfi coast is perfect. But Paul has given up his acting career and is writing a novel, and said he'd prefer the seclusion of Ravensburg—'

She broke off, repeated her mother's question, 'What does Paul look like?'

'Well…' she hesitated before answering it, 'I suppose he slightly resembles Father. Tall, ten years older than me, and rugged. But that's where the comparison ends,' she rushed. 'He's better looking and doesn't dominate me, and loves me just for myself. A man I can depend on…'

'But you would hate him, Father,' she again scraped William Ryan's inscription. 'He'd be a challenge to you. If only you knew how liberating that feels. I'm no longer your little girl, I'm a fulfilled woman, and getting real pleasure – at long last – in anything I can do to upset you. Even in death…' Her voice tailed off as she remembered.

Beneath her shining black, one-strap sandaled feet and knee length white socks, the fresh mounded grave opens up. Wearing a black dress with a black lace collar – and the other few mourners long gone – she's twelve years old again, standing alone with tears streaming down her face, in the gray tomb-stoned cemetery alongside thirty-eight year old William Ryan, a rugged man, some six foot tall, looking down at her mother's coffin. The brass coffin plate reads:

ELIZABETH RYAN
AGED 37

'There will never be anyone else for me, Karen.' Her father's voice is gravelly, his expression emotionless. Behind him, distant thunder rolls, lightning flashes, silhouetting him against the sky. 'And there was never anyone else but me for your mother. My prayer for you is that you will one day have what we had. A marriage built on mutual respect, not on empty sentiment.' Ryan turns her to face him, grips her shoulders. 'Physical love is a gift, Karen, to be shared only between a husband and wife, and not to be indulged in on a whim. Promise me. Promise me.'

He turns her to look down at the coffin. Pours earth into her hand, demands of her. 'Swear it, Karen. Swear it on your mother's body. Pour the earth.'

Frightened, Karen sprinkles the earth on to the coffin. 'I swear it, Father. I swear it.'

Karen's mind came back to now, the grave returned. 'But that's not why you made me swear it, was it, Daddy? You wanted me all to yourself. And not your little girl any more–'

Her voice broke and she returned to her mother. 'Poor you, Mom, married to *him*. It's no wonder you didn't live long. And now having to have him with you for all eternity! That would be Hell. Yes, I know I should have had him cremated and scattered. But then, you must understand, he would have blown away, dispersed by the wind, and I would have had nowhere to come to and talk to him. To tell him how much I hate him. Hate him.'

He puts his black leather driving glove back on and returns his gaze to Karen as she caresses her mother's name again before she leaves. He whispers at her in a voice cold with menace.

'Say your last goodbyes to them – Karen *Ryan*.' He glances at his gold Rolex watch, he loved gold. 'And add, "See you soon".'

Karen rose to her feet. An instinct made her turn her head. She saw the truck looking down on her. Black. Ominous. Its headlights came on, like eyes glaring at her, accentuating the dark day and seeming to silhouette the gray tombstones surrounding her, making it seem that the gargoyles and angels were closing in on her, as if their spread wings were stretching out to reach and envelop her, and keep her bound in their granite grip.

Suddenly frightened, she spun from the grave and hurried away, half running as she weaved her way between the threatening gray stones to reach the security of her car outside the black gates, the tops of their railings showing above the thick undergrowth choking the dirt track, making them look to her now like prison gates, fencing her inside the hollowed burial ground.

She began to run for them. The truck seemed to swivel as if on a turntable, its shining, staring eyes following her. Menacing. Its engine revved to a roar as its driver flattened and lifted his foot off the gas pedal, then flattened and lifted it again. Panicking now, she forced her way through the tendrils stretching out to hold her back, the brambles tore at her coat.

As if sensing her panic, the black ravens perched on The Hanging Tree swooped down on her, their raucous croaking blending in with roaring of the truck, their sharp claws brushing her hair as they dived in low over her head. She shielded herself with her arms. A raven swooped at her and pecked her wrist, drawing blood. She flayed at it, beating it off, and reached the inset gate. Struggling through it, she dug the car key out of her pocket and unlocked the door. Fighting off another raven, she scrambled inside her coupe and slammed the door shut on it.

Croaking in victory now, the ravens flew away, back to The Hanging Tree, and re-perched on its white branches, silent again, the hollowed cemetery returned to their keeping.

Ignoring her bloodied wrist, and the red drops from it spattered on her white coat sleeve, she feverishly inserted her key into the ignition and glanced at the embankment.

The black truck was gone.

She started her engine. Throttling it, she did a screeching U-turn into the narrow country road and sped off the way she had come.

Getting the hell away from there and back home to Paul.

-2-

White pines towering over her on both sides of the road, Karen entered the first corner too fast, hit her brakes and her BMW slewed into it, almost mounting a grassy bank.

With a squeal of her tires she stopped, took a deep breath to calm herself, stretched for a CD, inserted it in the player and listened to Beethoven's *Moonlight Sonata*, feeling her tension ease as its relaxing music took her back to Positano and lying with Paul on the beach in the late evening, hearing the waves break gently on the shore, and a full moon hanging over them in the dark blue sky above, its reflection mirrored on the clear waters of the Mediterranean, and behind them gaily colored villas descending a rocky hillside in tiers to the azure, sun-glistening waters below, so much the opposite of gray, overcast Ravensburg, it was hard to believe she was there but days ago.

She checked her wrist. It was still bleeding. Getting a small handkerchief from her pocket, she pressed it to the cut, cursing the raven that pecked her, and almost crying as she examined the red drops on the sleeve of her new white coat. Her beautiful Gucci! $8,000! Ruined!

She switched Beethoven off.

If she could get hold of that raven, she'd wring its scrawny neck. And that of the Jeep driver who had caused her to panic – hiding behind its black windshield, switching on his headlights, its beams cutting into the darkened cemetery, illuminating her, scaring her half to death. That could only have been deliberate. But why? Why?

Under her handkerchief the cut was throbbing. What if she got blood poisoning? Or rabies?

Could she *get* rabies from a bird cut? Did she need a tetanus shot? It was years since her last one and the nearest hospital was all of forty twisting miles away. What about old Doc Willowby, who'd withdrawn from the world ten years ago to live a hermit's existence in a shack deep in the woods, hanging over a stream and small falls? The juices he extracted from his antibacterial leaves could save Paul and her the journey…

No, the track to Doc's place was over seven miles away. The best thing to do was to get back to Paul and see what he advised. And there was still the Jeep…

What if it suddenly reappeared?

Peering at the dark forest surrounding her, getting to feel more and more frightened the more she thought about its ominous all-over blackness, she stamped her foot on the gas pedal, spinning her wheels, then shot away from the side of the road and around the corner into a short straight.

Up ahead of her, hiding in trees, was the Jeep.

Instinctively, she flattened her gas pedal almost to the floor. The Jeep's headlights came on and again like glaring eyes, seemed to follow her as she sped past. Glancing back in her rear mirror as she entered the next corner, she saw it exit the trees and come after her.

Sliding into the corner too fast again, she managed to straighten out, and looked once more in her mirror and saw the black Jeep appear in it, its driver smoothly rounding the bend, in control of his truck, catching her up, his headlights full on.

Oh, God, oh, God, why was he chasing her? What did he want with her? And why her? As for the truck, there was something evil about it. Its blackness. Its headlights, fixed hypnotic on her in her mirror. She forced herself to look away and saw another bend rushing up at her.

Again she entered it too fast, her car whiplashing as she exited it. Managing to correct it she checked in her mirror. The Jeep driver ironed the corner, continuing to close up on her. Another two short straights and two bends sped by, and as they exited the second he was right on her tail.

He rammed her.

She screamed, almost losing control of her car as it snaked down the straight.

He rammed her again, harder, jolting her, her seat belt cut into her shoulder, but this time she managed to keep her grip on the steering wheel as they entered the next bend, not quite so severe. Her more powerful engine opened up a slight gap, but ahead of them was an S-bend. Coming out of it the Jeep would be back on her tail, ramming her again, either trying to force her to crash or getting a sadistic pleasuring in terrorizing her. If the latter, the sonofabitch was succeeding. Her heart was pounding, the palms of her hands gripping the wheel were wet with sweat.

Paul, oh, Paul, why didn't I bring you with me?

'Call home,' she yelled at her car's computer screen.

The dial tone was immediately answered, thank God!

'Paul Archer.'

'Paul!' she screamed at the screen.

'Karen, what's wrong?' Paul cut across her, responding to her panic, his deep voice urgent yet reassuring, even over a phone connection, and more than two miles away from her.

'I'm being chased—'

'Chased? What do you mean?'

'By a black truck. With black windows.'

Glancing in her mirror as she neared the S-bend, she saw for the first time that the Jeep had no front license plate. Added to its blackness – not a sliver of chrome – and its all black windows that made it even more evil-looking.

'It's got no license plates!'

Entering the S-bend at speed, she didn't hear Paul's reply. Skidding, slithering, she managed to get through it, but as she exited into the next short straight, the Jeep was back behind her.

It rammed her again.

'It's ramming me!' she screamed to Paul.

'Pull away,' Paul shouted back. 'Your BM's faster than a truck.'

She accelerated, somehow keeping control of her sliding coupe around another bend, but lost speed snaking out of it into a long straight.

The Jeep overtook her and drove alongside her.

Up ahead she saw Carvers Gulch on her side of the road. The Jeep angled in at her, its side pressing against hers, forcing her toward its almost sheer descent, to send her over the edge and plunging down to her death on to the rocks below. Through the Jeep's black windows she could *feel* the driver's eyes fixed menacingly on her, *feel* him getting actual pleasure at the anticipation of her car flying out of control over the side, and the mangled wreck that in seconds would be her car, a metal coffin with her body crushed inside it.

'He's forcing me down Carvers Gulch,' she shrieked, stamping her foot down on her brake pedal. Her wheels locked and her car slid inexorably across the road toward the gully.

'Oh, God, I'm going over the edge.'

Sitting before an open laptop, its screen blank, on an otherwise clear desk in William Ryan's old study, holding an old fashioned corded phone to his ear, and a portrait of Ryan looking down at him, stern of face, from the wall above, Paul Archer heard Karen scream her last words. 'Oh, God, I'm going over the edge.' It was too late to shout back, whatever was going to happen to her was inevitable, no words of his could save her now.

He listened to the screech of locked wheels coming over the phone line, followed by silence. Then came Karen's voice. 'My brakes held but with a wheel over the edge. I daren't move in case I start to slide.'

'Damn!' Paul swore. A rugged man, just over six feet, good-looking rather than handsome, wearing jeans and denim shirt, fashion brands not Levis, 'What about the Jeep?' he demanded.

'It went past me 'round the next bend. He tried to kill me, Paul,' she was almost crying. 'He tried to kill me—' She broke off and screamed. 'Oh, God, he's coming back!'

Paul jammed the phone to his ear, interpreting the sounds as best as he could as he listened to what was happening to Karen at this very same moment.

With mounting horror, Karen watched the black Jeep come nearer and nearer, aiming for her, the driver slowing down as though savoring the moment of impact before sending her to her death.

But with a front wheel hanging over the gulch – if she moved that could happen anyway.

Her engine was still idling. Taking her foot off the brake she slammed the gas pedal, her rear wheels sprayed grit as they fought to grip, then the BMW shot forward cutting across the front of the Jeep as it angled in at her. Its front fender clipped her rear one, the BMW swerved toward an embankment on the other side of the road that, if it drove into it, would bring it to a juddering halt. Desperately spinning the steering wheel, Karen controlled it and raced for the bend.

Glancing in her rear mirror as she entered it, she saw the black Jeep make a U-turn and come after her.

Oh, God! Oh, God!

She exited the bend into a longer stretch of road. With her bigger engine, she could surely now open enough of a gap to keep him behind her until she reached home and Paul, and she would safe.

She looked again in her mirror. The Jeep was catching up on her.

Fuck! Fuck! Fuck! Whoever the sonofabitch was, he must have a supercharged engine under his hood.

'He's coming after me again,' she screamed at her car phone.

'Lock your doors,' Paul yelled back.

Fearfully, she locked them.

Sam King sat in his parked white Ford Fusion by the side of the road. A silver BMW coupe flashed past him. He caught a glimpse of the young woman driver. Shoulder length tawny hair, she glanced desperately at him as she went by. Close on her tail was an old Jeep Wrangler, all over black, and black windows raised, hiding the driver.

Sam, a Chicago cop, detective, Organized Crime, taking a solitary vacation in a cabin in nearby Ravensburg, seeking its isolation to be alone with his thoughts, switched on his engine. About forty years old, lean, wearing a dark blue shirt under a dark blue sleeveless padded jacket, dark blue slacks, he eased from the side of the road and drove off in pursuit.

Glancing again in her mirror, Karen saw the white car in the near distance, slowly catching up on the Jeep, and breathed a sigh of relief that its driver had realized her plight and come after them.

'Thank God,' she yelled at her phone. 'Another car's coming up behind us.'

'How far are you from home?' Paul's tense voice told her how uptight he was.

'About a mile. Approaching Ravens Pond—'

The Jeep rammed her coupe, jerking her so hard her seat belt dug into her again and cut off the rest of her reply. Recovering, she screamed again at her phone. 'He's still ramming me, trying to make me crash. Help me, Paul,' she pleaded. 'What do I do now?'

In his study, the phone lay on the desk where Paul had dropped it, the line still open. From it came Karen's voice, 'Help me, Paul. What do I do now?'

The study window overlooked a country road. Looking left, a front wing of the house jutted out, clapboard, substantial, showing that the whole was large. Once painted white, its freshness was long gone, telling that William Ryan, although wealthy when he was alive, was also thrifty, clearly not believing in any needless expenditure.

A dark blue SUV shot out of the dirt driveway beyond the front wing of the house, and sped off down the road as Paul burnt his tires to get to Ravens Pond.

In his rear mirror, the Jeep driver saw a white car closing up on him, then up ahead spied a sharp bend bordered by a coppice, thick trunked fir trees interspersed with slender saplings. I couldn't have wished for a better spot, he malignly gloated. I'll angle in on her, clip her rear fender and send her crashing into them – and speed off, leaving it for the driver behind to stop and try to render her aid. Except that try was the operative word. With more firs than saplings, the odds were more than stacked in his favor that she would slide out of control into one of them – head-on if the gods of retribution were looking down at them – but even if it wasn't head-on, at that speed there was no way she could survive such a crash.

Karen Ryan would be dead and he will have succeeded.

Entering the corner, Karen saw the Jeep in her rear mirror pulling out and angling in on her.

'Paul, Paul,' she screamed at her screen phone. But again Paul failed to reply.

At that same moment a truck trundled around the corner toward her. Instinctively braking to avoid it, she skidded out of control into the coppice.

The Jeep driver locked his wheels, saw he was sliding straight at a fir tree, took his foot off the brake pedal as he fought to control the Jeep, and entered the coppice at speed behind the BMW.

The driver of the truck, a vintage Dodge Ram, swerved to avoid the silver coupe and crashed into woods on the opposite side of the road, straight into the trunk of an oak tree.

Plowing through the coppice, flattening saplings but miraculously missing any fir trees, Karen came to a halt stuck in thick mud on the edge of Ravens Pond. Dark. Forbidding.

Behind her the Jeep hit a rise and flew over her coupe into the pool. For a moment it floated, then it started to sink. Its black door handle jerked up and down on the outside as the driver tried desperately to open it from inside.

'No,' Karen screeched at it, 'drown, you bastard, drown.'

She watched the door fail to open and the Jeep sink ever lower, but then his window started to roll down. Realizing he might yet crawl out of the cab and escape, she hammered on her steering wheel in rage, but then saw the window stop with a gap but inches wide. Gloved hands gripped it to force it down, but the water seeped in through the gap and the Jeep sank below the surface.

Even as she exhilarated in the certain torment of his last drowning moments, her BMW started to slowly slide through the mud toward the dark pool. Local folklore had it that Ravens Pond was bottomless.

'Paul,' she shrieked. 'Paul, where are you?'

Unclipping her safety belt, she reached to unlock her door. An agonizing pain shot through her back. She couldn't move. She screamed as, inch by slow inch, her BMW slid nearer the pool.

A crow landed on her hood. It was entirely black, shiny feathers, legs, talons and bill, even its eyes were black. A bird so black was said to signify death. Karen screamed again. The crow cawed.

And continued to caw the more she screamed.

Sam saw the Jeep lose control and follow the silver coupe into the coppice.

Slamming on his brakes, his car went into a sliding U-turn, backwards into the stand of trees. It hit a fir, his side on, and bounced off.

Dazed, Sam looked into his rear mirror and saw the Jeep sink below the surface of the pond, and the BMW slowly sliding toward it. On its hood, peering into the coupe through its windshield was a black crow. It seemed to Sam to be cawing.

A dark blue SUV braked to a stop alongside his Fusion as if out of nowhere. Sam shook his head, trying to clear it, but was only dimly aware of the driver leaping from it and running for the pond, yelling at the BMW as it slid slowly into its waters.

Reaching the pool, the driver hurriedly kicked off his shoes and dived in.

Only the upper part of the BMW was now above the surface of the pond, water was creeping up inside it and over the young woman's shoulders, leaving just her face and hair showing. Sam could dimly see through her window that she was screaming. The crow, like a dark harbinger that had fulfilled its purpose, flew off to re-join other black crows, silent witnesses perched on the branches of an oak tree overlooking the pool.

Sam glanced back across the road at the Dodge truck, saw the driver struggle out of it and fall to his knees, then get to his feet. Looking to be in his late twenties, wearing a brown leather jacket, army camouflage blouse, trousers, suede desert boots, he half ran, half staggered across the road.

Still dazed, Sam looked again in his rear mirror.

The SUV driver was swimming on his side on the surface of the pool, pulling at the almost submerged BMW's driver's door handle and kicking at its window, trying, but failing, to break it. Swimming on the passenger's side of the car, also pulling at its door handle and kicking at its window, was another man who must have been in the SUV with him.

The BMW sank, sucking air with it as it went under.

Leaving only ripples on the black surface of the pond.

-3-

The Dodge driver staggered to Sam's car. Sam unclipped his safety belt but couldn't open his door, the impact with the tree had jammed it. He glanced again in his mirror and saw the SUV driver dive under the water after the BMW. The other man, wearing what looked like a black polo neck sweater, stayed on the surface treading water.

The Dodge driver, 5' 10"-ish, good looking, well built, crew cut hair – a combat soldier and tough with it, Sam reckoned, home from abroad on furlough – yanked at Sam's car door but failed to budge it. Sam managed to crack his window down. 'Can you swim?' he yelled through the slit.

'Sure I can,' the soldier picked up on the urgency in Sam's voice.

'Coupe's gone under–'

'Karen!'

The soldier spun away, cutting Sam off. Watching the scene unfold in his mirror, he saw the soldier half run, half stumble, to the edge of the pond. Tearing off his jacket and boots, he hesitated…precious seconds passed…and then he dived into the pool, straight down into its murky depths, cold enough to maybe clear his head, but too late to help save her, Sam thought.

Still groggy, he clambered over his gearshift, out through his passenger door, lurched to the pond. Peering into it, trying to penetrate its blackness at what was happening beneath its surface, she hasn't a snowball's chance in hell of coming out of it alive, he brooded.

As her car sank slowly deeper, the water inside reached just below Karen's mouth, then it stopped rising, leaving a pocket of air for her to breathe. She tried to stretch up in her seat, to have all her face above the water. The agonizing pain shot through her back, preventing her.

She screamed again. Water seeped into her mouth. Choking, she spat out the foul tasting stuff, gulped in air and stared desperately out at the engulfing blackness, with only a faint light coming from the pool's surface far above her, and her car slowly sinking further away from it.

A wave of panic swept over her, and her heart was pounding so fast she could feel it as she realized she was going to die, die in the dark depths of a black pond, drowning as the air pocket she was breathing diminished, and the unrelenting water would creep up over her mouth and up her nostrils and down into her lungs, as it once had when she was fifteen and tried to escape her father and end it all by drowning herself in the bath – after first taking some tranks she'd got from a young pusher in her class at school on the promise of a quick feel behind the sheds she hadn't kept – leaving her father to live the rest of his life alone, ruing the way he had mistreated her. The remembrance of it flashed before her eyes – but wasn't it said that the whole of our life flashes before our eyes as we die, she despaired, recalling the burning sensation as the bath water filled her nostrils, and made her choke and retch up the contents of her stomach and swear never to try to kill herself again, but get her own back on him some other way.

As her BMW continued to slowly sink, she wanted to scream…and scream…and scream, but fought it off, not wanting the vile water filling her mouth again.

Paul loomed down through the cloudy water to her. She almost cried with relief seeing him. He signaled he was going to kick her window in and she took a deep breath, ready for when the glass shattered and the water outside would pour in and suck out her pocket of air. Paul kicked at the glass. His stockinged feet made no impact. He grabbed her side mirror as her car sank lower, taking him down with it, kicked again, looked despairingly in at her as he failed.

Now reconciled to dying, Karen mouthed to him, 'I love you.'

Paul angrily shook his head, not willing for her to drown, for it all to end so terribly this way under the depths of a static pool, and let go the mirror to try again.

The shape of a man in army camouflage plunged down to them through the watery gloom. Pushing Paul aside, he raised his knees karate style. Taking another deep breath, she put her hands over her face to protect it, but slitted her eyes and peered between her fingers.

The soldier hesitated…

She screamed at him. He kicked at the window. Again, she snatched a deep breath. The glass shattered. He pulled her out of the car. The pain in her back was excruciating but she wrapped her arms about his neck from behind as he stretched out cupped hands and rapidly flippered his feet, propelling them both up toward the surface with Paul close behind them.

Below them, the BMW sank to the bottom of the pond, where the black Jeep sat in thick weeds.

Its cab window was fully open.

Standing at the pool's edge, Sam waited for the soldier or the SUV driver to rise first and confirm the young woman's fate. With the other man now out of the pond and standing near him, black sweater, black slacks clinging wet to him, fists clenching and unclenching betraying his tension, Sam gazed at the dark pool. She surely couldn't have survived down there this long time.

Tawny hair plastered to her head, mascara running down her face, she and the soldier broke the pool's surface, her arms clasped around his neck. The SUV driver came up alongside them and took her — somewhat possessively it seemed to Sam – from her rescuer.

She gulped air and screamed. 'Paul! My back!'

Using a one arm stroke, the SUV driver swam with her for the bank, the soldier swimming alongside them, supporting her from behind. She and her rescuers reached the side of the pond, placed their arms under her shoulders and thighs and gently lifted her, but she still cried out in pain. Carrying her to some bushes, they lowered her on to the grass under their leafy protection. The SUV driver tried to remove her coat. She cried out again, begging him not to move her. He knelt beside her, rubbing her arms and her legs to restore her circulation.

Sam fixed on her face, etching every feature of it in his mind – her eyes, her brows, her nose, her mouth, her chin, vulnerable and crying out in pain. By rights, Karen Ryan should now be dead. Only by a miracle had she risen from the pond's watery grave.

The man alongside Sam turned away to go to them. Removing his cellphone from a pocket of his padded jacket, Sam took off the jacket and gave it to him. 'Put this over her.' The man hurried to her, knelt beside her opposite the SUV driver, excluding the soldier, and wrapped the jacket over her upper body.

The soldier crossed over to Sam, and he saw for the first time the large knife with a serrated edge hanging in a scabbard on his right side. Dialing out on his cellphone, Sam extended his hand to him as his call rang out. 'Sam King. I didn't think she'd make it. Whoever she is, she owes you her life.'

'Michael Rossi,' the soldier said curt, taking Sam's hand and releasing it. 'She's Karen Ryan. Now Karen Archer. Recently married. Lives a mile down the road. Lucky I was passing—'

A female voice answered Sam's call. 'Ambulance,' he requested. 'A woman's been hurt in a car crash. She can't move.' He glanced at the soldier. 'Do you know where we are, exactly?'

Michael Rossi took the phone. 'Ravens Corner, two miles south of Ravensburg,' he directed and gave Sam the phone back. 'And call the police,' Sam added into it, 'she was deliberately run off the road by another driver.' He listened to the operator's affirmative, switched off his phone and called over to the SUV driver. 'Ambulance is on its way.' The SUV driver raised his hand in acknowledgement.

Sam turned back to the soldier. 'You from around here?'

'Ravensburg.'

'Hank's garage – does he have a recovery truck?' Sam indicated the pond. 'There's a body and Jeep down there the police are going to be interested in.'

'As long as he gets paid. He's bit of a tightwad, Hank.'

'I'll pay him myself if needs be,' Sam said. 'If only to be sure the guy drowned.' He scrolled down his list of contact numbers and pressed Call. As he waited for it to be answered, the soldier asked. 'Here on vacation?'

'Short break.'

'Yeah, staying in one of Hank's cabins. I live across the way. Seen you through my window, heading off into the woods. No hunting rifle or rods though.'

'I chose here for the peace and quiet,' Sam said, drily.

A man's voice answered the phone. 'Hank,' Sam said into it, 'It's Sam. I'm at Ravens Corner. There's been a car crash. Two autos gone under a pond here—'

'One of them's Karen, Hank,' Rossi shouted into the phone. 'She's been hurt. Tell Susan.'

The voice on the other end of the line questioned Sam. 'Yes, that was Michael, Hank,' Sam confirmed. 'He was passing and dived in and saved her…Typical of him, you say?' he glanced at the soldier. 'Well, he looks the part…No, I don't think it's too bad, ricked her back, I suspect, but the other driver's still down there…Yeah, too late for him, Hank – assuming it's a man – but we need your recovery truck…Sure the police will pay for it, we do in Chicago…Ten minutes? Fine.'

Switching off his phone, Sam answered Rossi's questioning look. 'Police. Chicago. You?'

Sam saw an immediate barrier against him in Rossi's eyes, and heard it in the terse change of tone in his voice as he replied. 'Ex-marine. Got wounded in 'Ghan. Quit while I was ahead. Now living in my pa's old house. Deciding my future. Thinking of applying to the forest rangers.'

'After what you just did,' Sam said, 'I hope they take you.'

He glanced across at where the SUV driver was lying alongside Karen Ryan, holding her to him and trying to stop her shivering. He said something to the man in black. Having taught himself to lip-read now he was with Organized Crime – it helped to know what suspects were mouthing to each other – Sam saw he was telling the man he had clothes in his SUV he'd not yet unloaded, that might help to keep her warm. The man got to his feet and hurried to get them.

Sam indicated at them. 'They from around here, too?'

'Only Karen.'

'What about the two men?'

Sam heard scorn in Rossi's voice. 'The taller one's her new husband. Name's Archer, according to Hank. Years older than her. The other one, Hale, was his best man. Hank says that Susan–'

'Susan?' Sam questioned.

'Karen's cousin. Owns the antique shop. She was going to watch the house while they were away, but Hale stayed in it instead. Fuck knows why.'

'You don't sound too happy about it?' Sam said. 'Or with Mrs. Archer herself, come to that?'

'Nothing to do with me who she spreads her legs for. If she wants to make a fool of herself, that's up to her.'

Seeing how grouchy Rossi was about it, Sam didn't pursue it. 'Best get out of those clothes before they dry on you.'

'I've known worse, life in the marines hardens you. But Hank's going to need me to go down there again and fix his hook to both autos – and you said you wanted to be sure he drowned.'

'I shouldn't think there's much doubt about it,' Sam drawled. 'Not unless he holds the world record for underwater breath holding. But the police will want to know.'

'I take it you're staying on until they get here, to tell them what happened.'

'Yep.'

'It'll be either Solon Springs or Mignon,' Michael said. 'They're both forty miles by road, but still the nearest. I'll get back to my truck and run the heater until Hank gets here.'

As he turned away to head off, Hale returned with items of clothing. Giving Archer a dark blue overcoat and a dark blue padded jacket, he peeled off his sweater and black thermal undershirt, revealing a slim but surprisingly well toned upper body, and put on a green toweling robe. Archer wrapped the overcoat around Karen, put on the padded jacket and zipped it up to his neck.

Rossi walked past them, ignoring Karen, picked up his jacket and boots from where they were still lying at the edge of the pool, and made for his truck.

Sam headed back for his car to wait for the recovery truck.

-4-

'That's as much as I can tell you,' Sam told the Mignon patrol cop.

The cop looked up from his notebook. 'You're with the Chicago police you say, Sam?'

Wearing his jacket – inside out, its lining was damp from Karen's wet clothes – Sam produced his badge. 'Organized Crime, for my sins.'

'You're far from the windy city, Sam?'

'I'm here on a short vacation.' Sam cracked a wry grin, 'Some vacation, huh?'

'That's how it goes, Sam.' The cop indicated Hank's archaic recovery truck at the side of the pool. 'You know you've no authority here to request a recovery vehicle.'

'Sure, but I thought it best to get both raised a.s.a.p.'

The cop put away his notebook. 'You also know I have to include it in my report?'

'Sure. If there's an enquiry into it, I'll attend.'

'Fine. Being there's no fatality – other than maybe the driver – it could take us a day or so to collect the Jeep and check it for prints. But if he or she's a *corpus delecti*,' he gave Sam a card, 'we'll send a van for it.' He strolled back to his car parked by the edge of the coppice, got in, said something to his partner at the wheel, and they settled into their seats, waiting for the ambulance parked alongside them to leave the scene. Sam tore up the card and scattered the pieces.

Wrapped in blankets, her clothes removed by the paramedics, Karen was being stretchered to it. Still wearing his padded jacket, Archer was walking alongside her holding her hand. Hale sat hunched on the grass watching them, covered by a blanket over his green toweling robe. Karen's once white, but now dirt-gray Gucci coat, was lying sodden and forgotten under a bush. Tossed aside on to it was her gold Cartier watch.

Sam heard Archer say to Karen. 'Sorry I can't ride with you, *amante*, but as Morgan doesn't drive I can't leave him and the Lexus here.' He questioned one of the medics, the medic nodded in reply and Archer turned back to her, 'I just want to talk to the guy who called emergency, but I'll see you off first, then catch you up.' She clutched his hand and gave him a flitting smile.

Amante – lover – a word he'd probably picked up on honeymoon – pretentious jerk, Sam said to himself, instantly disliking the man, and turned away and surveyed the scene.

Rossi's Dodge Ram up against an oak tree on the other side of the road. His Ford Fusion up against the fir. Archer's Lexus alongside it. Ambulance, police car on a grass verge. All it needed, Sam thought, was for Santa Claus and his red-nosed reindeers to fly in, and Ravens Corner would look like Times Square at goddamn Christmas-time.

Picking up a blanket given to him by the medics, he headed back to the pond.

Reaching it, the silver coupe, weeds stuck to it, had been winched out of the pond and lowered onto the bank. On his recovery truck, Hank, scrawny, wearing a red plaid shirt and denim overalls, a Milwaukee Brewers baseball cap worn slantwise on his wispy grey-haired head, and chewing a toothpick, was waiting for Rossi to surface and signal he'd hooked-up the Jeep.

'He's been under long time,' Hank shouted across to Sam. 'Hope he's okay.'

Rossi suddenly whooshed up from the black depths clutching his serrated-edged knife. He gulped air, gave Hank a thumbs-up, sheathed his knife and swam crawl style to Sam. Hank started to winch up. The cable tautened as it took the weight of the Jeep.

Rising out of the pool and on to the bank in one movement, Rossi lay back recovering his breath, then sat up. Sam put the blanket around him.

'Any sign of him?' Sam questioned.

'Nope,' Rossi said. 'Cab window was open, not a thing inside, like it was fucking vacuumed.

Only thing I found was this.' Pulling a wet, black leather glove from under his belt, he handed it to Sam. 'It was floating down as I was coming up. Maybe it can be checked for prints?'

Sam gave it a cursory glance. 'Doubt it. Not leather. More so when it's dried out. Still, I'll send it to Chicago – the Mignon cop didn't seem too interested. What's it like down there?"

'Black. Cold. Deep. Weeds a mile high, like being in a jungle.'

'Maybe he got caught up in them?'

'Maybe, but it's so fucking murky I couldn't see no more than a foot in front of me, and had to hack through them by touch.' He started to shiver.

'Now you're done here, get yourself home for a whiskey and hot bath,' Sam said.

Rising to his feet, Rossi saw Karen's stretcher reach the ambulance and Archer holding her hand. 'How's she?' he asked, more like he was obliged to enquire than concerned.

A red coupe with the lines of an outdated Jaguar, braked to a stop behind the police car, curbing Sam's reply. A woman, dark hair, slim, seemingly young and pretty even from a distance, dressed chic in a light gray, tight-legged trouser suit, got out, ran to Karen, grasped her hand. The medics waited for her and Karen to exchange words, the woman embraced her and stood aside for them to lift the stretcher into the ambulance. Letting go of Karen's hand, Archer crossed to the woman.

'That Susan, Karen's cousin?' Sam asked.

'Yep,' Rossi confirmed.

'They close?'

'Like sisters.' Rossi hesitated, then decided to elaborate. 'Except, when Susan was sixteen, something happened between their pas. Susan's ended up broke and strung himself up from The Hanging Tree. She had to go and live with them, but from what I heard, she couldn't live under Ryan's rules, and blamed him for her pa's death, so she ran off to Chicago when she was eighteen with some guy. But the jerk couldn't keep it zipped and she came back to Ravensburg.'

'That when she started her antiques shop?'

'Her pa's old house. Now lives over it, selling stuff to a few tourists who pass through here and stop off. And maybe a little pissed off,' he added, 'for Karen ending up rich when Ryan died, and her still poor, driving a coop like Karen, except hers is an old Jag and Karen's was Ryan's latest BMW. They were the sleazebag's status symbol, though God only knows why, there was only my pa and Hank around here to show off to and both hated his guts.'

Sam made no reply to this. 'Does Karen help her out financially?'

'No idea. Been away ten years.'

Still looking at Susan Ryan as the ambulance and police car drove off, Sam saw her covertly take Archer's hand. Archer glanced around, saw Sam and Rossi watching them, said something to her and she dropped his hand. Turning her head and seeing them, she returned to her car.

'Close cousins, you say?' Sam said. 'They share everything?'

'Naw,' Michael said dismissively. 'Susan would never two-time Karen. She probably needed comforting, worrying about her.'

The red Jag sped off after the ambulance. Archer turned away and made for the pool. 'Before he gets here,' Sam questioned, 'what can you tell me about him?'

'Zilch. First time I've seen him.' Rossi said, bitterness returning to his voice. He hesitated, and decided to lay it all out. 'Okay…when I heard Ryan had died, I came back hoping Karen and me could pick up again from when we–' he checked himself. 'But then heard she and Susan had gone to Italy on vacation, only for her to meet Archer in Chicago and marry him just like that,' he viciously snapped his fingers, 'knowing fuck all about him, and dropped Susan like a stone – like Ryan did to her pa – and took the jack-shit away with her instead.'

'Her marrying Archer still seems personal with you,' Sam said.

'As I said before,' Rossi dead-panned, 'it's no skin off my nose who she does it with.'

Seeing through his veneer, Sam didn't pursue it. 'How about his friend?' he indicated Hale.

'Know zilch about him, except he's a theater designer, according to Hank – not what you'd call a man's job,' Rossi scorned.

Archer was now less than fifty yards away. Not wanting Rossi to be around in this mood, Sam prompted him. 'Whiskey and a hot bath. But maybe we can talk more later when I get back to my cabin? I've a bottle of Jim Beam Black we could share.'

'Sure.' Rossi made off, walking straight past Archer. Reaching Sam, Archer offered him his hand. 'Paul Archer.'

Sam returned his grasp. 'Sam King.'

They looked at the dark pond together for a moment in silence. Archer broke it. 'You live around here?'

'A short vacation in one of Hank's cabins, and was passing when it happened. Michael Rossi, the soldier, tells me she's your wife. I hope she's going to be okay?'

'In as much as she's lucky to be alive, but we won't know if she's done any lasting damage to her back until she's been x-rayed. We've been married less than three weeks. I don't know what I'd have done if she'd—' Archer choked on his words, recovered his composure, and indicated at Rossi making for his truck. 'Thank God he was also passing. I wanted to thank him.'

'Michael? You'll get another chance. He lives in Ravensburg – across from Hank's place.'

'I'll go see him as soon I can.' Archer indicated at the pond, 'I hope the swine drowned,' he said viciously.

'It's more than likely,' said Sam, 'Michael says he somehow got out of his cab but reckons he must have got caught up in the weeds – they're as thick as a jungle down there.'

'I only pray his body's found,' Archer grated, 'for me to rest easy. I'd hate to think he got free and will never pay for it – forcing her off the road the way he did.'

'If he drowned, he's already paid,' Sam said. 'But if he got free,' he showed Archer the leather glove, 'this could have his prints on it. I'll send it to Chicago—'

'Chicago?' Archer interjected. 'Forgive me, but it's not for you to decide where to—'

'I should've mentioned it,' Sam cut across him. 'I'm with the Chicago police.'

'Police?' Archer suddenly sounded tense. 'You've come a long way for a short vacation?'

'Yeah. Some vacation, huh?'

Archer took a moment to absorb this, then indicated the glove. 'Shouldn't you have given it to the Mignon police?'

'Probably,' Sam shrugged, 'but Chicago will deal with it quicker. Mignon will have to send it to Madison to check. That could take days, maybe weeks.'

'How do you know it's his?'

'It was floating down as Michael was coming up.'

'Then it's likely Karen's. Looking at it closer, it could be one of a pair she may have been wearing when she left the house earlier—'

'It's a man's glove.'

'In that case, send it to Chicago,' Archer said. 'The sooner we know who he was—'

'Or still is,' Sam cut across him again.

'—or by some miracle he got free – the sooner the police can find him, the sooner we can put it behind us.'

Sam returned his gaze to the pond and pointed to the taut cable. 'Jeep's on its way up. I'll ask Hank to give it a check when he gets it back to his garage – maybe he'll find something inside that could give Chicago the guy's name.'

The Jeep surfaced, weeds stuck to it, water pouring out of the cab window and from under and around the door. Hank lowered it to the ground, alongside Karen's BMW.

'Though I doubt it,' Sam added. 'Michael says the cab's as clean as a new pin.' He indicated the Jeep. 'And removing both licenses plates suggests it was planned.'

'Planned?' Archer came back at him sharp as the crack of a whip.

'Removing them points to it,' Sam said again. 'And why he still ran Mrs. Archer off the road, though I was on his tail. He banked on me stopping to go to her aid, letting him get clean away.'

Turning to the Jeep before Archer could reply, Sam opened the cab door. The last of the water trickled out as they both looked inside. 'As Michael said, it's like he scrubbed it out before setting off, making sure there'd be no trace of anything left behind if he ditched it and it was found.' He pulled at a trailing weed. 'Recognize it by any chance?'

'Hardly. Like you, I'm from Chicago, not here. But planned?' Archer repeated his question. 'You're surely not saying he tried to kill Karen deliberately?'

Cursorily examining the weed as if it might hold a clue, Sam said, 'Seeing it from behind them, there was no doubting it.' Tossing the weed aside, he indicated at the black windows. 'Nor is it from around here. Vehicles with tinted windows can't be licensed in Wisconsin.'

He turned his head and glanced at Hale. 'Your friend from Chicago, too?'

Archer nodded. 'Morgan? He was my best man at our wedding. Been looking after the house while we were away. But getting back to him trying to kill Karen—'

'Hope you'll both be happy,' said Sam.

'Thanks,' Archer said, curt, realizing Sam wasn't going to expand any further. 'Let me know if Chicago find any prints on the glove.'

'Will do,' Sam nodded.

Turning away, Archer returned to Hale. They got in the Lexus and drove off, leaving Sam alone with Hank, the Jeep, and the silver BMW coupe.

Twisting the glove in his hand like he was slowly strangling someone, Sam hurled it into the pond and watched it sink below the surface.

Hank descended from his recovery truck and crossed over to him. 'Settled into your cabin, Sam?' he asked, toothpick in his mouth chewed flat. 'Any ideas how long you'll be staying?'

'Depends on how my plans pan out, Hank,' Sam replied.

As day slowly turned to dusk, the pond grew blacker and more sinister, and its environs returned to its natural silence.

He emerged from the bushes, picked up the abandoned Gucci coat and Cartier watch, saw the watch had stopped, ruined by being under the water, almost caressingly stroked its gold surround, pocketed it and re-entered the bushes, rustling them.

Crows flew up cawing in protest. One swooped at him. He swatted it to the ground with the coat, ground its head into the earth with his heel, and faded into the surroundings.

The wheeling crows cawed louder, raucous, angry.

Timber wolves howled in the distance as if in answer.

-5-

A cold wind coming in from the Arctic over northern Canada and across Lake Superior, unusual this early in October when the humidity normally stayed high, buffeted Paul's SUV as he drove Karen home from hospital. Driving rain lashed the windshield and in it were flecks of early snow, making vision almost impossible despite the wipers trying frantically to swish it aside.

Using her left hand rather than her right – not wanting to stretch the tissue adhesive on her wrist wound from that damn raven – Karen wrapped an old coat Paul had brought her from home tighter around her. Under the coat she was wearing an old sweater and skirt Paul had also brought her, and flat shoes and no make-up – he'd not brought her any make-up either, or any of her new clothes – and her hair was straight and lifeless. God, she must look a mess. Whereas *Paul…*

Under a tan sheepskin jacket, collar pulled up, *he* was immaculate, wearing pale-blue denim designer shirt and jeans, new or yesterday's already washed, dried and ironed.

She controlled her resentment. 'God, the weather! To think the sun is shining in Positano.'

He replied as if his mind was elsewhere. 'We'll go back there when my book's finished.'

'Can't wait.' Ignoring the dull sedated pain in her back, she placed her left hand under his sheepskin and felt for his penis, squeezed it, held it a moment, got no response and released it. 'What's wrong with you today, Paul,' she demanded, 'you've been off with me since you arrived to drive me home. You weren't like this on honeymoon.' She gave it another squeeze. 'Then, you always rose to the occasion–'

'It's just that I'm worried about you, *amante*,' Paul gently removed her hand. 'Besides, we're not in Italy any more, we're in Ravensburg, the middle of nowhere – and only yesterday somebody tried to kill you. If it hadn't have been for Michael Rossi, you'd now be dead.'

'Except he's at the bottom of Ravens Pond,' she flared at Paul's rejection, 'drowned and no longer a threat.'

'Maybe. But just in case he somehow escaped, we need to find out who he was. *Why* he tried to kill you. For him to be caught before he tries again.'

'Tries again?' she scorned. 'He was locked in his cab, I saw him, and even if he wasn't inside it anymore, as Michael says, and managed to get out, he couldn't possibly have held his breath for that long – and at that depth. He *must* have drowned.' She narrowed her eyes at him 'But that's not your reason, is it? It's the way I'm dressed and wearing no make-up.' After twenty-seven years of living under her father's subjection, and now having at last experienced the sheer mind-blowing, orgasmic ecstasy of love-making, she wasn't willing to give up, and slid her hand up once more between his tight-jeaned thighs. 'But what's underneath is still the same.'

Paul clamped his hand on hers.

'No, Karen,' he said, 'that's not the reason. This is reality time, no longer honeymoon time. Yesterday,' he repeated, 'somebody tried to kill you. He set out...' he stressed the words slowly, 'in an unmarked Jeep, with black windows so no one could see him, with the sole intention of killing you. That Chicago cop said it must have been planned. I didn't accept it at first, but I now have to agree that all the evidence points to it. However unlikely it may be to you that he escaped – if he did, he could try again. So, before he does, we must find out who he was and prevent him, or we'll always be looking over our–'

'I don't want to talk about him, he's dead,' she snapped. 'I just want some reassurance that life is back to normal.'

'Well, inside my jeans isn't where to find it,' Paul placed her hand back on her lap. 'Until we know he *is* dead – or, if he's still alive, have him arrested – our life will never be normal.'

'But why should somebody want to kill me?' she protested. 'I've not harmed anyone.'

'Nevertheless, someone did, and though he failed, he nearly crippled you for good. So much so that as they warned at the hospital, rather than risk further damage, you're going to have to take it easy for the next few weeks or more, and not put any unnecessary pressure on your spine.'

'I'm not going to let it spoil what we've got either.' She changed her tactics and caressed the back of his neck. 'We can always do the me-on-top position. We were pretty good at it – and only a few days ago – *if* you can cast your mind back to then, the mood you're in.'

'For God's sake, Karen,' Paul lifted her hand off his shoulder and moved it aside, 'come back down to Earth. You surely don't want to be on crutches the rest of your life.'

'But it's only badly bruised.' Feeling spurned, she huddled into her seat. 'The consultant said it will heal in a short time.'

'He also said – only provided you rest,' Paul stressed. 'And until then, that means me taking care of you.'

'But it will interfere with your book and I don't want that to happen.'

'You will always come first, you know that.'

'Fine, you win,' Karen snapped – for the moment – but tonight in bed, she envisioned, she would use all her sex appeal on him…

It had been exhilarating to discover she *had* sex appeal, and equally exhilarating to find she could use it. 'Come here before you send me crazy,' Paul had groaned at her as he lay on the king sized bed in their Positano hotel suite in his blue summer slacks and shirt, watching her admire herself in the long mirror, wearing nothing but her white, fur-collared Gucci coat and stilettos, and letting the coat slide to the carpeted floor but leaving her stilettos on, and approving her shapely body and her long legs and tawny triangle of pubic hair, its top line so straight it looked like it had been shaved that way, except it hadn't, it was natural – well, maybe trimmed just a little.

'Now,' Paul had demanded, unzipping his fly…

And she'd gone to him still wearing her stilettos…and sat on his already erect pommel, and ridden him – and straightaway found that she preferred the on-top position, because that way, she immediately realized, *she* was in control, bending forward in the saddle, leaning back…riding him fast…then slow…and stopping and seeing the look of agony on his face when she did that, and the look of relief when she started riding him once more, slowly again at first, then gradually faster as she felt herself coming – but still *her* in control, seeing his frenzied expression telling her he was nearing climax too – and only then had she let herself go and they'd come together and collapsed in each other's arms…

Yes, she thought, she liked the on-top position. She liked being in control. In which case, she could wait, and tonight she would let him get into bed first, then she would do a strip-tease out of her clothes and into her sheer black nightie and slowly approach the bed with the light from the bedside lamp shining through it, accentuating her bushy pudendum that always turned him on, and *then* see if he could refuse her…

She banished the thought before it drove her crazy.

'How's the book coming along?' she asked.

'Great. Another five months, maybe six, and I can start thinking about an agent.'

'That soon?' Karen replied, surprised. 'What with the research, the writing and all the editing,

I thought it took at least a year to write a book. You are coming along well with it. Do you like it?'

'So far, yes, I do.'

'When may I read it?'

'You sure you want to? It should end up at over five hundred pages. Maybe six.'

Hearing the patronizing tone in his voice, Karen flared up again. 'What's six hundred pages? *Anna Karenina's* only just less than a thousand, *War and Peace* well over – and I've read them both. Twice.' She forced herself to calm down. 'There was nothing else to do in Ravensburg in between doing my art course, except read.'

Paul's answering smile was as patronizing. She dug the fingernails of her left hand deep into the leather of her seat to stay calm.

'Then after I've edited and polished it a few times' he conceded. 'The final draft, maybe.'

She dug deeper, inflicting pain on herself as she pulled the quicks under her nails far back.

'We're home,' Paul said, causing her to stop before she went too far and pulled a nail right off – as she had done a couple of times before, when her father had particularly angered her. Peering through the rain sheeted windshield as they rounded a bend into a straight, she saw the clapboard house in the near distance – house, not home, not with the memories of *him* still filling it – set at a forty-five degree angle to the road where it briefly straightened out, then disappeared again around the next corner back into the dark forest.

T-shaped, with the wide part at the front, and the narrower wing at the rear, in the center of a grass-earthed clearing, it was large with a wide front door opening on to a roofed, railed open deck that ran around the entire house. Wooden steps led down to a front parking area of hard earth with a dirt track leading up to it. Bordered by bushes, and beyond them oak trees, and further back the dark forest again, the latter encircled the whole like a prison perimeter wall.

Seeing its name CLANRYAN carved in bold, black letters on an oak sign swinging on chains from a branch of a leafless yellow birch tree at the start of the track, her heart sank.

CLANRYAN was another name for HELL to her, the Celtic Clan Ryan motto: *malo more quam foedari* – 'I would rather die than be dishonored or disgraced' – indoctrinated into her by her father ever since he became obsessed with tracing his ancient Irish roots, even though he'd not set a foot out of Wisconsin – other than Chicago – in his entire life, gripping her young shoulders to drive it home. '*Death before dishonor*, Karen,' he'd stress. 'The Clan Ryan motto, by which we live.'

Well, to hell with your motto, Father. It's dishonor before death for me every time. Drive on past the goddamn place, she willed Paul. Forget your goddamn novel, it's probably crap anyway compared to the books I've read, like *Rebecca*, say – Miss Goody Two Shoes No-Name was a real wimp, but I loved Rebecca. Although she was dead in the book, she was so defiant when she was alive, so much her own person and too much for her boring husband to handle – as for making him frame himself for her death, that was priceless. Du Maurier should have let her get away with it and let him hang. So drive past and let's get back to Positano – I've got more than enough for us to live well on for the next thirty or more years, and beyond that who cares. After a miserable existence until now – and that's all it was, an existence – I want to live life to the full while I can.

The rain and flecks of snow suddenly stopped as if a faucet in the sky had been switched off. And despite the dark clouds still hanging overhead, it just as suddenly dispelled her mood, banishing her resentment at Paul for his earlier condescension. 'It's a sign,' she said.

'A sign? A sign of what, exactly?' She detected a hint of amusement at her in his voice, but managed to ignore it and kept herself calm.

'That the gods are looking down on us, sending us their blessing.'

'Who needs their blessing, being with you is blessing enough,' Paul gripped her hand, and by so doing restored how much she loved him in her thoughts.

They turned into the dirt drive. Parked in front of the house, Karen saw her BMW, weeds still stuck to it, and a cold feeling went down her spine. 'We need to get rid of that though, or it will be a constant reminder of yesterday.' She forced the memory away. 'But until then, once we're inside, alone together, and can't see it–'

Her voice tailed off as Morgan exited onto the front porch to greet them. Purple shirt collar over a purple crew-neck sweater, purple slacks with knife sharp creases, all the same shade, and cream slip-on shoes, he was the antithesis of a natty dresser but didn't know it, or was color blind to it.

She fought to keep the returning anger out of her voice. 'Morgan is *still* here? You said he was going back to Chicago when we got back from Italy.'

'I kept it as a surprise,' Paul said, parking the Lexus next to the BMW. 'I asked him to stay on to help take care of you – just for a couple of weeks, until the bruising to your spine has gone. And for me to maybe spend a few hours a day on my book – but only if that's okay with you?'

'Sure,' she gritted, and tried to lean across to dutifully kiss him, but her back prevented her stretching that far. Paul patted her hand as he would a child's, got out of the SUV, and unloaded a folding wheelchair from the rear as Morgan reached them. She saw him give Paul an almost imperceptible raise of his eyebrows, asking Paul what kind of mood she was in. Paul returned him an equally brief shake of his head: Watch yourself.

She dug her nails deeper into her leather seat as she again fought to control her temper.

Morgan opened her door. 'Welcome home, Karen,' he greeted her.

'What an unexpected surprise seeing you, Morgan.'

'A pleasant one, I hope, nonetheless,' Morgan smiled.

'But of course,' she said, but was unable to return his smile.

Paul unfolded the wheelchair, brought it to her door, put one arm under her shoulders, the other under her thighs, and lifted her out of her car seat into it.

'This is so annoying,' she snapped.

'But fortunately, not lasting,' Morgan tried to calm her, realizing that Paul's relayed message about her mood was only too true. 'A month from now, Karen, you'll be performing cartwheels.'

'I'd be surprised if I could, Morgan. I never was able to before, not even as a child.'

Morgan forced a laugh. Taking a blanket from Paul, he tucked it about her legs and smoothed it out, hinting there was something of the precisian about him.

'Paul says you're staying on to help me, Morgan?'

'That's what a best man's for,' he cautiously replied.

'Thank you,' she obliged. 'And for trying to save me yesterday. I didn't get the chance to say it yesterday at the hospital.'

'I'm just so grateful you're not permanently injured.'

Giving Morgan the wheelchair to push, Paul returned to the rear of the SUV for a pair of crutches and a bag with her still damp clothes from Ravens Pond.

'What about your set designs, Morgan?' she asked him over her shoulder. 'Won't the theatre be wanting them?' *And fuck off back to Chicago with them, and leave Paul and me on our own.*

'I brought them with me to work on,' he replied, 'but unfortunately forgot my cell charger and it's flat. So being that your studio has a landline extension, I've taken the liberty of working there. I hope that's all right? I've taken care not to touch any of your paintings.'

Feeling it was anything but all right, that her private sanctuary had been trespassed, 'Of course,' she said, now digging her fingernails into the wheelchair's plastic leather seat.

'I've cooked you an early Thanksgiving dinner to welcome you home,' Morgan tried to alter her mood. 'A succulent turkey, cornbread dressing, yams, collared greens. I hope you're hungry?'

The roar of an approaching car saved her from another forced reply. Susan's coupe raced up to the house and braked to a sudden stop. Flinging the door open and slamming it shut behind her, Susan hurried to them. Wearing a light brown, three-quarter length faux shearing coat with a spread collar, left open to reveal a white, polo-necked sweater that accentuated her bust, narrow-leg black jeans with open-strap black stilettoes that made her legs appear to go on forever – she looks like a million fucking dollars, Karen thought, feeling even more conscious of how she herself looked. Despite the loss of her Gucci coat, amongst all her other new clothes in her wardrobe, she had black designer jeans, slim-leg, superbly cut, that made her legs look much longer, and made Susan's black jeans look like cheap denims. Her resentment with Paul for bringing her old clothes instead of her chic ones resurfaced.

'Sorry I'm late,' Susan apologized. 'I called you to let you know, Paul, but your cell's dead.'

'I failed to restore it after Ravens Pond,' Paul said. 'It's not water resistant.'

'Well, you won't get another in Ravenscroft,' Susan laughed. Turning to Karen, she hugged her. 'And how are you feeling today?'

'Better now that I'm home and have you and Morgan with us,' Karen forced herself to reply.

Paul had given Susan his cell number? Why? For what reason? They had known each other only briefly in Chicago, and Susan had driven straight home after the wedding? *Why would she need Paul's?*

'We were going to start without you,' Morgan said to Susan, an underlying bite in his banter.

'Not true,' Paul laughed. Carrying the bag in his right hand, he tucked the crutches under the same arm, giving Susan his free elbow to hold. 'No way would we have started without you.'

'Thank you, Paul,' Susan said, and for the briefest of moments they held each other's gaze.

It was long enough for Karen to pick up on the warmth between them. Digging her finger nails deeper into the plastic leather, she slowly scratched it, stretching the quicks, stopping only when she could no longer tolerate the pain.

'Paul's more than a cousin-in-law, Morgan,' Susan retorted back to Morgan as she and Paul lead the way to the house.' She looked up at Paul again. 'He's the brother I never had.'

Morgan abruptly swiveled the wheelchair about and followed them toward the house. From behind them, Karen saw that Susan's hold of Paul's arm was anything but sisterly.

She dug her nails deeper into the plastic leather of her chair, tearing through it and stretching her quicks to their limit.

The pain was acute.

She kept stretching them.

-6-

The brown and green brocaded dining room drapes were not fully drawn, hanging heavy to the oak planked floor, worn in places and in need of staining and polishing. Between the gap in the drapes it was dark outside, low black clouds were passing over an all but obscured three-quarter moon. The only other light to punctuate the night sky was the North Star trying to peer through wispy holes in the almost solid cover, only for them to close up again.

Dinner over, Karen and Susan were sitting opposite Paul and Morgan around a long rectangular oak table, drinking coffee. The two men had their backs to the kitchen door. Karen's crutches were propped against the wall behind her. William Ryan's carver chair stood at the head of the table as if daring anyone to sit in it again – it was *his*, and would always be his, and his alone.

Having restored her make-up, eye shadow and mascara, and washed and blow-dried her hair, Karen had changed into a simple yet chic navy blue dress with slanting pockets, tight fitting to show off her figure and small waist, but to her annoyance her bruised spine had forced her to reject her stilettos and wear flat shoes. Whereas Susan was still looking all long legged in her high heels.

Hanging up on a wall beside Karen was another large-framed portrait of William Ryan. Though she kept trying not to glance at him, she could feel him drawing her to do so – and see his stern face looking down at her, censorious of her new image. 'You wouldn't be allowed to dress, or paint your face like that, not if *I* was alive,' he seemed to be saying.

She turned her face away, only to see the oak replica of the Clan Ryan ancient heraldic shield he had commissioned – three silver griffins embossed in an inverted triangle on a blood red back-ground – hanging up over a cast-iron fireplace in keeping with the antiquity of the house. Revered by her father's warlike Celtic ancestors, the mythical griffin had to them symbolized courage and bravery – but *he* had chosen them because they were also mythologically regarded as protectors of treasure – in a word, *wealth* – and had the Clan Ryan motto: *Malo More Quam Foedari*, etched into a bronze plaque below the blood red shield.

Though he was no longer here, his presence still seemed to fill the house – even to declaring it was still his with the relief sculpture of another griffin he'd had carved over the front door. When she was a child she had dreaded walking under it, imagining its talons stretching down to grasp her in a viselike grip. She'd had nightmares about it. But then, she'd had other nightmares, too, and in those it was always *he* who dominated, and *they* had been even more cringing than the griffin…

Susan's voice broke into her thoughts. 'You must have some idea who he was, Kay,' her cousin protested, exasperated by Karen's curt reply to a question she'd just asked her, 'he tried to kill you. At Carvers Gulch and Ravens Wood, and you still ended up in its pond. If it wasn't for Michael you'd have drowned. No one could be that determined to get you on a passing whim. He must not only have known you, but had some grudge against you. And not just a grudge, but a huge one.'

'I said I don't want to talk about it,' Karen flared, making an angry gesture with her left hand and catching it on the edge of the table. 'Hell!' she exclaimed and clutched her forefinger, bound in a band-aid, its surface stained with dried blood.

'Take care, *amante*,' Paul said. 'You don't want your nail going septic, as well as a bad back.'

'I didn't pull it half off on purpose, Paul,' she retorted. 'All I did was catch it on something when Morgan was helping me out of the wheelchair.'

'I'll fix it in the morning,' Morgan said hurriedly, trying to defuse her mood.

'No need,' she snapped, 'I'll be using the crutches. Would you all get off my back.'

'I'm sorry, Kay,' Susan persisted, 'but I'm not giving up on it. What if he wasn't trapped down there, as you want to believe? What if he swam free?'

'I said the same when we were driving back from hospital, Susan,' Paul remarked. 'Yet he *must* have drowned...*Surely?* I didn't see him surface.' But he didn't sound convinced of this.

At the far end of the room a half open door led into the kitchen in the rear wing of the house. Through the gap it could be seen it was large and had a cast iron cooking range and two cast iron porcelain enameled sinks, both with hot and cold brass faucets, one for rinsing dishes, the other for washing them, wooden draining boards either side. William Ryan clearly hadn't given a thought to modernizing Clanryan. 'No need,' such an obdurate man would have said, 'it's all functional. My money is best invested in money, making more money.' At the far end of the kitchen a solid wooden door led out to the rear deck.

'Nevertheless, Paul,' Susan insisted, 'until we know for certain, we still have to consider the possibility he may have survived. If so, he could still be out there, waiting for another chance.'

'I very much doubt it,' Morgan entered the exchange. 'He was probably just some passing joy rider, high on drink, or on drugs, getting a kick out of frightening Karen – and who's now paid the price for his foolery. '

'A *joyrider*,' Susan scorned. 'Watching her in the graveyard? Waiting for her on the road she'd take to drive home? Black windows hiding him? No plates to identify him? I don't think so.'

Morgan stood, impatient with Susan for her insistence, and placed dishes on a tray to take to the kitchen. 'In *which* case,' he said to her in a caustic tone, 'and in the *highly* unlikely event he *is* still alive…*and* tries again…' turning to Karen he gave her a reassuring smile, 'he won't get past Paul and me. We'll make damn sure of that.'

Karen didn't respond. Looking upset by this, Morgan exited to the kitchen, leaving the door open. Pushing his chair back, Paul stood up and gathered more dishes. 'I'm still torn,' he said to Susan. 'A part of me still says he can't possibly have survived, the other agrees with you that he may, by some miracle, have done so. But if he did,' he reassured her, 'I promise you no harm will come to Karen now she's safe back home with me. You have my word on it.'

'That's more than good enough for me, Paul.' Susan stretched out her hand and clasped his.

Seeing Karen watching them, and a dark look come into her face, Paul picked up his dishes and followed Morgan into the kitchen, closing the door with his foot and leaving her and Susan alone.

Susan glanced at Karen – she averted her face. But knowing her well, having seen her mood swings when she was forced to live with her and William Ryan, Susan saw the anger in her eyes. Not only could she sense the atmosphere in the room, she could *feel* it. She realized she had to be the first to break it.

'Karen...' she said. The one word was enough.

'I hope that what happened yesterday won't affect Paul's writing.' Karen cut across her. 'He doesn't like being dependent on me, and has his heart set on his book being a success.'

Detecting the message – Paul is mine, lay off – Susan replied in kind, 'It will, Kay, Paul's not one to accept failure, he'll work on it until it's word perfect,' but then realized her statement could be interpreted she'd known Paul before and hastened to rectify it. 'When we three first met it was clear from the start that you were the one he'd fallen for–'

'And gave *you* his phone number,' Karen accused, vicious.

'That's only because he's worried about you,' Susan came back at her. 'That you'll be lonely now you've returned from Italy and he shuts himself away in his study, writing for hours on end. He's asked would I call him when the shop's quiet and check if you need company, without you knowing he's anxious about you. God, Kay, count yourself fortunate, I wish I had someone who put me first. But that's typical of my luck,' she failed to mask her bitterness. 'It rarely fails me.'

To her surprise, Karen clutched her hand. 'I'm so sorry, Sue,' she said. She sounded genuine. It was impossible to understand the suddenness of her cousin's mood swings, always had been.

From the kitchen came the sound of Paul's and Morgan's voices, indistinct through the clatter of dishes and pans being rinsed, washed, and placed on a draining board to be wiped dry.

'Hey, that's what cousins are for,' Susan responded. 'Paul just wasn't attracted to me – not that way, at least, only as two people who like each other in a brother and sister-like way, but nothing more. Destiny, Kay,' she gave Karen a wry smile. 'Except I'm never dealt a straight hand.'

Standing outside on the front deck, he peered through the gap in the drapes into the dining room, and fixed his manic eyes on Karen Ryan as she clutched her cousin's hand.

'I'll get you next time, *whore*,' he exuded hate at her. 'But first I'm going to make you suffer, like you made me suffer…choking that foul water…drowning in it…blackness all around me. What you made me go through will be nothing compared to what I'm going to inflict on you.'

In his hand he held a rock.

He tested its weight.

And made for the rear of the house.

In the dining room, Susan's bitterness dispelled. 'I'm just glad to see you looking so happy,' she squeezed Karen's hand back. 'Being married seems to really suit you, Kay.'

'It would suit you, too,' Karen returned, deliberately resurrecting an episode in her cousin's life that she would rather be kept buried. 'You deserved better than Peter. He was a skunk.'

Susan pulled her hand away. 'Fate again, Kay. Penis Pete was destined to take off with the first bimbo to stroke his ego – as good a word as any for his one and only attribute, which was nowhere near as big as his conceit. As I said, it's the way my cards were dealt. Take our dads,' again her bitterness rose the surface. 'The same week yours ends their partnership, he hits a lucky streak and makes millions. My dad goes broke and takes his own life. His and my shit luck,' her ironic laugh was almost savage. 'Just *pray* the fan never hits you with it.' She abruptly pushed her chair away from the table, scraping its legs on the planked floor. 'God,' she said, 'I could just do with a stiff drink.'

Paul entered the room, holding something behind his back. 'I'm surplus to requirement in the kitchen,' he said, 'but guess what I found stashed under some loose floorboards? No?' He revealed his hand, clutching a rich-ambered bottle by its long neck. 'Courvoisier – and not just a Courvoisier, but only a VSOP, the best.'

'Hallelujah,' Susan said. 'Let's hope it's a sign my luck's changed at long last.'

'Oh, this isn't all,' Paul said, 'there's another two bottles of it, plus three bottles of Bushmills and three Jack Daniels. Looks like he was a secret tippler, your father,' he said to Karen, 'looking down at us all judgmental from his portraits in every room of the house. Maybe he had other vices you didn't know about. Or maybe a whole secret life–'

'Paul,' Susan hastily cut across him. 'Just get some glasses.'

From the kitchen came a sudden loud splintering of glass being smashed – then Morgan yelled: '*Someone's hurled a rock through the window. I can see him running off across the clearing.*'

Paul dumped the Courvoisier on the table and ran into the kitchen. From outside on the deck, Morgan shouted to him: 'He went into the woods.'

Susan hurried out of the room. Grabbing her crutches, Karen went after her.

Entering the kitchen, shards of glass, large and small and tiny slivers, covered the surface of a working table under the shattered window and were scattered across the floor. In their midst was a jagged rock the size of a baseball.

Paul and Morgan were out on the rear deck peering into the darkness. Turning and seeing Karen crutching across the kitchen behind Susan, Paul yelled, 'For God's sake, Sue, don't let Karen out here. Stop her from seeing it.'

Susan turned to block her. Karen pushed past her and crutched out onto the deck.

Light from the broken window dimly shone on a leafless oak tree standing alone in the middle of the rear clearing, crows nests perched on its topmost branches. Hanging by its neck from a withy tied to a lower branch was a large rag doll, arms outstretched crucifix-like, fastened with strands of withy to a crosspiece, a broken branch. It was wearing Karen's Gucci coat. Its shoulder length dark brown hair was parted, Christ-like, in the center. On its head was a crown of thorny brambles.

But its face was garishly painted, thick black mascara eyebrows and lashes, purple eye shadow, rouged cheeks and leering crimson lips.

Karen recoiled in horror. '*Cut it down! Cut it down!*'

Paul ran into the kitchen, broken glass crunching under his feet. Susan reached out for Karen and held her. Turning away from the macabre effigy, Karen buried her face into Susan's shoulder and clung to her. Susan stroked her head, trying to soothe her as she moaned, 'Oh, God! He's still alive! And still out there, after me!' Pulling away, she begged Susan, 'But why? Why me?'

Paul exited the kitchen with a carving knife, crossed to the oak, stuck the blade into the trunk below a low branch, grabbed the branch and pulled himself up into the tree. Yanking the carving knife out of the trunk, he wormed along another branch to the rag doll. Crows flew up, cawing in protest. One larger than the rest swooped down at Paul. He slashed at it with the knife. Angrily croaking, it flew away and re-joined the others as they soared higher above the oak and hovered over it, wings beating and cawing in raucous chorus. 'What is it with this damn house and crows?' Paul called down. He cut through the withy and the rag doll fell to the ground. Lowering himself from the branch, he landed by the doll, picked it up and brought it to the deck and dropped it. It lay there, arms tied to the crosspiece, its stuffed legs splayed out.

Karen covered her eyes with a hand, but then peered at it through her fingers over Susan's shoulder and recoiled: '*Hide it! Hide it!*'

The three looked at the doll. The white coat was open from the waist. Sewn on its rag crutch to look like pubic hair, was a hide patch of animal hair. It had been repeatedly slashed, revealing its genital cloth insides, and daubed with red paint for blood.

'Call Hank,' Susan handed Paul a slim cellphone from the back pocket of her tight black jeans. 'Get him to send that Chicago cop here.'

Morgan picked up the doll with open repulsion, tossed it over the deck rail and wiped his hand with a spotless handkerchief.

Paul brought up Hank's number among Susan's stored contacts and called it, and cut across Hank as he answered it.

'Hank. Paul Archer, Karen Ryan's husband. Can you get an urgent message to that Chicago cop in your cabin? Ask him would he mind driving here?' He paused in mid-sentence as Hank questioned him, then answered. 'That Jeep driver didn't drown – he's been here and left a calling card…A particularly sick one, Hank. Ask him to hurry.' He cut the call and returned Susan her cellphone.

Karen crutched to him and fell against him. 'Oh, God, Paul,' she pleaded, her body trembling. 'Who is he? Why me? What does he have against me?'

'I don't know, Karen,' he held her tight. 'But whoever he is, he won't get to you.'

She looked up into his face, seeking his reassurance that he would protect her – and saw him flit Susan a message with his eyes.

She squeezed her split left fingernail with the thumb and first finger of her right hand.

The pain was excruciating.

Blood seeped through the band-aid.

She kept squeezing it.

-7-

The sitting-room fireplace was in dark oak, tall, wide, carved with large swirls, a heavy fireplace, solemn even, declaring the personality of the man who had chosen it, nothing frivolous about such a man. The wide mantel was plain, no ornaments on it. Such a man would have had no place in his life for ornaments. Even more, they would have detracted from the portrait above the mantel, set in a large, old gold frame.

It was a family portrait, posed, photographic, William Ryan, Elisabeth Ryan, and Karen at the age of twelve, set against a mottled, dark brown studio background. Wearing a black suit, William Ryan dominated it, standing behind a hard-backed chair on which sat Elizabeth Ryan in a long, high collared black dress, a three-string choker of pearls around her neck. Her fine cheekbones, the soft curve of her lips, the delicate line of her jaw told that she was once a beautiful woman, but already, at thirty-seven, her dark hair was flecked with grey, her features were pinched, old before her time, the face a sick woman. Karen was standing at her left side wearing a calf-length black dress with a white collar. Her eyes expressed a deep love for her mother, yet there was also the pain of seeing her mother's suffering, the eyes of a child older than her twelve years, clutching her mother's left hand, not wanting to let go of her. It was a dark picture, William Ryan gripping the top of Elizabeth Ryan's chair with his right hand, and his left gripping Karen's left shoulder like a griffin's talons, declaring that both were his,

his possessions, but a discerning eye would see that Karen's shoulder was lower than her right, shrinking away from his grasp.

The room was large, some 30-feet square. It had three windows, draped with the same brown and green brocaded material as in the dining room, again no expenditure wasted, not on *fabrics*. The front window when the drapes were pulled back, looked out at the track leading up to the house. The window on the far wall overlooked the side clearing, and beyond it the country road running past the house. The rear window looked out at the kitchen wing of the house and the back clearing. Seen through the half open door to a wide main hall, the top half of the front door was opaque glass. Across the hall was the door into the dining room, and from between it and the sitting room a wide staircase climbed up to a large square landing.

Sipping a generous glass of Courvoisier, and with the bottle on a side table nearby, Susan stood at the rear window peering between the drapes at Michael Rossi shining a flashlight at the ground around the foot of the leafless oak tree. He was again wearing his combats. A crow swooped at him, angrily cawing. Michael swiped at it with his flashlight. It flew away, screeching in protest.

It was the same crow that had earlier swooped at Paul, she knew it only too well. '*What is it with this damn house and crows?*' Paul had shouted. Well she could tell him, she brooded, remembering back to her first night in Clanryan after her dad had died, and being woken up by the noise of their cawing below the back bedroom she'd been given as her own. Although she was a young woman in body, she was then only fifteen and still innocent.

Getting out of bed and peeping through the drapes, William Ryan was tossing them scraps of food as they flocked around him. One crow, larger than the others, its plumage looking blacker and shinier and with longer tail feathers, was perched on Ryan's shoulder and it alone was being fed by hand, then it would nuzzle Ryan's face, thanking him, like there was a bond between the two.

As if sensing her in the window, Ryan glanced up and she quickly closed the drapes and got back into bed – but minutes later she heard the door open and William Ryan entered her room, sat on the edge of her bed and switched on her bedside light. Crows were predators. She little realized that she was going to lose her innocence to one blacker than them all...

'If you're wondering why I was feeding the crows, Susan,' he said to her in that gravelly voice she would soon come to hate, 'or rather, *my* crows, as I call them, it's because they bring me good luck. Luck that began the day I saw one with an injured wing by the rear porch – the one you saw on my shoulder. I was going to kill it, but a voice inside me told me not to...'

He reached for her hand, and his skin was surprisingly smooth, giving her a cringing feeling down her spine at its touch, and she tried to withdraw hers but he held on to it.

'...Until then, all I knew about crows came from myth, birds of ill omen that ate the flesh of ancient warriors fallen in battle, and carried their souls to the land of the dead. And so I read up on them, to see if there was any record of what happened to anyone who'd mistreated them...'

He stroked her hand. It was like being stroked by moist silk. Again she tried to pull her hand away. Again he wouldn't release it.

'...There were too many to count, but the one that stood out was Alexander the Great himself who had a raven guide him and his armies across a desert to Babylon, but as he stood at its gates it kept flying around him and he killed it with his sword...'

Still sitting on the side of the bed, he edged nearer to her. She tried to move back on her pillow but the bedhead prevented her.

'…After battle, Alexander always drank wine to celebrate his victories, but this time he collapsed and died in agony. Well, crows are of the same family, *corvus genus*, as ravens and *that* was enough for me, and instead of killing it, I made it a moss bed and began to restore it to health…'

He stretched out his other hand, it was as smooth as the other, and now cupped hers between his, making her flinch.

'…That same day my fortunes changed. Some bad investments I'd made suddenly picked up and kept rising, and I later sold them at a huge profit…'

His top hand started to stroke the back of hers, like he was massaging her, and she felt panic rising within her.

'…So, when my crow recovered, I clipped its flight feathers to make sure it stayed at Clanryan and maybe bring me even more luck than it already had – it was about the time your father and I agreed to go our separate ways…'

Agreed? Bullshit! It was you who dumped my Dad, you lying hypocrite. Now that you were making big money you wanted it all to yourself and because of it he's gone bust and hung himself. Well, I'm going to get my own back on you one day, Uncle William, no matter how long it takes – and will you get your hands off me, you scuzzy creep.

'…As I figured,' he kept stroking her, 'it was able to fly up only into the oak tree and roosted there. I gave him a name – a secret name that only he and I know – and every night I go out on the porch and call to him, and he flies down and sits on my shoulder and listens to me, and answers "yes" or "no" to anything I ask him by nodding or shaking his head…'

Stop pawing me, you sicko.

'...On that same day he was joined by a mate – they stay together for life, crows – and since then *all* my stock ventures have come off, and I am where I am today because of that crow. Soon more joined him, and there are now so many here that Clanryan is encircled by them...'

You're talking about them like they're an army and you're their general, you nut.

'...and nesting on most of the trees around here it sometimes seems, driving the ravens out of even Ravensburg – the place that took its name from them – so that the few ravens left around here now just inhabit just the cemetery, guarding the dead as it were...'

You among them one day, Uncle William, and the sooner the better if I had my way.

'...They also, for me, confirm what is said about crows – that they're so intelligent, they not only recognize people by their features, but warn other crows when strangers are about, especially those they sense to be a threat to them...'

He moved her hand and placed it on the inside of his knee. She tried to pull it away. Again he kept his hand clamped down on it.

'...But the crows on my oak are special, and as you saw from your window a moment ago, every Friday I give them a singular treat – cheese, biscuits soaked in blood from whatever animal I can find to kill in the woods – and when I go out to them they're waiting for me – it's as if they can count every seventh day – and from all the cawing that greets me, it's clear they recognize me...'

It's the food they're greeting, you weirdo, not you – and will you let go my hand and get out of my room, you're scaring me.

'...My crow is their leader, I see him marshaling them. He uses a distinctive *ko* sound to tell them what to do...' he mimicked the call

'…and they fly off to obey him and return here, like they regard Clanryan as their own. I fear how they will react when I'm gone, it wouldn't surprise me if they take everyone else but me to be their enemy and try to drive them away – though I hope not, for Karen's sake.'

He moved her clamped hand higher up his inner thigh.

'I'm sorry about your father, Susan, 'he said, 'but now that you're here, you are my responsibility and for this you must get to know me better…'

And he guided her hand to his–

'Sure it's a sick way of telling us he's still alive, Mr. Archer.'

Her spine shivering as she recollected that dread night, Sam King's voice brought her back to now as he agreed with something Paul had just said.

-8-

Banishing her nightmare, Susan gulped some Courvoisier and looked into the room where a log fire crackled and blazed in the fireplace's gray cast-iron fret. Wearing his dark blue jacket, shirt, slacks, and facing into the room, Sam stood to one side of the fire for Karen – sitting on a long, brown leather couch with Paul holding her hand – to feel the warming comfort of the flames. Morgan Hale sat in an armchair nearby.

'Sure it's a sick way of telling us he's still alive, Mr. Archer. But now you've said he was watching Mrs. Archer in the cemetery – and waiting for her on her way back home,' Sam said, 'it confirms for me that yesterday was planned.'

'And the rag doll, Detective King?' Morgan Hale questioned. 'Paul calls it sick. I would call it repugnant, blasphemous. Christ on the Cross and a painted whore – depicted as one in the same effigy. He's clearly sending us some message by it.'

Even more – Sam was about to ask – where did he get the rag doll from, out here in the middle of nowhere, and the hide patch and the needle and thread to sew it on with? – but Paul cut in first.

'You're reading too much into it, Morgan. The guy's a flake. The only message he's sending us is that he's still alive…' he clutched Karen's hand tighter '…and still intent on harming Karen.'

'I agree with you about his *intention*, Paul,' Morgan said, 'but I still believe there's a deeper meaning to embodying someone who was sinless, with a whore that epitomizes sin.'

'What about Minong?' Paul turned to Sam. 'Now we know he's alive and still pursuing Karen, couldn't they send a patrol car to at least try to search for him? They're only thirty miles away.'

'Thirty miles as an arrow flies,' Sam agreed, deciding to delay his question, and curious to see if anyone else asked it, 'forty miles or more along your roads. But I doubt they'd send anyone out this time of night – not for some sick joker, as they'll see it, dangling a rag doll from a tree.'

'Joker!' Paul erupted. 'Almost drowning Karen, and now hanging up an effigy of Christ on the cross, painted to look like a whore! What more proof could they want?'

'Stop saying *whore*, Paul,' Karen begged, almost in tears, 'that's worse than the Christ thing. And it was wearing my Gucci. I paid eight thousand dollars for it and it's ruined.'

Susan looked in sharply from the window as they all looked at Karen, no one quite believing they'd heard her aright.

'As for my Cartier watch, God knows where *that's* gone.'

Paul was the first to react. 'Sorry, *amante*,' he stroked her hair – Susan took another gulp of cognac, looked back through the window. 'I should have chosen my words more carefully. I was stressing the gravity of it to Detective King.'

'No need, Mr. Archer,' Sam took his lead from him, 'but Mignon will likely see the effigy as nothing more than him trying to scare Karen, and even though what happened yesterday at Ravens Pond almost turned disastrous, I doubt it will be enough for them to give you full protection.'

'Good God alive, no police protection.' Morgan sat up in his chair, appalled. 'Living out here is like being suspended back in time. Other than Ravensburg – and that's little more than a one-horse trading post reminiscent of the old Wild West – we're isolated, no one for miles around.'

'It's nothing like Chicago, that's for sure Mr. Hale,' Sam agreed, 'but when things are normal it has its compensations, if only for its peace–'

'Peace!' Morgan protested, 'smashing a window in the dead of night! As for calling emergency should he return, my cell phone kept cutting off before it went flat. And every landline here – with the exception of this room,' he indicated to a cordless in a charger on a side table by the window looking out on to the road, 'are all cradled with stretch cords would you believe, like something out of Noah's Ark, and subject to static interference.'

'This extension is one of dear Uncle William's three concessions to modernity,' Susan said, looking into the room, 'the other two were a laptop for his dubious share dealings.' She crossed the room to refill her glass. 'And his constantly updated BMW for us to see how wealthy he was on the backs of others like my Dad, his own brother,' her bitterness was evident in her tone, 'knowing damn well he couldn't take the stigma of being made bankrupt, that he would rather take his own life. Yet, he still ended their partnership.' Topping up her glass, she returned to the window and looked out again, sipping her cognac and brooding.

'That's unfair, Sue,' Karen objected, though but tokenly. 'I may not have liked the way Father ended their relationship, but he couldn't keep covering Uncle John's bad investments.'

'That's easy for you to say,' Susan said, not turning her face, 'having inherited all his money.'

'Okay, both,' Paul interjected. 'I don't mean to be abrupt, but what's past is past. What we need to think about now is the Jeep driver and how to stop him.'

'Please God,' Karen clutched his arm, her eight thousand dollar Gucci gone from her mind.

'Michael seems to be very much involved in this, Detective King,' Susan said, looking out at Michael as he probed the nearby woods with his flashlight. 'Rescuing Karen yesterday, and now checking outside.'

'He was in Hank's when Mr. Archer called,' Sam said. 'Said he'd come with me. His fender's dented but his truck's okay, and he followed me in case it was needed.'

'I still don't think we've given enough thought to the significance of him depicting the effigy as Christ on the Cross,' Morgan returned to his earlier comment.

'And a *whore*,' Susan added without turning her head.

Karen angrily sat up to remonstrate with her. Paul drew her back into his arms and resumed stroking her hair. Like he was soothing a vexed child, Sam thought.

Ignoring Susan's remark, Morgan continued. 'To me, it seems he wants to terrorize her first.'

'Oh, God, oh, God, he's an animal,' Karen twisted the band aid on her forefinger.

'Psychopath, more like, Karen,' Morgan said. 'Only a sick mind would depict Christ as a whore.'

'And where did he get the rag doll from in the first place?' Paul asked. At last, Sam thought.

'Guilty I'm afraid,' Susan turned away from the window. 'It's a Victorian doll I have for sale. And the fur patch, and needle and thread to sew it on, came, I suspect, from a stuffed pine marten and an old etui case. Sorry,' she said, sounding more matter of fact than apologetic, 'I should have said sooner, he must have entered my shop last night, but I didn't want to distract you all from—'

'It would have helped if you had,' Morgan snapped at her. 'The question of where he could have found them out here in the wild, has been on my mind ever since I saw it. It's a bit late now to tell us you had a break in.'

'I wasn't aware of it, not until I saw it dangling from the tree.'

'And how did he break in?'

'My shop door was unlocked. With no crime around here, I often forget to secure it.'

'But how did he know the doll was there?' Morgan demanded, having now assumed the role of her interrogator.

'It was sitting on a table in full view of the window. He must have entered while I was asleep. I have a brass bell over the door but didn't hear it ring.'

'And this morning?'

'My mind was with Karen, I didn't notice it had gone. What is this Morgan?' Susan suddenly objected. 'Are you seriously suggesting I'm in this with him?'

That's how it looks, Sam thought as Morgan shrugged and sank back into his chair.

Karen reburied her face in Paul's chest. He caressed her nape. Susan downed her cognac and looked back through the window and crossed her arms over her shoulders as if comforting herself.

'Could be you're right about him, Mr. Hale,' said Sam. 'It would take a twisted mind to think of crucifying a rag doll just to tell us he still means to–'

Checking himself before saying 'kill Mrs. Archer', he turned to Karen, her face still in Paul's chest. 'Do you have somewhere else you can stay, Mrs. Archer – well away from here?'

'Oh, yes, Paul,' Karen raised her face to his. 'Back to Italy? Or the Thompson Hotel? There, he wouldn't be able to get to me – not in a city, surrounded by people.'

'It would be just as easy for him to get to you in crowded city like Chicago, *amante*, especially as we've no idea what he looks like, then get clean away. If he *is* a psychopath, as Morgan thinks, he's not going to give up wherever we go, not until he's caught. We can't live in hotels forever.'

'Then it seems I've no choice, Mr. King,' Karen said, despair in her voice. She glanced up at her father in the portrait and suddenly, from nowhere it seemed to Sam, a hidden side of her surfaced. 'What's more,' a steely edge now entered her voice and she sat up, 'my father wouldn't have let anyone drive him out of his home, nor is he going to drive me out either.'

'I still think Mignon should give us some kind of back-up,' Paul said to Sam.

Susan turned sharply from the window and looked at Paul. Sam stored her reaction in his mind and replied to him. 'I still doubt they'll consider that this kook–'

'Psycho,' Morgan cut across him.

'–that he's done enough,' Sam said, 'to warrant them giving you twenty-four seven protection.'

'Then what the hell will it take them?' /Paul protested. 'Him succeeding in killing–'

'Paul!' Susan interjected as she saw Karen dig her nails into a cushion, as she once had when she herself lived here, and witnessed her pulling one off when William Ryan particularly angered her one day, tearing the quick from her finger, and blood seeping from it. She had already almost pulled one off earlier today for some reason, and they didn't need another. 'You're not in Chicago now, but as far from any police presence as you can get in Wisconsin.'

'Except it's not so easy, not when it's Karen's life on the line,' Paul said. He grasped her hand. 'It's just that I love you so much, *amante*.'

Susan refaced the window, knocked back the dregs of her cognac.

'I don't know whether you'd agree to this as a compromise?' Sam said.

'Right now, detective, any suggestion would be welcome,' Paul replied.

'Until you can find a security company to provide you with around the clock protection, I'll ask Rossi to share it with me. He's just bumming around at the moment. If he agrees, he can take the day watch, I'll do the night. And if this kook returns, we might even get a chance to nab him.'

'Oh, yes, Mr. King, thank you,' Karen said.

'My name's Sam.'

'Only if you call me Karen, Sam.'

'Sure, Karen,' said Sam.

'Then we'll take you up on it, detective,' Paul agreed, 'at least, for a few days – until we find someone to take over from you–'

'Michael's coming in,' Susan said.

Sam exited to the hall. Rossi entered through the front door. Their voices mumbled together as Sam put the proposition to him. They both came back into the sitting room.

'He's okay with it,' Sam said.

Karen mouthed to Michael, 'Thank you.'

He gave her a curt nod back, curt enough for Sam to realize he still had feelings for her and was hurting seeing her sitting so close to Paul.

'Find anything?' Sam questioned him.

'Some footprints,' he replied. 'I'm no cop, but I reckon they're too messed up to be of use.'

'You're both going to want paying for this,' Paul said.

'It's on the house,' Michael said, still curt and avoiding looking at Karen.

'That goes for me,' said Sam.

'Then in the absence of police protection,' Paul responded, 'thank you both.'

'And from me, Sam,' Karen said. 'With you and Michael outside, and Paul and Morgan inside,

I'll feel safe.'

'Four men enough for you, Kay?' Susan said with a brittle laugh. Crossing to the side window, she peered through the drapes at the fir trees on the other side of the dark country road, their tops dimly visible against the cloudy night sky and bending in a strengthening wind.

Seeing Karen tense up to retaliate, Sam cut in. 'Still on this kook, are you *certain* you've never crossed anyone, Karen?'

She tore her sharp gaze away from Susan. 'I'm positive, Sam.'

'My wife doesn't make enemies, detective,' Paul said.

'She couldn't if she tried,' Morgan gave her an ingratiating smile that she seemed not to see.

'Then is it possible he lost out in some deal he and your father were involved in?' Sam asked, 'and he's after revenge? Except in his twisted mind, he's now set on getting it from you instead.'

She hesitated before replying. 'Sure, my father was a hard man to do business with, Sam, and shrewd, but honest to the nth degree. He never defrauded anyone in his life.'

Seeing Susan turn sharply in from the window at Karen's assertion, clearly intent on making another sarcastic remark, Sam got in first and turned to Rossi. 'Then we'll get back outside.'

Rossi made for the hall. Sam followed him, but paused as his eyes went to the portrait over the mantel and fixed on William Ryan, seeing his thin lips, eyes that showed no feeling, his hands placed possessively on Karen's shoulder. Poor child, he thought, having to live alone in this house with such a man–

'I was ten,' Karen said behind him.

'So was Emma,' Sam grated, and exited the room and out through the front door after Rossi.

'What was that about?' asked Morgan.

No one answered.

No one knew.

Morgan glanced at his watch, a gold Rolex. 'It's getting late Paul, if we're going to board up the window,' he said.

-9-

Sam was sitting behind the wheel of his parked car outside Clanryan, with Rossi alongside him in the passenger seat. The dent in the Fusion's door had been beaten out. The rag doll sat in the rear behind them, crown of brambles on its head, crimson lips leering out of a window. Rossi's truck, front fender bent, was parked alongside the Ford. Other than a faint sliver of light showing through a crack in the drapes covering Clanryan's sitting room window, blackness enveloped them. Heavy clouds hung low in the night sky, scudding over the dark forest encircling the house, its faded white exterior standing faint and stark and alone against a sable backcloth.

'Norman Bates would have loved it here,' Sam said.

'Who's Norman Bates?' Rossi asked.

'*Psycho*. The shower scene. Stabbing Janet Leigh over and over again with a butcher's knife.'

'*That* Norman. I thought it was someone you knew. I saw the movie when I was on downtime in 'Ghan. It was in black and white though.'

'Hitchcock shot it like that. More atmospheric.'

'Her blood would have been better in color – all that red. Did you send the glove to Chicago?'

'Yesterday,' said Sam. 'They should have it today. Tomorrow at the latest.'

'How long will it take for them to send you their findings?'

'A week, maybe more. They'll have more urgent things to check first.'

'Do you think it will come up with his prints?'

'I doubt it,' Sam said.

'And unlike Cinder-fucking-rella,' Rossi said, 'we've no one to try it on for size.'

They looked through their windows at the surrounding darkness, and the low clouds passing over the encompassing forest, the tops of the fir trees swaying in the wind.

'It's getting stronger,' Rossi said. 'Seems we're heading for a storm.'

From somewhere in the distant north, over Lake Superior to the cold plains of central Canada, came a dim rumble of thunder, and for a split second, sheet lightning illuminated the night sky.

'Looks that way,' Sam agreed.

'Let me do the night shift.'

'This personal?' Sam asked.

'Guess so,' Rossi said, seemingly reluctant to say why, but telling it anyway. 'Had a crush on her in high school and wanted her to be my girl. Asked her out on a date and she said yes—'

'Same with me,' Sam said. 'She was the cheerleader, prettiest girl in college.'

'But then she went and asked Ryan would it be okay,' Rossi continued, deaf to Sam.

Sam was just as oblivious to what Rossi was saying.' We married. I loved her 'til the day she died. Still do...' he screwed his eyes shut with the pain of it. 'Cancer,' he said with a choke in his voice and saw Rossi wasn't listening.

'He warned me off with his fists. I was fifteen.' Sam heard the venom in Rossi's voice. 'Half killed me, the shit. Lucky for him he croaked it before I got back from 'Ghan, or I'd have fucking done it for him.'

'How'd he die?'

'Broke his lousy neck falling downstairs, according to Hank. More's the pity. I got at least ten of the Taliban bastards when I was out in 'Ghan. I was a sniper. Felt nothing. But Ryan? I'd have fucking enjoyed it.'

'And spent the next sixty years in stir for murder, Michael,' Sam said, using Rossi's first name for the first time.

'Beat the hell out of me,' Michael grated, still not hearing Sam, 'yelling I wasn't good enough for her. Pity he's not still alive, I'd have paid him back, and once I started on him, I wouldn't have known when to stop...' His voice tailed off and he simmered down, realizing he had betrayed how vindictive he still felt. 'When I heard he'd died I came home, hoping to pick up with her again...'

He brooded on it some more.

'Women!' he suddenly snarled again, bitterness back in his voice, 'you never know where the fuck you are with them. Breaking class for a feel behind the school sheds, but no further. I'd have waited for her, though,' he flared. 'Except she goes and marries a fucking stranger, years old than her...'

He was angry now, vicious.

'What's more, he looks like her fucking pa. That's got to be sick, don't you think, dropping them for a guy who looks like your fucking pa? Like it's incest. And only three days after meeting the prick. Women like that – fucking cock teasers – they should be–'

He stopped himself in mid-sentence and gave Sam an apologetic grimace. 'Sorry about that. Got carried away there for a moment.'

'That's okay,' Sam said, 'we've all been there in our different ways. Telling it can often help relieve it. The hell of it is when talking's not enough. When it's inside you so deep, the only way to relieve it is to do something about it...'

Sam paused, lost in his own thoughts again.

'…except it gets worse when you realize that what you'd planned to do is a step too far – yet something inside you is still *driving* you to do it – even though you know you're going to have to live with it the rest of your life.'

Realizing that Sam was talking about himself – about something that had happened to him in the past which he'd maybe not yet resolved – Michael hesitated to go further with this conversation, not wanting to probe into what was clearly troubling Sam, and returned to why they were sitting in the dark in his car outside Clanryan approaching midnight. 'I came in on the tail end of you all talking inside, and it set me thinking.'

Sam brought his mind back to Michael. 'About what exactly?'

'Who's trying to kill Karen and why.'

'And what did you come up with?'

'That maybe he's a hired hitman – working for someone else with a grudge, not himself? And going with what you were saying – against her sonofabitch pa, not Karen. He was a nasty piece of shit, Ryan, and must have made enemies.'

'Someone like you, you mean, Michael,' Sam said. 'Especially the way you feel about him? Karen, too, from what you've just been saying about her? Maybe it's you that's hired him?'

'Hey,' Michael protested. 'It was me that saved her.'

'You had little choice, not with witnesses present–'

'Witnesses be fucked. I could have drowned down there, what with the weeds so thick.'

'As you keep telling me. But it makes a perfect alibi should he succeed at his next attempt. It's also a bit too pat, you arriving on the scene at the very same time, and from the opposite direction.'

'So what if I was,' Michael flared again, 'I was returning home from a drive.'

'Simmer down,' Sam said, 'I was just ribbing you, and adding some hypothesizing to get your dander up and help you get her out of your system.'

'Yeah?' Michael responded. 'Well, if we're hypothesizing what about you? Being a cop you'd know where to find a hitman. And then you also turn up in this neck of the woods, four hundred miles from Chicago, and again at the exact time it happened. Maybe it's you that's got the grudge?'

'Against *Karen*?' Sam scorned the thought. 'I never knew she existed until yesterday.'

'No, against Ryan,' Michael repeated. 'Except, with him being dead, the only way is for you to have Karen done in instead. Maybe that's what was troubling you a moment ago, not knowing whether or not to go through with it?'

'Ryan?' Sam said, curt. 'I never met the man.'

'Got you there, Sam,' Michael grinned. 'Just ribbing, same as you. Think it's called hoisted by your own petard. Whatever a petard is?'

'It's a historical word for a small bomb that blows up right in your own face.' Sam replied, returning Michael's grin. 'But you sure as hell got me with it, right enough,'

A silence pervaded Sam's Fusion as both brooded with their thoughts. Michael broke it.

'Still hypothesizing, Sam – and also assuming he *is* a hitman – what about it being Archer who has the motive? Hank says he was broke when Karen met him, and with her having just come into Ryan's millions, maybe he married her for her money? Getting someone to kill her would–'

'Eliminate him as a suspect,' Sam finished it for him.

Paul and Morgan exited the front door, Paul carrying a toolbox and Morgan with a flashlight. They headed along the deck for the kitchen, Morgan beaming the way for Paul to see.

'Him and his homo friend,' Michael said. 'Working together.'

'You don't like Morgan?'

'Wouldn't last two minutes in the marines,' Michael derided.

A second silence pervaded the car. This time it was Sam who broke it. 'Of course, if we're *still* hypothesizing, there's also Susan. Her dad lost everything because of Ryan, and went and killed himself. Now that Karen's suddenly rich, but she's still having to count every cent in order to exist, maybe jealousy's made her vindictive—'

'No, not Susan,' Michael rejected the thought. 'She's one of the straightest I know, and sexy looking with it. If she was a couple of years younger I could go for her myself.' He visibly drove the thought of it from his mind. 'No, you can forget Susan, she thinks of Karen as a sister.'

'Except the way she was talking she seems to hate Ryan as much dead as when he was alive. And begrudges Karen coming into his money. Her story about the rag doll sounded suspect, too.'

'No, you're way off track there, Sam. You can definitely rule Susan out.'

'In that case, Marine Rossi,' Sam said, 'having rounded up all the usual suspects – as Claude Rains says in *Casablanca* – we're no wiser. Not unless this psycho, as Hale calls him, tries again and we manage to catch him. But for tonight, get a good night's sleep. You need to be focused when you're protecting someone.'

Michael hesitated, reluctant to leave it at this, then half opened the door: 'See you at eight?'

'Sure,' Sam said. 'Do you have a gun of some kind?'

Michael pulled his serrated bladed knife from its sheath and brandished it. 'This is all I need.'

'That's okay for close combat,' Sam said. 'With a gun you can take him from a distance.'

'I've got an old Colt forty-five of my grandpa's. And my pa's hunting rifle. Both kept oiled.'

'I won't ask if you've got a license for the Colt,' said Sam. 'Bring it with you tomorrow.'

'Will do,' Michael said. Re-sheathing his knife, he got out of Sam's Fusion, crossed to his Dodge Ram, got in it and closed the door, ignited its engine, switched on his lights and drove off.

Left alone, Sam went back to that terrible day imprinted into his memory, when his own world ended and he no longer wanted to live anymore, and the tears welled up in his eyes. Surrounded by the blackness of the night, he stared through his curtain of pain at the isolated clapboard house.

'A life for a life,' he whispered.

Somewhere out there in the darkness, a timber wolf howled.

It sounded to Sam like the wolf was hunting alone.

Outside the pack.

-10-

Bridling her resentment at Karen's, '*He never defrauded anyone in his life*' - that certainly wasn't true of the way William Ryan had treated her father – Susan sat on the sitting room sofa and held her cousin's hand. 'You sure there's no one you've ever ticked off, Kay? Some loony ex-boyfriend?'

From the kitchen came the sounds of the window being boarded up.

'You know damn well he wouldn't let me have one, Sue,' Karen indicated at William Ryan frowning down at them from above the mantelpiece. 'Death before dishonor and all his clan Ryan crap. Besides, living in Ravensburg there was only Michael, and you know what father did to him.' She blurted out the lie of it, not wanting Susan to know she'd enjoyed petting with Michael in the shrubbery behind the school sheds, eagerly playing hooky from classes to get there – and as many times a week as she could. 'Paul was the first to ever touch me.'

'At twenty-seven!' Susan protested. 'You've got to be joking. I know you didn't get a chance after he wouldn't let you go to college, but I assumed you'd at least experimented in high school. I did, despite–' Biting her tongue, she glanced up at him in the family portrait, *hating* him still.

'God's truth, Kay,' Karen crossed herself, praying, though she didn't believe in Him, that He wouldn't punish her for invoking the lie.

She indicated at her father again. His frown, it somehow seemed to her, had deepened. 'You know what he was like. The day we buried Mom, he made me swear over her coffin–'

She checked herself from going any further.

'I'm sorry Kay,' Susan clasped her hand. 'I should have realized. 'I loved your mom, but not him.' She inwardly shuddered at her dread memories of William Ryan. 'Especially the evenings I was left alone with him after you were sent to bed before me–'

Susan again bit her tongue. She didn't want anyone, especially Karen, to ever know.

Sitting in his Ford Fusion, Sam could hear the sound of hammering coming from the kitchen wing of the house as Paul and Morgan boarded it up – one guess as to which of them would be holding the flashlight for the other to do the work, Sam thought.

Pulling out his leather wallet from an inside pocket of his jacket, he opened it and looked at a photograph of Emma and her Mom – the last one of them together, taken a year before Gina began feeling ill. Gina – short for Luigiana, his teasing name for her was Luigi – was half Italian from her mother's side. Lustrous dark hair, tanned skin and slim, and sensuous curves in all the right places, she was the most beautiful woman he'd ever seen. Emma had inherited her soft brown eyes, eyes that had held such warmth – but now no longer would, because of–

He stroked Emma's face, yearning for her…

Paul and Morgan appeared from around the far corner of the dining room. Morgan shone the flashlight on the front facing windows and checked they were shut tight. Paul acknowledged Sam with a curt nod and entered the house. Morgan gave him a friendlier nod and followed Paul inside. Reflected light lit up the hallway as they entered the sitting room, then went out as they closed the door behind them.

Sam replaced the photo in his wallet and settled into his car seat for the night. From all around him there was nothing but silence and blackness. Clanryan was still barely discernible against the dark woods and the night sky from which no stars were shining, not even the North Star any more.

And the moon had long disappeared behind the low hanging clouds.

A light switched on in the main hall. Moments later, another light came on in the bedroom above the sitting room. Sam looked up and saw Paul enter the room, then Karen on crutches. Paul crossed to the window. Without looking down at Sam, he closed the drapes.

From the far distance came another rumble of thunder, a flash of sheet lightning momentarily silhouetted Clanryan against the encircling forest as the approaching storm came slowly nearer. It was not a large storm as storms go, cold winds from the north meeting a warmer wind from the east and driving it inexorably onwards, extending from its center like the curved horns of a bison, and the storm center moved with them, its wind increasing in strength and the cold north air thrusting itself under the warmer eastern air, ensuring that when it arrived it would be torrential. Above it rode menacing clouds, bringing thunder and lightning with them, and bursts of drumming rain and hail. Soon it would cross the Canadian border and over Lake Superior, the wind at its center blowing in a circle and creating a swell that would cause the level of the lake to rise and go before it, swirling over dark waters darkened even more by the storm itself, sucking them up into heavy rain that would pour steadily, unremittingly down. A mountain barrier could have stopped it, the storm would have risen over it and passed over north Wisconsin and gone further south. But north Wisconsin was flat and would bear the brunt of it.

A sudden gust of wind, precursor of the storm, came from nowhere and passed over the roof of the forest, bending the tops of the fir trees and whistled through the leafless branches of the oak tree, and the black crows perched on them squawked in protest…and then went instantly quiet as if something imminent, something ominous was about to happen.

Sam felt for his revolver in his shoulder holster under his jacket, making sure it was there.

In the bedroom, Paul placed a glass of water and a small bottle of pills on the bedside table, took a folded black lace nightdress from under Karen's pillow and spread it on the duvet. She sat on the edge of the bed, placed her crutches on the floor, and extended her arms out for him to undress her.

'I'm just going to say goodnight to Susan,' Paul said.

'But Paul–' she protested.

'Start without me, I'll only be a moment,' he said and he exited out to the landing, closing the door behind him.

It was a large, square landing. Opening directly on to it were the doors to four bedrooms, two in the back of the house, two in the front. One of them – Karen's – was over the front of the sitting room, the other was over the front of the dining room, and both looked down on the parking area. The bedroom behind Karen's was over the rear of the sitting room, the other back bedroom across the landing was over the rear of the dining room. Between these two rooms a corridor led over the kitchen wing to a study that had once been

William Ryan's but was now Paul's, overlooking the side clearing and the country road. Opposite it was Karen's studio, overlooking the back clearing enclosed by fir trees. At the end of the corridor a window looked out over both the back and side clearings, and the country road where it emerged out of the forest from Ravensburg.

Paul ran down the stairs to where Susan was waiting for him in the hall and held her hand. She put the first finger of her other hand to her lips and pointed up to Karen's bedroom, telling him to be careful of what he said.

Paul nodded and questioned her in a normal voice. 'See you sometime tomorrow, Susan?'

'Possibly,' Susan replied for Karen to hear.

He embraced her, she kissed him fully on the lips and pulled away. 'I hope Karen gets a good night's sleep,' she said out loud. 'Call me first thing in the morning and let me know.' She opened the door, her hand still lingering in his.

'Without fail,' Paul whispered.

Sam saw the front door of the house open. Susan and Paul appeared in the doorway. Her hand was in his, and lingered there, her arm outstretched before letting go, turning away, and heading for her red coupe, glancing nervously at the surrounding dark trees.

Sam lowered his window. 'Everything okay inside, Miss Ryan?' he called out.

'Considering,' Susan replied as she kept walking.

'I'll make sure Karen gets a quiet night,' Sam said.

'Thank you, Detective King.' She reached her coupe and got in. 'Goodnight.'

'Goodnight,' Sam replied.

She closed her door, ignited her engine, switched on her lights and drove off, waving to Paul through her open window.

Sam looked at Paul standing in the doorway, waving back to her as she headed down the dirt track, then glanced up at Karen's window and saw her peering through the drapes at Susan driving away – the roof over the porch was hiding Paul from her view. Susan exited out of the drive on to the road and turned for Ravensburg and was swallowed up by the forest. Paul closed the front door.

'Close cousins, huh?' Sam said to himself. 'Maybe Karen doesn't realize how close?'

He looked up at her in the window. She looked down at him…and the face Sam now saw was Emma's. She was wearing her black dress with white lace collar. She gently shook her head at him, telling him not to seek vengeance, and smiled at him, the smile of someone at peace.

Sam buried his face in his hands.

He was hiding in the thick shrubbery behind Sam's Ford Fusion.

His eyes moved from him to Karen Ryan in her bedroom window.

'*Whore*,' he whispered, hatred in his voice.

He hoped the effigy had terrified her. Terrified her out of her wits. And part paid her back for what she had made him suffer, choking and almost drowning in that putrid pond. In the hours after he recovered from the dreadful experience, he had brooded about how to pay her back, and then recalled seeing the rag doll in the antique shop while having to wait for her to return from Italy, and send her plunging to her death over Carvers Gulch the first chance he would get, which, as fate had decreed it, was the very next day, her going to the cemetery had been heaven-sent–

Except it had failed…failed…failed…failed.

With an effort he controlled himself. Nevertheless, the doll had been perfect. Returning to the pond for her coat and watch, it had been easy getting into the shop with the door left unlocked. As for cutting the patch of fur from the pine marten and sewing it on, a few tacks was all it had taken. Nor had the mascara, eye shadow, rouge, lipstick been a problem, he always had his own with him. As for the crown of brambles, it grew in abundance by the wayside, and there he had it: an effigy of the Christ to represent her need for forgiveness for her carnal sin – and his own need to achieve reparation from the whore she really was.

Add her coat for there to be no mistake about who the effigy stood for – he'd conflicted within himself about adding the Cartier, too, for there to be no possible doubt and give it an artistic touch, but despite it being ruined he couldn't part with its gold. Still, the finished embodiment was a work of genius, sure to make her terrified of him, and in dread of what he would do to her next.

He glanced at his gold Rolex watch – a Submariner, water resistant.

Not much longer to wait.

Say four hours for all inside to be asleep.

He looked up at in her bedroom window.

'I'm coming for you, *whore*,' he whispered.

And headed for the back of the house.

Still looking down at Sam, curious why he was burying his face in his hands, Karen saw the rag doll leering up at her from the back of his car and hurriedly shut the drapes, crutched back to her bed and sat waiting for Paul to return and undress her.

And as soon as she was naked, stark naked, she brooded, feeling an anticipatory tingle down there, she would slowly, seductively, part her legs for him, and *then* see if he could resist her…

Paul entered the room and crossed over to her.

Impulsively, she stretched for his hand. 'Thank you.'

'For what?' Paul smiled, amused by her almost childlike earnestness.

'For being you,' she squeezed his hand. 'For being strong. Until I met you, I never felt safe.'

'Shucks, pardner,' Paul affected a cowboy drawl. 'Twern't nothing.'

'I'm being serious, Paul,' Karen said, more like a child again than the woman she now was.

'You're everything to me.'

Seeing how intense she was, Paul dropped the play-acting. 'No, it's me who should be serious, and more appreciative of your support. I'm not cut out to be an actor. Writing was always my dream.'

'Then we were meant for each other?' she entreated. 'A perfect couple?'

'Sure,' Paul said.

Hurt by his casual reply, expecting it to be an emphatic response from his heart, she almost let go his hand, but then seeing him standing there in front of her, legs slightly parted, his crotch only a short stretch away from her hand, she fought off the temptation to reach out and cup it, and raised her arms again for him to undress her.

Paul reached for the phial on the bedside table, tapped a red and yellow capsule from it into his hand and proffered it and the glass of water to her.

'Sleeping pill. From the hospital. After all that's happened to you over the last couple of days, you need to wipe it from your mind. The best guarantee for that is a long night's sleep. Oblivion.'

Sleeping pill!

A fucking sleeping pill!

Oblivion!

After what she'd been hoping for!

She snatched the glass and slammed it back on table. '*Shove it up your rectum.*'

Paul turned away, crossed to the window and peered through the drapes, trying to stay calm. She damn well *had* to take it, or their plans for after she was asleep, dead to this world, would be ruined.

All was quiet outside. In his car, Sam King had his face buried in his hands. He couldn't give a toss why the goddamn cop was doing this, but him guarding the house could help persuade her to take the damn pill.

She had to take it.

He faced back into the room. 'The Chicago cop's outside, looking alert. No one will get past him.' Crossing back to the bed, he reoffered her the pill. 'You really *must* get a good night's sleep.'

She hit it out of his hand. '*I told you what to do with it. Shove it up your—*'

'Karen,' he cut across her, trying to reason with her. 'I'm only thinking of you.'

She forced herself to simmer down and thrust her arms up. 'Then help me get into my nightie, and I'll take it after you come to bed.' Long after, she thought, after I've fucked you rotten.

'I'm going to sleep in the room behind you,' he said, 'I want to be sure you get a long rest.' He tapped another pill out of the phial. 'So, please take one.'

Immediately panicking at the thought of being alone in this big room without him, her rancor dissipated. 'No, Paul, please,' she begged, grabbing his arm, 'Stay with me and just hold me then. *Please.* We don't have to do anything. I'll feel safer and sleep better if you're with me.'

'No, Karen,' he pulled his hand out of her grasp. 'With your back, it's better you sleep alone. I'll only be next door should you wake up, except you won't – not after taking this pill.' He placed it aside on the table and picked up her nightdress off the bed. 'I'll just help you into this–'

She snatched the nightdress from him. 'I can undress myself.'

'Karen!' Paul put on an injured air, trying to apply subtlety now instead of reasoning, 'I'm only sleeping in the next room because I'm *concerned* about you.'

'Then go to Susan's and sleep with her, she's even further away.'

'Susan? Whatever put that thought into your head?'

'Who else would she have been waving back to as she drove away – Morgan? I don't think so. Susan likes her men to be men, not like Morgan. She thinks I don't know she's been sneaking off to Chicago for months now for dirty weekends – like it's a *great, big, secret*. And knowing her as I do, probably with some married man she's met. And now she's lining you up.'

'Karen,' he protested. 'That's unwarranted–'

'Come to that,' she flew at him, her darker nature in total control of her now – she wanted to make wild accusations, 'maybe it's you she's been–'

'Karen!'

'God, is that all you can say, Paul. Karen! Karen!'

'Please! You're being unreasonable–'

'Fuck off, Paul.'

Paul stood there in shock now, not having witnessed this extreme side of her before.

'I said fuck off. I'm not getting undressed while you're watching.'

'Karen!'

'Fuck off!' she screamed. 'Fuck off! Fuck off!'

Paul spun away and exited the room out on to the landing.

'And leave the door open,' she shrieked after him.

Paul half closed the door behind him and went up the corridor to his study.

Snatching up the pills bottle, she hurled it across the room, cursing herself for having lost it.

When it flared she seemed to have no control over it. She started to feel panicky. Having now seen this other side of her, would Paul shrug it aside as just a tantrum and forget it? If he loved her the way he said he did then he would...*surely*...and attribute it to all the pressure she was under.

It was Clanryan, her father's presence still filled the house. She'd felt it the moment she entered the house again on getting back from honeymoon, as if from beyond the grave, he was determined she would never be happy.

But he was dead.

Dead. Dead. Dead.

And she was glad he was dead.

She wished he'd died sooner.

For her to be free of him sooner.

All those wasted years gone.

When they could have been enjoyed.

Sitting there on the bed, she rocked herself.

Wouldn't he *ever* leave her alone.

God, Paul was right.

She needed oblivion more than being fucked.

Oblivion from *him, him, him*.

Reaching for the pill that Paul had left on the table, she swallowed it without water and tore at her black lace nightdress. 'There's no *fucking* point wearing *this*,' she swore, reducing it to tatters and hurling it to the floor. Crutching to a mahogany chest of drawers, she yanked out a pair of pale blue pajamas, loose fitting, shapeless, changed into them and got under her duvet and wrapped it around her.

Her right hand went inside her pajamas pants to her clitoris. She needed comforting as well as oblivion. She stroked it, quickened her finger as she felt her eyelids get heavy and she came. It wasn't eruptive, more gentle and sensual, but it was nice.

She curled herself up and snuggled her face into her pillow.

He crept across the grass making for the kitchen window. As he neared the oak tree he heard one of the crows in it give a low growl – a single growl rapidly repeated – telling the others in the tree that it was one person approaching – Beware!

The other crows added their growls to the first's. He couldn't see them against the dark sky, but it immediately became a chorus of growls, growing in intensity out of the darkness into harsh caws, threatening him that if he came any came nearer they would attack, screaming as they dived off the branches at him, talons outstretched to claw his face to ribbons and drive him off.

He made for the porch, and as he climbed the steps to the rear deck away from them, the same crow gave a different sound – more of a sharp ko than a caw – and the others obeyed him and went silent, but he could sense them still watching him through the darkness, their black eyes fixed on him, each one vigilant to ensure that whatever he was up to was no threat to them.

Pulling a flashlight out of a pocket, he shielded its beam with his hand and shone it on the boards.

From the oak came a combined rustle of feathers as the light made them agitated again.

He checked the slats. They were mostly old, partly rotting, and badly nailed down. He'd have them off in no time. He placed a hand on the bottom slat and switched off the flashlight.

The rustle of feathers died down, but he could still feel them watching.

He inserted his crowbar by touch under the slat.

A distant flash of sheet lightning silhouetted the oak against the night sky.

There must have been at least fifty crows – all ebony black – perched on its leafless branches and all looking silently down at him, watching his every move.

From the same crow again – it looked bigger, with larger tail feathers, than the others gathered around him – came the gravelly voice of a man.

'My name is Midas,' it said, mimicking the one who had trained him to say it. 'My name is Midas.'

Hearing it, his blood ran cold.

And then the sky went dark again.

He could still sense their presence.

But he could no longer see them.

He prized at the first slat.

-11-

The boarding over the window had been removed.

Inside the kitchen, he took all the carving knives out of their rack, laid them out on a working surface and deliberated over them, deciding which to use.

Choosing a large one with a double-edged blade, he swished it through the air, imagining himself slicing her with it and causing her such pain, before finally ending it by cutting her throat, then lifting what was left of her nightdress, exposing her genitalia – and slicing and slicing it until the whore would never be able to use it again.

But of course she wouldn't be able to use it again, he exulted.

She'd be *dead. Dead. Dead.*

Replacing the other knives in the rack, he picked up the one he'd chosen, crept into the dining room and over to the door to the hall. Cracking it open, he hid behind it, stroking the carving blade, feeling its sharpness.

He heard someone descend the stairs and peered through the thin gap between the door's iron hinges. It was Paul.

Switching off the upstairs landing light, Paul glanced at the door as if knowing he was behind it. Clutching the knife, he thought Paul was going to enter, but then the sitting room door opened and closed, leaving the hall light on, illuminating the way up to her bedroom.

He waited.

From the sitting room came the sound of orchestra music. He knew it, *Moonlight Serenade,* slow music to dance to from way back in the forties. Exiting the dining room he crept upstairs, holding the carving knife thrust at arm's length by his side.

Karen's eyelids grew heavier as music drifted up from the sitting room below her. Soothing to listen to, it reminded her of lying on the beach in Positano, listening to *Moonlight Serenade* with Paul. She smiled to herself. First thing in the morning, she would say *"sorry"* to him, he would forgive her, and all would be well between them again.

Through her half open door, the light from the hall below cast his shadow on the wall, slowly creeping up the stairs, clutching a large knife in his hand.

Eyes closed, she didn't see it. Still smiling to herself, she fell asleep.

The shadow came higher up the stairs and peered through the banisters into her room.

He looked at her lying oblivious in her bed.

One slit of her throat and she would be dead.

But being dead she wouldn't have suffered enough for what she had put him through.

She had to suffer even more before he ended her life.

An eye for an eye, a tooth for a tooth.

Your suffering for my suffering, you *whore.*

It was justified.

He crept back down the stairs to wait until the house was in darkness and all was still.

In his Ford Fusion, Sam heard the dance music coming from the house. *Moonlight Serenade,* one of Gina's favorites, she and he sometimes used to dance to it, slowly, only shuffling really, holding each other tight after Emma had gone to bed.

Gina, only thirty-seven…*cancer.*

Emma, only twelve…*hit-and-run driver.*

One *evil.* The other *vile.*

Both had deprived him of the two he loved most in the world.

There was nothing he could do about the cancer. There was never anything he could have done about the cancer. It was always beyond his control.

There was nothing he could do about the hit-and-run driver either.

It too was beyond his control.

But there was one thing not beyond his control…

The music ended.

Sam up looked at Karen's bedroom, as if waiting for something to happen behind its window, drapes closed, no light shining behind them, telling that the room was in darkness.

Below Karen, the sitting room door opened, Paul and Morgan exited into the hall. Paul turned off the hall light and switched on the landing light and they came upstairs.

Morgan waited out on the landing, Paul entered Karen's bedroom. He checked the bedside table, saw the pill had gone and peered at Karen. She was lying on her side, body curled up under the duvet, face on the pillow, out to this world. For some reason, she had a smile on her face. He crept out of the room, closed the door, and under it the landing light went out.

Leaving the house in darkness.

A door closed and all was still.

Karen turned onto her back, her smile faded, her hands lashed out as if fighting off some night- mare presence from approaching her bed. Just as suddenly she stopped and returned on to her side, her face nestled back into the pillow, and she sank again into a deep sleep.

Her door cracked open.

He crept in, a flashlight beam punctuated the darkness.

A floorboard creaked as he approached her bed.

She didn't move.

From his left hand dangled something that was blacker than the darkness of the room.

He placed it next to her face, dipped his finger into it and wrote on the pillow, staining it.

He shone his light on her and looked down at her lying there, sleeping, pulled the carving knife out from inside his clothing and suspended it over her, drawing out the moment.

'*Whore*,' he whispered.

The knife flashed down.

He looked her, all still now.

He smiled. Gloated.

And crept out of the room.

-two-

-12-

Sam switched off Fox 11 News weather bulletin on his car radio and looked up at the dark dawn sky. The storm was still moving slow, still hadn't grown in size, and with no mountains to stop it was still headed for north Wisconsin, sending forewarnings of what was to come – gusts of wind, showers of rain that started then stopped, and a drop in the temperature. Sam shivered, huddled into his jacket, feeling the cold after a night awake without his car heater on. The pressure at the center of the storm was falling, its cold front had overtaken its warm front and was containing it, then in its own time would release it. The rain would be heavy, in places stormy, in other places its frontal winds would be gale intensity, and the polar air still piling up behind it over Ontario would bring sleet and snow and slate gray clouds containing lightning and thunder that, as yet, were still some distance off. But as sure as fate they would arrive. Sam slapped his arms across his chest to restore circulation. What a time of the year to be spending a night in a car in north Wisconsin, surrounded on all sides by a dark forest, and only a Norman Bates-like clapboard house to look at.

At the rear of the house, the crows in the oak tree were creating a hell of a din. Something was clearly bothering them, he brooded – "murder", the collective name for a group of crows couldn't be more apt for them – they were screaming fit to murder, the kind of collective screaming that was made either in anger, or in grief – or both.

Through the glazed glass front door, a light switched on on the upstairs landing, then Karen's bedroom window, still draped, lit up. Moments later, the hall light came on and the blurred shape of a man wearing mauve hurtled down the stairs. He struggled to unlock the door, yanked it open and Morgan Hale, in mauve pajamas and mauve slippers, came running out on to the front porch yelling to Sam, 'He's got into Karen's room. It's ghastly. Ghastly.'

Sam shot out of his car and ran for the house, took the porch steps in two bounds and into the front hall and tore up the stairs. Behind him, he heard Morgan say, 'I need a brandy', and go into the sitting room.

Sam burst into the bedroom. Wearing a dark blue toweling robe over dark blue pajama trousers, Paul was standing at the foot of the bed holding Karen, wearing pale blue pajamas, in his arms and stroking her head and "shushing" her "*amante*", trying to calm her as she clung to him, shivering, her face streaked with blood.

'What the hell's happened?' Sam asked. From Morgan's reaction he'd thought to see Karen not just murdered in her bed – but killed in a most brutal way.

Paul moved aside for Sam to see the bed, the duvet hurled aside.

A dead crow lay in its own blood on one side of a hollow made in a pillow by Karen's head. On the other side of the hollow, buried into the pillow, was a carving knife. Above the hollow, printed in the crow's blood, were the words:

NEXT TIME

The knife was buried less an inch from where Karen's head would have been. Had she moved while it was descending, it would have entered her skull. The crow's blood staining the pillow told that it was freshly killed when it was placed there, its neck cut in half and held together only by its black feathered skin. And likely explained the din from the crows in the oak – still protesting at its vicious butchery and at its killer, even though he was long gone from them by now.

But having somehow got into the house and crept upstairs to Karen's room, and with her lying asleep at his mercy, why instead of killing her had he tableaued such a macabre scene? The insanity of it went through Sam's mind–

'How in the hell did he get past you, detective?' Paul demanded. 'How come you didn't see or hear him?'

'This house has eight walls, Mr. Archer,' Sam returned, 'six of them with windows, and I've got only one pair of eyes.' Indicating the words on the pillow, he expressed the more glaring question, 'But however he got in, why didn't he–'

He stopped himself before asking, 'Why didn't he kill her?' – realizing that waking up and seeing a carving knife buried an inch from her face in her pillow, and a dead crow with a slit throat lying on it, and the words NEXT TIME written in blood above it, could spook most women out of their wits – but then he saw that Karen was too much in shock to hear what he was saying.

'It doesn't make any sense,' he said to Paul.

'Sense doesn't come into it,' Paul grated. 'As Morgan said from the beginning, we're dealing with someone who's evidently not right in the head. Loco. Deranged.'

Sam glanced at the pillow next to Karen's and saw no depression in it. 'I see you didn't stay the night with her, Mr. Archer. Knowing he was still out there, I hardly thought you'd let her sleep alone.'

'Yes, okay, detective,' Paul said, curt. 'I should have stayed with her.'

'No, it's not okay!' Karen erupted out of her stupor, pushing Paul away and hitting his chest with her clenched fists. 'It's no fucking way okay!' she flared, surprising Sam with her language, and her ferocity, almost beside herself, it seemed. This was a side of her he'd not seen before. She kept hitting Paul. 'I asked you, begged you to stay with me.'

'I'm so sorry, *amante*,' he pulled her, resisting, to him again. She struggled to get out of his arms. Then just as suddenly she gave in and collapsed into them and buried her face into his chest, her arms around his waist and clutched him tight.

Stroking her head, Paul turned to Sam. 'I thought it best for Karen to get a good night's sleep. I slept in the next room with the door half open should she want me, and woke early to check on her. She was asleep, but then I saw–' he choked, unable to relate the scene that met his eyes. 'I called Morgan and he came running. When he saw it – the knife in her pillow…' Paul turned to the bed, taking Karen with him, '…the dead crow–'

'Oh, no,' Karen moaned, looking at the dead bird in horror. 'It's Midas's mate.'

'Who in God's name is Midas?' Paul demanded.

'*His* – my father's – lucky crow. I can tell her by the white patches on her tail feathers. Midas will make Clanryan will suffer for this,' she whimpered, believing what she was saying.

'Nonsense, *amante*,' Paul said, trying to pacify her. 'There's no more to crows than any other bird.'

'Not Midas,' Karen clung to Paul, clearly in awe of Midas. 'My father swore he's as intelligent as us. Ever since he settled here, he brought him nothing but good luck.'

'A coincidence,' Paul insisted, 'nothing more.'

'He'll be wanting revenge for this.' She repeated, staring awestruck at the dead crow.

'Karen, *please*,' Paul protested, getting exasperated by her persistence.

'More to the point,' Sam said, 'how did the kook catch it to kill it?'

'What does it matter how?' she turned on Sam now. 'All that matters is that he did. From the very first day we got back here, things have been going from bad to worse. And he's going to try again.' Karen pointed at her pillow. '*Next time*. It's written in her blood.'

'Karen, *please*,' Paul repeated. 'You surely don't believe such superstitious baloney—'

The sudden ringing of the bedside phone pierced the room.

Shriiiiiiilll...

Sam and Paul exchanged glances. That someone was calling so early in the morning, before dawn had fully broken and it was still dark outside, made its insistence stridence sound ominous.

Shriiiiiiilll...

Karen looked at the ringing phone as if transfixed by it.

'Why doesn't Morgan answer it?' Paul snapped, making no move to pick it up.

Shriiiiiiilll...

Sam snatched up the corded black receiver from its cradle. 'Clanryan.'

'I could have easily killed her.' His voice was a whisper. Venomous.

Sam nodded to them it was him. Paul drew Karen closer.

'Then why didn't you?' asked Sam, wanting to keep him on the line – he could slip up and say something that might reveal more about himself.

'I decided to slit her pillow instead of her throat.'

'Why?' Sam asked again. 'You tried twice, so why not last night?'

'Because she made me suffer.' The whispered voice was vicious now. 'I almost drowned. Water choking me, blackness all around me. Now she's going to suffer...*suffer*...' the voice rose to a scream, then a whisper again. 'Until death itself will be a mercy to her ...*the whore!*'

'Except there'll be no next time,' said Sam.

'Oh, but there will. I've waited long for atonement. And now, as promised, the end is near.'

'Yours, not hers.'

'Next time I *will* kill her. Nothing is surer.'

'There's no way you'll get near her again.'

'It will be soon,' the voice whispered. 'Very soon.'

The line went dead.

Sam replaced the receiver in its cradle. 'He cut me off.'

Karen pulled away from Paul, 'I'm not staying another night here,' she flared. 'We're leaving – now! And going back to–'

'Now's not the time to be making decisions, *amante*,' Paul gripped her shoulders. 'You're too – we're too emotional. We need to think things through calmly.'

'Calmly!' she was half sobbing now. 'It's not your life he's threatening.'

'I only wish it was me, *amante*,' he stroked her face, 'and not you. But we should still talk it through first.'

'What is there to talk about?' she implored him. 'He wants to kill me!'

'Paul! Paul!' They heard Morgan running up the stairs. Still in his mauve pajamas and no robe, he burst into the bedroom. 'He pulled the boarding off the kitchen window–'

'So now we know,' Sam said to Paul.

'He's also just phoned,' Paul told Morgan. 'Detective King answered it.'

'I saw him,' Morgan blurted, words spilling out in his agitation. 'I had to go to the kitchen for more cognac, and in the shock of seeing how he'd got in, I didn't switch on the light and saw him standing at the edge of the woods watching the house and holding something to his ear. It must have been a cellphone because the kitchen extension rang, and then it stopped and he started talking into it. All I could make out was that he was tall, about six feet at a guess, wearing dark clothes. But then he must have seen me and vanished into the woods.'

'What about the outside door?' Sam asked. 'Was it open?'

'Closed and locked on the inside.'

Sam turned to Paul. 'He must have got out the same way he got in.'

'Or the window outside my study?' said Paul.

Sam exited out to the landing and saw the window at the end of the corridor. The door to Paul's bedroom was open. His double bed was still rumpled from when he woke up to check on Karen. Both the other bedroom doors were closed, one would be Morgan's – but Paul said that Morgan 'came running' when he called to him earlier, Sam brooded as he headed up the corridor. Pausing to close the door behind him seemed somewhat contradictory, to say the least.

Like all the others in the house, the window was a sash. The bottom half was pulled up. There were blood smears on the inside and outside sills. They would be from the dead crow. He had clearly got out this way and down the adjoining drainpipe and into the woods. There was no blood on the pipe, it must all have smeared off on the sills. It was too dark out there to see beyond the tree line, but Sam got the feeling that his eyes were staring at him from the edge of the forest.

The crows in the oak tree were still creating bedlam, one sounding louder and angrier than the others. That would be Midas, Sam thought. Karen hadn't been fanciful when she said he'd be mad as holy hell about his mate. Closing the window, he returned to her room.

'It was open,' he said as he entered, 'and blood on the sills. That's the way he took, sure enough.'

'It must have been,' Morgan said. 'I checked it last night before turning in and it was shut then. I wanted to be sure that Karen would be safe – this house is so dated, not even a burglar alarm.'

Karen dropped onto the bed as if her knees had given under her, 'I'm getting away from here today, Paul, as far away as I can.' She reached for her bedside phone. 'I'm calling O'Hare now.'

Paul clasped her hand and sat beside her. She tried to pull it away, he held on to it. 'I still think it best that we talk it through, *amante*. But later, when it's light and with clearer minds—'

'Talk things through!' Karen yanked her hand away. 'Fuck you, Paul, fuck you! It's *me* he's trying to kill, not you!'

This time her flare-up didn't surprise Sam. He realized this was the real Karen – or at least the Karen she kept hidden under a veneer of being elegantly confident, and yet vulnerable –

Sam broke off there. Both faces – confident yet vulnerable – were in opposition to each other. And now her flare-up. How many Karen Archer's were there? How many sides did she have?

Paul put his arm around her shoulder. She tried to shrug it off but he pulled her closer. 'We'll make sure he doesn't get to you again, *amante*. If he's crazy enough to try, he'll find—'

'He'll find what!' Her voice was still fractious, but creeping into it was a plea to be reassured. 'That he can break in here just as easily next time.'

'No,' Paul tilted her face up to his. 'Trust me on this, *amante*, he won't get to you again. Meantime, I think the best thing now is for you to get a few more hours sleep, at least until it gets light—'

'Sleep!' she erupted again, close to breaking point once more. 'Are you mad! How can I sleep here, and in the same bed, after he—'

'I'll stay with you,' Paul insisted. He gestured with his eyes to Morgan, indicating the bottle of pills lying on the floor near the window.

'I agree with Paul, Karen,' Morgan said, handing the bottle to Paul. 'I'll get you a clean duvet, sheets and pillows. With fresh linen it won't feel the same bed.'

'Sam?' she pleaded up to him.

'It's still early outside,' Sam said. 'It's best you sleep on it first.'

Searching their faces again, Karen resigned herself. She reached for the glass on her bedside table and extended her other hand to Paul for the pill. He unscrewed the phial cap, ejected a red and yellow capsule and broke it in half. 'I'm only giving you half a pill,' he said. 'Just enough to help you get back to sleep, and better able to make the right decision when you wake up and it's daylight again.' She swallowed the half pill and returned him the glass. He replaced it and the phial back on the table and helped her to her feet, leaving his arm tight around her shoulders.

Morgan began stripping the bed. Taking fastidious hold of the carving knife by its handle, he placed it on the table, tilted the pillow and let the dead crow fall on to the undersheet, and rolled it around the decapitated bird. Hurling the pillows out on to the landing, he picked up the duvet and undersheet and exited the room.

'Burn them and the damn crow with them,' Paul said to him. Morgan kicked the pillows down the stairs and descended after them. 'And bring a facecloth and towel to wash Karen's face,' Paul called to him.

Karen's hands jerked up to her face. She lowered them, looked horrified at the blood on them, then saw the carving knife, stained red with the crow's blood, on the bedside table.

'Get it out of my sight!' she screamed at Sam.

Sam picked it up by its point. 'I'll send it to Chicago,' he said to Paul. 'He may have slipped up and left his prints on it.'

Karen tore herself away from Paul and sat back on the bed, rocking herself to and fro as she waited for Morgan to return with new bedding. Paul sat alongside her and held her again. 'What are the chances?' he asked Sam, indicating the knife held between Sam's first finger and thumb.

'Slim,' Sam said. 'Same as the gloves I sent them yesterday.'

'Get it out of my fucking sight!' Karen screamed again, covering her face with her hands.

Sam wrapped it in a large handkerchief, stuffed it under his jacket and paused at the door. 'I'll do some quick repairs to the boarding, and as soon as Michael takes over I'll get back to Hank's and ask him does he know someone who can come today to replace the window.'

'Thanks,' Paul said.

Sam exited the room and went downstairs into the sitting room. Crossing to the cordless landline he pressed CALLS and checked the screen for the number of the one he'd just answered.

There was no record of it.

No record? How was it possible to have an incoming call and not have it listed. Yet it didn't appear on the screen.

He scrolled down the previous calls.

The last one was an outgoing call: (715) 862-1945, 00.32am Today.

Half an hour past midnight. An odd hour for someone in this house to be calling out...

The one before was an incoming call: WITHHELD, 11.49am Mon.

The same morning the Jeep drove Karen off the road into Ravens Pond…

The one previous was also an incoming call: (715) 862-1945, 11.26 am Mon.

23 mins before the WITHHELD call…

The one before that was an outgoing call: (715) 862-1945, 4.53 pm Sun.

It was almost an open line between here and that number Sam thought.

Scrolling back, he stared at the screen, brooding again as to how there was no record of the call he'd just answered. He replaced the phone in its cradle and peered through the drapes.

Dawn was climbing above the dark forest, yet the sky was getting blacker. The oncoming storm, though slow to peak, was still headed this way. Complex in its build up, when it finally reached it could be mega-scale…or spend itself out from within and pass by, leaving little or no destruction.

Only time would tell.

He glanced at the country road as it wound its way out of the trees, and straightened as it went past Clanryan, then disappeared back into forest. Nothing had driven past in all the time he'd been sitting outside keeping watch on the house. It was not just the back of beyond, he thought to himself, it was the back of the back of beyond, and the nearest police – other than himself, Sam gave a grim smile – were all of forty twisting miles away, and the only habitation – if it could be called that – in all directions, north, south, east and west, was Ravensburg.

Why Ryan had brought his young wife to this god-forsaken place and then remained here after Karen was born, subjecting them both to a life of loneliness, only Ryan knew, unless it had given him a feeling – an irrational feeling, Sam thought in his mind – of being king of all he surveyed, all being nothing more than a wooded wilderness, and maybe given him an imaginary sense of power, when in truth, as Sam knew for himself only too well, he'd been a man with no guts – no guts at all.

But whatever his reason, it had left Karen isolated out here and almost defenseless, and a man she didn't know hiding somewhere nearby, determined to kill her and tenacious enough to succeed – unless she could later persuade Paul to change his mind and take her away. Still, by the time she awoke it would be too late for them to go today – time enough for him to carry out his threat of NEXT TIME.

Exiting the sitting room and out of the house and down the porch steps, Sam bent his body to the strengthening wind as he walked to his car.

The storm was coming, with the disposition of a capricious woman, cold and warm combined in one body. Preparing herself to strike, but only when *she* was ready. Unlike the national weather channel that gave universal names for only large storms, Fox 11 weather news gave names to all north Wisconsin storms, alternating between women's and men's names. This one was a woman's, and by coincidence started with K – Katie.

A better name for it, Sam thought, would have been Karen.

He settled into his car seat to wait for Michael.

From the back of the house, the crows were now silent.

Creating, by their very silence, an ominous stillness that hung over Clanryan.

Like a portent of things still to come.

If one believed the things that were said about crows.

-13-

Shriiiiiiilll...

The strident sound of the bedside phone ringing brought Karen slowly back to consciousness, yet it was a relief, banishing the vivid nightmare she was having of a man who wanted to kill her standing over her bed with a featureless face – like that of Munch's *The Scream*, white eyes with no pupils and flecked red veins – staring down at her from under a black cowled robe, and holding a Grim Reaper's scythe that slowly metamorphosed into a double-edged carving knife.

Shriiiiiiilll...

'Paul,' she muttered, lying on her side not fully awake, eyes still shut. 'The phone.'

He didn't answer, didn't stretch across her to pick up the receiver.

'Paul,' she repeated, more insistent now, feeling her temper rise.

There was still no response from him. Was he expecting her to do it!

'Paul!' She stretched her hand behind her to shake him.

He wasn't there.

Her eyes opened in alarm. She turned her head and saw the hollow on top of the duvet where he'd been lying. Her aggravation dissipated, panic replaced it. He had promised to stay with her until she woke up. She turned her face back and stared at the ringing phone.

Shriiiiiiilll...

It sounded even more strident now, as if insistent it should be answered.

She sat up. The bedroom door was closed. 'Paul!' she screamed at it. 'Paul!'

There was no answering voice. The house was silent. Silent as the grave, the thought came from nowhere into her mind, making her spine go cold.

Shriiiiiiilll...

'Paul!' she screamed again.

The stillness from behind her door was eerie now. Turning to the ringing phone she forced herself to think calmly, logically about who could possibly be ringing. She glanced at the bedside clock. 9.44. The daylight penetrating into her room through the drapes was somehow comforting. As was knowing that Michael would be below her window in his truck. She glanced again at the clock. Quarter to ten in the morning. It would be Susan – it had to be Susan, calling to see if she'd had a restful night's sleep, and unaware of last night's dread events – not knowing he had crept into her room, nor about the dead crow on her pillow, or the carving knife buried in it, or the writing in blood, or about this morning's call from him. Having immediately lain down with her to ensure she got back to sleep, it was unlikely that Paul had phoned her yet, to let her know.

She lifted the receiver, her movements lethargic from the effect of the sleeping pill: 'Susan.'

From down the line came the sound of breathing. Slow, sinister breathing.

Hearing it, she was paralyzed by the dread realization it was him. Unable to release the phone, she heard his voice come from it, sibilant like that of a cobra before it strikes.

'I see your drapes are still closed. I hope I didn't wake you.'

Karen looked at her window. He was out there at this very moment, staring at her room.

'Leave me alone!' she shrieked into the mouthpiece.

'I did – last night,' the voice whispered. 'You looked so peaceful I granted you a stay of execution. Until the next time. And *then* you will die.'

'Leave me alone,' she shrieked at him again.

'But I must have atonement. And the only way I can achieve it is by your death.'

'Why me?' she was whimpering now.

'You are the only one who can give me reparation.'

'But I don't even know who you are.'

'You will. Just before I kill you.'

'Please, please, no,' she begged.

'Too late to beg,' whispered the voice. 'It's inevitable.'

She slammed the receiver down on its cradle. '*Paul!*' she screamed. '*Paul!*'

The same deathly silence pervaded the house. Hurling her duvet aside, she grabbed her crutches propped against the wall by her side of the bed and hobbled out on to the landing. All was still, no sound from anywhere upstairs or downstairs.

'*Paul!*' she shrieked. Crutching to his room, she flung the door open. His bed was unmade from when he'd got up earlier this morning to check on her – but no Paul.

She crossed to Morgan's rear bedroom door opposite and rapped on it, frantic now. '*Morgan!* Again no reply. She opened it. His bed was meticulously neat, looking as if it hadn't been slept in, hardly a crease in the duvet cover and the pillow plumped up – but no Morgan.

She crutched along the corridor to Paul's study. '*Paul!*' she screamed, throwing the door open. He wasn't there. She turned to her own studio and entered the room. '*Morgan!*' Again, no Morgan.

Half painted canvases she'd not had the patience to finish, were propped against the walls. In the middle of the floor was an easel with a blank canvas, not yet started on. Discarded brushes and squeezed tubes were scattered across a table. Half open drawers in a pine chest held messy sketchpads. On top of the chest was her father's laptop – she'd moved it out of the study for Paul to know the room was his now, no trace of William Ryan having ever occupied it. But Morgan had clearly been here earlier – the bottom half of the sash window was open. She crutched to it to close it.

From the top of a cupboard a crow cawed threateningly at her. She looked up and saw Midas, wings spread open, poised to fly at her, and instantly knew why he was in the house. He'd come seeking vengeance for the death of his mate. 'My name is Midas,' he said in her father's gravelly voice and swooped at her, talons outstretched, angrily cawing.

She hit him to the floor with her crutch. It was done instinctively, impassively, with no fear in her at his sudden attack. Midas lay there, broken wings flapping, unable to rise. Using her other crutch as a prop, she lowered herself and knelt beside him, wrung his neck, and tossed him through the open window. 'Fuck you, Midas,' she said.

From outside came the sound of angry cawing. Pulling herself up on her crutches, she looked through the open window. Midas's dead body was already surrounded by his crows from the oak, all angrily protesting. More from the perimeter trees were swooping down and joining them.

A large crow resembling Midas enough to be his offspring, suddenly looked up and saw her in the window. Immediately assuming the leadership of the murder, the one to avenge Midas's killing, he soared into the sky, high above the oak, and dived at her. She waited – and slammed the window closed. He hit the central strut in full flight and dropped to the ground. Dead, she hoped, looking down at the crows as their shrieking increased. 'Fucking crows,' she said. One by one they went silent and looked up at her. She felt the hatred in their black eyes, but none challenged her now.

'Fuck you all,' she said to them, locking the window latch, and with suddenness reverted back to the Karen of before. '*Paul!*', she shrieked and crutched backwards out of the room…

…into a man standing in the corridor.

Petrified, she screamed. From behind, he clamped his hand to her mouth. 'Ssh,' he whispered, and slowly turned her to face him.

Paul.

Seeing him, she freaked. Dropping her crutches, she beat at him with clenched fists. 'I thought you were him, I thought you were him. Where were you, where were you? I've been calling you.'

'Well, I'm here now,' Paul said, gripping her shoulders, forcing her to drop her arms. 'Susan rang earlier, you were still asleep. I took it in my study so as not to disturb you, told her all that had happened, and that I'd given you another half pill to help you get off again. She said she'd phone you later, and I went down to pay the workmen for replacing the window. I'm sorry if I–'

'He's called again!' she shrieked across him. 'The phone woke me up–'

'It was him!' Paul's voice rose in disbelief. 'I heard it ring in the kitchen, but just as I got to it, it cut off. I thought it was Susan calling back–'

'Yes, it was him, it was him, it was him!' she screamed again. 'It kept ringing and ringing and you weren't there and I…' she choked on her words, '…I picked it up.'

He held her to him. She tried to push him away. He wouldn't let go. She gave in and collapsed into his arms.

'You should have called Morgan,' he stroked her hair.

'I did,' Karen replied, her voice like that of a little girl lost now. 'He wasn't there, either.'

'Blast him,' Paul swore. 'He promised to–' He yelled down the stairs. 'Morgan!'

There was no reply from Morgan.

'Morgan!' Paul yelled again.

Morgan rushed out of the dining room. 'What's happened? I was in the washroom, rinsing the duvet cover–'

'He's called again,' Paul grated down to him. 'Karen answered it.'

'Oh, poor you, Karen,' said Morgan, aghast. He started up the stairs, intent on consoling her. 'I heard it ring and assumed *you'd* answered it, Paul–'

'No!' Paul stopped him. 'Call the damn cop.'

'He's gone back to his cabin to sleep. Michael's outside.'

'Then fucking call Michael!' Paul snarled, failing to control his spleen at Morgan's inaction.

Morgan turned to the front door and hurled it open.

Sitting in his truck, Michael was talking on his cellphone to Sam.

'The window's been replaced,' Michael said, 'the workmen have left and all's quiet here–'

He saw the front door hurl open. Morgan Hale emerged in an obvious panic. Michael wound his window down. 'He's phoned Karen again,' Morgan shouted to him.

'I don't know if you heard that,' Michael said to Sam. 'He's called again.'

He cut off Sam's reply, jumped down from his truck and ran for the house.

Replacing his cellphone in his jacket pocket, Sam prized himself off his bed and sat on its edge and looked at the carving knife lying tossed aside on a table, still wrapped in his handkerchief.

Through his window, Ravensburg could be seen to be but a few clapboard buildings – sparsely spaced. Hank's gas station, repairs shop and general stores. Michael's small house and "Ryan Antiques" across the road. A previous one-horse trading post, suspended back in time.

He got to his feet, picked up the carving knife and walked out of the cabin and into his white Ford Fusion, switched on the engine and drove away in no hurry.

In a corner of the cabin, the rag doll sat leering in an old rocking chair.

Susan stood behind the Dickensian-style paned door of her antique shop, watching Sam drive off, and holding a cordless landline phone in her hand.

She pressed REDIAL. The phone called the last number. The ringing tone was cut short and an angry voice snarled down the line. 'When I get my hands on you, you sicko, I'll–'

'It's Susan, Paul,' Susan cut across him.

'Sorry, Sue, I thought it was him again,' Paul replied, terse. 'He's just called Karen. I'll call you back.' The line went dead.

Susan fingers hovered over the keys, deciding whether or not to make another call.

-14-

Clanryan. Mid-morning. In the sitting room, all five were silent with their own thoughts.

Sam was standing, as before, below the portrait of William Ryan gripping Elizabeth Ryan's high-back chair with one hand, his other on 12-year old Karen's shoulder. Sam could feel Ryan's eyes boring into the back of his head, forever master of CLANRYAN.

Michael was standing just inside in the open doorway, Morgan was sitting in his usual armchair, wearing pale blue today – or was it pale green, it was difficult to tell – open-collared shirt, V-necked sweater, knife-creased slacks, the same cream-colored slip-ons as yesterday. Looking like a tailor's dummy, Sam thought.

Paul and Karen were sitting on the couch, Paul immaculate as ever in his light blue fine-denim jacket and jeans – how he'd found the inclination, or the time, to bother about himself after all that happened to Karen this morning, was beyond Sam.

But the biggest enigma was Karen herself. Crutches by her side, she was sitting as close to Paul as she could get, her right arm tucked under his left, and instead of putting on any old clothes after all she'd been subjected to over the last forty-eight hours, she had taken time to decide on a close fitting white sweater that gave her the bust line of a pin-up model, and tight black jeans – my "sexy jeans" was how Gina described them, Sam recalled with an ache in his heart, whenever she wore hers to look particularly good for him, though Gina always looked good to him whatever she had on, or off, for that matter – and white pumps with wedge heels, as if competing, the thought struck Sam, with the way Susan Ryan looked yesterday. Her make-up immaculately applied, too.

It was as if she was many personalities in one, Sam brooded, recalling all the varying moods he'd now seen her exhibit. Most women would be nervous wrecks after all she'd been put through.

Being watched from a sinister black truck, when she was all alone in a cemetery.

Chased by it along a country road, a fender glued to her tail and her car rammed.

Almost forced over the edge of a gulch to her certain death.

Driven into the trees at Ravens Corner where she'd have been killed if she'd hit one head on.

Almost drowned in Ravens Pond – had it not been for Michael Rossi rescuing her.

Him creeping into her bedroom last night and plunging a carving knife into her pillow one side of her head, leaving a slit dead crow the other side, and the message NEXT TIME in its blood above it.

And now two phone calls from him – one he'd taken himself – the other she'd picked up, saying he was still going to kill her, that she was his atonement, his reparation, whatever he meant by that.

She was…Sam searched for an apt word for her…she was a contradiction, clinging to Paul for support, yet had found the will power to deliberately dress up for him – and exhibit, there was no other word for it – that whatever her cousin had, she had more of.

Glancing through the window and seeing layers of dark clouds moving in different directions across the distant sky – one weather front moving against another, a sure sign that depending on which of them was the more dominant, the promised storm would be here within the next twenty-four hours or so – made Sam think of them as an analogy of her varying moods: light one minute, dark the next. Maybe it was caused by her inheriting opposing traits from her parents. Light from her mother, dark from Ryan, conflicting within her for ascendency, but with Ryan's influence the greater because of her having lived alone with him, influenced by him after her mother's death. If so, perhaps he should feel sympathy for her, a child living alone with such a man, far removed from the companionship of other children her own age, subject to his domineering say. One had only to see how many portraits there were of him in this house – stern of face, condemnatory even – to realize how overpowering the man must have been–

'Have you sent the knife to Chicago for testing, detective?' Paul broke into his thoughts.

'I've not yet had the chance, Mr. Archer. I'll send it later today.'

'Later could be too late,' Paul replied. 'We need him identified now, before he tries again.'

'Soon as I get back to Ravensburg,' Sam said. Crossing to the window overlooking the road, he took the wrapped carving knife from his jacket pocket and placed it on the phone table, picked up the cordless receiver and checked the screen for CALLS made or received since he last checked.

It showed four more. All incoming. All from (715) 862-1945.

The last one was at 9.57am this morning.

The one before that was at 9.36am, 22 minutes earlier.

The one before that was at 9.21am, just 15 minutes previous.

And the fourth as early as 6.53am.

6.53 – it was only minutes before Paul checked on Karen, and saw the knife in her pillow and the message NEXT TIME in blood – and straight after it had come the call he himself had answered...

Coincidence? Sam brooded. His second call had also come only minutes after the call at 9.36.

He scrolled back. No, there was no record of his second call either. *How in the hell had he blocked them?*

He scrolled down again, confirming that the rest of the calls were those he'd already seen, and decided to start querying them with the one received this morning at 6.53am.

'Most of the calls here are either to or from the same number, Mr. Archer – 862-1945?'

'Susan,' said Karen. 'But I've called her only once–'

'They're all personal, detective,' Paul cut in, 'and of no relevance to his calls'.

'It's the police procedure I'd use in Chicago, Mr. Archer,' Sam said.

'We're anxious to answer any question you want to ask us, Sam,' Karen stressed. Sam sensed she wanted to hear Paul's answers for herself.

'Relating to him, amante,' said Paul. 'But Susan's calls are private.'

'We've nothing to hide, Paul,' Karen countered, 'not from Sam. Surely?'

'Of course not,' Paul swiftly returned. It sounded to Sam that his reassurance was forced. He refaced Sam. 'Which one first, detective?'

Sam glanced at the screen. 'Miss Ryan's call at six fifty-three this morning. Why so early?'

'With all that's happening here, detective, I don't regard seven minutes to seven as early. But to answer you – she was anxious to know what kind of a night Karen had after yesterday. I heard the phone ring, and as there's no extension in the bedroom I'm in, I hurried to my study to take it before it woke Karen. I didn't know then he'd got into her room, and I told Susan she'd had a good night – I had no reason to think otherwise – but on my way back to bed I checked in on Karen and saw it all – the carving knife, the dead crow, the message in blood on her pillow, and called Morgan, and he ran outside and called Michael–'

'But if I recall right, Mr. Archer,' Sam interjected, 'you said you went straight to Karen's room when you woke up?'

'Which I did,' Paul said. 'As soon as I ended Susan's call.'

'Yet only minutes after your conversation with her, he made his first call here, which I took?'

'That would be about right, detective. Your point being…?'

'None, Mr. Archer, merely remarking on the fact.' Sam glanced again at the screen. 'And the call you made to her six hours earlier? Thirty-two minutes past midnight? And with all respect, Mr. Archer, I would regard that as late.'

Sam saw Karen's body stiffen. 'I wanted to make sure she got home safe last night,' Paul said. 'With this madman on the loose I needed to be certain, for Karen's sake. Susan's like a sister to her.'

Sam saw the tenseness go out of Karen. Glancing again at the screen, he decided to go back further and clear up the previous calls. 'And the withheld call at 11.49am, on Monday morning?'

'That would be Karen, phoning from her car – just before he tried to force her off the road and into Carvers Gulch.'

'Oh, God, yes,' Karen gripped Paul's arm. 'He was on my tail, ramming me. I was desperate. Calling Paul was the only thing I could think of.'

'And the call at 11.26, twenty-three minutes before that – from Miss Ryan again? Karen would probably have been at the cemetery at that time.'

'No,' she answered before Paul. 'I was just reaching it. I remember glancing at my dashboard clock and it was 11.25.'

'She wanted to speak to Karen,' Paul replied to Sam's question. 'I told her she'd taken flowers to her mother's grave. She said she'd ring back and ended the –'

'It was another ten minutes before I saw him in his black truck watching me at the graveside,' Karen interjected. 'He glared his lights at me and I –' she choked on her words.

'And then I got Karen's call from her car telling me she was being tailed,' Paul added.

Seeing Karen go rigid at the recollection of it, Sam quickly asked, 'And the one to Miss Ryan at 4.53pm Sunday?'

'That was me,' Karen found voice to say, 'letting her know we were back from honeymoon.'

'Okay,' said Sam, scrolling up the screen, 'which brings us back to the calls after his first one this morning, starting with Miss Ryan's call...' he glanced at the screen, 'at 9.21am – some two and half hours later?'

'Is all this necessary, detective?' Paul questioned.

'Just covering all the bases, Mr. Archer,' Sam said.

'It was to see whether Karen was awake yet,' Paul replied, curt. 'I was lying with her and she was deep into her second sleep. I grabbed the phone before it could ring twice, but it disturbed her and made her restless, so it was now me having to whisper to Susan that I would call her back.'

'Without even telling her what had happened here during the night?'

'I've just explained that detective. I didn't want to wake Karen.'

'Nevertheless, Miss Ryan still called you back – only fifteen minutes later, at 9.36am?'

Sam saw Karen tense up again as she waited for Paul's answer.

'She'd sensed something was wrong when she rang at 9.21, but Karen was sleeping soundly once more, so I crept out of bed and took it in my study, and now told her all that had happened – that he'd broken in, the carving knife, the crow, the message, and that he'd phoned here some two and half hours earlier. She wanted to come right over, but I told her I'd given Karen half of another sleeping pill, and I'd call her back to let her know when she was awake. I then went down to pay the men for the window, and was out on the deck when I heard the kitchen phone ring, but before I could get to it, Karen picked it up–'

'I wish I hadn't,' Karen shuddered. 'His voice, it's –' she broke off and shuddered again.

Sam gave her a moment to gather herself. 'And what time would it have been, Karen? Would you happen to remember?'

'9.44. I looked at my bedside clock before answering it, to see how late in the morning it was.'

'That would place him at eight minutes, no more, after Miss Ryan's call here at 9.36–'

'Detective King,' Paul cut in, curt. 'This is the second time you've stressed that both his calls here came only minutes after a previous call from Susan. I hope you're not inferring–'

'Sorry if I'm giving that impression, Mr. Archer. I'm just summarizing the sequence of the calls made to and from here in my mind.' And before Paul could reply, Sam glanced again at the screen. 'The next was also an incoming call – from Miss Ryan again, her last this morning, at 9.57?'

'She saw you drive out of Ravensburg in a hurry,' Paul replied with ill-humor, 'and panicked that something else had happened to Karen after her previous call. But like I said, he'd just made his second call to Karen and I again had to say I'd call her back — but I've not yet had the chance. She must be worried out of her mind.'

Karen yanked her hand out of his. 'God, hearing you so concerned how Susan must be feeling, Paul, after all that's happened to me, makes me ask myself why I'm so fucking traumatized.'

Paul took her hand back. 'I didn't mean it to sound like that, *amante*, I was replying as briefly as I could for Detective King.'

Seeing Karen's jaw tighten, Sam moved on before she could reply. 'Appreciated, Mr. Archer.'

He scrolled the screen back and showed it to Paul. 'This shows the call that Miss Ryan made here at 6.53am this morning, but as you can see there's no record of the call he made here only minutes after.' He scrolled again and re-showed the screen to Paul. 'And this shows Miss Ryan's later call at 9.36 — and again there's no record of the call he made, eight minutes later, at 9.44—'

'Detective,' Paul cut in again. 'Would you not keep inferring that Miss Ryan—'

And he was at the cemetery only ten minutes after she called Paul at 11.26, Karen thought. *It could of course have been a coincidence, but it was an odd coincidence, nonetheless.*

'I'm not, Mr. Archer,' said Sam. 'It's just that the screen doesn't show either of his calls.'

'Which implies what?' Paul demanded.

'Just how in the hell is he blocking them?'

Paul absorbed this. 'You're right, detective, that *is* odd.' He thought a moment. 'Hiding out in the woods, as he must be, he has to be using a cell, so maybe it has something to do with weak signals, surrounded as he is by trees?'

'But if his calls are getting through,' Sam said, 'they should also show up on the screen—'

'Well, I just hope the wolves get him,' Morgan venomously cut across him.

Reminded of Morgan Hale's presence in the room, Sam put his perplexity aside for a moment. 'I also noticed you've not made any calls while you've been here, Mr. Hale, not even to Chicago?'

'But I thought that was why you chose to work in my studio, Morgan?' Karen questioned him. 'Because it has a landline extension you could use, what with your cellphone being flat?'

'No, it was in case I needed to call out,' Morgan stressed. 'As it happened, I didn't.'

'Yet you had a number of withheld calls,' Sam said. 'The last one the day before Karen and Mr. Archer got back from Italy?'

'The theater, to discuss my designs. As were all the previous calls. But there was never a need for me to call them back.'

There was a word to describe the way Morgan was replying, Sam thought. It came to him – glib. It was as if he'd anticipated being questioned and rehearsed his answers. But maybe he was being biased, he just couldn't take to the man. Dismissing it, this was no time for personal prejudice, he now included all in the room as he returned to the two unrecorded calls.

'Which brings us back to how is he blocking his calls?'

'I agree with Paul, detective' Morgan said. 'He has to be using a cellphone. I saw him earlier on the edge of the woods, don't forget, holding one to his ear—'

'No,' Michael cut in, 'it can't be his cell.'

'And why not?' Morgan snapped at him, as if his word was being questioned.

'It's at the bottom of Ravens Pond,' Michael said. 'I saw it in the weeds – gold-cased – when I was down there, hooking Hank up to the Jeep. But I had to come up for air.'

'Why in the hell didn't you go down again and recover it?' Paul turned on him. 'It could have given us the man's name–'

'I would have done,' Michael's hackles shot to the surface, 'but the Jeep was on its way up by then, and without it as a marker, there was no way I would have found it again.'

'Mr. Archer's just concerned, Michael,' Sam said, 'not blaming you.' Paul remained deadpan, making no attempt to excuse his reaction. 'Yet it makes it even more baffling,' Sam reflected. 'If he's without a cellphone, he must be using a landline.'

'But there are only two others around here, Sam,' Karen said. 'Hank's and Susan's.'

'Hank's had his cut off,' Michael said. 'It was corded. With his gas station, stores and chalets to look after, he finds it easier to use a cell.'

'Then that leaves only Susan's…' Karen's voice tailed off as she realized the implication of what she was saying, added to the coincidences of him phoning only ten minutes after Susan had called…and again him being at the cemetery not long after she herself had got there.

'No, it can't possibly be Susan's, Karen,' Paul said. 'That again is as good as implying she's in this with him. Sheltering him, even. And that's absurd, as I've said to Detective King.'

'Yes, of course it is. Sorry, Susan…' Karen apologized to her absent cousin. But Sam saw that she said it without conviction.

'Well, I insist I saw him talking into one,' Morgan repeated. 'So he must have another.'

'But if he had, Mr. Hale,' Sam reasoned, 'he was under the water so long it would be useless.'

'Maybe he's using a phone booth?' Michael said. 'There's still one at Cobbs Bend. I saw it as I was passing the other day. But it's years old and I don't know if it's working.'

'How far is Cobbs Bend?' Sam queried.

'Half a mile, maybe.'

'Half a mile?' said Sam. 'That's surely too far for him to be using.'

And when he called me, Karen was about to say, he knew my bedroom drapes were closed, but decided to wait until she could somehow get to talk Sam on his own about his obvious suspicions over Susan's calls, and maybe dampen her own suspicions about them.

'And yet he's still calling here,' Sam added. 'And in some way able to block his number?'

'Then he must be using the one at Cobbs Bend,' Michael repeated.

Sam was forced to agree. 'I guess he must be.'

'Well, whatever I saw,' Morgan joined in again, implying by his tone he'd not been mistaken in what he'd seen, 'he's hiding close by. When I checked around the house this morning, I found a dead crow beneath Karen's studio window – its neck had been wrung. Only a psychopath could have done such a thing. Whatever his abhorrence with crows, it hadn't long been killed, and when I picked it up by its feet and threw it as far away as I could, the others – one in particular – created a most vociferous protest. But it proves he must be out there somewhere.' The gaining wind outside rattled the windows. 'Though how he can possibly survive out there in this foul weather,' Morgan shuddered at the thought, 'I can't begin to imagine.'

Only one dead crow, not two, Karen brooded. So, son of Midas was still alive. She'd hoped she'd killed him, too, leaving them without a leader, for them to fly away from Clanryan for good, taking all reminder of *him*, her father, with them – other than his staring portraits everywhere, that is, *and* his clan Ryan shield, *and* his griffins. If she had been intending to stay on here – which she wasn't, it was still back to Positano for her, and as soon as Sam and Michael had gone she would be phoning O'Hare – but if she had been staying on she would have trashed them, *and* the heavy old furniture, *and* the old fireplaces, *and* the old kitchen range, *and* the old cast iron log boiler, *and* the ugly old cast iron radiators, everything damned thing that reminded her of all the excruciating years she'd had to endure here alone with him—

'Another possible reason for his calls not being recorded, detective,' Paul cut into her dark thoughts, 'is that the landline here is so dated – as Morgan has previously pointed out. Get Mignon to put a tap on it.'

'They drove over yesterday and gave the jeep a cursory check,' Sam said, 'but found it to be clean and lost all interest in it, especially as there was no fatality. I now liaise with Chicago on it. As for a tap on the line, that's easier said than done. Permission could take days.'

'You have to be kidding!' Morgan exclaimed.

'Afraid not, Mr. Hale,' said Sam.

'In that case,' Paul persisted, 'even though the Jeep has no license plates, is there no other way of tracing it? Engine, chassis number…'

'Except if he's not its first owner, tracing him won't be easy. And again, it could take days.'

'Good God alive,' Morgan cut across him, 'talk about living out in the backwoods!'

'We appreciate all you and Michael have done for us, Sam,' Karen broke into their exchange, wanting him and Michael to now go, for her to phone O'Hare and put thousands of miles between her and all her conflicting thoughts running through her mind about Susan. 'But we'll be leaving in a few hours and going back to Positano – staying in Chicago tonight and flying out tomorrow.'

Paul gripped her hands. From the pained expression on his face, Sam guessed what he was going to say. 'I was giving it some thought while you were asleep, *amante*, agonizing over it. God knows I love you, and would do anything in the world to protect you. But if you're not here, he'll have no cause to stay either. But when we return, so could he.'

'I've no intention of returning!' Karen flared, 'I'm staying there for good this time! Whether you want to come with me or not is up to you!'

'You can't mean that,' Paul protested. 'Not with what we mean to each other.'

'Oh, but I do. It's my fucking life at stake here, not yours.'

'No, *amante*, hear me out first,' he insisted. 'If he's so determined to get you, it shouldn't be hard for him to find us wherever we've gone. While he remains free, you won't be safe. But if we want him out of our lives for good, then the only way to help catch him is for us to stay here–'

'Stay here!' she screamed at him. 'If you think I'm staying here for even one more day, you must be off your fucking mind!'

'But it's the only way he can be caught,' Paul persisted. 'I realize we can't remain here constantly living under protection, nor spend the rest of our lives with his shadow always hanging over us. But neither will moving elsewhere guarantee he won't find us and come after us.'

'Oh, God,' Karen hands flew to her face, like she was trying to blot out Paul's argument. 'Let me think,' she begged…then lowered her hands and looked at Sam. 'Sam, what do you think?'

'Mr. Archer's right,' said Sam. 'Or you'll be forever looking over your shoulder.'

'Much as I regret saying this Karen,' Morgan said from the depths of his arm chair, 'and God knows I don't want you subjected to any more trauma, but I agree with Paul and Detective King.'

'Michael?' Karen looked across the room at him.

'Not for me to say,' Michael grated, like it was being forced out of him. 'But running away's no answer, the only way to stop him is for him to be caught. And the best chance of that is here.'

She pondered a long moment, her inner conflict mirrored in her eyes, then exhaled a long breath.

'I guess you're all right,' she said, but her reluctance to agree with them was evident in her voice, 'If that's the only way to catch him, then it seems I've no choice but to stay.'

Paul held her. 'You're doing the right thing, *amante*.'

Karen returned his embrace, holding on to him as if for grim life.

At Ryan Antiques, Susan was looking through a window at Hank's clapboard garage on the edge of town, where Hank was giving the black Jeep a leisurely going over.

An old Volvo estate car, maroon, pulled up outside. The driver, an elderly man with gray wavy hair, wearing a fawn cavalry coat, a spotted green cravat and a cream shirt, twill trousers and suede shoes, hurried around the car to open the door for a stout woman with blue-rinse hair and rimless blue-tinted spectacles and a fake mink coat to get out. Clearly passing tourists, they made for the Dickensian bow-shaped window and browsed at the antiques on show.

Ignoring them, Susan picked up a pair of antique binoculars from a nearby table and focused them on Hank, and saw him examine something on the driver's window. Picking up his spectacles and ball point pen from a bench, he perused whatever it was and jotted it on the back of his hand.

Stretching for her phone, she called up REDIAL and was about to press it when the brass bell hanging above her door jangled and the tourists entered. 'Can I help you?' Susan asked, abrupt.

'We're just looking,' said blue rinse and they started to idly browse.

Spotted cravat, who clearly thought he looked like a Hollywood matinee idol of old, picked up a tomahawk. 'Chippewa?' he said to Susan, inferring by his tone that if anyone knew his antiques, he did.

'Ojibwas, to give them their proper name,' Susan snapped. 'Over two hundred years old.'

Taken aback, the man turned away and rejoined his wife, muttering something about Susan to her as she continued browsing.

On edge to make her call, Susan refocused her binoculars on Hank. He had the cab door open and was bending inside searching the floor. Straightening up, holding something small between his thumb and first finger, he removed his spectacles and held a lens like a magnifying glass close to the object and scrutinized it.

Susan glared at blue rinse's and spotted cravat's backs, willing them to stop shamming they were going to buy anything and go.

She needed to make the phone call.

-15-

Sam opened the handkerchief on the phone table and looked at the double-edged bladed carving knife. 'Let's hope Chicago find his prints or DNA on it. Tracing chassis and engine numbers is too long a shot.' Seeing Karen re-tense up in Paul's arms as she stared at the knife, Sam covered it again with the handkerchief and left it on the table.

'I can take it to Hank's now and make sure it goes today,' Michael said, still standing inside the doorway. 'I can be there and back in twenty minutes.'

'I'll be going back myself in a short while,' Sam replied.

'I still can't understand his threat about making Karen suffer,' Paul said. 'He's the one who caused himself to almost drown in Ravens Pond.'

'If Mr. Hale's right he's a psycho,' said Sam, 'causing pain gives them a sort of sick pleasure. That would be reason enough for him.'

'I suggest there's even more to his threat than that, detective,' Morgan sat up in his arm chair. 'His use of words such as atonement and reparation infers he's seeking revenge for some injustice that's been done to him. Or at least, he considers has been done to him."

'But Karen can't possibly be the cause of any injustice he's suffered, Morgan.' Paul objected. 'How could she, living out here with just her father all her life?'

'Nevertheless,' Morgan insisted, 'it would seem that his failure to kill her by forcing her off the road the other day has so incensed him as to inflict as much anguish on Karen as he can before he tries again. It's the only explanation for his "next time" message, and leaving the dead crow on her pillow last night, instead of ending her life there and then.'

'Oh, God,' Karen clutched Paul's arm. 'What if he tries to break in again tonight?'

'He won't, *amante*,' Paul squeezed her hand. 'He'll know we'll be on our guard. And I'll stay with you until you're asleep.'

'Staying with me until morning would ensure it more,' Karen flared and pulled away from him.

'And I still think it's best you have the bed to yourself,' he insisted

'Getting back to that Christ on the Cross mock-up, detective,' Morgan interjected. 'I can't rid myself of the feeling that it holds the answer to it all.'

'Except I was never very good in school at religious studies, Mr. Hale,' said Sam.

'Christ died for the sins of others, detective. A sacrifice for their iniquities,' Morgan replied, with an air of imparting his knowledge about him that jarred Sam.

'That much I learned, Mr. Hale,' he said, trying not to show it, 'but you still think it's William Ryan he's got the grudge against, and Karen has now taken his place in the kook's mind?'

'Exactly,' Morgan returned. '*She* is the propitiation for her father's sin, whatever he regards that so-called sin to be.'

'Are we back to saying that Karen is just a scapegoat for something that Ryan once did to him?' Paul cut in. 'If so, I don't agree. In my opinion it's Karen herself he has the grievance with – though God only knows why. The Christ-like effigy, and his use of biblical words, are nothing more than a cover to hide it.'

'Except I doubt it's Karen who's harmed him enough to drive him to such extreme measures,' Morgan rejoined. 'And rather than seek justice, as he sees it, the legal way, he's seeking himself to avenge the wrong done to him. Not only that, but by taking the law into his own hands, it suggests his lust for revenge is so extreme he's going way beyond the biblical concept of retributive justice – eye for an eye, tooth for a tooth – and wants to mentally torment her before exacting the ultimate punishment – her death.'

'Oh, God, but why...' Karen dug her fingernails into her seat cushion – as if to prevent herself from screaming, it seemed to Sam. 'If it's my father who wronged him, why kill me?'

'Because what he's now seeking – at least, in my opinion,' Morgan replied, 'is akin to a form of reprisal known as altruistic punishment.' There was an increasing air of pontification about Morgan as he spelt out what he meant by this. 'Seeking revenge against the one who stands in the evildoer's place. And the nearest he can get to your father – the perpetrator of the original crime as he will regard it – is you, Karen. His daughter. The one who has inherited his wealth.'

'Then what about–' Paul started to ask, but then checked himself. 'I'm sorry, *amante*,' he said to Karen, 'but it has to be asked,' and refaced Morgan. 'What about the whore side of it, Morgan? How does that fit in with your reckoning?'

'Only that the rag doll being painted to look like one is so contradictory, not just to the Savior himself, but also to Karen, confirms for me that the man's a psychopath, trying to mentally torture her – and I don't believe it has any more significance than that.'

'I agree with Mr. Hale,' said Sam. He turned to her. 'Are you sure your father never crossed anyone, Karen? Money makes enemies.'

'I can only repeat what I said before, Sam,' she said, digging her finger nails deeper into her cushion. 'He may have ruffled a few feathers in his dealings, but he was honest as the day is long.'

But if he did cross someone, I wish I'd known it before I – before he died. I would have made sure he was the one who would suffer, not me. Why should I have to pay for his fucking sins?

'I still don't agree,' Paul persisted. 'From all that's been happening to her, I still believe that for some inexplicable reason, it's Karen he has the grudge against. And the Christ-like doll, and words like reparation, are merely to conceal it.'

'Extending that thought, Mr. Archer – of it all being a cover,' Sam said, 'it could also be that he's not trying to kill her for himself, but he's a hitman, hired by someone else with a grudge–'

'A *hitman?*' Paul looked aghast at him.

'It can't be ruled out. And this psycho stuff's just a blind to divert us from who's paying him?'

'Then why didn't he kill Karen last night?' Paul came back at him. 'Why leave the knife in her pillow instead? Why the crow, a portent of death? And why the phone calls since – saying he wants to make her suffer first. No, detective, none of it fits in with him being a hired killer.'

'It doesn't negate it either,' said Sam, 'especially if it's the one paying him who's dictating the shots and making the calls? And maybe from a distance away. It would explain there being no local landline to phone from. And give him an alibi for when his man tried to force Karen off the road.'

'It still doesn't explain how the calls are being blocked, Sam,' Michael cut in.

'That's true, Michael.' Sam said. 'It doesn't.'

'Listening to all this is too much for me,' Karen cut in, her voice trembling. 'All I know is that it's me he wants to kill. Except I've never harmed anyone – only Hank,' she forced a flitting smile, 'when he caught me taking a packet of gum, but I was only eight and he forgave me.'

'With all respect, detective,' Morgan re-entered the discussion, and still grandiloquent with it, 'I believe you can exclude all notion of him being a hitman – as you call it. His use of such words as reparation and atonement, confirms for me that he has his own personal motive for wanting revenge. That's it's for himself alone and not for anyone else. Nor – to quote him – will he be satisfied until he has caused Karen more suffering first, and only then will he–'

He paused as Karen buried her face in her hands. Sam saw she had changed the band-aid on her finger with a new one. However she had managed to injure herself yesterday, it was clearing up.

'I'm sorry if this is distressing for Karen to hear,' Morgan continued, 'but if he's to be stopped, we need to try to find out as much as we can about him – even though it may be only an educated guess,' he added as an aside that said his participation in it ensured it would at the least be that. 'I appreciate that whether it's for something her father did to him – or whether it was Karen – is pure speculation. The whore image suggests Karen – though why a whore is beyond me, you couldn't find anyone nicer. Yet on the other hand, the word reparation still suggests her father. If so, then with Ryan being a speculator, it can be assumed the man lost money because of him. But whether the sum involved was large or small is of little relevance. It could be tens of thousands, or as little as a hundred dollars–'

'My father never dealt in hundreds of dollars,' Karen protested, raising her face.

'With respect, Karen, that's not my point–' Morgan returned.

'Mr. Hale's hypothesizing, Karen,' Michael cut in, with a note of sarcasm aimed at Morgan, who was clearly bugging Michael as much as he was Sam. 'Sam does it all the time.' It was the first time Michael had used her name to her over the last couple of days and Karen looked up at him, but his face stayed cold.

Morgan gave him a withering glance and continued. 'As Michael rightly says, I acknowledge that this is all hypothesis, but at this moment we've little else to go on. The point I was making is that whatever the sum, it was all he had in the world, and that in itself would give him sufficient motive to seek revenge. And being – to repeat – that Ryan is dead, Karen has now taken his place as the substitute for her father's sins, his propitiation, his scapegoat, call it what you will.'

The room was silent as Morgan waited for Sam or Paul to respond.

'It's certainly something to think about, Mr. Hale,' Sam finally said.

'Too much conjecture,' said Paul. 'The only thing that matters to me is that he's intent on harming Karen, not *why* – and I intend to ensure he doesn't succeed.'

'But surely, Paul,' Morgan persisted, a petulant tone entering his voice, 'if only we can work out his motive, we might then be able to–' he abruptly stopped in mid-sentence as if there was no point continuing, and in a clear huff got to his feet. 'I'm going to make myself a coffee. Anyone else?'

No one did. Morgan exited the sitting room to the dining room and made for the kitchen.

Sam picked up the carving knife from the phone table, and though Karen might again react to it, he opened the handkerchief and pondered over the double-edged blade.

'Karen? Are you sure you've never–'

'No!' Karen flared. 'How many more times do I have to say I can't think why anyone would want to harm me. For myself, or for anything my father may have done—'

Shriiiiiiilll...

They all turned to the shrilling phone. They all seemed hypnotized by it.

Sam looked at Paul to answer it.

Shriiiiiiilll...

'It's him,' Karen whimpered. 'I know it is.'

'Would you answer it, detective?' Paul said.

Sam picked up the receiver and waited for the caller to speak first.

'I assume it's you, Sam?' the voice whispered

'And what do I call you?' Sam asked.

Paul put his arm around Karen as if shielding her from him, though he wasn't in the room.

'Why not call me John, Sam.'

'Smith?' said Sam. 'Or Doe?'

'Very droll, Sam,' said the whisper. 'How is she bearing up, Sam? Knowing that *nothing* is going to stop me from killing her.'

'She's bearing up fine, John,' Sam replied, aware of Karen and Paul watching him, listening to his every word. 'Knowing you'll slip up and be caught.'

'I don't think so, Sam,' whispered the voice. 'You're no nearer to catching me now than you ever will be.'

'But why Karen, John?' Sam probed, trying again to see if he could be tripped up into saying something, anything that might reveal who he was.

'I've explained this, Sam. Retribution. Life for a life. Blood for blood. And I'm her executioner.' The whispered voice paused. 'I watched her get dressed this morning, Sam. Tell her she shouldn't open her drapes so wide – the *whore*. Overtight sweater. Overtight jeans. And briefs so brief that any last shred of decency she had left has long gone.'

Sam crossed to the front window below Karen's bedroom window and searched the woods opposite for some vantage point from where the caller could have watched Karen earlier, but there was just a dark wall of close standing pines. 'Listen up you sonofabitch–'

The phone went dead.

'The bastard cut me off again,' Sam swore.

Karen buried her face on Paul's chest. 'Oh, God, I can't take much more of this, Paul.'

Stroking her hair, Paul looked at Sam. 'At least we now know his first name.'

'I wouldn't put much stock to it,' said Sam.

Paul nodded, assimilating this. 'Any record of his call this time?'

'I'll check,' Sam's finger hovered over the keypad. 'But I reckon we can forget all thought of him calling from a distance away.'

He cut off the phone he'd used to call Sam, flipped open his cell, entered IMAGES, and studied a wedding photo of Karen alone, smiling and clutching a wedding posy of red roses.

'Soon,' he said, 'very soon. But only after you've suffered more.'

They had discussed it, even argued about it since it all went wrong and he had almost lost his own life in Ravens Pond, sinking below its filthy waters as the Jeep sank lower and lower into its depths, its blackness surrounding him, filling him with such fear as he had never before experienced, realizing he was going to die.

'Kill her tonight,' he was told. 'You've had your revenge with the effigy. Finish it.'

But looking at her through the banisters lying oblivious in her bed, he'd again relived the foul water seeping into his cab, and into his nose, and into his mouth, choking him, and would have drowned had the window not suddenly pulled down at his last desperate attempt.

And he'd wanted to make her suffer for it to the very extreme of her sanity

So, he'd returned to the kitchen, found a tin of moldy cookies and gone out onto the deck and scattered them, waited for some crows to fly down for them, grabbed the nearest and greediest one and slit its throat, and gone back inside to punish her more for what she had put him through.

But she hadn't yet been punished anywhere near enough. No, she was going to experience far greater suffering before he was satisfied. Only then would he kill her and it would be excruciating, pushing the knife deeper and deeper into her with every slow inch.

'*Whore,*' he said, switching off the cellphone and checking the time on his Rolex watch.

When it was finally over, he would buy himself another gold necklace and gold bracelet to go with it – and another gold watch, a luxury Bulgari he'd long coveted.

And only then would they celebrate.

Sam called up CALLS on the phone's screen – again, no record of his call. The last call showing was yet another from (715) 862-1945. Seeing the time of it, Sam checked it against his watch, and realized it was made but a minute or so ago.

Coincidence?

He pressed RECALL. It rang at the other end of the line.

'Ryan Antiques.'

'It's me, Miss Ryan, Sam King. I'm at Karen's. Did you just call?'

'Yes, to talk to Paul,' Susan replied, 'but the line was engaged.'

Sam extended the phone to Paul. 'Miss Ryan wants to speak to you.'

Karen dug her fingernails further into her couch cushion and dragged them back.

Watching her do it, Sam saw blood come through her band aid and realized she was deliberately inflicting pain on herself – like a self-harmer, Sam thought – hurting herself, and that she was doing it because Susan was wanting to speak to Paul. He also realized it was her jealously, and maybe this was why she had injured herself yesterday. That her jealousy could be so extreme over such a small matter amazed Sam. To say she was complex was putting it mildly. He'd heard of people having split personalities. As he understood it, this meant two. How many did Karen Ryan have?

Paul went to take the call but then saw the new blood on Karen's band-aid. 'I'll call her back.'

'He'll call you back, Miss Ryan. The kook's phoned again.'

'Oh, God,' Susan exclaimed. Her reaction sounded genuine. 'Tell Karen I'll be right over.'

Sam turned to Karen. 'Miss Ryan says she'll be right over.'

'Tell her there's no need,' Karen replied, curt. 'I've got Paul.'

Sam relayed the message. 'Karen said—'

'I heard what she said,' Susan replied and ended the call.

By the tone of Susan Ryan's voice in response, Sam brooded, it seemed that jealousy cut both ways between the two.

He returned to checking CALLS on the screen.

The previous call was still from Susan at 9.57am.

'Again, no record of the call he's just made...' Sam said out loud. He turned to them all in the room. 'How the hell does he *do* that? And where in the hell is he making them from?'

'Cobbs Bend, Sam?' Michael suggested.

'Worth a try,' Sam said.

As they exited through the front door, slamming it behind them in their hurry, Morgan Hale came from the dining room and entered the sitting room, gingerly holding a heavy mug of coffee by its thick handle. 'There's not a china cup to be found in this house—' he said, and broke off as he saw Karen clinging to Paul. 'What's happened?'

'He's called again,' Paul said.

'Oh, poor you, Karen!' Morgan exclaimed. 'I heard it ring but thought it must be Susan.'

'They're checking the phone booth at Cobbs Bend.'

Morgan crossed to the window overlooking the road and watched Michael's truck lead Sam's car down the dirt track and speed off around the corner into the dark forest.

'The knife!' Karen screamed, pointing to the carving knife lying open on Sam's handkerchief on the telephone table. 'Get rid of it! Get rid of it!'

Morgan gingerly picked it up, wrapped it back in the handkerchief, opened a drawer, put the knife inside it, and hastily shut the drawer on it like it was contaminated.

Ahead of Sam, Michael's taillights came on as he slowed to a stop alongside an old pay-phone booth on the side of the road, almost hidden by surrounding brush and fir trees.

Sam pulled up behind the Dodge truck, got out of his Ford Fusion and stood with Michael in front of the empty booth. It was almost archaic. Square, frame mostly grey, the top two panels on both sides in clear glass and the bottom two in red. Its door, hinged in the middle, was all glass, and above it, in white letters on a small glass panel in similar red, was TELEPHONE, and the same at the top of both sides, under a flat roof.

'I'd no idea booths like this still existed.' Sam said. 'I thought they'd got rid of them years ago.'

'This is north Wisconsin,' said Michael as if that was reason enough.

Sam entered the booth, picked up the receiver and listened for a dialing tone. 'Line's dead,' he said. Replacing the receiver, he returned to Michael's side.

'Maybe he knows how to disconnect it?' Michael said, 'and re-connects it when he uses it?'

'Unlikely,' Sam replied.

Michael stepped inside the booth, pretended to look at the incoming cable for any signs it had been tampered with, glanced at the panel and made a mental note of the number. The first six digits, area code 715 862, were the same as his. The last four, 1966, were easy to remember. He rejoined Sam outside.

'While I'm here I'll check around,' Sam said, 'just in case. You get back. I don't want to leave Karen alone too long.'

'Archer and Hale are with her.

'Exactly. On their own.'

'Yeah, sure,' Michael said. He turned to go.

'He knew my name, Michael,' Sam suddenly said.

Michael looked back.

'He called me Sam,' Sam repeated.

'So what?' Michael asked. 'It's your name.'

'There are only five others in Ravensburg, apart from Karen, who know it. There's you–'

'Like I said before, Sam, you can cross me off.'

'Just talking aloud, Michael. As well as you…'

Michael looked like he was going to again protest, but held back.

'…there's Paul and Morgan, and Susan – who's now back to being the only one around here with a landline.'

'I keep telling you, Sam. You can forget Susan.'

'And Hank,' Sam ignored him, 'but we can rule him out.'

'Except he could have called in there for provisions and casually mentioned you, knowing you're staying in the cabin,' Michael returned, 'and Hank gave him your name without thinking.'

'It's a possibility,' Sam agreed, 'I'll ask Hank later. But sticking to our hitman thinking for the moment, that just leaves Paul and Morgan and Susan–'

'And you, Sam. You keep leaving yourself out of the equation. If he was working for you, he could know your name. '

'I'm not in the equation,' Sam said. 'As I said before – I never knew William Ryan.'

'Yeah, sure, Sam.'

But the way Michael said it was like he knew something different and was holding it back.

-16-

Karen sat in an easy chair pulled up near the hearth, looking into a blazing log fire that Paul had lit for her, drawing comfort from it. Her crutches were on the floor by her feet. Paul and Morgan were standing at the front window looking down the drive, talking in low voices.

Michael's truck drove up to the house. He got out, ran up the porch steps and in through the front door, entered the sitting room and remained standing, as always, inside the doorway.

'Anything?' Paul asked, his tension evident in his abrupt tone.

'Line's dead,' Michael said. 'But Sam's searching around for a sign he may have used it.'

Karen grabbed her crutches and pulled herself up out of her chair. 'I can't sit here doing nothing,' she snapped, the comforting effect of the fire dispelled in an instant. 'I'm going to do some painting.'

Paul crossed to help her.

'I can manage on my own,' she flew at him, crutching past Michael without glancing at him and into the hall. Putting the crutches under her right arm and grabbing the handrail at the foot of the stairs with her left hand, she started to drag herself up the risers one at a time.

Paul saw Michael's hesitation as he watched her struggle – torn as to whether or not to help her. 'She's fine,' Paul said, curt. 'Painting helps take her mind off things.'

How would you know, dickhead? Michael thought, *you've only known her three weeks, I've known her for years, and in more ways than one.*

Turning away, he exited the house.

Still standing at the front window, Paul and Morgan watched him reach his truck. With his hand on the door handle, he looked up at Karen's bedroom window.

'Jealous she married you?' Morgan said, his eyes still on Michael as he got into his cab.

'Could be,' Paul replied. 'Jealousy's a strong motive.' Crossing to the phone table, he picked up the receiver and dialed out. It rang at the other end of the line. Paul spoke into it as soon as it was picked up. 'You called me earlier,' he said, keeping his voice low.

'Hank's checked the Jeep,' Susan replied. 'He found something on the window and jotted it down. He also found something on the floor of the cab—'

'Could you make out what was on the window?' Paul queried, still speaking in an undertone.

'From the way Hank peered at it, I'd guess it was etched into the glass.'

'Ten to one, the license number,' Paul replied. 'What about the other?'

'It was too small to make out...Paul,' she blurted, 'when are we going to—'

'Karen's calling me from her room,' Paul cut across her.

'Paul—'

'I have to go.' He ended the call and turned to Morgan. 'Hank's found something etched on the Jeep's window.'

'The license number...' Morgan left his question in mid-air.

'It's the only thing it could be. He also found something on the floor of the cab, but it was too small for her to make out.'

'I thought King said the cab was pristine clean,' said Morgan.

'So did I,' said Paul.

Back in his truck, Michael took a cellphone from the pocket of his leather jacket, dialed *31 to block his user ID, then: (715) 862-1945. It rang at the other end of the line. Cobbs Bend payphone wasn't dead as Sam had said. He let it ring. Sam didn't answer it. Whatever his reason for saying he wanted to search around, either he was ignoring it…or he was in the forest out of earshot…or he'd driven off somewhere else.

Michael replaced the cellphone in his jacket, reached into his glove compartment and took out the gold-cased cellphone he'd recovered from Ravens Pond, switched it on and called up IMAGES.

The screen showed what was clearly a self-photo of a man, in his late 30s at a guess, standing outside a log cabin, surrounded by woods. Handsome, but with a mean look about him. It was in the eyes, Michael brooded, cold and fixed, staring into the lens the way a psychopath might stare.

He cleared the screen and called up the only contact stored – listed as MY NUMBER.

It rang out and went straight to voice mail. A hard voice said: 'Leave a message.'

No risk of him being discovered if the cellphone fell into the wrong hands, Michael thought.

He left an equally terse message, 'Rossi. I recovered your phone. Lucky it's waterproof. We need to talk.' He switched off the phone and reflected.

Returning to Ravensburg after seven years in the marines, and finding from Hank that Karen, at twenty-five, was still living in Clanryan under William Ryan's domination, he'd kicked about for a few days, hoping to see her, but realized it was hopeless and moved to the lights of Chicago.

But with no skills other than those he'd learned in the marines, and that was mostly how to kill – especially with a knife, he was a natural with a knife, he could creep up on an enemy without making a sound, and dispose of them with a swift slice of their throat before they could yell out – he drifted into crime and slowly found himself headed for hell – but unlike Audie Murphy, there was no "To Hell and Back", only "To Hell and no coming Back", ending in him recently avoiding a life sentence in Marion Penitentiary for murder – but only from lack of hard evidence.

That was the crux for him, he didn't want to come that close again.

And then he'd heard William Ryan had died, and it had engendered a hope that with Karen now free of him at last, and free to make her own decisions, she could be more than glad for them to get back together. It wasn't the money she'd inherited – though that would be more than welcome – it was Karen herself, he'd loved her since high school, and – recalling how she'd let him feel her up in their teens and starting to get a boner on even now thinking about it – he'd hoped she'd loved him back. Okay, so she'd never let him go all the way, but now he was older he'd assumed she felt the same as him then, but had been holding back, keeping herself for him until they were more mature, hoping her father would finally allow her to be with him.

Well, how much more stupid could he have been?

Bussing it, thumbing it, trudging it, sleeping rough, he'd finally got back to Ravensburg, only to find she had up and married someone else, the *bitch*. Some stranger she'd known for only three days! And so he'd shut himself in his father's old house and simmered and come up with his plan for revenge and decided to put it into action as soon as she got back from honeymoon, no time to change his mind.

But then, with so many others there at Ravens Pond observing him, he'd found himself having to dive in and rescue her. Total irony, he thought – if that was the right expression – he who wanted her dead having to save her.

And now, even more ironic, he was outside her house – guarding it. Who would have thought of that? But again, it was perfect for his plan. Who would suspect that the one who rescued her from drowning, the one now guarding the house, could be the very one wanting it to be executed.

"Executed…" yeah, he liked that, executed was exactly what he had planned for her.

She shouldn't have married the prick – a complete and total prick like Paul Archer, he thought. By doing so, she had left him with no other choice.

He re-called the solitary MY NUMBER and again got the hard voice: 'Leave a message.'

'Rossi again,' he stressed. 'Call me back.'

He returned to IMAGES and called up a second photo.

It was of Karen, smiling, holding a wedding posy of red roses.

To think he once loved her, Michael thought.

No more, he now hated her.

Hated her to death.

He heard a message come through on his cellphone. He checked – two waiting him. He hadn't heard the first.

'Rossi. I recovered your phone. Lucky it's waterproof. We need to talk,' was the first message. 'Rossi again. Call me back,' was the second. He sounded like he was getting more and more tense.

Well, he didn't need to talk to Rossi.

Nor did he need to call him back.

His course was set and he was adhering to it.

He deleted both calls.

-17-

Sitting in his Ford Fusion beside Ravens Pond, Sam stared at it – dark, sinister, the low-hanging black clouds bringing the approaching storm ever nearer, making it look even more sinister.

He thought back to two days ago, trying to remember something he'd seen in his rear mirror after crashing into the tree, and slowly coming to as Karen's coupé slowly sank below the pond's surface – but it was stored deep in his subconscious and his subconscious was refusing to release it.

The only things he could remember were vague.

Paul's SUV slamming to a halt alongside him.

Paul running for the pond, shouting something that Sam's mind's ear wouldn't relinquish.

Paul and Morgan Hale in the water trying desperately to open Karen's door.

The coupe submerging as Karen looked panic stricken through her window.

Paul going in after it and Morgan Hale treading water.

Michael reaching the pond and hesitating.

Digging deep, Sam now re-saw this in his mind's eye.

Michael had hesitated before diving in.

Why?

Was that what he was trying to recall.

No, it wasn't, his subconscious was at least telling him that.

It was something else.

Sam tried to force himself to remember, but wasn't able to. Instead his mind went back even further, to the scene that constantly haunted him.

He was standing alone by Gina's re-opened grave, no Emma holding his hand. Emma was in the small white coffin being lowered into the grave to re-join her Mom.

REUNITED was what he had decided to have carved on their headstone.

"Reunited", what a mockery. He had little thought that his two most loved ones would ever be reunited in death. Their bodies cold in their grave. With no realization that they were being reunited. Because after Death there was only Death. Nothing more. No awareness. Only Death.

It was there, watching Emma's coffin reach the bottom of the grave and the earth scattered on top of it, remorselessly covering it and hiding her forever from his sight, when he determined that the vow he'd made to Emma in the moment of his grief, would become more than words.

And he once more relived the day Emma died…

It's a gray rainy day. Windshield wipers beating, Sam's car is a Ford Taurus as he and Emma, sitting in the front seat beside him, drive through Highwood, a Chicago neighborhood. Sam's wearing his police dress uniform. Emma, a pretty girl, but ten years old, the apple of his eye, is wearing a black velvet dress with a white lace collar that he chose for her to attend her mother's funeral.

Emma's brooding in silence. Her tears have dried up, though still staining her face.

'Why did Mommy have to die?' she suddenly begged Sam.

'I don't know, sweetheart,' Sam replied, a catch in his voice. 'I wish I had the answer.'

'Is she in Heaven now?' In her voice was an unspoken plea for her Daddy to answer 'Yes.'

'If anyone deserves to be in Heaven, sweetheart, Mommy does.'

A silver coupe shot out of the right arm of an intersection at speed. The driver swerved to try to miss Sam's car, but hit Emma's door side on and glanced off, sending the Taurus sliding into a concrete wall, crumpling Sam's door. The coupe locked its wheels and slid to a stop.

Dazed by the impact, almost smothered by his safety airbag, Sam struggled to stay conscious and popped the bag with the needle of his police badge. He looked over at Emma. Still sitting in her seat, safety belt tight, airbag inflated, she was inert, blood trickling from her nose and mouth.

Desperately, Sam popped her airbag and felt her wrist pulse, throat. Nothing. He put his ear to her heart. Not even a faintest of beats. Unclipping both safety belts, he pulled Emma to him, put his mouth over hers. Panicking now, he tried to breathe life into her. It was no use. Emma was dead.

Sam cradled her body and rocked her to him, tears streaming down his face, in too much of a shock to even whisper her name, even though he felt like screaming it – *Emma! Emma!* – out loud.

Emma's buckled door opened. A man, rugged and seemingly tall, peered in.

'Are you okay?' he blurted, then went silent as he took in the scene. His initial facial reaction was one of shock, but was quickly replaced by panic. Slamming Emma's door, he ran for his silver coupe, scrambled inside and sped off.

Sam's windshield wipers, despite the collision, continued to swish through the curtain of rain, obscuring his vision. He made out only the letters WRY in the silver coupe's license plate.

'I'll find you,' Sam choked through his tears. 'I'll find you…and make you pay for this. A life for a life.'

He'd not taken long to find the full license number of the silver coupé, a BMW – WRYAN1 – or the driver's name – William Ryan – and began plotting his revenge. Life for a life. Ryan's life for Emma's. A punishment fitting the crime. Nor was he concerned if he was caught. With Gina and Emma both dead, his life was over anyway.

But before he could carry out his revenge, Ryan was dead.

Not by his hands though and he'd felt cheated.

He had brooded over Emma's photograph for days…and then decided.

Daughter for daughter.

It was still a life for a life.

Poetic justice.

And when, as he waited for her by the side of the road, he saw her flash past with the Jeep on her tail, he had followed them, and though she'd somehow missed all the trees, she'd ended up in Ravens Pond, with Paul and Morgan failing to save her. Watching it all in his rear mirror, he had thought that the God he didn't believe in was answering his prayers. '*Vengeance is Mine*', sayeth the Lord, wasn't that what it said in the Bible? And by allowing Karen Ryan to drown, *HE*, GOD, was ensuring that he, Sam King, would be free of all blame. Only for it to go wrong when Michael Rossi happened to be driving past only moments earlier. And against all the odds, rescued her.

And now, in sublime negation of his resolution to still get justice for Emma's death, he was protecting her from him, supposed to ensure he wouldn't succeed the next time. Sam gave a grim smile. Could anything be more macabre than the one who wanted Karen Ryan dead protecting her? And as to why he'd not killed her last night when she was lying there at his mercy, was beyond him.

Nevertheless, Emma would be avenged, Sam again vowed, he'd make sure of that.

He'd thought the pain of losing Gina so young was the worse pain he could ever experience, but losing Emma was worse. It wasn't natural – it wasn't right – for a child to die before a parent. There would be no more of her infectious laughter filling the house, no more impish blue eyes as they played games together, no more tucking her up in bed at night and reading her stories.

The tears flowed down Sam's cheeks.

He wiped them away.

There was no going back now.

Switching on his engine, he drove off.

Behind him, the dark pond was silent.

The black clouds were coming nearer.

Crows suddenly flew up, cawing, as if disturbed.

Inside his car, Sam didn't hear them.

And his tears continued to flow.

-18-

In her studio, Karen painted a new canvas with savage strokes. It was a landscape. Dominating it, was a dark pond, its waters still, making the painting look sinister. Surrounded by stark trees, and hearing the black daubed crows circling above them cawing in her ears, she suddenly realized it was of Ravens Pond, and slashed it, and slashed it with shrieking blood red paint, obliterating it.

She picked up her old phone from its black cradle, jabbed her finger into the numbered holes in its round silver plate and savagely dialed out. She heard it ring and being picked up.

'Paul?' Susan whispered.

'It's Karen,' she snapped back at her, instantly incensed. 'What made you think it was Paul?'

'I saw your number on my screen,' Susan hastened to reply, now using her normal voice, 'and assumed it was Paul calling back again.'

'Again? Why? Did he call you before?

'To tell me about your latest phone call.'

She detected that Susan's response was rushed, as if her dear cousin was thinking it up on the spot. 'But Sam King's already told you that,' she felt her bile rising. 'After you called here and he rang you back – less than an hour ago.'

'Yes...yes, he did...' came Susan's edgy reply, '...hang on a moment.'

Hearing only silence now on the other end of the line, Karen drummed her fingers on a nearby worktable, getting angrier and angrier.

In Ryan Antiques, Susan cupped her hand over the mouthpiece, and tried to quickly think how to answer Karen. She removed her hand and spoke back into the phone.

'Sorry, I had tourists here. They've only just left.' They'd left ages ago. 'Paul wanted to tell me more than Sam King had earlier. It must have been traumatic for you. But he can't hide out in the woods forever, Kay, when he comes out he'll be caught for sure. Meanwhile,' she hastened to change the subject, 'I asked a Chicago friend to find out about King. He has quite a tragic past…'

Karen drummed her fingers harder on the table, too on edge to fully hear what Susan was saying about Sam. 'That was tough,' she cut in, brusque. 'But I've forgotten now why I called you.'

She'd wanted to subtly question her about her phoning Clanryan the morning of the cemetery and Paul telling her where she'd gone, and only ten minutes later the black Jeep appeared, looking down at her from the ridge.

'If I remember it, I'll ring you back,' she said.

'No need,' Susan replied, sounding relieved their call was over. 'I'll be over as soon as I close up. I'll let you know when I'm on the way.'

Karen replaced her phone on its cradle, grabbed the expunged painting off the easel and hurled it across the studio. The front doorbell rang, then voices came from the hall. Crutching out on to the landing, she saw Sam follow Paul into the sitting room and stand inside the doorway, his back visible to Karen. She couldn't see Paul, but heard him say, 'Find anything?'

'No luck,' Sam said.

Sliding down her crutches, she sat on the top riser and peered through the banisters at Sam's back in the doorway.

'What now?' Paul asked from inside the room.

'I'll get back to my cabin,' Sam replied, 'and check whether Chicago's come up with anything on the engine or chassis numbers.' Paul didn't respond. 'But what's bugging me,' Sam continued, 'is that I still can't figure out why his calls aren't listed.'

'Have you checked with the phone company?' Paul asked.

'Drew a blank there, too,' Sam replied, terse.

'Then I don't know what else to suggest,' Paul said.

'Nor me,' said Sam. 'I've also been giving some thought to his use of the word "reparation". If it's not for something her father did to him, maybe his grudge is against you, Mr. Archer, now you're married to Karen? Any skeletons you wish to share?'

'He also said "an eye for an eye, tooth for a tooth" detective,' said Paul. 'Retributive justice as Morgan calls it, which rules me out. My misdemeanors are many, but they don't include murder. The guy's just sick.'

'It was Mr. Hale that said an eye for an eye, tooth for a tooth,' Sam said, 'What he said, last time he called, was "life for a life, blood for blood".'

'Then it must be her father,' Paul returned. 'Karen has most certainly not killed anyone, so I guess William Ryan must have. Altruistic punishment, to again quote Morgan. Seeking revenge against the one who stands in his place.'

'And brings us back to whether he's been hired by someone else with a grudge against Ryan,' Sam added. 'Hopefully, when Chicago gets the knife they'll be able to find some–' He stopped in mid-sentence. 'The knife. I left it right there on the table, next to the phone.'

'Maybe Morgan put it somewhere,' Paul replied. 'He's in the dining room, working on his set designs. I'll call him.'

From behind the closed dining room door suddenly came piano music, sinister, grim tonality dominating it and seeming to fill the house.

Sam hesitated. 'No, don't disturb him,' he said, 'I'll pick it up later.' He turned away and exited the house, closing the door behind him.

Karen remained sitting on the stairs, looking at the closed door to the dining room, repelled by the music coming from behind it. It sounded eerie, funereal almost, brooding.

Why had Sam gone without the knife?

And why did Paul tell Sam he didn't know where it was, knowing that Morgan had put it in the phone table drawer away from her, when she screamed at him to get it out of her sight?

Both questions churned in her mind.

But she was unable to fathom their reasons.

And her mind switched to the dread realization that another night lay ahead of her.

For him to try again.

The piano music from the dining room built up, sounding more and more sinister.

Karen put her hands to her ears, but failed to block it out.

-19-

Paul exited the sitting room and saw her on the top riser. She removed her hands. The music was getting more frenzied, it sounded like the pianist was going berserk.

'How long have you been there?' he called up to her. 'Did you hear what Detective King had to say?'

She descended the stairs still sitting, bringing her crutches with her.

'Let me help you.' Paul extended his hand.

'I can manage on my own,' she said, curt. Reaching the bottom riser, she placed the feet of her crutches on the hall floor and struggled to pull herself up and stand with them. Paul again held out his hand to help her. She thrust it away. Realizing her mood hadn't changed, he moved aside.

Morgan exited the dining room into the hall. Behind him the music was building up to a crescendo as the pianist's fingers sped frenetically over the keyboard. 'I thought I detected voices,' Morgan said.

'Over that music?' Paul attempted to be jovial 'You must have the ears of a bat.'

'It's Rachmaninov's "Prelude in C Sharp Minor", as you well know, Paul, being it's one of my favorite pieces.' He turned to Karen. 'I brought my CD player with me especially to play it. Despite its intensity, in a contrary way it helps me relax.' Before she could make the pithy response already on her lips, he added. 'Now you're back home again, Karen, I've moved my work from your studio on to the dining table, if that's alright with you?' Without waiting for a reply, 'Either of you like a coffee?' he asked. 'No?' he answered for them. 'Then I'll get back to my designs.' Re-entering the room, he closed the door, muffling the piano piece as it climaxed, and then softened down.

Karen crutched into the sitting room. Paul followed, puffed up a cushion for her to sit by him on the couch. She sat in another chair.

'I'm afraid Morgan has his own peculiar taste in music,' Paul remarked, trying to dispel the tense atmosphere she'd brought into the room. 'The piece he's listening to now, so he told me, was once called "The Day of Judgment".'

'I could have done without knowing that,' she bit back at him, instantly regretting her outburst, she needed to be calm to outwit him.

'Sorry, *amante*, I should have thought first.'

'And I shouldn't have snapped,' she forced herself to say and added as an aside, 'I've just been talking to Susan. She said you've not long called her.'

He sat facing her on the couch before replying. 'Just to reassure her that you were getting over his last call,' he said dismissively.

'Susan said it was about an antique necklace you're wanting to give me,' she lied, watching his face for his reaction,.

'Damn!' Paul mimed a flicker of annoyance. 'I wanted to keep it a surprise.'

'It was a really sweet thought,' she responded. 'Thank you. But I already have enough necklaces. I'll tell her when she gets here.'

'It will probably be better if you leave it to me to tell her,' he returned, a tad too hastily. 'She'll have realized she slipped up as soon as she said it. We don't want to make her feel worse.'

'Then I won't,' she said, and saw him visibly relax.

'Thanks. Best if it comes from me. Especially as I asked her to keep it to herself.'

'I won't say a word,' she promised, not sure whether or not she would keep it.

You bastard, she thought, her inner anger flaring up again, now you're lying to me as well as having lied to Sam about the carving knife. But if you and Susan are in this together, you'll not get away with it. You'll both pay for it. Beyond measure. Believe me on that.

Paul leant forward, clearly on edge to change the subject. 'If you're up to it, I'd like to talk some more about this psychopath, as Morgan calls him—'

'I'm not,' she cut across him.

'It's just that whether he's a hitman, as King suggests,' he persisted, 'or acting alone, perhaps your father did cross someone?'

'No,' she fought to control herself, she was getting tired of saying this, 'he was as straight as a die. His only partner was Susan's father. And that ended years ago.'

'Yes, she told me,' he said.

He saw suspicion reflected in her face and realized he'd slipped up and hurriedly continued. 'Then being that we must rely on King's and Rossi's protection until we can get someone to replace them, we'll have to hope they get the chance to catch him. For your sake especially, and for us to restart our new life together.' He hesitated. 'And for me to get back to my book,' he added, as if reluctant to mention it. 'I've not touched it since Monday.'

Picking up on his deliberate pause, Karen realized he was anxious to make himself scarce in case she questioned him some more about what Susan had said about their fathers. 'Then why not go and work on it now?'

'No, *amante*,' Paul protested, keeping up his act. 'I don't want to leave you on your own.'

'I'll be fine,' she insisted, wanting herself to be alone to think. 'And Morgan's only across the hall,' she indicated to the dining room where the music had now stopped.

'Well…if you're sure?'

'Of course I'm sure,' she gritted, holding back from wanting to scream it at him.

'In that case…' He crossed over to her, pecked her on her cheek and made for the hall, pausing in the doorway. 'Call me if you need me.'

Digging her fingernails into her seat cushion, she forced herself to give him a fleeting smile. 'For goodness sake, Paul, go.'

He turned away and ran up the stairs to the landing and along the corridor. She heard his study door close.

Alone in the room, her mind throbbed as she brooded about them…Paul and Susan…Susan and Paul…not wanting to go where her racing thoughts were taking her – not only that they were in this together, but more than this, the possibility…the probability even they were lovers…

Unable to take the pulsating thought of it any more – the graphic images she was getting in her head of them making frenetic love on a king sized bed – and needing something to distract her mind away from it, she crutched to the bookshelves, took down a photo album and sat on the couch. With one eye on the green light on the phone charger to see if it flickered, telling her that Paul was calling Susan on his study extension about the necklace, she opened it at a well-thumbed page.

The first photograph showed her standing on the front porch of CLANRYAN at the age of twelve, holding her Mom's hand as she sat, looking frail, in a wheelchair – while above their heads was that fucking griffin, poised with talons extended as if hovering over both its prey. She looked away from it, back to her Mom's still beautiful, though wan face…

It was a picture that had haunted her ever since her Mom died, drawing her to gaze at it over and over again. It was the last one her father took of them together before her Mom was confined to her bed, then dying a month later, leaving her to live alone with him…

She dragged her eyes away from it to the second photo showing her Mom's fresh grave, earth mounded six feet by three, with four wreaths on it. Her father's, a huge one, as if even in death he was declaring his possession of her Mom's body, then her own small wreath, and one from Uncle John and Susan, and the fourth from Hank – just four wreaths…a testament in themselves of how lonely her Mom's life had been, living out there with him in the wilds. Whatever had possessed her to marry him, sentencing herself to a life with no friends, no neighbors? Maybe it had been more a physical attraction than love? – like her with Paul, as she was coming to realize.

Whatever, her Mom had paid the price for it, old by the age of thirty, and dead at thirty-seven…

Karen lowered the album. Was this what was in store for her, too? That unless she got away from here it would kill her, just like it had killed her Mom…

But there again – and the realization came to her that this wasn't the first time she'd thought about it since getting back from Italy – did she want the rest of her life anywhere to be with Paul? Forgetting, for a moment, his lies about Susan and her suspicions about them both – but it would be hell to pay for both if she found they were right – Paul hadn't been the same here as he was in Positano, he'd been almost like another person from the first day they got back, indifferent even.

Maybe it was CLANRYAN, she brooded, her father's presence dominating the house, making Paul feel he was living in someone else's home – even though it was he who'd insisted he wanted to be closeted away here from the world to write his fucking book – a book he wouldn't even let her read, not even snatches of it, like it was some precious jewel that only he should see.

Even more, she continued to brood, her mind now full of conflicting thoughts, it was as if he didn't want to sleep with her any more, glad of the excuse to be on his own in the next room, another bed – though maybe she was being unfair to him here, she conceded, letting her sleep on her own because of her injured spine was perhaps the sensible thing to do…

But that was the issue – she didn't want to be sensible, she wanted to be excited, she wanted to be aroused, to be loved – okay, maybe not a full fucking with her sprained back – but feeling her up and giving her an orgasm or two – or even better, three – wouldn't go amiss, and might help to take her mind away from the terrifying reality that somebody out there wanted to kill her…

Though again, when it came to him – a man who wanted her dead, for God's sake – Paul had been obstinate over this, too. Insisting on staying here, refusing to do what to her was the obvious thing to do. Get away from Clanryan for good and fly back to Italy. There he had been a different man, passionate, not able to get enough of her…

Or had he?

Maybe that was the way it had seemed to her. Other than her youthful fumblings with Michael she'd been inexperienced. What had she really known about making love? It had all been new to her, exciting, out of this world, sleeping naked with a man, being felt by a man, being fucked by a man – no, she hadn't meant to say "a man", she'd meant to say Paul…but again, thinking about it now from the reality of being back in Ravensburg - and previously reading erotic magazines she'd bought online after her father died - maybe there had been a sort of following a guide book about his lovemaking, always the same routine, no variety. Do this first, that second, press the right buttons in the right order until we achieve lift off then relax, mission accomplished – all so goddamned repetitive. Maybe he wasn't so skilled after all? Maybe it was her, aching for it, and because she'd orgasmed – so willingly and so many times she'd lost count – thinking she'd achieved the ultimate? Perhaps he wasn't as endowed as she'd thought. Maybe there were men out there she'd not yet had the chance to meet, men who were better at it than Paul, more passionate, more skillful? Men the same age as her, or even better, younger than her, who could keep up with her needs? Whereas Paul, thirteen years older than her – now was the time to think about it, before it was too late – might get even more indifferent than he'd suddenly become? – look at the way he was with her on the way home from hospital, not even letting her hold his penis. Well, if so, maybe now was the moment to accept she'd made a mistake – pressurized by Susan, the interfering bitch, telling her in Chicago in her older sister way, that she and Paul were made for each other, rushing her into marrying him – far too hastily, looking back at it, and yet another suspicion to add to all the others about her and Paul. Well, if she'd made a mistake – and the more she thought about it, the more convinced she was that she had – it was time to start planning how to get out of it. A quick divorce, pay him off- ?

No, why the hell should she pay him off?

What about telling him that she had changed her mind about staying here until the psycho was caught? Kill two birds with one stone, as it were? Insist she wanted to get far away from here and back to Positano after all. And once they were there, she could think of some cliffs that were ideal for an unfortunate accident…yes, okay, she brooded, there were places to get rid of his body around Ravensburg, too, but Morgan was here, and it wouldn't be so easy to carry out…

No, Positano was better, where they would be alone – one push, such a tragedy – and when her time of mourning was over – a month, but no more, wearing widow's weeds, all black, designer of course – buy a villa there and look for another man, maybe Italian, she'd heard they were fabulous lovers, the Italians, and it would be Goodbye Paul, Hello Paulo…Even better, why stop at Paulo? Why not two, or three, or maybe more?

Yes, the more she thought of it, more would be even better…

Feeling herself getting excited by the thought, she turned to the next page in the album. A studio photo again, just like the portrait on the wall, except it was just her and her father, only a month after her Mom died. In it, she was again wearing the black dress with its black lace collar and looking lost, cowed even, sitting in the high backed chair her Mom had sat in, her father standing behind her, his hand on her shoulder. His possessive pose was the same as in the portrait on the wall…except her Mom was missing. She studied it for the thousandth time. It was like he was saying: 'So she's gone. But I still own you.'

She slammed the album shut, hurled it aside, and glanced again at the light on the charger. It wasn't flickering. Paul wasn't risking a call.

Sitting at his laptop, Paul decided the title for his book and typed it on the screen in front of him:

LOVE IS LETHAL

PAUL ARCHER

He scrolled down to page 1. And opened the file with a letter:

As we agreed, marriage is but part one of the plan. It doesn't affect, or lessen my love for you. My heart, my very soul are yours. For eternity.

He paused and looked at the landline. Cursing the loss of his cellphone, he pondered whether to call Susan to agree their story about the necklace – angry with her for having been so stupid as to say it, and make him have to think fast his response to Karen. But with Sam King checking every call, he didn't want to have to think up yet another excuse for phoning her. He returned to the letter:

When it's finally over …

With his set designs spread across the dining room table, Morgan opened a slim folder and listed figures on a blank, lined pad:

> 1) 1,364,000
>
> 2) 1,938,000

He added a third figure, brooded over it, savagely crossed it out, and added a fourth figure

> 3) ~~2,500,000 ???~~
>
> 4) 3,000,000 ???

He totaled the three uncrossed figures:

> $ 6,302,000

Though openly pleased with the total figure, the crossed-out ~~$2,500,000~~ still angered him.

He crossed it out again…and again…and again…obliterating it.

Sitting in his Dodge truck, Michael switched on the gold-cased cellphone to IMAGES, and again brought up the wedding photograph of Karen with her posy of red roses.

He studied it, his conflicting emotions about her expressed on his face, one moment longing, the next hate. He hastily cleared it off the screen and replaced it with the one of the man standing outside a log cabin surrounded by woods, and again fixed on the eyes. They were mean, real mean.

Taking a notebook and ballpoint pen from a top pocket of his leather jacket, he began making notes, pausing to deliberate between each entry.

Sam lay fully clothed on a bed in his cabin, trying but failing to get some sleep.

His cellphone rang alongside him on the bed. He stretched for it. 'Sam King.'

'I've got the Jeep's license number, Sam,' Hank's voice drawled in his ear. 'It was engraved on the driver's window.' Sam didn't respond, as if he wasn't expecting this.

'Sam?' Hank prompted.

'Hang on a moment, Hank,' Sam replied. He sat up, transferred the phone to his left hand and reached into a jacket pocket for his note pad and ballpoint pen attached to it. 'Okay, give it me.'

Hank read out the license over the line. Sam jotted it down:

CHICAGO

PAXTON 1

'Thanks, Hank,' said Sam.

'I also found something on the cab floor,' Hank added. 'It may mean nothing, but it's a mite peculiar. Thought I should mention it.'

'Sure.'

'It's the body of what looks like a butterfly. At a guess, an Admiral. But it looks like its wings and legs and feelers were pulled off. Anyone who could do that, Sam, must be sick in the head.'

'You're damn right about that, Hank,' Sam said, 'but thanks for the number.' Ending the call, he brooded over it, then called up a contact stored on his cellphone.

'Detective Quinlan, Organized Crime,' a man's gruff voice answered.

'It's Sam, Bert,' Sam replied, and listened as Quinlan briefly questioned him.

'It's quiet,' Sam responded, 'but it's just what I need after Gina and Emma…Thanks, Bert. Sorry to ask you, I know how busy you are, but could you do me a favor? Guy in a Jeep truck drove off from the gas station by where I'm staying without paying. I took his license number and told the owner, I'd get his details. I realize I'm putting on you, but if you could? Thanks, Bert, I owe you…Chicago Paxton One. Would you text them? Thanks again, much appreciated.'

Sam lay back on the pillow, left hand still holding the phone, and the first finger of his right hand hovering over it, brooding whether or not to dial out.

-20-

Karen stretched across the couch for her photo album and reopened it at the one of herself in the black dress with the black collar, sitting in the high-backed chair with her father's hand clamped on her shoulder. She looked at it in silence, then said viciously to William Ryan. 'I hope you felt every riser as you fell down them, all the way from the top to the hall. And hearing your fucking neck snap when you hit the bottom was like I was finally out of prison. Bliss.'

She heard Paul coming down the stairs and slammed the album shut.

'I can't concentrate,' he said, entering the room, 'not with this sicko on the loose.' He crossed over to her. 'Are you okay?'

The concern in his voice didn't match the disquiet in his eyes. It's not me he's worried about, she thought, it's whether I'll still mention the necklace to Susan before he can warn her.

'Don't let him interfere with your writing, Paul,' she faked a brave voice. 'Sam and Michael won't let him break in again and I've no intention of going outside. He can't stay out in the woods much longer, not with this storm on the way. Either he'll be forced into the open, or he'll give up and we won't hear from him again. Then can we go back to Positano…' she affected a hesitant tone as she almost begged, '…and start all over again there?'

Well, I will, she thought, thinking of that cliff that was waiting for him.

'Sure we will,' he agreed – too hastily. The disquiet was still in his eyes, she saw it, savoring the stress she was causing him. 'Meantime, I'll put my book on hold – no, I insist,' he cut across her as she feigned she was going to protest, 'you're far more important.' He forced a smile at her, 'I'm relieved you're now thinking things through.'

Oh, I am, I am, she exulted, yet at the same time feeling dispassion about what she was planning to do to him.

He crossed to the drinks cabinet. 'Small cognac, *amante*, with just a dash of soda?'

And now he's putting on his charm act for me, she thought. No need to, Paul dearest, I'm way ahead of you.

'No thanks.'

'Mind if I do?' he asked, hand hovering over a Jack Daniels bottle.

'Of course not.'

As he poured himself a generous slug of Tennessee whiskey, neat, Morgan entered the sitting room from the dining room. 'Try as I will, I just can't focus on my designs today.'

'You, too?' Paul said. 'Drink?'

'Courvoisier.'

Paul decanted some into a goblet and gave it to Morgan. Cupping it in his hand, Morgan gently swirled it and breathed in the bouquet, then tasted it. 'Perfect.' He crossed to the front window and looked out at the encircling woods, the tops of the fir trees bending in the strengthening wind. 'He must be close by. He always seems to know what Karen is doing.'

Paul joined him. They both looked out, Morgan sipping his cognac.

Michael was sitting in his truck, a brown scarf wrapped around his neck, his breath exhaling from his mouth and nose like spurts of vapory mist, clouding his windshield and causing him to sporadically clear patches in it to see through. His wipers were sweeping at the light rain falling on it. Swirling leaves were scurrying across the parking space, and around and under the truck.

'Looks like the temperature's taken a sudden drop,' Morgan commented, 'I'd rather it be Rossi out there than me.'

'It's not so bad we can't take a look around?' said Paul. 'See if we can find somewhere from where he could be watching?'

'Depends what your definition of not so bad is,' Morgan said, 'it looks pretty cold to me. But there again, I'd rather be doing something than just sitting around.'

Downing his Jack Daniels, Paul turned to Karen. 'Will you be okay? We won't be gone long.'

A sudden feeling of panic swept over her. 'I'd rather you didn't,' she said. Acting composed when Paul and Morgan were with her was one thing, being left on her own was another. Clanryan was a creepy old house at most times, but when the roof timbers and floorboards creaked as they were now with the wind intensifying and getting under them, it was especially so – even more, it held too many bad memories she had no wish to dwell on.

'Five minutes?' Paul assured her. 'I can ask Michael to come in if you like?'

Five minutes, okay, she could live with that, no time to show weakness, not with what she had in mind for him. 'No, I'll be all right on my own. But don't be any longer,' she begged, adding her little girl lost tone to her voice.

'We won't.' He crossed to her to kiss her cheek. Reflexively, she averted her face and it landed nowhere. I shouldn't have done that, she thought, I want him to think I'm now fine with him. She clutched his hand, 'Promise?'

'Promise,' Paul said, gripping her hand back. Releasing it, he turned to Morgan. 'I'll take the woods to the front and left of the house. You take the right and the rear, and we'll meet up on the front porch.' He gripped Karen's hand again. 'We'll be back before you know it. I'll ask Michael to keep a close eye on the house while we're gone.'

He and Morgan exited to the hall, grabbed their parkas off their pegs and put them on. Paul's was black, lightly padded. He zipped it up under his chin but didn't raise his hood. Morgan's was sky-blue, thickly padded with a fur lined hood. He raised it over his head to cover his forehead almost to his eyes, and also pulled his zip up to the top, leaving little of his face exposed.

In the corner by the front door was a brass stand of William Ryan's walking sticks – still there from when took his evening walks, squire of Clanryan, wearing a Deerstalker hat and long check coat with a matching shoulder cape. Morgan selected one with a heavy nobbly head like an Irish shillelagh, clutched it like a club and tested its weight on his palm, and followed Paul out on to the front porch, closing the door behind him.

Crutching to the window, she watched Paul cross to the truck and say something to Michael. Michael nodded. Paul made for the woods to the left of the house. Morgan headed for the woods to the right.

Now left alone in Clanryan, she felt edgy. The silence was oppressive, every groan of the timber-framed house magnified in her ears, making it sound like someone was creeping up on her. A shiver ran up her spine. Needing something to occupy her mind, she searched the bookshelves for something to read, rejected them all and returned to the window.

Still in his truck, Michael was dialing out on a cellphone. Raising it to his ear, he shielded it with a cupped hand, as if trying to hide that he was calling someone – and for some reason kept glancing at the house as he waited for it to be answered.

Momentarily puzzled by his odd behavior she turned away from the window, crossed to her landline phone and called Susan's number, telling herself as it rang at the other end of the line to act normal when Susan answered, aiming to trap her into another lie.

Michael ended his call and brought up the third and last image stored on the gold cased cellphone.

It was of Karen kneeling at her parents' grave. Taken looking down at her and the cemetery from a higher vantage point, she was arranging flowers in the rose.

He brooded over it, scrolled to the image of the mean-looking man, then looked out at Clanryan as if expecting something to happen inside.

Susan was locking her shop door, on her way out, when her phone rang. She went back inside, saw the caller's number and answered it, 'Karen?', in case it was her.

'I was calling to see if you'd left, Sue.' She sounded edgy to Susan, though she was clearly trying to act normal – whatever normal was with Karen. 'Had you not replied, I'd have known you had.'

'You sound nervy? Is everything okay?'

'Yes and no,' Karen replied. 'It's just that I'm in the house on my own. Paul and Morgan have gone outside to check around the house.' She gave what was patently a forced laugh. 'It's not as if he's going to try to break in while they're gone – and Michael's outside…' Her voice tailed off.

Susan returned to the door and closed it, talking into the phone. 'I've a couple of things still to do here, Kay. They won't take more than a few minutes–'

'That's okay, Sue,' Karen said. 'But before you go, I wanted to quickly ask you about–'

'Ask me when I get there,' Susan cut across her. 'I'll call you back when I'm leaving.'

'Fine,' Karen returned. She gave another forced laugh, 'It's not like I'm not going anywhere,' and ended the call.

Not going anywhere? Susan said to herself. You damn well are, Karen dearest, and the sooner the better. And I won't be poor as a church mouse cousin Susan any more.

From memory, she punched a cellphone number, and waited for it to be answered.

Karen replaced her landline in its charger and looked out through the side window at the country road emerging out of the dark forest and straightening as it passed Clanryan, then disappearing back into the trees around another bend. The clouds above them had joined to form one dark expanse, low and thick, coming nearer with a slow almost majestic pace, and beneath it scudded a lower stratus that seemed to be skimming over the top of the forest and releasing a curtain of fine rain.

There was no sign of Paul or Morgan.

Angry with herself for failing to extend her conversation, Karen brooded over her next gambit. Should she bring up the antique necklace again later, when Paul and Susan were together with her in the same room? Or should she keep playing cat and mouse with them and say nothing, and watch them squirm – knowing she had already caught Paul out in one lie, and on edge as to her reason for doing so.

Had she guessed they were lovers, they'd be asking themselves?

Because if she found out they were, she continued to brood, then after pushing Paul over that Positano cliff, it would be Susan's turn to die.

But how? How? How?

And it came to her, just like that.

After phoning Susan with the sad news, and paying for her to fly out to attend Paul's funeral, she'd ask her to live with her in Positano for good. The bitch would jump at the chance. They'd both then return to Ravensburg, put Clanryan and Ryan Antiques up for sale and leave for Italy together, making a show of saying goodbye to Hank – and on the way to O'Hare she would kill Susan, too. Stop for a break, hit her on the head with a wrench, and keep hitting and hitting her until she was as dead as could be, then drag her body into the forest and let the wolves and the crows have her.

And once she was back in Positano, Karen brooded, Hank and any friends Susan might have in Chicago – doubtful, who could possibly like the conniving slut, and as for men friends, all she'd be to them would be a casual lay – would all think she now lived in Italy. She herself could even write a letter from her to Hank, she calculated, saying how thrilled she was to be living out there, and after that she'd soon be forgotten, a just ending for her, the fucking husband stealer.

My husband, you treacherous bitch.

Turning away from the window and looking across the empty room and, beyond it, the empty front hall, and beyond that the large empty dining room, and beyond that the large empty kitchen, she was suddenly aware of the silence, not a sound to be heard apart from the rising wind rattling the windows, and making an eerie sound as it whined along the deck surrounding Clanryan.

Hastily turning on the radio, she searched the channels until she found one playing classical music and lay on the couch with a cushion under her head, letting the soothing sounds of violins seep into her ears and through her body, trying to relax the tension inside her.

The cymbals suddenly clashed making her start, and the music became discordant. Rising to her feet she switched the radio off. Made edgy again by the ominous silence, she wandered about the room, picking up pieces of china her Mom had collected over the years, gently brushing with her fingers a Dresden mirror she had particularly loved and seeing her own face reflected in it, pale as if the light tan she'd acquired in Italy had drained away, sunken dark lines under her staring eyes–

Shriiiiiiilll…

Startled by the strident sound, she knocked the mirror aside. It fell off the chest of drawers to the floor, shattering into bits about her feet. She stared at them in horror, recalling how much her Mom had treasured the piece, feeling she had violated a precious memory of her.

Shriiiiiiilll…

Realizing it was Susan phoning to say she was on the way, she picked it up. 'Susan.'

'You're all on your own inside the house,' the familiar voice whispered.

Karen froze, unable to move or to speak.

'Just you, no husband to protect you,' the chilling voice continued. 'Nor his friend. I watched them leave And saw the knife being hidden from you earlier…Open the drawer.'

Almost as if hypnotized by the whispered command she opened the telephone table drawer and stared at the shape of the carving knife wrapped inside the handkerchief.

'Unwrap it. Look at it.'

Obeying the voice like she was in a trance, she slowly unwrapped the handkerchief, exposing the double-edged knife with the dried crow's blood on its blade.

'I'm going to slice you up with it. Just like the rag doll. Blood for blood,' the voice hissed the words, venom in his tone. 'There's no one outside protecting you either. Now would be the time to come and get you, don't you think?'

She dropped the phone, crutched to the front window and peered out. Michael's cab was empty, nor was he anywhere to be seen. Nor, again, was there any sign of Paul or Morgan.

Desperately, she crutched out into the hall and locked and bolted the front door, then back into the sitting room to the phone table. Tremulously taking the carving knife by its handle, she turned to face the hall like a cornered animal, as if expecting him to burst in through the front door.

From the phone lying by her feet, his voice whispered, 'Retribution will soon be mine.'

She slammed it with the foot of a crutch. It slid across the floor, his sibilant voice still coming from it. 'I'm coming for you, whore.' His whisper changed to a scream, '*Whore! Whore!*'

Sobbing, she hobbled to it, slid down her crutches and knelt on the floor, switched off his evil voice and hurled the phone away. It hit the back of Morgan's chair and fell on to the seat cushion.

Still kneeling and clutching the carving knife, she re-faced the hall. There was no way he could get in. The front door was locked. All the windows were locked–

The back door? Was that locked?

Pulling herself to her feet with her crutches, she stumbled to the hall and into the dining room, and looked through to the kitchen.

The back door was wide open.

Half tripping in her desperation to get to it, she crutched into the kitchen and across the floor and lunged to close it.

One of her crutches slipped from under her and she fell, sprawling to the floor.

Jerked out of her hand, the carving knife slid across the floor to the door.

Lying there flat on her face, she saw a man's shoes and trousered ankles enter from outside.

His hand reached for the carving knife and he straightened up.

He crossed the floor and the shoes stopped by her face.

He loomed over her.

His hand held the knife low to plunge it into her.

The other hand grabbed her arm and pulled her to her feet.

Not wanting to see his face – it would be evil, she knew it would be – she closed her eyes and screamed, praying that Paul, or Michael, or Morgan would hear her before he stabbed her.

'*Ssh,*' his voice whispered.

She screamed again.

'It's only me, *amante.*'

She cracked her eyes open and saw Paul looking at her. Stretching past her, he put the knife on the working table next to Morgan's shillelagh-like walking stick, opened his wet parka and held her to his denim-shirted chest. 'It's all right,' he said, stroking her hair, 'It's all right. I'm here.'

She pulled away from him, beat at him with clenched fists. He clutched her wrists. She fought to release them, but he held them. She collapsed against him, sobbing again. He put his arms back around her. 'I'm sorry, *amante,* I didn't mean to frighten you.'

'He's called again,' she whimpered.

'When?' Paul demanded. 'You mean now?'

'Yes, yes. As soon as you left me.'

'The bastard,' he grated. 'He must have been watching the house and saw us leave–'

Shriiiiiiilll…

The strident sound of the kitchen phone, an old-fashioned instrument with a coiled cord, resting on a wall-mounted cradle, pierced the room.

Pulling away from him, Karen put her hands over her ears. 'Don't answer it! Don't answer it!' she begged him through her tears. 'It's him. It's him again.'

Paul crossed to the phone, grabbed the receiver and snarled into it. 'Listen up, you sicko–'

'Paul! It's me!' Susan's voice cut across him. 'What's happened?'

Michael came from around the front left corner of the house, body bent against the strengthening wind and struggled along the deck, past the sitting room and dining room windows to the kitchen.

Her screams had stopped. She'd sounded terrified. But only silence now came from the kitchen.

Had he finally got to her?

Reaching the kitchen window, Michael saw Paul talking into the wall-mounted phone. Karen was standing near to him. She was still alive.

He spun away and headed back to his truck. Reaching it he got into his cab, slammed the door shut, reached into his glove compartment for the gold cased cellphone, pressed REDIAL, and heard an engaged tone. He hurled the phone aside. It hit the passenger door and fell to the floor, the engaged signal still coming from it.

'Fuck, fuck, fuck,' Michael slammed his clenched fist again and again into his steering wheel.

Why the fuck did Paul have to get to her first?

'What's happened?' Susan repeated over the phone. 'Paul?'

Seeing Karen trembling, Paul hurriedly replied, 'He's phoned again. Karen answered it. I'll call you back.'

'I'll be right over,' Susan said and put her receiver down.

Replacing the phone on its wall-mounted cradle, Paul held Karen tight again, feeling her still trembling in his arms. 'It was Susan. She's on her way.'

She tried to pull away from him but his grip stayed viselike and her body subsided against his. 'I asked you, begged you not to leave me,' she accused him, her voice on the edge of breaking again.

'I'm sorry, *amante*,' Paul said, his tone gentle with her, contrite. 'So sorry.'

'I was alone. You and Morgan weren't there. Michael wasn't outside.'

'He was when we left the house,' Paul said, less apologetic now, partly justifying his decision to leave her alone.

'He's not now,' she snapped back, suddenly changing from being abject to accusing.

Paul took her hand and led her into the dining room and to the window. They looked out and saw Michael in his truck. 'He's still there,' Paul said, his tone suggesting she'd been mistaken.

She was about to retaliate when Michael stretched across his passenger seat, taking him almost from their sight as he grasped for something on the floor.

'Maybe that's what he was doing?' Paul suggested, 'and you weren't able to see him?'

'No,' she insisted. 'I looked for him but there was no sign of him anywhere.'

Paul pulled a wry face, clearly believing she was mistaken. Anger welled up inside her, but then she saw Michael straighten up and dial out on whatever he'd recovered – a cellphone. The anger drained out of her as a sudden terrible thought came into her mind.

No. Surely? Not Michael?

'He's calling someone,' she voiced her fear as he raised the phone to his ear and again shielded it with his cupped hand as he waited for it to be answered. 'I saw him call someone earlier, too, just before that evil voice phoned me. Maybe it's Michael who's hired him? Watching the house, he'd know when I was alone and could be letting him know.'

'It couldn't be,' Paul said. 'Michael was in the sitting room with us once when the sicko called. And he saved you from drowning.'

'Maybe he had no choice, not with you swimming alongside him ...' Her voice tailed off as she recalled something.

'And he hesitated, Paul. He hesitated before breaking my window.'

'Yes. Yes, he did…' Paul reflected, but then shook his head. 'No, it couldn't be,' he repeated. 'Why would Michael Rossi want you dead?'

'What if he came back here hoping to take up with me for my money, but found I'd married you? Her voice shook as the thought took hold of her. 'That would more than make Michael vindictive. When he was younger, he could hold a grudge for months if things went against him.'

'Well, our phone's not ringing,' Paul deliberated, now sounding like he was being swayed by her argument. 'Whoever he's calling, it's not here.'

Michael removed the phone from his ear as his call clearly wasn't answered, and replaced it in his glove compartment.

'We have to tell Sam.' Karen said, her voice still shaking at the thought of it being Michael who wanted her dead.

'Sure, soon as he gets here,' Paul said. 'Meantime, after what you've just experienced you need a brandy.' Clasping her hand, he led her into the front hall, hung up his parka back on its peg, and they entered the sitting room just as Morgan came around the front left corner of the house.

Leaning into the wind, Morgan struggled along the deck to the front door. Finding it locked, he continued past the dining room window, around the right corner of the house to the back door, and entered the kitchen. Seeing the carving knife on the table he snatched it, opened the sink cupboard and threw it inside, shut the door on it and turned to enter the dining room, but then saw his walking stick lying across the table. Grabbing it, he crossed the dining room to the front hall, replaced the stick in the stand, hung his parka on a peg and entered the sitting room.

'I saw no sign of –' He stopped mid-sentence as he saw Karen sitting, looking ashen, in the chair by the hearth, and Paul decanting cognac into a goblet and handing it to her. Snatching it from Paul, she gulped some down.

'He's called again,' Paul said over his shoulder. 'We shouldn't have left her.'

Morgan stepped toward her. 'Damn. I'm so sorry, Karen.'

'Give her a moment,' Paul said.

'Of course,' Morgan said and subsided into his usual chair. 'Have you called King?'

'After I first check whether he's slipped up this time and left his number.'

'I doubt it,' Morgan said.

Paul crossed to the phone and checked the list of recorded calls, and replaced the phone back on its charger. 'No,' he said. 'The last one is Susan's, she called a minute ago. There's no record of his call before that.'

'Best call King,' Morgan repeated.

'I'm doing it,' Paul snapped and dialed out.

Sitting on the couch, sipping her brandy and watching them, Karen brooded.

Michael?

Could it be Michael who wanted her dead? If so, was it from jealousy? But, no, surely…all they'd been to each other was a teenage groping, and more than twelve years ago. No, if it was Michael, it had be her father's money…

Money…she thought…Money.

Hooding her eyelids, she studied Paul from under them as he waited, phone gripped to his ear, for Sam to answer, and her suspicion of him and Susan came back into her head.

Were they lovers? Plotting to get their hands on her money after she'd been killed?

Her eyes moved to Morgan Hale sitting in his chair. And what about him?

Could he, too, be complicit in Paul's and Susan's intrigues?

She rocked herself back and forth in her chair as her thoughts whirled about inside her head.

It was getting to be that Sam King was the only one she could trust.

Sam was still lying fully clothed on his bed in his cabin, looking at the photo of Emma with Gina. The wind outside was getting stronger, rain spattering on the window.

His cellphone alongside him rang. He reached for it and switched it on. 'Sam King.'

'Paul Archer, detective,' Paul's voice came over the line.

'What's wrong?' Sam asked, detecting the tension in Paul's voice.

'He's called again,' Paul replied. 'Karen answered it.'

'How is she?'

'Not good.'

'Have you checked whether–'

'No record of it.'

'I was sleeping when you rang,' Sam said. 'I'll be there as soon as I can.'

'Sure,' Paul said and ended the call.

Sam lay back, brooding. Hearing a car start up, he got off the bed, went to the window, saw Susan's red Jaguar coupe speed away from her antique shop and be swallowed up as it entered the forest.

His cellphone bleeped with an incoming message. He looked at the screen.

On it was the image of a handsome, though mean-looking man – in his mid-30s, Sam judged. He had cruel eyes.

Sam scrolled down and read Bert Quinlan's brief data about him.

John Paxton. 34. Chicago. Actor (small roles)
Served two terms (1 & 3) for aggravated assault
May be armed

Sam opened his bedside cabinet drawer, took out a note pad and wrote RAVENSBURG on the top left of the first page, and Karen's, Paul's, Morgan's, Susan's and Michael's names under it. He then wrote CHICAGO on the bottom right of the page, with Paxton's name under it, and encircled them, drew an arrowed line from them up to RAVENSBURG and Karen, and also encircled them. Next, he drew an arrowed line from CHICAGO and Paxton, to Paul, Morgan, Susan, Michael, encircled them, too, and put a question mark behind their names.

Drawing an arrow up from them to Karen, he studied the final sketch.

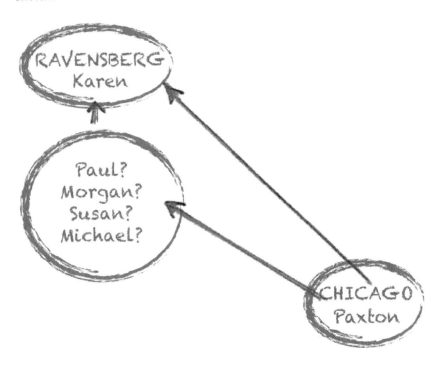

He brooded over the four names in the circle below Karen.

Paul?

Morgan?

Susan?

Michael?

Then, in a grim, almost inaudible voice, Sam said, 'And me, too.'

-21-

The meal that Morgan had rustled up was over. Karen was sitting at the dining table wrapped in her thoughts and her food untouched, the dark storm gathering outside matching her mood, and seemingly unaware of Morgan bustling around her clearing dishes on to a tray.

Except that though her thoughts were deep inside her brooding mind, she was aware of Paul and Susan standing at the front window, talking in low voices as they pretended to be looking out at the approaching storm. Paul was good at it – as an actor, he would be – his gaze fixed on outside, mannerisms and posture casual, but she wasn't fooled by him. Susan however, was standing part sideways and unable to prevent herself from sometimes snatching glances at her to see if she was watching them – yet not realizing that she was, intently so, from the hooded corners of her eyes.

What's more, from the anxious look Susan kept giving her each time she turned her face, she knew what they were talking about, could almost read their conversation.

Paul: 'Well, that's what she told me. That you said I'd called you about an antique necklace I was giving her as a surprise gift.'

Susan (voice trembling, knowing from the past about my moods, Karen thought): 'But why would she say that? Do you think she suspects us? If so, we'd best watch our backs. She can turn vicious in an instant.'

Paul (muttering from the corner of his mouth): 'As I'm realizing. I never saw this side of her in Italy, or in Chicago, either. Only when we got back here to Clanryan.'

Susan (muttering back): If anything crosses her – watch out! I once saw her kill a red squirrel that ran into the kitchen through the open door. She grabbed it by its tail, smashed its head against the wall and threw it out and carried on with what she was doing as if nothing had happened. And she was still only twelve when she did that.'

What in the fuck did you expect me to do with it? Karen thought. *Give it a saucer of warm milk and some nuts and keep it as a pet?*

Susan (glancing back at her again and quickly averting her gaze): 'I think she's watching us.'

The bitch, Karen simmered, but I've given her enough to make her edgy. Turning her eyes from them, she felt them being pulled to the Clan Ryan shield on the wall, and its motto: "I would rather die before being dishonored or disgraced", and at the same time felt her father's eyes boring into the back of her head from his portrait hanging up on the wall behind her …

Suddenly, in the dark recesses of her mind, she was taken back to when she was a child.

Unable to resist, like she was two persons in one, her grown up self, and twelve years old again, she heard herself saying, in a little girl's voice, 'Mommy, please don't be dead. Please come back, Mommy, He's opening my door and coming into my bedroom.'

At the same time she was also aware – in a strange, distant way – of Susan hurrying across the room, and sitting alongside her and holding her in her arms and placing her head on her shoulder and stroking it, as the little girl's voice still emanated from somewhere within her.

'What do you want?' she pleaded to the one entering her room.

In her mind's ear, she heard the gravelly voice reply. 'You know what I want. The same as I always want.'

'Go away,' she whimpered back. 'Go away.'

Still like she was in a dream, yet conscious of what was going on around her, she saw Paul and Morgan exchange glances, and heard Paul whisper to Susan: 'What's happening to her?'

Susan gestured him away and kept holding her tight, stroking her head.

Raising her face, she pleaded with Susan, but it wasn't the Susan of now, it was the Susan she had turned to so many times in the past, from when she was a twelve-year-old child.

'Make him stop, Sue …' her voice tailed off, she shuddered. 'Stop him getting into my bed.'

She buried her face in her hands, trying blocking out the fraught memory as she came back to the present, aware of Susan stroking her hair, and warning Paul and Morgan away with her eyes.

'I want to be told that what's happening to me now is a bad dream, Sue,' she whimpered on Susan's shoulder. 'That whoever he is, he will go away, like I made the other bad dream go away and never come back again.'

'I had the same dream, Kay, when I lived here with you,' Susan murmured. 'But yours will fade as mine did, and disappear like it never happened.'

Susan's words entered Karen's consciousness. She looked up stunned at her cousin, realizing for the first time she'd gone through the same nightmare, then clutched Susan's hand as they sat together in tacit silence, their pasts filling their thoughts, the present for the moment forgotten.

Moments passed, then Paul motioned to Susan. She looked up at him. He questioned her with his eyes. She flicked hers at him in reply. Responding, he and Morgan picked up dishes and took them to the kitchen, closing the door behind them.

Susan rested Karen's face back on her shoulder. 'It will all soon be over, Kay,' she whispered. 'I promise.'

-22-

Despite the darkness outside, the oilcloth drapes were not fully closed over the kitchen window as Morgan put the last of the washed and dried dishes away in a wall cupboard. On a working table below it an old electric percolator brewed coffee. Next to it was a tray laid with a white cloth. On it were four mugs and teaspoons, a bowl of sugar and a jug of milk.

He reached for the percolator, poured coffee into the mugs, and from a trouser pocket pulled out a spotless white handkerchief, neatly folded, and unwrapped it, revealing one of Karen's red and yellow sleeping capsules. He separated the two halves over one of the mugs and poured white powder into the coffee. Stirring it until the powder dissolved, he rinsed the spoon under a hot water faucet, dried it, and replaced it on the tray, dropped the capsule halves into the enamel sink and ran the hot water over them until they melted, and flushed the sink.

He picked up the tray and made for the door to the dining room.

In the dining room, Susan was still sitting alongside Karen, clutching her hand, and Paul facing them across the table.

'He can't hold out there much longer, Kay,' Susan said. 'Listen to it,' she indicated outside to the sound of the gusts venting their fury against Clanryan's clapboard walls – finding gaps in the sash windows and ruffling the closed drapes. 'What food he had with him must be gone by now. He'll be getting desperate, giving Sam King and Michael more chance to catch him.' She gripped Karen's hand. 'It won't be for much longer.'

Her suspicions about her cousin and Paul again filling her mind, 'I wish I could believe it, Sue,' Karen said.

Paul stretched out his arm and grasped Karen's other hand. 'You must, *amante*. Susan, myself and Morgan, Detective King and Rossi, we'll all make sure he doesn't get to you again, and once he's caught our lives can get back to normal.'

Normal!, Karen thought, repulsed now by even the touch of his hand, but leaving hers in his not to let him know. *What the fuck is normal! Two weeks in Positano, shagging. Back to shitty Ravensburg, chased by a psycho and almost drowned. Him getting into my room, leaving a carving knife and bloodied dead crow by my face on my pillow. And now shagging me is taboo. Not that I want it from you any more, Paul, with your amante this, your amante that. So, I'll tell you what normal is, when I've got rid of you and can finally have a life of my own–*

Morgan entered from the kitchen carrying mugs on a tray and breaking her thoughts. Closing the door behind him, he crossed to the table. 'Coffee,' he said unnecessarily, placing a mug next to Karen and putting the tray by Paul and Susan. 'It doesn't matter which, they're both the same,' he said to them, sat next to Paul and offered Karen the jug of milk. 'Milk, Karen?'

'No thanks, Morgan, I'll have it black.' Pulling her hand away from Paul's, she stretched for the coffee mug, forcing Susan to release her other hand.

Morgan extended the bowl to her. 'Sugar, then?'

'Again, no, thanks.'

'You sure?' Morgan moved the bowl nearer her. 'Sugar's a restorative, recommended in times of trauma. It reduces the cortisone levels, the stress hormone.'

'In that case,' she said, if only to shut Morgan the fuck up. Spooning two sugars into her coffee and stirring it, she saw Morgan give Paul an almost imperceptible nod. Paul pushed his chair back, abruptly stood up, crossed to the front window, cracked open the drapes and peered out.

Now what? Karen thought, then saw Morgan watching her out of the corner of his eye as she raised her mug to her mouth. *Has he put something in my coffee*, the suspicion flashed to her mind, *and that's why he's so insistent on me taking sugar – to hide the taste? Whatever it is, it can't be lethal, they can't risk openly committing murder, but a sleeping pill in my coffee will ensure I fall into a deep sleep. Then carry me up to bed and Paul can knife me as I lie there – Morgan doesn't have the guts – knowing the psycho will be blamed for it, with no suspicion falling on them…*

She paused with the mug to her lips, and saw the suspense in Morgan's eyes as she breathed in the aroma of the coffee. She sipped it. Morgan visibly relaxed. She lowered the mug back on to the table. 'Too hot,' she said and caught the tightening of his jaw in frustration. It was only for a split second, but she caught it.

I'm right, she thought. *Morgan's in it with them. And I'm trapped in here with all three. Now what can I do?*

'King's late tonight,' Paul said, providing her solution as he again peered through the drapes.

Sam! Sam's my answer, she brooded. *I'll play them along until he gets here, then signal him from my bedroom to come below my window, tell him these three bastards are planning to kill me and get him to take me away from here. And on the way to his place, tell him my suspicions about Michael, too.*

'How are your designs progressing, Morgan?' she asked, indicating to them rolled up on the bottom half of an antique American dresser, its three shelves above lined with vintage Wisconsin china plates.

'You can't possibly want to see my work?' Morgan protested. 'Not at a time like this?'

'Please,' she put on her little girl lost act. 'It will help take my mind off things.'

'Well, if you're sure.' He seemed reluctant to concede, but crossed to the dresser and brought his designs to the table and spread them out on its surface, pinning the corners down with the salt and pepper glass shakers and two dispensers from a four-piece condiment set.

'I rather like them,' Morgan said, pride in his work now suddenly over-ruling all else. 'Though I doubt those Chicago philistines who commissioned me will.'

'I'm sure they'll love them,' she rejoined, still playing her part. 'And use my studio. I won't be wanting it until this nightmare is over.'

'I prefer working here, if that's alright with you.' Morgan replied. 'The table's bigger and also next to the kitchen, and allows me to be creative at both my fortes – my designs, and my cooking – at the same time.'

'Which theater, Morgan?' Susan cut in.

Pretending to be interested, the bitch, Karen brewed. *Well, Sam will be here any minute now.*

'One of those avant-garde theaters on Monroe Street,' Morgan pulled a disparaging face. 'It's under new management and this is their first production.'

'What's the play?' Susan studied the top sheet.

It's all a charade, Karen thought. *The three of them acting their parts.*

'It's more a merger of musical and ballet rather than a play, very Gene Kelly,' Morgan preened. 'This is the set for the opening scene.'

He stood back and looked at the design with hands on hips, his evident pride in it momentarily now taking precedence.

'King's here,' Paul said from the window.

At last, Karen said to herself.

Crutching to Paul's side, and ensuring her shoulder didn't touch his, she parted the drapes a little more and saw Sam's car reach the house and stop.

Sam got out. Battling against the wind, he crossed to Michael's truck, took his cellphone from his jacket pocket, showed Michael the screen and asked him a question.

'Looks like he's heard something,' Paul said. 'He'll probably be coming in.'

Change of plan, Karen thought. *I'll have to think of a pretext to get Sam aside and talk to him on his own. And tell him about the spiked coffee to prove I'm right.*

Watching Michael shake his head in reply to Sam, and knowing his body language from all those years ago, she picked up on him being too vehement, as if he did know what was on Sam's screen, but was denying it – she stored it for when she could somehow get Sam alone.

Pocketing his cellphone, Sam made for the house. Michael extracted something from his leather jacket and briefly wrote on it, then mused at what he'd jotted down.

'Rossi keeps making notes in a pad,' Paul muttered to her, 'and looking about him, as if he's checking no one's watching. Like it's a big secret.'

'We all have our secrets, Paul,' she said, as Sam climbed the porch steps to the front door. 'But the more hidden they are, the more danger of slipping up and being caught out.'

She felt Paul's eyes on her as he pondered what she meant by that, but then he turned away to open the front door for Sam as the bell rang.

She crutched back across the room to face Sam when he entered. Morgan rolled up his designs in an evident dudgeon at having to end his presentation. Susan stayed sitting at the table.

Out in the hall, Paul opened the door. The wind howled in as Sam came inside. Paul slammed the door closed. 'We're in the dining room, detective.'

Sam preceded Paul into the room, running his fingers through his wind-blown hair. 'It's coming up a fine storm,' he said and turned to her. 'He's called you again, Karen?'

It was a rhetorical question. She nodded, trying to think of some pretext to get him on his own.

'I'm guessing you have some news for us?' Paul said. 'We saw you question Michael.'

Sam produced a notebook. 'Chicago's traced his name.' He glanced at his notes, 'Paxton,' he read out, like he needed to be reminded of it and looked up. 'John Paxton. Ever heard your father mention him, Karen?'

She shook her head. 'No, Sam. Never.'

'How about you, Miss Ryan? In connection with your own father, maybe?'

'My father died over ten years ago, detective,' Susan said, brusque.

'Ten years?' Sam repeated. 'That long?' He turned to Morgan. 'Mr. Hale?'

'I don't see how this is any way connected to me, detective,' Morgan replied testily, replacing her mug and the other three on the tray and sliding it nearer to take to the kitchen.

I'm watching you, you creep. No way will you get rid of the evidence.

'Only that Paxton's also from Chicago, Mr. Hale.'

'As are over three million others,' Morgan retorted. 'Including you, detective.'

'Sure,' said Sam. 'How about you, Mr. Archer?'

'Like Morgan,' Paul snapped, 'I don't understand why you're asking us about him.'

'Sorry, Mr. Archer, I should have explained. It's just that Paxton's an actor, same as you. That narrows the chances of you having met him considerably from Mr. Hale's three million. You, too, Mr. Hale. Being a set designer I'm guessing you move in more or less the same circles.'

Oh, God, I'm right. They know him and hired him to kill me, and now they're intending to do it themselves and him to take the rap. I must talk to Sam. And fuck them hearing me. It's my life at stake here.

'If you think Morgan and I have anything to do with what's happening here, detective,' Paul said angrily, 'then come straight out with it, rather than imply it. '

'I'm not implying anything, Mr. Archer. Just saying that you or Mr. Hale might have met this Paxton sometime – without either of you realizing it, maybe? It's a small world.'

'Sam–' she tried to intrude.

'If coming from Chicago makes us suspects,' Paul retorted, cutting across her, 'then as Morgan said, you're also from there. Except you're idling about here, supposedly on vacation, yet at the wrong time of the year, but just happened to be at the scene when this Paxton tried to run Karen off the road. For all we know about you, you could have a motive. And being with Organized Crime you'd know exactly where to find a hitman – as you call them.'

Oh, God, oh, God, that's right, Sam would. What if it's Sam, not Paul and Morgan? Except, Sam doesn't have a motive. But again, the way it's evolving so rapidly around me, maybe it's not one I know of. What with shock after shock coming at me from all directions, anything's possible.

Paul's voice intruded into her whirling thoughts. 'Rossi can't be dismissed either. Returning here in the hope of maybe picking up with Karen again, only to find she's married me, he could get to Chicago in less than eight hours – and even less to find someone like Paxton.'

Oh, God! Yes! Michael! He could simmer for days when I wouldn't let him go all the way.

What if he's another one who wants me dead?

Paul?

Morgan?

Susan?

Michael?

And now, far-fetched though it may be, Sam, too?

If I want to stay alive – and I do, please, God, I do – there's only one way out of this and that's through my own wits, and my own wits alone. I'm not saying a word to Sam.

'And going from the sublime to the ridiculous, if it's not far for Michael, then nor would it be for Susan,' said Morgan, reinforcing her suspicion about her cousin.

'Thanks for just making me a prime suspect, Morgan,' Susan snapped at him and turned to Sam. 'But aren't we getting away from the real suspect here, detective? Paxton, you said his name is?'

'You're right, Miss Ryan,' Sam said. Producing his cellphone from a jacket pocket, he called up an image on his screen. 'This is him – if Paxton's his real name,' he added and showed it to Paul.

Paul glanced at it. 'Never met him.'

Sam showed the image to Morgan. 'Mr. Hale?'

'Definitely not, detective,' Morgan grimaced. 'Nor would I wish to, judging by his eyes. There's absolutely no feeling in them. As for those gold necklaces and bracelets,' Morgan looked away, showing his distaste.

Sam stretched the cellphone across the table to Susan. 'How about you, Miss Ryan? Ever seen him before? In Hank's maybe, buying provisions?'

'Never.' Susan looked away from the photo. 'And like Morgan, nor would I wish to.'

Karen flipped. Crutching across to Sam, she snatched the phone from him, looked at Paxton's image, and recoiled in horror. 'This is him! This is the sick psycho who tried to drown me? Who crept into my room and…'

Choking on her words, she raised her arm to hurl the phone away. Sam grabbed it from her. She spun on her crutches and returned to near the kitchen door. But Sam saw she was trembling, like she was cracking up – as much from fear as from tension.

'So, what happens next, detective?' Morgan asked, picking up the tray to take to the kitchen.

'Chicago's checking him out, Mr. Hale,' Sam said.

'Surely we now know enough about him for Mignon to help find him?' Paul questioned.

'I'll call them,' said Sam. 'Meantime, Chicago are checking for any connection between him and Karen's father, though it's still possible it's Karen he has the problem with, his continued use,' he hesitated, clearly unsure how to say this, 'sorry about this, Karen, his use of the word whore–'

Karen flipped again. 'If I hear that said about me again, I'll…I'll…'

Susan reached out for her. Karen backed away from her, up to the kitchen door – as if she wanted to flee from the room, from the very house itself come to that, Sam thought and returned to Paul.

'This Paxton's complex, Mr. Archer. It's like he has an abhorrence with Karen's sexuality, even to how…' he hesitated, 'how she dresses.'

'Which proves that Morgan's right about him, detective,' Paul said. 'He's a psycho, whether or not he's doing it for himself or been hired by someone else.'

'You're probably right,' Sam agreed. 'But for you all to know – he has a record and could be armed. Chicago's also checking whether Paxton is his name, or if it's an–'

'Won't his fingerprints on the carving knife tell them?' Susan asked.

'They will, Miss Ryan, if there's any on it,' Sam said. 'I'll send it them later. Except with all that's been happening, I can't remember where I put it–'

'It's on the kitchen table!' Karen snapped. 'Paul left it there earlier.' Hurling the door open she crutched into the kitchen – and screamed. 'It's gone! Oh, God, oh, God, it's gone!'

Paul crossed to her and held her tight. She didn't resist and buried her face in his chest.

'Blame me, Karen,' Morgan said, berating himself as entered the kitchen with the tray of mugs.

'Just seeing the gruesome thing sickened me. I hid it from my sight.' He put the tray down, opened the sink cupboard and stared horror stricken into it. 'It's not there! But I placed it inside!'

Pulling away from Paul, Karen looked wildly around her. 'He's been in here? When? When?'

'It must have been a moment ago,' Morgan replied. 'After I made the coffee–'

'When we were in the next room!' She was near to collapse now. 'With only a door between us!'

'I'm so sorry, Karen,' Morgan said, almost beside himself with guilt, and turning to Sam. 'It's my fault, detective,' he spilled out his words in self-reproach, 'I took some garbage out while the coffee brewed and must have forgotten to re-lock the door after I came back in.'

'And the drapes cracked open, Mr. Hale,' Sam said, 'for him to see the kitchen was clear.'

'It's okay, Morgan,' Paul cut in, seeing how overwrought Morgan was. 'No one's blaming you.' He saw Karen shivering. 'Another stiff brandy for you,' he said to her. Taking her arm, he led her unresisting in the dining room. Susan hurried to them, took Karen from him and the three continued through to the front hall and into the sitting room.

Sam went out onto the rear deck. 'Michael!' he called out to him, still sitting in his truck.

Left alone in the kitchen, Morgan turned on the hot water faucet and rinsed Karen's mug.

Out on the deck, Michael came running. Sam instructed him in a low voice.

Michael hurried off. Sam re-entered the kitchen.

'So, he's again got a carving knife,' he said to Morgan.

'And seemingly a psychotic fixation to use one,' said Morgan.

-23-

Karen was sitting between Paul and Susan on the couch, feeling imprisoned by them as she sipped her brandy. Morgan was watching her from his chair opposite like he was her warden.

Outside, the wind was rattling the loose fitting sash windows, taking her mind back to the dark evening when they'd returned to Clanryan after burying her Mom and the storm that had threatened all that day finally broke, rattling the windows then too, billowing the drapes as her father sat beside her and gripped her hand like a vice. 'Well, Karen,' he said in his gravelly voice. 'Your mother has left us alone together in Clanryan. It will be lonely here without her. The only way we will get through it is by consoling each other.' And her father had placed her hand on–

Sam entered the room. Shuddering, she banished the dread memory and returned her thoughts to now. Clanryan was still her prison. She had to get away. As far from Paxton's menace outside as possible. And far from Paul and Susan and Morgan too. And not knowing who she could trust, there was also Sam and Michael to be reckoned with. She had to escape all six of them. *Six.* An unlucky number so it was said. Especially when repeated: *Six Six Six*, the number of The Beast, symbolizing Satan and Hell – and Clanryan was getting to be more like Hell to her than ever it was, even when *he* was alive.

But to get away, especially from the three inside, she needed to buy herself time to crystallize the plan forming in her mind. And the only way to buy herself time was to drive a wedge between them.

Glancing out of the corner of her eye at Susan, she's the weak link, Karen brooded, and I know how to do it, she decided, refocusing her gaze back to Sam as he casually questioned Morgan.

'Out of curiosity, Mr. Hale, how did you get to Ravensburg after Karen and Mr. Archer left for Italy? Chicago's over four hundred miles and you don't seem to have any transport of your own.'

Karen felt Paul stiffen beside her. 'I keep saying this, detective,' he grated before Morgan could reply, 'but Paxton's your suspect not Morgan - nor myself if you intend questioning me, too.'

'Sure, Mr. Archer. I was being conversational, nothing more.'

'It's fine, Paul,' Morgan said and answered Sam. 'I hired a taxicab service to drive me here.'

'That must have set you back some,' Sam returned.

'Twelve hundred dollars, including tip,' Morgan shrugged, dismissing the sum. 'But well worth it. Paul has been a good friend to me. And though I've known Karen for but a short time,' he smiled across at her, 'I've become very fond of her.' Seeming not to notice that she didn't return his smile, he added to Sam. 'Minding the house was the least I could do.'

'Getting back to Paxton, detective,' Paul intervened.

'Yes, Sam,' Karen cut in. Draining her cognac in a gulp, she felt it restore something of her old self, and now entered the exchange to deceive them all into thinking that the only thing on her mind was Paxton and his threat to her life. 'There are many things about him puzzling me.'

'Me, too, Karen,' Sam said. 'But ask yours first and I'll see if I can answer them.'

Clutching her glass, Karen sat up to feel less hemmed in by Paul and Susan. 'To start with,' she began, 'whether or not he's being paid by someone else, he drives here all the way from Chicago—'

'You want to suggest here, detective,' Paul interjected, 'that he may have given Morgan a lift?'

'Except I still have the receipt for the taxicab,' Morgan said in good humor, 'should there be any doubt.'

'There's none, Mr. Hale,' Sam said, ignoring Paul's jibe. 'You were saying, Karen?'

'That having driven from Chicago, it's still only mid-morning when he's watching me in the cemetery. So, either he drove through the night – or the previous day and slept in his truck.'

'One or the other,' Sam agreed.

'So, how did he know that's where I'd be – and that early in the morning? I didn't return from Italy until the evening before.'

'He could have been hiding nearby watching the house,' Sam reasoned, 'and followed you there some distance behind and you didn't see him.'

'Maybe…' her voice tailed off, unconvinced. 'Then how did he know I would be here?' she challenged him. 'What if we'd decided to extend our stay in Italy? I wanted to, but Paul was on edge to get back to his book.'

'I wouldn't say I was on edge, *amante*,' Paul objected.

'Oh, Paul, you know you were,' she said over-sweetly,' you were mostly all packed the day before.'

Sam hastily stepped in. 'Maybe he didn't know you were away, Karen? Him being here the same time you got back was just a coincidence?'

'No, it would be too much of a coincidence, Sam. He must have known it from someone—'

'That implies Paul, or Morgan, or myself, Kay?' Susan said, curt.

'I'm not implying anything, Sue,' Karen returned. 'Just telling Sam the things that are puzzling me about him, and hoping that as a detective he can provide some answers.'

But she was still being over-sweet and Sam swiftly stepped in again. 'What else, Karen?'

'His change of mindset, Sam, after what happened at Ravens Pond.'

'In what way?'

'Before then all he wanted, it seems, was to kill me. First, by forcing me off the road at Carvers Gulch, making it look like I'd accidentally driven over the edge–'

'I think I know what's troubling you, Karen,' Morgan entered the conversation.

'But in case someone did see him,' Karen continued, ignoring him, 'he'd already removed his license plates so the truck couldn't be identified. They would have had to stop and see whether by some miracle I was alive, and he would have driven off – only now it would be a hit and run.'

'And by the time Mignon could be called to the scene,' Morgan insisted on having his say, 'and driven the forty miles here and put out an APB on him, he could be halfway back to Chicago with his plates replaced, just one truck in a crowd.'

'Or gotten rid of it and be picked up by whoever hired him,' said Sam.

'And the same later, when you came into it, Sam,' Karen said. 'Had I have gone into the trees at Ravens Corner, you too would have had to stop and he'd still have got away.'

'I don't understand the purpose of this, *amante?* Paul cut in. 'You're only repeating what we already know.'

'But having failed to kill me there,' she continued with Sam, 'his mindset now changes.'

'You're right, Karen,' Morgan interjected again. 'I hadn't realized it before, not even when we were discussing it previously, but it's only *after* Ravens Pond that saying he needs reparation becomes a motive. Before that, killing you was all he wanted to do.'

'That's what's bothering me,' she still addressed Sam. 'There was nothing of reparation in his mind before then, Sam.'

'And now we're getting all these phone calls from him,' said Morgan, insisting on being part of the exchange, and using "we're" to denote his involvement in it all, 'with his threats of seeking retribution first.'

'And even though he risked getting into my bedroom, Sam, and still had hours to be on his way back to Chicago after killing me, he didn't. Yet at first, that was all he wanted. Instead he goes to the extreme of creating a grisly scene: a dead crow with its neck cut off.'

'You're right, Karen,' Sam agreed, 'making you suffer, as he calls it, is suddenly as vital to him as killing you, if not more so.' He brooded a moment. 'Of course, it's still possible his grudge may not be against you or your father.' He turned to Paul. 'Have you given more thought, Mr. Archer, to it being you he's–'

'How many times do I have to say this, detective–'

'I'm not suggesting it's something big, Mr. Archer, just that it's big to him – as Mr. Hale said yesterday.'

'And I'm suggesting we end all this surmising, detective, and focus on Paxton,' Paul said.

He clutched Karen's hand. It brought her mind back to her intention to drive a wedge between him and Susan. She shivered for them to think that the mention of Paxton had reminded her of him being out there wanting to kill her.

Susan took her from Paul and stroked her head, like she was a child again.

Stroke away, bitch, it makes no difference. You've still got yours coming.

'See how distressing all this is to her, detective?' Paul turned on Sam. 'Catching Paxton is what we should be concentrating on, not his motive. That can come after, when he's facing trial.'

Susan raised Karen's face. 'Until then, Kay,' she said in a low voice, full of concern. 'Maybe you should go somewhere well away from here?'

Karen put on a despairing look. 'But if he's so determined to kill me, Sue, he's going to find me wherever I try to hide.'

'Even so,' Susan insisted. 'I still think it would be safer for you than staying on in Clanryan.'

'Yes, *amante*,' Paul cut in, 'I've been rethinking it, and agree with Susan. Maybe it would be best if you go back to Positano. And Susan can go with you while Morgan and I remain here with Detective King. Once he's caught, we can join you both. Book the flights tomorrow.'

Sam saw an immediate suspicion in Karen's eyes – he could almost hear her think: *Why has Paul changed his mind? And wanting Susan to come with me? What have they got planned for me out there?*

He watched her expression change to one of wiliness – like a cunning chess player thinking three moves ahead. Again he thought that never before had he met someone who could so quickly alter from one mood to another. He waited, fascinated, for her reply.

'No, I think it's best I stay, Paul' she said. 'Here I not only have you and Morgan to protect me, I also have Sam and Michael. If Paxton somehow found out I'd gone back to Italy, he could come after me, and maybe be left with no choice but to kill Susan, too. No, when I think it through, we're both safer here.'

Watching for Paul's response, Sam saw him and Susan exchange a swift glance.

Paul turned to Sam. 'Won't you reason with her, detective?'

'It's Karen's decision,' Sam said. 'I also happen to agree with her.'

An expression of frustration flitted across Susan's face, as if something that she and Paul had conceived had failed. It was only fleeting and immediately replaced by a look of concern, but Sam caught it.

'Whatever Karen thinks is best,' she gripped Karen's hand. Sam saw that Karen didn't return it.

'Then I'll go and grab some sleep before relieving Michael,' Sam said and made for the door, but paused and turned back to Paul. 'And there's no record of his last call?'

'None, detective,' Paul snapped.'

'How the hell does he do that?' Sam said out loud to himself. He exited the room and then the house, closing the front door behind him.

With her hand unresponsive in Susan's, Karen mentally planned the words she would use to drive the first wedge between her cousin and Paul.

Sam descended the porch steps. The clouds hanging over the forest were lower still, with a thin mist covering the tops of the firs releasing a curtain of fine rain, and the strengthening wind was gusting it like a swirling cloak across the road and sweeping over Clanryan and the parking space.

Michael was searching the edge of the shrubbery with his flashlight. His probing was desultory, maybe caused by the rain, Sam thought. Zipping up his jacket, he crossed to him. 'Find anything.'

'Zilch,' Michael said.

'Your mind seems elsewhere, Michael.'

'It's personal,' Michael grated.

'Fine,' Sam said. 'I'm going back to the cabin. I asked Chicago to check up on something. My cellphone keeps breaking up here, but it's fine there. I'll be back as soon as I can.'

'Sure,' Michael said and called after him as Sam turned away. 'Did you find any sign of him near the phone booth?'

Sam looked back. 'None I could see. No footprints or broken twigs. But I'm no tracker and that's not to say there weren't.'

'I called it.'

'I didn't hear it.'

'It rang out.'

'Maybe there's a line fault – and that's why it was dead when I checked it, and also why his calls aren't being recorded here. But I didn't hang about there long. How soon after did you call?'

'Soon as I got back here. Say ten minutes.'

'I'd gone by then.' Sam made for his Ford Fusion again.

'Did Hank tell you if anyone's been asking about you?'

'I clean forgot to check,' Sam replied over his shoulder. 'I'll do it before going to my cabin.'

'He could also have got your name from Archer?' Michael persisted. 'Or his homo buddy?'

'Or Miss Ryan?' Sam said.

'No, not Susan.' Michael protested. 'Like I said, there's no way she's involved in any of this.'

'If you say so, Michael,' Sam responded.

Michael watched him get into his car, switch on his lights and drive out onto the road and from sight into the forest. Delving into a jacket pocket for the gold-cased cellphone, he called up IMAGES and studied Paxton's face.

'No need to check with Hank, Sam,' he said. 'I know exactly how Paxton knows your name.'

-24-

Pulling her hand out of Susan's tight grip, Karen rose from the couch, holding her empty cognac glass and crossed to the side window. She peered through the drapes. A hole had appeared in the black clouds above them, the rain had suddenly stopped and the wind dropped, leaving a stillness that lay heavy like an invisible shroud of death over the dark surrounding forest.

To her right she could dimly see the road to Ravensburg disappearing into the trees, heading back into the still oncoming storm. The road to her left heading south appeared lighter through the gloom, no more than 40 twisting miles to negotiate before reaching the straighter 360 or so miles along Routes 53 and 94 and beyond, that would take her direct to Chicago and O'Hare – her escape route to safety.

Tomorrow, she thought. All she had to do was survive here one more night.

Behind her, Paul rose from his chair and asked. 'Another cognac, *amante*?'

'No.' She didn't turn her face.

Susan?'

'I'm fine, Paul,' said Susan.

'Morgan?'

'A Courvoisier would be more than welcome,' Morgan replied from the depths of his chair.

Turning from the window, Karen waited for Paul to pour Morgan's cognac and a Jack Daniels for himself. 'I'd like to talk to Susan, Paul,' she said. 'Alone. Cousin talk.'

She saw the edginess in Paul's eyes and his fingers grip both glasses, wondering what she was up to now. Knowing her antique necklace story was a fabrication, she could sense his mind racing: What did she want with Susan on her own? What more was she going to say to her? She saw his eyes flick to Susan. Her face was turned away from Karen, but she must have given him an "it's okay" response with her eyes. 'Sure,' he replied. 'We'll go tidy up the kitchen.'

Taking his Courvoisier from Paul, Morgan stood, 'We'll leave you to it,' he said, following Paul out of the room and closing the door behind him.

Left alone with her cousin, Karen crutched to Morgan's chair and sat facing Susan and started with small talk to make her edgier than she patently was, wondering what was coming.

'I was looking through old photos earlier. Do you remember our first Thanksgiving after your Dad died, when Father overcooked the turkey?'

'Overcooked it!' Susan said, tension evident in her voice. 'It was burnt black,'

'He wanted you to stay living with us. So did I, Sue,' Karen added a tone of regret.

'I'm sorry, Kay,' Susan tried to look contrite, 'I didn't want to leave you here alone, but having met Peter, it was my first chance to start a new life...' she pulled a wry face 'To my cost, with all his womanizing. I also had to get away from your father's ...' she hesitated, searching for an all-embracing word, 'his possessiveness ...' her voice tailed off, not wanting to recall any more about the nightmare two years she'd been forced to go through, living in Clanryan.

Oh, my odious father, Karen was again ashamed of being his daughter. She almost reached out to clutch her cousin's hand – but then *'you bitch'* exploded in her mind. She had to hold back from slapping her face instead. *Leaving me here alone with him knowing he'd keep making me do the same. Two years of it is all you had to endure. I had it over fifteen – fifteen years of hell, until finally I–*

She controlled herself and fixed her mind on drawing her two-faced bitch cousin in.

'He always felt bad about the way things turned out with him and your Dad. He was going to make it up to you by including you in his will–'

'Except, he didn't,' Susan almost spat the words.

'His accident happened before he had the chance.'

'Conveniently for you…'

Karen heard the inference in her voice and again had to resist slapping her face.

'…especially him falling down the stairs like that…'

She dug her fingernails into her seat cushion.

'…timely for you, as it turned out,' Susan continued, 'though not for him…'

The intimation was clearly there. She dug her nails in deeper.

'…But you're his daughter. It was right it all went to you.'

Control yourself, she said to herself. *Don't let her get to you. Fix on driving a wedge between her and Paul. Pretend to give her what she's after. Money. Get her confused, torn as to who best to go with.*

Paul…or me.

She pulled her nails out of the cushion, stretched across and clutched Susan's hand. 'Despite the protection I'm getting from you all, Sue, should this Paxton succeed in getting to me, it would be unfair on you if everything I own goes to Paul. Although we're married, I've known him only three weeks, whereas you're family, more like my sister than cousin. Clanryan will go to him, but I'm leaving you half my investments, as Father should have with Uncle John – and they're worth far more than this old clapboard of a house.'

Seeing immediate suspicion in her cousin's eyes, Karen hastened to reassure her, clutching her hand tighter. 'I insist, Sue. I thought this through even when Paul and I were on honeymoon, and I'm calling my Chicago attorneys first thing tomorrow to see about making my will.'

From the phone in my studio, she thought, except it will be to the American Airlines desk at O'Hare, and then call for a taxicab to drive me there, and once I'm back in Positano and Paxton is caught, Paul can fly out and join me…and after I've got rid of him, it will be your turn next, you slut–

Shriiiiiiiilll…

Karen stared, hypnotized, at the shrilling phone, her cold resolve for Paul and Susan suddenly replaced by a cold shiver up her spine, feeling herself crumble inside.

Shriiiiiiiilll…

Still staring at it, she whimpered, 'Why doesn't Paul answer it?'

Susan crossed over to the table…and hesitated…torn by what Karen had just told her and unable to decide what to do…

Cupping his phone between his left ear and shoulder, he listened to his call ringing at the other end of the line, sliding his thumb along the carving knife's blade, caressing it, feeling its sharpness.

'Answer it, you whore,' he whispered. 'Answer it.'

On a flat surface in front of him was a photo of Karen, holding her wedding posy of red roses. He looked at it as he waited, vitriolic words on his tongue, for her voice to come down the line and hearing it become all tremulous with fear when she heard him whisper to her…instead he heard the phone being picked up and slammed down, and then only silence.

He brought the carving knife savagely down into her face.

'*Whore,*' he screamed. '*You whore.*'

He stabbed her face over and over again, '*Whore…! Whore…! Whore…!* puncturing it with knife cuts, reducing the photo to shreds.

Having ended the landline's strident shrilling by snatching it off its cradle, Susan slammed it back down.

Paul rushed into the sitting room and saw Karen trembling on the couch. Hurrying to her, he sat beside her and held her. She didn't resist, rocking herself back and to in his arms.

'Was it him?' he asked Susan. 'I was outside and didn't get to the kitchen in time to answer it.'

'I don't know,' Susan replied. 'I cut it off in case it was.'

'*It was him!*' Karen screamed, beating at Paul's chest. '*It was him! I know it! I know it.*'

Paul clasped her tighter. 'Check it out,' he said to Susan.

She searched CALLS and turned to him. 'No record of it.'

Karen tried to wrestle herself free from Paul's grasp, screaming again. '*I told you it was him!*'

Susan returned to the couch to help Paul control her. Morgan entered the room and hurried toward them. Paul shook his head, warning him away.

From under hooded lids, Karen watched them like an animal at bay wanting to escape from their clutches. Her other self told her how to. She stopped herself trembling, prized Paul's hands away from her and sat up, calm again.

'I'm alright now,' she said. 'It was just the initial shock, but I can feel a headache coming on. I'm going to my room, take an Advil, and lie down for a while.'

'*Amante*—' Paul protested.

'Don't fuss, Paul,' she said. Reaching for her crutches, she raised herself up from the couch and limped out of the room leaving the door open, and headed upstairs.

'What in the hell do you make of that?' Paul turned to both Susan and Morgan. 'One minute she's—' he left the sentence unfinished. 'The next she's—'

'It's the way she is,' Susan said in a low voice, realizing that Karen was not yet out of earshot. 'It's the way she's been ever since her mom died. But go after her and try giving her some love.'

'Sure,' Paul said and left the room.

Morgan sank into his armchair. 'Not the best of starts to their married life,' he said to Susan. 'When Paul first told me he'd met you, I thought you were the one he—'

Susan put a finger to her lips. 'I don't want Kay to ever know we knew each other before.'

'Especially when you came to Chicago,' Morgan lowered his voice, 'and spent the weekend together. What happened?'

'That weekend happened,' Susan replied. 'After it we realized that we were more suited to be friends than lovers…'

Morgan narrowed his eyes, behind them there was hate.

'…But Paul was just right for Karen, so I arranged for them to meet.'

They heard Paul returning downstairs. Turning off the stairs and landing lights and leaving the hall light on, he re-entered the room, closed the door behind him and crossed to the side table and poured himself a stiff Jack Daniels. 'She no longer wants me to stay with her tonight,' he said, 'said she prefers to be alone. I didn't dare argue,' he took a swig, 'she's back to being that tetchy.'

'It's hardly surprising with all that's happened to her since getting back from Italy,' Susan said.

'No, it's more than that. It's like she's not the same person here as she was there. Since we got back it's as if…well…it's as if she's two people in one. At times it can be almost frightening.'

'Mrs. Jekyll and Miss Hyde,' Morgan said in an acerbic aside.

'So would you be Morgan,' Susan snapped, 'if you'd had her childhood.'

Paul looked at her, surprised to hear her defend Karen. Seeing his reaction, Susan decided to tell Karen's background now. 'Get me a brandy, Paul, and I'll explain.'

Paul returned to the side table, poured a glass of Courvoisier, crossed back and extended it to her. She snatched it, drank some and began.

'Her mom was the nicest person you could wish to meet, but her father could be both dark and light. In his younger days – according to my Dad – he was a good-looking man, and charmed Karen's mom away from the bustle of Chicago to live with him here, in this isolated Gothic heap.'

Paul sat beside her and raised his glass to take another drink. She put her hand on his arm and stopped him. It was a reflex act, but nonetheless proprietary and Morgan narrowed his eyes again.

'But she was soon unhappy,' Susan continued, 'except by then she was pregnant with Karen, and with both her parents dead she had nowhere to go to and stayed. So, she went to Doc Willowby and he gave her an old Native American potion for her not to have another child – she confided all this to my Dad, he was her only friend – and she tried to make the best of it, but in the end it killed her – she was only thirty-seven. It left Karen alone with her father – though I lived here with them for two years, and I can tell you it was hell.'

Recollecting it, she gulped more cognac.

'But I escaped, and Karen's only break from him was high school. Even then, he drove her there every morning and was waiting outside for her every afternoon. And that's how it was for her – if it had been me, I'd have gone crazy.'

She tossed back the dregs of her drink.

'The result is that though it's her mother in her that's mostly on the surface, when his nature takes over – watch out. Especially here in Clanryan, the place seems to bring out the worst in her – it's like his presence is in every room. And she's had to live with this ever since she was twelve, when her mom died. It seemed to traumatize her – to the extent it's as if she's both of them. One minute her mother. The next, him.'

'Then Miss Oedipus and Miss Electra,' said Morgan, in an equally acerbic aside.

'Anything but,' Susan returned. 'She hated him. Who wouldn't. He was…evil.' Angry with Morgan for his snide comments, she turned away from him. 'And now she's got this Paxton to contend with,' she said to Paul, 'and his constant mind threats.'

'Then let's hope he'll soon be caught,' Paul replied, draining his Jack Daniels.

'And the sooner the better,' Morgan said. 'For us all to get back to normal.' He stood up. 'I'm going to make myself a hot tea. Either of you want one?'

'No thanks, Morgan,' Paul said.

Susan waited for Morgan to leave the room. 'She's not mentioned the necklace,' she whispered to Paul, 'not a word. She makes me on edge when she's like this. It's like living with a time bomb, knowing it's going to blow up, but not knowing when.'

She meant this.

One side of Karen scared her bad.

But her mind was still with what the other Karen had said to her.

Driving past Ravens Pond on his way back to Clanryan, Sam stopped his car by the side of the road and looked at the pool, dark, forbidding, its surface rippling in the dropped wind blowing across it, and black-feathered crows perched on stark branches silhouetted against an ominous sky. Whoever would choose to live in an isolated house, surrounded as far as the eye could see by dense forest, with no one to talk to day after day, and the nearest habitation being a one-horse hicksville like Ravensburg, must be of a peculiar mentality, Sam thought.

Disturbed by the presence of his car, a crow cawed. Others joined in. In their raucous chorus was a distinct menace. You're violating our sacred space, be warned, it seemed to say.

Ignoring it, Sam looked at the pond.

Buried in his subconscious, something about when Karen drove into it was still bothering him.

Digging deep into the dim recesses of his mind, he tried to recall what it was.

In his rear mirror, her car slowly sank below the water.

There was no sign of the Jeep, it had already gone under.

Paul's SUV stopped alongside him.

Paul leapt out and ran for the pond, shouting something.

In a daze from sliding his car into a tree, Sam couldn't hear what it was...

Again, he tried to recall it, knowing it was vital, but he still couldn't hear what Paul was shouting.

He could recollect looking in his rear mirror and seeing Paul dive into the pool.

And then Morgan and him in the water trying together to rescue Karen from her sinking car.

But other than that, all else was locked away in his mind.

An insistent tapping cut into his thoughts. He looked up.

A black crow was on his hood, tapping the windshield with its black beak as if trying to get his attention. Seeing Sam look up, it stopped and stared at Sam with his black eyes.

It's like he's trying to tell me something, Sam thought.

The Greeks may have regarded them as symbols of good fortune and the Celts as omens of bad tidings, but if the evil-looking birds stood for anything, the Native Americans closer to home were likely nearer the truth calling them 'Tricksters' – seeming to promise good luck but delivering bad.

Sam looked at the crow, black eyes staring hypnotically back at him, and the word "trickster" kept resounding in his mind.

Trickster. Trickster. Duplicity.

It had some connection, he knew, to what was locked in his mind.

He tried again to recall what it was.

Trickster. Duplicity.

The crow cawed once, long and strident, and flew away.

The storm was coming in darker now and would break tomorrow. The hole in the clouds had almost closed up, leaving a wispy chink that showed a pale sun beyond it trying to get through. But then the clouds closed and the mantle above was black again and low over the forest – and the sun stayed hidden.

Sam switched on his engine and drove away.

-25-

Karen sat on the bed, wanting to kill Paul and Susan. The room was dim, the only light coming from the bedside table lamp, and a thin crack filtering under the closed door from the hall below. The drapes were half open to the stygian night outside. The dark cloud overhead was one mass again as it drifted sluggishly past her window, but the rain had not yet resumed and rivulets of water were slowly meandering down the panes.

She crutched to a wardrobe and from the top shelf withdrew a cardboard box. Inside it was an oilskin package. Unwrapping it, she pulled out her father's Colt 45 and a box of bullets, dexterously inserted six bullets into its chambers and put it under her pillow. Should Paxton get into her room again tonight – she doubted it though, Sam couldn't risk the finger pointing at him if he let the man get past him twice – but should he, she would put all six into him, "fill him full of lead" as the saying went, two in his chest, two in his stomach, one in his balls, and the final one in the middle of his forehead. That was one thing she could at least be grateful to her father for, he'd taught her how to shoot – Colt 45 and hunting rifle.

Meantime, as soon as it was morning she would call O'Hare, and by tomorrow evening she would be flying to safety far from this goddamn place and planning to return only the once – sadly, oh, so very sadly, in her planned all black widow's weeds, within only days of Paul flying out to join her and tragically falling over that cliff – to bring Susan bitch back to Positano to live with her – except her dearest cousin wouldn't make it, because the wolves and the crows would be feasting on her body deep in the forest where she would have dumped it…

Karen sat there, living the thought of them getting what was due to them – particularly Susan.

It would be like a rewrite of *My Cousin Rachel,* except it would be *My Cousin Susan,* but with no broken body found on the rocks below – that was just for Paul – only her bones stripped bare of all flesh, never to be found.

She saw a car's headlights come up the track and cut out in front of the house. She knew it was Sam returning to take over from Michael, but still checked her bedside clock. 8:32. Switching off her bedside light, she crutched to the window, peered out, and saw Michael cross to meet Sam as he got out of his car.

She studied Michael's muscular body. Now that he was a man – an ex-soldier who'd served overseas and likely experienced with women – what would he be like to screw, she pondered? No more youthful petting she felt sure, like they'd done behind the school sheds – except she wouldn't let his penis near her, repulsed as she was by what her father was making her–

Shuddering, she dismissed the memory.

Nonetheless, it was strange how she'd been okay with Paul's – well, more than okay, insatiable really. From the first time she'd not been able to get enough of it. But then, knowing her father was safely interred under six feet of earth, maybe that had been her catharsis – a psychological cleansing from all her dread years with him.

She turned her eyes to Sam. And what would he be like in bed? Good-looking, nice body under his jacket, good shoulders, taut waist, walked and moved lithe like an athlete, married before and therefore experienced – maybe he'd be an athlete between the sheets, too?

When Paul's gone the world will be my oyster, she thought, mentally undressing both Michael and Sam. She silently cracked her window open to hear what they were saying to each other.

'Find anything?' Sam queried.

'Not a thing,' Michael replied. 'Has anyone asked Hank about you?'

'Nope.'

'Did Chicago reply?'

'Yep.'

'What about?'

'You, Michael,' said Sam. 'Seems you left the marines over two years ago, not recently – on a bad conduct discharge after aggravated assault on an officer and spending six months in the brig–'

'It was worth it,' Michael grated. 'Bastard ordered me on a suicide mission, with no hope of me coming out of it alive.'

'Not for me to judge,' Sam replied. 'But since then you've been living on the edge of the law in Chicago, questioned more than once for auto-theft but nothing proved. Last time you were taken in was for murder – but neither the owner – or the truck – were ever found and you weren't charged. Except it was a Jeep – black, like Paxton's. Some coincidence don't you think?

Sam left the question in mid-air. Michael didn't reply. Sam continued.

'Another coincidence is that it happened not long after Karen inherited – and about that same time you went off the police radar.'

Sam waited for a response from Michael. Again, Michael made none.

'But now you're back in Ravensburg, with no visible means of how you got here, according to Hank, but feeling mighty cut up when you heard that Karen had married someone else.'

She felt herself tremble, whether from chagrin or anger she couldn't determine. But she'd been right in her suspicions. Not only was Michael capable of murder, he'd actually committed murder, and what was more, he did have a grudge against her.

But was it deep enough for him to want her dead?

She opened her window a little more to hear Michael's reply to Sam.

'Yeah?' he said, not seeming to be in any way phased by Sam's findings. 'The reason I came home, Sam, is because I decided to go straight. No more to it than that. As for getting here, it was by bussing it, hitching it and fucking footslogging it, mile after fucking mile after fucking mile.'

His voice now changed to be accusatory. 'But being we're talking coincidences Sam, how's this for one? That last time I was picked up, I was sitting in the back of a patrol car when it was called to a fatal car crash.'

Michael paused to stress his next words.

'What's more, I saw the driver. He was holding his little daughter in his arms and looked a lot like you, Sam, wearing a police uniform. I heard him describe the car that hit him, and by another coincidence, Sam, it was a silver coupe, just like Ryan's, except the cop said the guy that caused the crash just drove off, and he was too traumatized to read the license plate.'

Karen stood there rooted in shock, but dimly hearing Michael continue.

'But say he had, he might have wanted to take the law into his own hands, don't you think, Sam? Life for a life, as Paxton says he's after. And I'm guessing that as a cop, he'd know where to find a hitman.' Michael paused again. 'So, why are you here in Ravensburg, Sam?'

The two men faced each other in silence, letting their accusations speak for them now.

Karen moved away from the window, her mind whirling with all she'd heard, now knowing that Sam did have a reason for wanting her dead. His daughter's death, caused by her own father. It would give him more than enough cause…

Michael, too…Except with Michael, the life for a life, blood for blood threat didn't make any sense – yet, when another student once crossed him in school, then like a cur with a bone he wouldn't let it go until he'd retaliated – in more than kind, he'd half killed the boy. What if his nature was still the same? What if in his eyes she had crossed him by marrying Paul? Was it enough for him to want her dead, just out of anger and spite?

Bombarded by so many conflicting thoughts, she tried to control her rising panic, but uppermost was a claustrophobic realization, amounting to fear, that she was all alone in Clanryan with five people – five people – each with their own motive for wanting her dead…

Paul and Susan – for her money.

Morgan – for his cut of it.

Michael – from malice.

Sam – revenge for his daughter's death.

And adding Paxton to them…hired by one or more of them…that made six.

No it made more than six. It made Six, Six, Six.

Six motives. Six stone hearts. Six people all wanting to kill her.

Could anything be more hellish than this.

Feeling like a hunted quarry surrounded on all sides, she heard Michael say a curt 'goodnight' to Sam.

'Goodnight,' Sam returned, equally brusque.

She forced herself back to the window. Sam was standing motionless watching Michael drive off. But as if sensing her looking down at him, he turned and stared up at her window.

She retreated into the room, hoping its darkness had prevented him from seeing her.

Then, standing back, she peered out again.

He was still looking up at her window.

He'd seen her the first time, she knew it for certain.

The only thing to do was out-bluff him.

She opened the side window wide. 'Goodnight, Sam,' she called down to him.

'Goodnight, Karen,' Sam said. 'Sleep tight.'

But his voice was cold, and was there a hidden meaning in his "sleep tight"?

Was he saying "dead to this world"?

She shut the window, closed the drapes, switched her bedside light back on and pulled the Colt from under her pillow. Gripping the 45, she sat in a stiff-backed wing chair in a corner of the room facing the door.

From the deep shrubbery facing the house, he saw a light come on in her room, then she appeared in the window, opened it and called down: 'Goodnight, Sam.'

Extracting the blood-stained carving knife from under his dark jacket, he lined up the blade on her throat and imagined himself slowly slicing her from ear to ear and her blood spurting out.

'Goodnight, Karen. Sleep tight,' King replied.

'Yes, sleep tight, *whore*,' he whispered, hate in his voice. 'Soon you'll be sleeping forever.'

She shut the window and closed the drapes.

Replacing the knife under his jacket he heard a faint sound as something fell to the ground. He searched with his hands for it, found it, picked it up and peered through the darkness at it. It was a plastic Wisconsin Regular Driving License with the required photo on the left side, a smaller one on the right, and between them the surname PAXTON and under it the first name JOHN, then his Chicago address, and below them height, weight, color of eyes, color of hair and DOB.

Cursing his uncharacteristic laxness in almost leaving such a vital clue behind him, his prints smeared on it, he replaced the license in his pocket and headed for the back of the house.

-26-

Karen rose from the wing chair, turned off her bedside lamp and cracked her bedroom door open, letting light from the hall below into the room, took the duvet off the bed and wrapped it around her like a comfort shawl, and returned to sit in the chair, the Colt 45 held tight in her hand.

Outside, a crow cawed. Others joined in. A raucous chorus. They went silent again. Ominous.

Oh, God, she thought, were the black, ill-omened birds really harbingers of death after all, as was said of them. Did they really have a sixth sense for knowing when someone was going to die?

She heard the sitting room door open and Paul's and Susan's voices coming from the hall.

'Good night, Paul,' Susan said. Karen could tell she was forcing her voice to sound normal.

'Good night, Susan,' Paul replied, his voice as forced as Susan's.

Pulling her duvet aside, she crutched to the door, quietly opened it, crept out to the landing and peered over the banister rail into the hall.

They were locked in an embrace – the two-faced shits. Susan pulled Paul's face down to hers and kissed him, ardent, and broke away.

'Tomorrow?' she questioned in a whisper. Paul nodded. Kissing her own finger, she put it to his lips for him to kiss it back – or rather suck it like he was sucking her fucking clitoris, the tacky prick – then she slowly, sensually withdrew it, opened the door and exited the house. Paul stayed in the doorway, watching her go.

Re-entering her bedroom, she peered through the drapes at Susan hurrying for her car, and saw her look back at the house and wave Paul a final goodnight. Seething with rage, Karen couldn't see him, hidden from her sight under the porch roof, but she just knew he was waving back.

Sam wound down his car window to say something to Susan.

Karen slightly opened her window to listen.

'Everything okay inside, Miss Ryan?' Sam asked.

'Considering all that's happening, detective,' Susan said. 'But thanks for all you're doing.'

'Just keeping my promise to Karen,' Sam returned.

'As long as you keep her from harm,' Susan put on a concerned cousin voice, 'at least until we can arrange for someone to take over from you. That's all we ask.'

'Rest assured, Miss Ryan,' Sam said. 'I will.'

Fucking conniving Judases, Karen simmered. Not just Susan and Sam, but all of them – Paul and Morgan, and Michael, too. And as for whichever of them was paying Paxton, then doubly so. And Susan's "until we can arrange for someone to take over from you", that was all crap. They'd made no attempt to find anyone. And why? Because they knew she'd soon be dead.

Well, think on, Judases – because tomorrow I'll be gone.

'Good night, Miss Ryan,' Sam called out as Susan reached her car.

'Good night, detective,' she replied. Getting into it and closing her door, she switched on her ignition and drove off down the track, her headlights cutting like lasers into the night, and out into the road and around the corner into the dark forest on her way back to Ravensburg,

Slouching back in his car seat, Sam settled down for the night.

Karen shut the window, closed the drapes tight and sank back into the wing chair clutching the Colt 45, wrapped the duvet tight around her again and sat there brooding.

"Tomorrow", Susan had whispered to Paul.

Exactly what had they planned for her tomorrow?

Whatever it was, it told her she was safe for tonight.

And tomorrow would be too late, she'd be gone.

Swing music suddenly drifted up from the sitting room.

Swing music! she seethed.

Despite their malign intentions for her, Paul and Morgan were listening to music. What's more, she now remembered its title, *Moonlight Serenade*, she'd not been allowed by her father to see the film on TV – a gooey biopic of some ancient bandleader's life, Miller something or other – nor had she really wanted to, other than to defy him. But that they were sitting below her listening to such sentimental pap, yet knowing Paxton was still out there somewhere, determined to kill her, made her see red…red…red…RED!

She sat up, finger on the Colt 45's trigger, and grabbed at her crutches to go downstairs and hurl the door open and blow them both to Kingdom Come, but then she paused…

I'm not spending the next sixty years in prison for them, she brooded. When I kill them, Susan too, it will be without any suspicion falling on me. I need to think it through calmly and not let my other self take control.

She sank back into the wing chair.

There was also Sam and Michael. They, too, had their own personal agendas for wanting her dead. Getting rid of just Paul and Susan and Morgan wasn't enough – she had to get rid of all five.

And what about Paxton?

No, by getting rid of all five, it ensured that whichever of them was paying him would then be dead, and he would crawl back to whatever rat-hole he had slithered out of.

Pity, she would have liked to kill him, too, and made him suffer, like he had made her suffer, but for her to get away with killing the others, it was a pleasure she would just have to forego.

No, not allowing her other side to rule her, she would have to confine it to just the five.

But paramount, surrounded by them as she was, a prisoner in Clanryan, it reinforced the fact she had to escape. She looked at her bedside phone – she could call O'Hare now while Paul and Morgan were listening to their pap music, and book her flight – and she could also make it just the one call by asking them to arrange a taxicab to come and pick her up…

She stretched her hand for the phone, and paused. No, the line engaged light would flash on the sitting room charger and would warn them. If only she had a cellphone, but her father wouldn't let her have one. Susan had offered to smuggle one in to her, but somehow he would have found out. She should have got one in Chicago, but was too excited at having met Paul. Recalling how excited she was, she was mortified with herself for being so naïve. Getting married! Getting a lover! How those dreams had been shattered, leaving her now in fear of her life.

In which case, best leave it until, say, 2.00 in the morning, by which time they'd be sound asleep, arrange for the cab to be here at 11.00 –

now that would be a shock for them – and with a stranger picking her up, none of them, Paul, Morgan, or Sam – no, it would be Michael on watch outside at 11.00 – none of them could stop her from going.

And once she was safely back in Positano she could buy her villa and plot her revenge.

Paul first – before or after buying her villa, it made no difference.

Then fly back for Susan.

Then Morgan.

Then Michael.

And finally, Sam.

She'd not yet thought of how she was going to kill Morgan and Michael and Sam, but as sure as hell was hot she would think of something fitting for them.

In fact, why not now? – starting with Morgan.

So…how to kill him…

A flash of inspiration came to her mind. She would have Paul cremated instead of buried and invite Morgan to her villa to join her in scattering his ashes. But first, she would buy a small yacht – not too grand to draw attention to herself, one she could easily sell later – learn to sail it, and have the ceremony out into the Mediterranean and ask him to perform it – he would wallow in it, weep over it – and as he was standing there, his back to her, sprinkling them, she would push him overboard, and keep him under with a boathook – if that's what they were called – until he'd drowned. With luck, his body wouldn't be found for months and by then he'd be a "floater" – a word she'd read in a crime novel – all bloated up like a balloon, rotted flesh half eaten by fish – maybe sharks, even better – his oh-so-immaculate clothes worn away by the salt water – how he would hate that – no hair left on his head, most of his teeth gone – she'd got that from the same book –

not that it would matter, his dental charts would be back in Chicago – and what was left of his unidentified body would be buried without ceremony and no name over it, in some faraway Italian graveyard.

Yes, that would a perfect ending for him, the creep.

And now, Michael…

He shouldn't be any problem, either. She could fly back to Chicago, book into a downtown hotel for one night, then call his home in Ravensburg and invite him to come visit her – with a hint that there would be more on offer for him than just a visit, and he'd be there in a flash – take him out for a meal, and tempt him into an alley first for a quick feel as a prelude to sleeping the night with her – he'd be up for that, for sure, in more ways than one – and then *"bang!"* – a.45 bullet into him and she'd be on her way back to O'Hare before his body was found, his fingerprints taken, his criminal past revealed, and presumed by the police to have been killed by an "ex-associate" – she'd seen that word in another crime book.

Two down. One to go.

Sam…

Now Sam would be more difficult…but there again, she brooded, maybe not. The difficult part would be to get him to fly out to Positano. But, cross fingers, maybe he'd still be harboring thoughts of killing her in revenge for his daughter and he would accept her invitation. Meantime, though it was mostly a holiday village, it must have a playground where pretty, little local Italian girls played and she would find it. Once he was staying with her in her villa, she would get him to go with her for walks and make sure they kept passing it, and what could be more understandable – to the emotional Italian mind, that is – than the sound of their laughter would remind Sam of his own daughter, to the point where he could bear it no longer. Stricken with grief – and tranquilized by sedatives that she'd tell the *polizia* he was taking for depression, and which she would put in a drink, coffee if he was teetotal – suicide would be their only conclusion for him blowing his brains out.

And that would be all five of them gone, she brooded, and no pattern to their deaths – other than they would be dead – no finger of suspicion pointing at her, or should that be fingers in the plural being that she'd be sending five to Hell. Sadly, there was, of course, no such place, but just the thought of them there, roasting in flames, was almost as gratifying.

She checked her watch again. 9:03. Secure in the thought that whatever Paul and Susan had planned for her wasn't until tomorrow, and there was still five hours to go before calling American Airlines, she might as well get some sleep, she had a ten and half hour flight ahead of her. And after making her call she could quietly pack a few clothes and other things she intended taking with her. As for Paxton again, if he was thinking of breaking in tonight, then following his pattern of last night, it wouldn't be until long after she was asleep, and seeing her bedroom light come on at 2.00 am, he'd have to abort it – but if he didn't, she'd be ready for him with her Colt 45, and shoot him right between his fucking eyes – just the one slug, regretfully, thinking about it some more, if it was to look like she was defending herself she'd have to dispense with the two in his chest, two in his stomach and one in his balls.

Rising from the chair, she undressed into her pajamas, got under the duvet, put the Colt 45 under her pillow, and screwed her eyes shut – and snapped them open as different dance music drifted up from the sitting room below. What the fuck was possessing Paul, didn't he have any conscience about tomorrow, at least play some Johnny Cash.

She stretched out a hand for her pills bottle, unscrewed the cap, popped a pill, broke it in half for her not to sleep too long, and swallowed it with a gulp of water from her glass. Replacing the phial and glass on her bedside table, she put her head back on the pillow, pulled the duvet over her ears and clutched her Colt.

Within minutes she felt the pill take effect. Her eyelids grew heavy, her body relaxed. But her subconscious refused to release her from her earlier thoughts and she lay there, seeing Paul's, and Susan's, and Morgan's, and Sam's and Michael's faces, imagining their deaths.

Paul falling, falling, down a cliff on to the rocks below and breaking every bone in his body.

Susan spread-eagled on the forest floor being eaten by ravenous wolves and crows – while still alive – she'd changed her mind about killing her right off and would break both her legs for her not to crawl away, strip her of all her clothing, and leave her half dead to feel the searing agony of her flesh being bitten and torn off her body in strips – a just ending for her, the bitch.

Morgan all naked and bloated being nibbled by fish, and chunks of him eaten by sharks.

Michael lying in a cold Chicago alley, a hole in his chest.

Sam slumped in a chair, half his head gone.

She fell asleep, a smile on her face…

Down in the hall, he crept from the dining room and up the stairs clutching the carving knife, the hall light casting his dark shadow on the wall.

Reaching the landing, he slowly opened Karen's door and stood there a long moment, his eyes riveted on her in bed, then he entered her room.

As he approached her, a floorboard creaked.

The noise partly woke her up. Peering through heavy, half-drugged eyelids she saw him creeping toward her, carving knife held high in his right hand.

Still gripping the Colt, she tried to raise it.

But paralyzed with fear, she couldn't move her arm.

He loomed over her.

She screamed, but her terror made it soundless.

The knife flashed down into her breast – again, and again, and again.

Her body jerked, gave a final twitch, and lay still.

He crept back out and downstairs into the dining room, closing the door behind him.

In the sitting room, the music ceased. Paul laughed at something Morgan said and they exited the room together. Paul switched on the landing light, turned off the hall light and they came upstairs. Paul peered into her darkened room, saw her lying motionless in her bed, nodded to Morgan and closed the door on her.

Inside the room, the thin band of light under the door went out.

Leaving the house in darkness.

And all was silent.

The son of Midas cawed.

Others joined in.

Then suddenly they ceased.

And silence again descended on Clanryan.

-three-

-27-

He swooped down, black wings outstretched, as if materializing like a herald of death out of the dark dawn sky, the son of Midas, landed on her window ledge and looked in with his black eyes at her lying inert in her bed. He rapped on the window with his black beak. She didn't move. He rapped harder. Still she didn't move. Launching himself off the sill, he flew back up into the sky, loudly cawing as if in victory, and faded into the murky canopy hanging low over Clanryan.

Karen suddenly flayed her arms about, beating off a crow from attacking her, then just as suddenly she opened her eyes and her hands frenziedly searched her breast. She could find no wounds – last night had been a nightmare – but still fearful, her eyes warily searched the room's dusk for a shadow that might be waiting there to harm her. Despite seeing no one, a cold terror swept over her and she started to shiver. Wrapping her duvet around her, she huddled into her mattress and heard Michael's truck come up to the house. He and Sam loudly exchanged words through opened windows to make themselves heard above the rising wind. Sam's car drove off down the dirt track and Country and western music – Tammy Wynette singing *Stand By Your Man,* for fuck's sake – drifted faintly up from Michael's car radio.

Reassured by it, her eyelids still heavy after the sleeping pill, she turned on her side, bringing the duvet with her, felt for her Colt 45 and allowed herself to fall back to sleep. Within moments, she was transported back to Positano, lying on a sunbed by the shimmering blue swimming pool of her new villa, and lying alongside her was a hunky Italian bodyguard. She reached out to touch him, he turned and smiled at her…his face was John Paxton's, his smile was cruel, his eyes were cold, and in his hand he held a bloodied carving knife–

She jerked out of her sleep, her heart was racing, and she looked wildly about her – the room was lighter now, no dark corners in which he could hide. Subsiding into her pillow, she looked at her bedside clock, saw it was 8.30, and was angry with herself for not having woken up at 2.00am and phoning O'Hare. Another day lost.

Outside, a vehicle drove up to the house. Its door slammed shut, she heard Sam say something to Michael, and his footsteps ran up the steps to the porch and the front door bell rang.

She flung back the duvet, quickly donned a light robe lying at the foot of the bed, grabbed her crutches and went out onto the landing. Hanging back, she peered down into the hall and saw Paul open the door for Sam. 'Detective King?'

'We need to talk, Mr. Archer,' said Sam. He sounded grim.

'Come right in,' Paul replied, standing aside for Sam to enter, and closed the door and preceded him into the sitting room.

'Good morning, Detective King,' Morgan's voice came from inside the room.

'I'm not sure it is, Mr. Hale,' Sam said, his voice monotonic, not returning Morgan's welcome nor using either of their first names, Karen discerned. She sat on the top stair riser from where she could see Sam's back standing just inside the doorway and heard him address Paul.

'I asked Chicago to dig further into Paxton's past, Mr. Archer. Care to say why you lied about not knowing him?'

Karen felt herself go rigid with shock.

'Starting from Ravens Pond. I'm assuming you recognized his truck? It was pretty distinctive despite it having no plates.'

From inside the room, Paul was silent.

'Any reason for not telling me?'

Even from where she sat, she heard Paul exhale in resignation. 'Okay, detective. I know how bad it makes me look, but I thought he'd drowned. No one should have survived that crash.'

'And when it was clear he had?' Sam demanded. 'After he got into Karen's room, and all the phone calls?

'By then I was stuck with it.'

'Even though disclosing his identity might have helped catch him?' There was anger in Sam's voice now. 'And saved Karen from all the hell she's gone through.'

'I know! I know!' Paul blurted. 'You can't make me feel any worse than I already do. But I was still hoping you'd be forced into killing him and wouldn't make the connection.'

'That Paxton was once engaged to your first wife?' said Sam.

Karen hooked her first finger and bit it hard to prevent herself from screaming.

Paul had been married before! Yet he hadn't told her, the shit. She wasn't his first wife. After all his honeyed words that she was his only love. And his impassioned cries as he climaxed on top of her that she was the best lay he'd ever had…

Lies! Lies! Lies! Lies!

'Instead she met you,' Sam continued, 'ditched Paxton and married you.'

'That about sums it up,' Paul said, a penitent tone now in his voice.

'Anything but, Mr. Archer, as you damn well know.' The anger was back in Sam's voice. 'It seems he didn't take it too good.'

'No, he didn't,' Paul said, like it was being dragged out of him. 'He threatened me.'

'Not just you, Mr. Archer.'

'Okay, Julia, too.'

'No, Mr. Archer, he did more than threaten.' Sam's tone was now steely. 'She was found dead in her bedroom. Not only murdered but mutilated, her genitals slashed like that effigy hanging from the tree.'

Karen clenched her teeth on her finger.

Paxton, the man who had got into her bedroom and stood over her with a carving knife, had not only killed Paul's first wife, he'd sliced her to pieces, and the same could have happened to her, her body cut to ribbons. And he was still out there, still threatening to do it to her. Oh, God, oh, God, she had to get away from here.

'Except Paxton claimed you did it,' Sam said. 'That you set him up, smashed the window to make it look like an intruder. Someone with a score to settle. Paxton, for instance. And being her ex-lover his prints were all over the bedroom, detracting from you as a main suspect.'

Oh, God, this was getting nightmarish. Paxton was saying that Paul had done it – killed Julia. And not only killed her, but hacked her to death. That Paul had Julia's blood on his hands. Hands that had been all over her body.

She felt sickened. She'd already found him out to be many things she'd not even considered him capable of when she married him – a barefaced liar, a deceitful cheat – but not in her wildest imaginations had she thought him capable of murder with his own hands.

'Paul was auditioning for a part in a play that afternoon, detective.' Morgan cut in. 'The police checked it out. Paxton undoubtedly killed her. He went out of his mind when she married Paul.'

'You knew about all this, Mr. Hale?' Sam turned on Morgan.

'It was when I first met Paul,' Morgan replied. 'He and Paxton were in a play I was designing the sets for.'

'So, which of you was going to be the first to tell me?' Sam asked.

'It should have been me,' Paul said. 'Julia was my wife—'

'And a two-timing slut,' said Morgan.

'Maybe,' Paul acknowledged. 'But she didn't deserve to die – nor like that.'

'No,' Morgan agreed. 'No one should die like that. But if you'd met Paxton, detective, you'd know there was almost an inevitability about it. He was an animal. A psychopath. And clearly still is. Killing Julia was only half his threat.'

'Only he wasn't charged,' Paul said. 'Not enough evidence. And keeping up the pretense that I did it. Swearing he would make me suffer the same way – by killing someone I loved. But then I met Karen and moved out here, far away from Chicago, hoping I'd put him behind me...'

'Except he's the kind of maniac who'd pursue you to the ends of the earth.' Morgan said.

It was as much as Karen could do to stop herself crutching downstairs and scratching Paul's eyes out. Even if he'd not killed Julia, he had deceived her – made her as a lamb to the slaughter.

'Maybe, but one of you should have been straight with me,' Sam said. 'If I'd known sooner I could have—'

'Okay, detective, point made,' Paul snapped, then immediately regretted it. 'Apologies, but it wasn't the best of marriages. Far from it, in fact. I'd left it behind me – and then was lucky to meet Karen and be given a chance to start a new life.'

Except your luck has run out as suddenly as it started, amante, and the whole of your life is going to pass before your eyes in seconds as you fall down that cliff, and then splat! as you break every fucking bone in your body on the rocks waiting for you below.

'And I was so sure you'd be forced into killing him if you found him,' Paul stressed, 'I didn't want it ruined by disclosing I was married before. Especially to someone as promiscuous as Julia.'

'Yeah, I can see what was behind your reasoning,' said Sam. 'But I wish you'd leveled with me. I was starting to think *you* may have hired him.'

'I can see that now,' Paul said. 'Inadequate though it is, I can only repeat that I apologize.'

Sam ignored the apology. 'At least this tells us he's no hitman hired by someone with a grudge, either against Karen or her father. That he's here for himself. And this is the meaning of his threat "life for a life" – Karen's life for Julia's, his concept of retribution.'

Karen felt the anger rise up inside her again, but then realized that by being here in Ravensburg, determined to carry out his threat, it meant that Paxton himself still believed it was Paul who'd killed Julia.

Had he?

Or was it nothing more than Paxton's obsession – all in his psychotic mind?

But there again, maybe Paul had killed her.

If so, why?

Because she was "a two-timing slut" as Morgan had said?

Or for some other reason?

Money maybe?

And what about Morgan?

He clearly knew Paul at that time? And maybe provided him with a false alibi for the time of Julia's death…

And what about Susan?

Did she know about Julia, and yet despite this was still in it with Paul now?

Her mind spinning with it all, Sam's voice broke into her brooding. 'It's Karen you should be apologizing to, Mr. Archer. You have to tell her all of this, and hope she can find it within herself to forgive you.'

Some hope, Karen pledged.

'As soon as she wakes up,' Paul said.

I am awake, Paul, both eyes open. As sure as Hell I'll think of a way to get out of here today. And as for that Positano cliff, it will still be waiting for you.

And then Morgan feeding the fishes.

And Susan devoured by the wolves.

Sam half turned to exit the sitting room and paused.

He's clearly looking at the portrait of me when I was twelve, obsessed over his daughter's death.

And Sam with his brains blown out.

And Michael lying stone cold dead in that Chicago alley.

Both have their reasons for wanting me killed.

And both of them are going to have to pay for it.

'To repeat, detective,' Paul said inside the room. 'I wish I could rewind and play it differently.'

'What's past is past, Mr. Archer,' Sam grated. 'As for the present, the problem is that once the wheel is set in motion, it's difficult to stop.'

Sam turned fully into the hall, saw her sitting at the top of the stairs and realized she must have overheard the conversation about Paul and Julia. 'I'm sorry, Karen,' he said and exited the house.

Karen watched his shape through the front door's opaque glass as he descended the porch steps and headed for Michael's truck, and got a sixth-sense feeling that his 'sorry' was not for what she had overheard, but was for something that was still to come and, to quote him, "once the wheel is set in motion, it's difficult to stop".

Was Sam involved with Paxton after all?

Paul exited from the sitting room, having heard Sam call up to her.

His jaw tightened as he looked at her for her reaction.

She looked back at him feeling nothing but hate for him.

By not telling her about Julia and Paxton, he was more than guilty.

He had betrayed her.

She gathered her thoughts to play the part of the injured wife.

'Well that ends the hitman theory,' Sam said, sitting with Michael in the cab of his truck. 'As far as Paul and Morgan are concerned that is. They may be guilty of the sin of omission, but not of commission. But not you, Michael,' he stressed, 'I made a further check and Paxton's name is linked with yours on police files.'

'News to me,' Michael replied without batting an eye. 'I never heard of him before, least not under that name. Nor does it let you off the hook, Sam. If his name's on police files, you'd know how and where to find him easier than me.'

There was a long silence between them, then Sam broke it. 'I'm going back to my cabin,' he said, opening the door. 'I need to get my head down for a couple of hours. I also need Chicago to check up on something else that's bothering me.'

Michael watched Sam speed off and dialed out on the gold cellphone.

It rang but wasn't answered.

He put it back in the glove compartment, opened his window.

And let the first drops of rain fall on his face like he was trying to wash himself free of sin.

-28-

'I take it you heard Sam King?' Paul looked up at her sitting on the top riser. 'I'm sorry, *amante*.' There was contrition in his voice, but she also detected anger, that he was furious she'd overheard, livid at her for eavesdropping on him, but was controlling it and putting on a remorseful face.

She adopted her little girl hurt act. 'Why couldn't you have told me it's you he wants to harm, Paul?' she asked, faking a broken voice. 'That I'm just his means to achieve it.'

'I'm so sorry,' he repeated, starting up the stairs to console her. 'But as I said to King, I thought he'd drowned. After that, I don't know what I was hoping for.'

He reached out a hand to hers, she yanked hers away, repulsed by his touch, and was suddenly unable to hold back her rage. 'You said it yourself,' she screamed at him, 'that Sam would be forced to kill him. That he'd do your dirty work for you. And with him dead it would go away, like it never happened. And I would never find out. Nor that you were married before, you…you…'

She feigned that words had failed her, but she said them inside her mind anyway, because that was exactly what she thought of him:…*you bastard, you shit, you prick, you louse…*

Paul looked abject, no words to offer in his defense – all a sham, she thought.

'You gambled with my life,' she was cold inside now, choosing her every word, but still maintaining her outward fury. 'Put me in the front seat…while you hid behind me, you…you…'

Again she said the words in her mind, even more contemptuous than before.

He reached for her hand again.

She grabbed at her crutch to hit him in the stomach with it and send him tumbling down the stairs, but a flash vision of her father falling down them and snapping his neck on the hall below, halted her, she didn't want the police stopping her from getting away from here – two stair deaths in the same house within a year of each other would look suspicious, when she killed him it must look like an accident – like all splattered on the rocks at the foot of that cliff.

His hand touched hers. She slapped his face. He rocked backwards and for a split second she thought he was going to fall, but then he grabbed at the handrail and pulled himself back up.

'Get away from me!' her scream was pretty well a screech now. 'Don't touch me!'

Morgan exited the sitting room. He was wearing purple again today, the creep, shirt, sweater, slacks, socks, slippers. 'If it's any help, Karen,' he tried to intervene, 'it was Paul who found Julia's body. It traumatized him. He blamed himself for not being there to protect her, and since then has never talked about it, not even to me, as if by doing so, it would go away.'

'And now it's all happening again,' Paul begged her to understand and dismissing her slap to his face 'Same man, same scenario, except it's with you, *amante*,' he stressed. 'But this time I am here, and I'll make sure he won't get to you. I love you, Karen. You're everything to me.'

'Barring those are the same words you once said to someone else, Paul,' she snapped back. 'Someone I knew nothing about…' she tailed off, suddenly femininely curious to know about the other woman who had previously shared his life. 'Did you love her? Was she beautiful?'

'Yes…' he hesitated to say it. 'Yes, she was beautiful, and yes, I loved her. But then I found out what kind of woman she was. And you're my life now.'

'Except it's in the hands of a man out there who wants to end it,' she flared. 'Because of you …you…' This time she couldn't withhold the words. '*You bastard, you prick, you shit!*'

He again stretched his hand to her. 'Karen–'

'Keep away from me, Paul.' she shrieked at him. 'I don't know you.'

Grabbing the banisters, she pulled herself to her feet, crutched into her bedroom and slammed the door shut.

Paul looked up the stairs, decided against going after her, and returned to the hall. Morgan put a consoling arm on his shoulder and they entered the sitting room and closed the door.

She sat looking at herself in her dressing table mirror and heard her own voice. 'Keep away from me, Paul. I don't know you.'

And more than anything, she wanted to know as much as she could about him and Julia.

He'd said she was beautiful, but did he marry her because he loved her?

Or because, like herself, she was wealthy?

Sam would have the answers. On reflection, it was clear now he wasn't involved with Paxton. Nor was Michael. He could drive her to Ravensburg. And for the moment, neither was there need to fear

Paxton himself – until this worsening storm had passed, he would be lying low. Then, after talking to Sam, she'd go to Susan's and call O'Hare from there – telling her she was phoning her attorney about him drawing up the will she'd mentioned to her, but she needed to be on her own while talking to him - and not have her listening, the bitch. Then back to Clanryan to pack some essentials, best coats, best dresses, tightest jeans, sexiest underwear, stilettos – when she got to Italy, she would replace everything she'd have to leave behind – and wait for the cab to arrive.

Then once she was back in Positano, phone Paul to say she had forgiven him and ask him to join her. And resume with her plan for his and Morgan's and Susan's swift demises – Sam's and Michael's, too, she'd not forgotten that both wanted her dead.

She hurriedly put on yesterday's dress, the blue with tight belt and slanting pockets, hesitated over whether to put on make-up, realized she had no time, and put on her new white leather trench coat, a Burberry, and a matching sou'wester styled hat with a turned back brim, stuffed the Colt in a large purse – in case Michael tried to make amorous advances to her in his truck – and exited on to the landing.

The murmur of Paul's and Morgan's voices came from the sitting room, the door was closed.

She quietly slid down to the hall, slowly opened the front door and crutched out onto the deck.

It was raining heavier now and the wind was increasing. She carefully negotiated the porch steps and struggled for Michael's truck, praying that neither Paul or Morgan would happen to glance through the sitting room window as she passed it.

Michael saw her, leapt out of his truck and ran to her.

'Take me to Sam's, Michael,' she urged. 'Before Paul sees me.'

Michael helped her to into his cab, gave her the crutches and closed the door, and saw Morgan exit the house, parka over his shoulders, hood over his head, and down the porch steps. Running around the truck to his door, Michael got in, slammed the door shut and turned on his engine.

Morgan reached the truck and jerked open Karen's door. 'Karen. Where you going?'

'Susan's,' she said, brusque.

'But what about Paxton?' Morgan demanded.

'I'll be safe with Michael.'

'Sure she will,' Michael said, engaging gear, and the truck moved off.

Morgan kept pace with it, keeping the door open. 'I don't think you should go—'

Michael increased speed and made down the dirt track, forcing Morgan to release the door.

It slammed shut with the truck's sudden acceleration.

In her side mirror, Karen saw Morgan standing there helpless, the rain beating down on him and then Paul arrived by his side without his parka and already drenched, hair plastered to his head – and clearly angry with Morgan for letting her go.

'Looks like there's trouble in Paradise,' said Michael, looking in his rear mirror as she placed her hand inside her purse and clutched her Colt 45.

-29-

Clanryan passed from Karen's sight in her rain spattered side mirror as they exited the dirt track into the road and turned right for Ravensburg. 'How's married life?' Michael asked in a scathing tone, not turning his face to her as he drove.

'Fine,' she said, brusque, wanting to be left alone.

'Getting much?' he asked, being deliberately offensive.

'Michael,' she said, 'just drive.' Clutching her revolver, she looked out of the window as they entered the dark forest and it closed in around them.

The grey cloud deck above was hanging heavy and low over the tops of the trees, with thinner wisps scudding beneath it. The rain was getting heavier with flecks of snow in it that were sticking to the uppermost pine needles, forming a fine white carpet over the roof of the forest, while on the ground the rain was creating shallow gullies that were merging into small rivulets flowing out on to the road.

The rain drumming on Michael's cab roof seemed to get louder by the silence inside. Karen stared through the window. They reached Ravens Corner. She could see Ravens Pond through the trees, its surface lashed by the rain, and she shivered as she recollected her car sinking under its dark waters, and remembered her panic turning to an acceptance that she was going to die.

'You'd have drowned there if I hadn't saved you,' said Michael, almost like a petulant child.

She faced in to him, 'I will always be grateful to you, Michael,' she said, and added, though she didn't mean it, 'Maybe if you'd returned home sooner, things could have turned out different.'

'They still can,' he seized the opening. 'If it's not working out for you, maybe we could—'

'It's too late, Michael.'

'It's never too late,' Michael persisted. 'Paxton can be taken care of. Then we can move away from here. California maybe—'

'No,' she said, her voice hard again, 'what's past is past,' and looked back through the window. Michael slammed his foot on the throttle in anger and the forest sped by and then opened up as they reached Carvers Gulch – the rain was gushing out of the trees on the other side and across the road and cascading down on to the rocks far below that had nearly been her death trap, and swelling the stream into a torrent.

She looked away and they now entered the stretch of corners where Paxton had driven on her tail and kept ramming her BMW, then passed where he had waited for her to drive by and emerged out of the trees and chased her. Her spine went cold as she relived it.

Around the next corner the cemetery came into view, the gargoyles and angels with their spread wings seeming greyer than ever under the overhanging cloud, and The Hanging Tree looking stark against the heavy sky, no ravens perched on its whitened branches today as the rain beat down on it and she brooded whether it would permeate down through the earth to where her mother lay in her wicker coffin and seep into it, making her bones wet. *I love you, Mom,* she silently whispered to herself. *Why couldn't you have lived for us to be best friends, and travel the world together just the two of us, and escaped from him...'*

'Ravensburg,' Michael said, brusque, breaking into her thoughts, and she looked ahead as they exited their last corner and Susan's clapboard shop and Hank's clapboard store came into view, on opposite sides of the road where it widened and passed between them, before narrowing again.

'I'll wait and drive you back,' Michael said, still curt, as they entered Hank's lodge park, five log cabins spaced apart, and drove across the packed earth surface for Sam's, the end one.

'I'll go with Susan,' Karen said.

'Fine,' said Michael, braking to a jarring stop by the steps to Sam's door.

In his cabin, "uh-huhing" to a voice on the other end of his cellphone line, Sam saw Michael's truck pull up outside with Karen in the front seat.

'Uh-huhing' again into his phone, he loquaciously added another 'uh-huh,' while at the same time watching Karen struggle out of the truck with her crutches and Michael making no attempt to help her. She placed them under her armpits. Michael stretched across his cab, slammed her door closed and sped off into the road and headed back for Clanryan.

'Sometime tomorrow – thanks, Bert,' Sam ended the call as Karen crutched up the steps to his cabin, buffeted by the wind and the rain.

Crossing to the door, Sam opened it for her to enter. Over her shoulder he saw Susan standing in the shadow of her bow window across the road, talking to someone on her landline phone.

'She's going into Sam King's cabin,' Susan said to her listener as she saw that Karen was wearing designer rainwear despite the horrendous weather.

Don't think I don't realize you've worn it just for me to see, cousin dearest, but sure as hell is hot, my time will come.

Her listener replied.

'Maybe,' she returned, 'but I just wish you'd told me about Julia from the start–'

Her listener cut across her.

'Yes, I realize how traumatic it must have been for you,' she said. 'But I still wish you'd shared it with me, rather than being forced to tell me now.'

He again replied.

'No…' Susan paused, 'it's not changed the way I feel. Well, maybe it has…' she hesitated. 'At least, dented my trust a little.'

He appealed for her understanding and reassured her.

It took Susan a moment to reply. 'Yes,' she finally said, 'me, too.' But the words sounded like they'd been wrung out of her and she ended the call.

Sam helped Karen into the cabin, clutching a large purse and water pouring off the rim of her sou'wester. 'You shouldn't be here on your own,' he said, 'not with Paxton on the loose.'

'I was safe with Michael,' she replied, not using Sam's first name. 'I've some questions to ask and hoping you'll have the answers. Susan can drive me back, I need to talk to her, too.'

'Best I take you.'

'There's no need for you to go out in this storm.'

'We'll argue about that later,' Sam said. 'Let me get you a chair.'

He turned away from her. Hidden before by his body, the rag doll leered up at her from an old rocking chair. She recoiled back on her crutches, recollecting it hanging from the oak's branch.

'Sorry about that,' Sam said. Grabbing the quilt off the bed, he threw it over the doll and slid a chair to her. Recovering, she sat on it, Sam sat on the edge of the bed. 'Fire away,' he said.

'Julia,' she questioned. 'Was she rich?'

'I can guess where you're going with this.' Sam said. He indicated his cellphone on the table. 'I got Chicago to check it out, they've just called back. Yes, she was. Very.'

As I thought, Karen brooded, her suspicion confirmed.

'Except, Paul didn't benefit. Her entire estate: house; investments; were locked up in a trust fund. She was only entitled to the income.'

Karen narrowed her eyes.

Maybe Julia didn't confide that to Paul. And that's why he found me as his next victim.

Sam gripped her arm. 'You're having a tough time. It's bound to cause you doubts.'

She put on her little girl lost act. "I don't know what to believe any more, Sam. It's one shock after another.'

He let go her arm, his voice hardened: 'I know just how it feels. I've been there.'

'I know you have, Sam,' she said, keeping up her act, 'and now I'm burdening you with mine.' She struggled to stand up on her crutches, so pathetic: 'I'll leave you alone. The last thing you need now is me bothering you.'

'I'll drive you to Miss Ryan's,' he said, brusque.

'It's only across the street.'

'In this weather, you'd drown before you're halfway there.'

Retaking her arm, he helped her to the door.

From inside her shop Susan watched Sam help Karen down the steps of his cabin and into his car. He handed her her crutches and got into his driver's seat, started the engine and the Fusion rolled off across the earthen parking space to the exit.

She pressed REDIAL on the landline still in her hand. The voice answered. 'Sam's driving her somewhere,' she said. 'Probably taking her back.'

Sam exited the lodge park and drove straight across the road to her door.

'No,' Susan whispered now. 'They're coming here.'

Sam helped Karen out of his car and to the shop's covered deck. He tried the door and found it locked.

The voice instructed her.

'Understood,' she said, still keeping her voice low. 'I'll let you know the moment we leave.'

She cut the call, put the landline next to her cellphone on an antique table, crossed to the door and opened it. 'Karen! Detective King!' she exclaimed as if surprised to see them. 'Has something happened?' she asked, putting on a concerned voice as Karen crutched inside.

'No, all's fine, Miss Ryan,' Sam replied, staying out on the deck.

'Susan,' Susan pertly admonished him to use her first name.

Sam didn't respond and turned to Karen, 'I'll be outside when you're ready.'

'Sue will take me,' Karen repeated.

'I'm going back there anyway,' Sam insisted. He indicated the sheets of rain being driven across the road by the rising wind. 'It will save Miss Ryan from coming out into it.' He turned away before Karen could reply, got back in his car and settled in his front seat to wait.

Susan closed the shop door. 'Sam King doesn't seem to approve of me for some reason. Not that I'll lose any sleep over it,' she shrugged. 'Paul called earlier. He said you were on your way here.'

Karen sat on an antique chair from where she could see Sam. 'Did he tell you why?'

'Yes, he did.'

Karen turned to her cousin and now took in that she was wearing a tan sweater and narrow leg black jeans even tighter than yesterday. More of a statement – a sexual one – than her own raincoat, Burberry though it was – the scheming bitch.

'He's truly upset, Kay. And wishes he'd told you from the start.'

'Did *you* know he was married before?' she asked, yet certain her cousin had known.

'No, Kay, how could I? I didn't know Paul existed until we met him together in Chicago, just three weeks ago. But being married before doesn't mean he doesn't love you.'

'*No?*' Karen stressed the word, expressing her disbelief.

'He fell for you the first time he saw you.'

'Me…or my money, Sue?'

'You, of course. Paul just couldn't–' Susan hastily corrected herself, 'wouldn't fake it, Kay,'

Karen heard her cousin's slip-up, but her expression gave nothing away.

'It's only since you both returned from Italy that I've come to know him,' Susan weighted her words, 'but I think I can safely say that.'

Come to know him as in the carnal sense, you two-faced bitch, and long before Italy, I'd stake my life on it.

'And to add to it all, Sue,' Karen reassumed her little girl lost act, 'he's known all along who was trying to kill me.'

Susan took her car keys out of a drawer of an antique dresser. 'I'm driving you home so you and he can talk things through.'

'Sam said he'd take me,' Karen kept up her act and indicated at Sam waiting outside in his car.

'No need,' Susan insisted, 'with this weather I'd closed up anyway.'

'Fine,' Karen capitulated, she didn't trust either of them any more than she trusted Michael, but with her Colt in her purse she'd feel safer with Susan than Sam. 'But may I first call my attorney about changing my will? I'd rather talk to him away from Clanryan. And in private,' she hesitated, 'if that's okay?'

'Sure.' Susan handed her the landline from the antique table. Her cellphone bleeped at the same time. She picked it up and stared at it in horror. 'No!' she stifled a scream. 'No!'

Karen dropped the landline back on the antique table and snatched the cell from her. On its screen was the image of a short-nightied young woman lying slashed and bloodied on a bedroom floor. Her genital area was a gory mess. Words beneath the image read:

PAUL DID THIS TO JULIA
I WILL DO THE SAME TO KAREN

'Oh, God – No!' Karen recoiled and raised the cellphone to hurl it to the floor and stamp on it.

Susan snatched it from her. 'No, Kay! Sam King will need to see it.'

Karen looked mutely up at Susan, fear etched on her face.

'That's it,' Susan said, 'I'm taking you away from here. Somewhere far, where we'll be alone together, just you and I, and you'll be safe.'

'There's nowhere safe,' Karen was almost whimpering, and no longer as part of her little girl act. 'He always knows where I am – even that I'm here with you now.'

'That's why we need to get you away from here,' Susan said. 'Somewhere secret no one but you and I will know. I'll drive you back to Clanryan. We'll pack a few things. And on the pretext of you coming here to stay with me, we'll head for O'Hare. But first I'll copy this for Sam King to keep up the pretense.'

Picking up her landline from the antique table, she made for her desk at the rear of the shop, replaced her landline in its charger, connected her cellphone to a printer and printed a copy of the image. Returning with it, she said, 'At least it tells us he has a cellphone, but God only knows where he's charging it from.'

Averting her gaze from the print of the mutilated woman, Karen saw Sam talking on his cell in his car. A sudden thought came to her. 'Sam's on his phone,' she said fearfully to Susan. 'Only he knew I was with you when the image was sent. You don't think it's Sam telling Paxton? Does he know your cell number?'

'Sure. I gave it him in case he ever needed it.'

'Then how else could Paxton have gotten it?'

'No, it couldn't be Sam.' But Susan sounded unsure of it and Karen felt her panic increase as she watched Sam talking into his cell.

Seeing her fear, Susan grabbed her hand to help her out of her chair. 'We're going back to pack your bags,' she said, but then let go Karen's hand. 'Sorry, I forgot. I arranged to see a dresser old man Barker wants to sell, his pumpkin harvest failed this year, he's desperate for cash. I'll quickly call him and tell him I can't make it today.'

Returning to her desk, Susan sat in her swivel chair with her back to Karen. At the same time, Karen saw Sam end his call and wait as if he was expecting another call.

Glancing at Susan, Karen watched her dial out on her landline.

Sam answered his cellphone, Susan spoke into her landline.

Sam listened to his cellphone and replied.

Susan listened to her landline.

It's like they're talking to each other, Karen brooded.

Susan looked down at her cellphone, part swiveled her chair, and briefly glanced back at her like she was likening her to whatever she was looking at on her screen.

Karen realized it was Julia's gory body. *As if Susan was imagining her dead the same way.*

With Susan's face still half turned toward her, Karen lip-read her words as she spoke again into her landline: 'Shall I delete it?'

Sam spoke into his cellphone. Susan asked: 'You sure?'

Sam replied. Susan said, 'We're leaving now,' and ended her call.

Sam ended his call and put his cellphone away.

Karen checked the Colt 45 in her bag, wondering whether to force Susan upstairs, tie her up, phone O'Hare and get them to send the taxicab here, then come down and tell Sam she'd changed her mind and was spending the day with her cousin, but with her having said over her cell, 'We're leaving now', it was too risky – Sam wouldn't believe her. She would deal with the bitch on their way to Chicago. Sam, too, with her Colt, should he follow them some distance behind.

Susan crossed back across the shop to her, pocketing her cellphone. 'That's old man Barker sorted,' she said. Taking a dark green raincoat off a nearby peg, she put it on, pulled up the hood over her head, and helped Karen, clutching her bag, out her out of her chair.

Karen crutched out on to the deck. Susan locked the door. 'I'll just tell Sam I'm taking you', she said, and crossed over to him. He lowered his window. She said something to him, Sam nodded, and she returned to Karen, helped her into her low Jaguar, got into her driver's seat, started the engine, reversed into the road, and headed out of town.

Watching them drive from sight, Sam called out on his cell, spoke a few words into it, ended the call, and drove after them.

-30-

Within a hundred yards of leaving Ravensburg behind them and entering the dark forest, the rain lashing the Jaguar's windshield eased a little. Susan switched on her beams, partly lighting up the road through the beating wipers, but making the surrounding trees seem even darker and towering over them, creating an impenetrable tunnel that had no discernible end.

Karen clutched her purse tighter in her lap, ready to pull out her Colt 45.

They exited a bend and the trees thinned out as they passed the cemetery clearing, and Karen looked at the tall padlocked gates imprisoning her Mom behind them in her wicker basket - and *him* lying above her in his heavy mahogany coffin, keeping her weighted under him just as much as when she was alive.

God, she hated him still. His death had done nothing to erase the dread memories.

'I'm glad he's dead, too,' Susan said as if reading her mind. Karen didn't turn her face, didn't reply. Susan saw she'd withdrawn into herself and left her alone…

Reliving the night her father died.

William Ryan came out of her bedroom, wearing a green and white tartan shirt and blue corduroy slacks and paused at the top of the landing to re-fasten his belt. Karen hurtled out of her room in a nightdress and shoved him in the back, sending him tumbling down the stairs. A big heavy man, he hit the hallway hard, she heard his neck snap, and he lay sprawled and inert by the front door.

There was no doubt but that he was dead.

'Goodbye, *Daddy*,' Karen said from the top of the stairs, then entered his bedroom, picked up his phone extension and dialed 911. A woman's voice answered.

'Oh, thank God,' Karen faked a tremulous voice. 'My Pop's fallen downstairs. He's lying in the hall. His neck's twisted. I think he's dead.'

The woman asked a question.

'Clanryan,' Karen shakily replied. 'Two miles south of Ravensburg,' and replaced the phone.

Exiting the room, she walked unhurriedly downstairs, sat alongside her father, spat in his face, wiped it with the hem of her nightdress, then cradled his head in her lap and calmly waited to hear the ambulance approach before she turned on the tears.

'Good riddance,' she said to him and spat into his face again.

'Good riddance to what?' Susan asked, bringing her back to now and the realization that she had spoken out loud. Looking through the window, she saw they were passing Ravens Pond again.

'Good riddance to when we've left Clanryan and its terrible memories for good,' Karen said.

'Amen to that,' Susan said with unmistakable fervor in her voice.

Amen indeed, except twenty miles is all the journey you'll be making, Susan dearest, to where the wolves can feast on you, and the birds and the maggots can pick your bones clean.

Susan glanced in her rear mirror. 'There's a vehicle coming up fast behind us.'

Karen looked in her side mirror and saw twin headlights bearing up on them. From the space between both lights, and their height in relation to Susan's low car, they looked to be the beam lights of a truck. It caught them up. Susan slowed for it to pass. It stayed glued to their tail.

Karen panicked. 'It's him,' she cried to Susan, and then recalled her saying 'We're leaving now', to whoever was on the other end of her phone line before they left the shop. Sam? Maybe. But it wasn't to old man Barker, that was for sure, because the driver on their tail was Paxton, she knew it was, and was equally sure she'd been set up.

She put her right hand inside her purse and gripped her Colt 45.

'If it doesn't want to pass, then fuck it,' Susan said, keeping up the sham and speeding up into the next bend.

And as before, just as he had three days earlier, Paxton stayed glued to their tail.

Karen tightened her hold on the Colt's butt and her first finger moved on to the trigger.

They exited the curve into a straight. The headlights moved left out of Karen's vision in her side mirror and the truck went past them and the driver tooted his horn.

Susan tooted back. 'It's just Hank,' she said.

From a vantage point overlooking the road from Ravensburg, a rifle held by black-leather gloved hands, was trained on a bend in the road, a finger hovered over the trigger.

Hank's truck appeared around the bend and went by.

Susan's car entered the bend in the rifle's sights.

The trigger finger tightened.

Susan's car rounded the bend and Clanryan came into view.

A bullet smashed through the windshield. It was unmistakably a bullet, it whined as it passed between them and out through the rear window.

Susan lost control of the car. Slamming on the brakes, it slid, snaking at speed on the wet road, mounted a bank and slammed head on into the trunk of a tree.

Both sat stunned in their seats, sleet lashing in through the broken windshield into their faces and running down their raincoats. Susan was the first to recover. 'That was a rifle,' she said, voice shaking. 'It must have been Paxton. A few inches either way, it would have got one of us.' She grasped Karen's hand. 'You okay?'

Too shaken to speak, Karen nodded.

Through her rain blurred vision she could just see Clanryan.

Michael was driving down the dirt track in his truck, speeding to get to them.

Paul exited the house, throwing on his parka, and ran across the grass clearing toward them.

Morgan emerged out on to the front deck and watched from under the covered porch.

Sam's car braked to a stop behind them.

He ran to the Jaguar and yanked Karen's door open.

'God,' he exclaimed as she turned her face to him. 'I never thought to see you alive. Not after that crash. Nor you Miss Ryan,' he added. 'What in the hell happened?'

-31-

Karen and Susan sat facing the sitting room fire, Paul handed them brandies, 'Down the hatch,' he said, 'after that close miss you both need it.'

Holding the snifter in both hands. Karen looked into the fire, brooding that Paxton had once more tried to kill her. She'd been wrong about him following her in the truck, but right about being set up – with all things a rifle aimed at her head, and only by a miracle had he missed.

Was Sam in it with Susan and Paul and Morgan?

Who knew anymore?

Her mind was spinning with it all.

But she still had to get away from here today.

Sitting near her on the sofa, Susan tossed her drink down in one and extended her glass back to Paul. He topped it up and gave it back to her. She took another slug. He sat next to Karen on the arm of the sofa and placed his hand on her shoulder. She pulled away from his touch.

From the kitchen, past the open sitting room door where Michael was standing as usual, came the sound of Morgan clattering dishes. Sam was peering through the side drapes at the trees across the road. Distant flashes of lightning were illuminating the dense roof of the stygian-black forest, rumbles of thunder rolled nearer with them, and the rain was lashing down again.

'Beats me where he can be hiding out in this weather,' Sam said.

If he was in it with Paxton, Karen brooded, then he was keeping up the pretense.

Her nerves on edge, she gulped some of her brandy and coughed as the raw spirit burned her throat.

Sam looked in. 'You okay, Karen?'

'How did he know I would be in Susan's car?' she asked in an accusatory voice.

'He must have seen you leave earlier and was waiting for you to return,' Sam replied easily. Turning to Susan, 'How about you, Miss Ryan?' he asked.

'Susan,' she reminded him again. 'A little shell-shocked Sam, considering I almost got killed.' She took another slug of brandy.

'Soon as this storm's over,' he said, 'I'll find the sonofabitch.' He glanced at the phone, impatient for it to ring.

'You still think he's going to call?' Paul asked.

'I'd bet my last dollar on it,' said Sam – proving he knew full well that Paxton would, Karen thought.

Susan extended him the printout of Julia's body. 'He sent this to my cellphone, Sam.'

Sam's face exhibited revulsion as he looked at Julia's body. 'I've seen some grisly killings,' he said, 'but that's the worst. It's butchery. He must be pathologically depraved.'

He showed it to Paul who turned away, unable to look at it. Michael glanced at it over Sam's shoulder and hastily drew back, appalled.

Sam read the wording under the image. 'He's still saying you did it, Paul.'

'That's absurd,' Paul replied. 'The sicko clearly took it himself after he killed her.'

Sam turned back to Susan. 'Send me a cell image of it, Susan. It will have his number on it.'

'Sure,' Susan said. Producing her phone, she entered IMAGES and looked at Sam with despair. 'I must have accidentally deleted it, Sam. How more stupid could I be.'

Karen raised her face from the fire and saw her cousin's remorseful expression.

Accidental. Like hell. She'd asked on her cell should she delete it, and Sam – if it was Sam? –must have told her to.

'Damn!' Sam swore. 'Chicago might have been able to pinpoint where he's talking to us from. Would you mind me sending them your cell instead? They may be able to get something from it.'

'Of course not, Sam,' Susan replied and extended her cellphone toward him.

Morgan entered with a tray of mugs and a coffee pot and placed it on a side table next to Susan.

'Would you pour,' he asked her, 'I have to get back to the kitchen. I thought an early dinner might help restore us.'

'Sure I will,' she said. Morgan left the room. Susan pocketed her cell and turned to the tray.

Watching her do this and Sam lower his arm, it confirmed Karen's suspicion about them, and she observed them both from under hooded eyes as Susan picked up the coffee pot.

'How do you like yours, Sam?' Susan asked with disarming amity.

'Black, please, Susan, no sugar,' Sam replied, pocketing the photo of Julia's body.

Susan poured, handed the mug to him and turned to Michael. 'Michael?'

'Cream, thanks, Miss Ryan,' said Michael. 'Two sugars.'

Shriiiiiiiilll…

'On time,' said Sam. Crossing the room to the telephone table, he placed his coffee mug on it, picked up the phone, pressed the conference button and said into the receiver. 'Sam King.'

His voice was heard by all in the room, venomous. 'I had her dead center in my sights, Sam.'

Sam nodded to Michael. He ran from the room and out through the front door.

Still sitting on the arm of the sofa, Paul replaced his arm on Karen's shoulder and tried to draw her nearer to him. She pulled away from him.

'Except you missed, John,' Sam said into the phone. 'Assuming you *are* John Paxton?' Sam added – knowing damn well he was, Karen simmered.

Seen through the front window, Michael leapt into his truck and slammed his door closed.

Was Michael in it with them, too, playing his role?

'So now you know my surname, too, Sam,' the voice replied. 'But I'll still call you Sam, if that's okay with you?

'Why change a habit,' Sam said.

'I'll get her next time, Sam.'

'There won't be a next time, John.'

Michael's truck sped off down the dirt track into the road and turned left into the forest.

'I decide that, Sam,' the voice spat out the words. 'Not you.'

'Over my dead body,' said Sam.

'It's not your dead body I want, Sam, it's the *whore's*.'

Paul's reached out again for Karen's hand. She slid nearer to Susan. Susan tried to grasp her other hand. Karen rose, crossed to Morgan's chair and sat in it, bent her legs up into her stomach and her arms around her knees, and pulled them tight to her.

'Archer killed the woman I loved,' the voice intensified for all to hear, 'And I'm going to kill the woman he loves.'

Paul slid off the sofa arm nearer to Susan and they sat looking at her. *Like vultures over their prey, waiting for when I'll be dead.*

'Whatever you believe about Julia's death, John,' Sam replied into the phone, 'this isn't the way to deal with it.'

'But the Good Book says a life for a life, Sam. The punishment must fit the crime. As a lawman, you must realize that.'

Sam looked at his watch, pretending to try to buy Michael more time. 'But why the mutilation, John? Help me to understand.'

'It's Archer you should be asking, Sam, not me. *He's* the one who knows why. And his *whore* will soon know how. But I have to go, Sam. Your sidekick must be close by now.'

Lightning flashed as Michael raced along a storm-lashed road. He cut his lights as he entered the next bend and slowed to a crawl. At the end of the straight he could just discern Cobbs Bend phone booth shrouded by rain.

He drove closer to it and stopped, got out of the truck, pulled out his revolver and crept to the booth. It was misted up but he could make out Paxton's shape inside leaning back against the door.

Michael flung it open. Paxton lunged at him. Michael shot. Paxton's head exploded, bits of it showered over him, his face, his hair, his clothes, and Paxton's inert body fell against him. It was a dummy made of an old coat draped over a cross-pieced two-branched frame, the remains of the head was a pumpkin impaled on the top of the central strut.

'Fuck and shit,' Michael cursed, wiping off bits of pumpkin.

Back in Clanryan, his voice gloated down the phone to Sam. 'Except I'm not using the same booth, Sam. We'll talk again soon.' He ended the call.

Sam slammed the phone back into its cradle: 'Damn him,' he swore. 'Damn him to hell.'

Sam's reaction was so angry, so vehement, Karen's suspicion of him began wavering again.

He studied the image of Julia's mutilated body on his cellphone – the one he had taken of her after he had killed her and she lay supine on the bedroom carpet, her blood oozing out of her and forming a red pool around her.

In his mind, he relived killing her as she backed away from him, trying to shield herself with her upraised arms as he stabbed her, and stabbed her, and stabbed her with a large carving knife.

She fell to the floor, her nightdress in shreds, her bloodied body lacerated with deep cuts.

He knelt alongside her, tore at what was left of her nightdress, exposing her revolting triangle of fair hair and hacked at her genitals – never again would she be able to use it, the *whore*.

Finally satisfied she had been punished for her sin, he took a second image of her lying there – having now paid the price for it.

He smiled as he remembered it, and recalled Sam.

Shriiiiiiilll…

Sam grabbed the phone off its charger. 'Listen up you sonofabitch–'

To the distant sound of rolling thunder in the background, Michael yelled back at him into the phone. 'The fucking turd rigged up a pumpkin dummy, Sam. I'm covered in the fucking stuff–'

'Get straight back, Michael,' Sam yelled across him. 'He used a different callbox.'

Fork lightning hit the ground near the front corner of the house. Above Karen's bedroom window, a connection box linked the phone wire from a pole close to the road, providing the mains line to Clanryan. An extension wire descended from this box and along the front wall from above the sitting room window to another box above the dining room window. A fork lightning tail struck close to the wire, jerking its connection plug out of its socket. The wire's whole length whipped back along the front deck to the corner of the house.

'Michael, you there?' Sam called into the phone. Hearing only static come from it, he replaced the phone and turned to the others: 'The line's gone dead.'

'Storm interference,' Paul speculated. 'As soon as it's passed over it should be restored.'

Hearing only static from his phone, he called up Julia's mutilated body on his cellphone screen.

In his imagination, Julia's face became Karen's as he stabbed and stabbed and stabbed her. She fell, all bloodied, to the floor, except that in his imagination she was still alive, helpless and at his mercy.

He knelt alongside her, tore open her nightdress and raised his carving knife. 'Your suffering is almost over, *whore*,' he whispered. 'Just a little slicing first, and then you'll pay with your life.'

'Let's hope that storm interference is all it is,' Sam said grimly. 'And not some trap of Paxton's–' the rest of his words died on his lips as a metallic tap came from the front window, like someone had rapped sharp and hard outside on the glass pane.

They all turned to stare at the closed drapes.

Another sharp tap.

Sam pulled his revolver and crossed to the window and cautiously parted the drapes.

Blown by the wind, the loose telephone wire snaked and leapt across the deck, the metal connection plug at its end hitting the window and recoiling and snapping against it again and again in the strong wind.

'That explains the dead line,' Sam said, closing the drapes. 'At least, he won't be calling again.'

And with Susan's car wrapped around a tree trunk, immobilized, Karen thought, and no way I can get my hands on Paul's SUV keys, I'm here yet another night.

Morgan entered the room. 'Did Michael catch him?

No one answered him.

'I take it he didn't, then?' Morgan said, sounding distinctly miffed at being ignored.

-32-

Lightning illuminated Clanryan, highlighting the poised griffin, talons raised high over the front door, and the black crows silently perched on the stark branches of the leafless oak tree, looking down like precursors of death on the rain-lashed clapboard house.

Sam and Michael appeared on the front deck from around its opposite corners. Their upper bodies protected from the driving rain by its covered roof, they checked the windows were secure and met on the front porch. Entering the house, they stood on the square of brown hessian rug on the wood planked hall and stamped the wet off their shoes. Sam entered the sitting room.

Karen was still sitting in Morgan's chair looking into the fire. Morgan was standing near Paul as he decanted Courvoisier into a goblet. Handing it to Morgan, Paul poured himself a tumbler of Jack Daniels. Susan was sitting on the sofa, clutching a half empty glass. All the drapes were still drawn. The rain was beating against the windows.

Paul looked around as Sam entered. 'Everything's secure,' Sam said. 'I'm staying for Michael to go and get cleaned up. He'll try to get someone to fix the line, hopefully as soon as tomorrow.' He turned to Susan, 'He can drive you home.'

'Paul's asked me to stay as company for Karen,' Susan replied. 'Would Michael ask Hank to tow my car in?'

'There's no need for you to stay,' Karen said, brusque. 'I'm going to my room when dinner's over. I've a headache coming on.'

'I think it's better that Susan does,' Paul said, but giving Sam the feeling that he wanted her to stay for himself rather than for Karen. 'The more of us there are in the house around you, amante, the safer you'll feel.'

Safer! I'm no safer inside this house than out there where Paxton is waiting for me.

Paul turned to Sam. 'Have dinner with us, detective? It's not right for you to be out there in weather like this.'

'Yes, Sam,' Susan added her voice to Paul's, 'please do.'

And now Sam wanting revenge for his daughter's death — all four locking me around the table, pretending to be fine on the surface and thinking dark thoughts about me in their minds.

'I'm making steak and baked potatoes, Sam,' Morgan joined in. 'It should warm us all up on a day like this.'

With sleeping powder in mine as before, Karen thought, determining she'd not touch hers.

'In that case, I will,' Sam agreed. 'It's one hell of a day, and I doubt Paxton's going to be out in it. He'll have found someplace dry to hunker up.'

Sam returned to the hall and hung up his jacket. 'See you in the morning, Michael.'

'I'll be back at eight,' Michael replied.

'And don't forget the report the line down,' said Sam. 'Tell them it's a police scene and urgent. If they need to check it, they can call Chicago Police, Organized Crime, Detective Bert Quinlan.'

'Sure,' Michael said and exited the house.

Sam re-entered the sitting room.

'Drink, detective?' Paul asked him.

'Just a splash of Jack Daniels, Mr. Archer.'

Paul poured it and handed Sam the tumbler, 'And call me Paul.'

Sam took the tumbler, 'Thanks, Paul,' and looked where to sit.

Morgan stood, 'Take my chair, Sam, I have to check the dinner.'

'Thanks, Morgan,' Sam said, accepting Morgan's invitation to call him by his first name, too, and sinking into the chair and tasting his drink.

They're all acting like it's a fucking party. Like it's an Irish wake before I'm even dead.

Morgan exited to the hall and into the dining room and through to the kitchen beyond.

Paul tossed back the rest of his drink and replaced his tumbler on the table. 'I just want to nip up to my study to check on something,' he said to Karen. 'Two minutes, no more.'

'Take as long as you want,' she replied, 'I don't need you constantly watching me.'

'Karen!' Paul protested.

'For fuck's sake, Paul, go.'

Paul hesitated, then exited, leaving a silence in the room after Karen's outburst.

Sam broke it. 'That bullet was a close call, Karen. I don't think you should venture out of the house again.'

'I won't, Sam,' Karen said.

But I'll be out of here for good tomorrow, once the line's been repaired.

Sam turned to Susan, 'And how are you now, Susan?'

'Still feeling shaky, Sam,' Susan held out a hand to show it trembling. 'It's not every day I get shot at.'

Feeling her nerves on edge, Karen stood. 'The wind's getting worse, I hope it won't prevent them repairing the line.' She started to crutch for the front window to peer outside.

280 | RICHARD REES

'Have you tried walking without your crutches, Karen?' Sam asked.

'I don't think I could,' she replied, brusque.

'Have you tried?' Sam insisted.

Taking up Sam's challenge, she willfully tossed her crutches aside and reached the window.

'See, you made it,' Sam said. 'Without needing help from anyone. Just keep trying.'

'Except *he's* out there somewhere,' Karen flared, 'wanting to kill me,' and she angrily parted the drapes wide.

A *crack*, like a rifle shot, exploded. She screamed and staggered back. Sam leapt from his chair and caught her. A second *crack* exploded. She screamed again and clung to Sam.

'It's okay, it's the loose wire,' Sam said and reclosed the drapes.

Paul burst into the room from upstairs and frowned as he saw Sam holding Karen.

'It was only the wire hitting the glass, Paul,' Susan hastily told him.' It sounded like gun shot.'

Sam released Karen. She walked back to Morgan's chair.

'Where are your crutches, Karen?' Paul demanded.

She sat down and ignored him.

Outside, his back pressed against the house's front wall – she'd almost caught him when she suddenly opened the drapes – the hood of a black parka raised over his head against the storm, he picked up the connection plug at the end of the telephone wire, crossed to the dining room window, inserted it into the inlet hole in the receptor box above, and let go the wire. It pulled out. He looked about him for something to utilize, saw a sliver of lightning-charred wood on the deck, picked it up and reinserted the plug, wedging the wire in place with the sliver.

He faded into the darkness as he headed along the deck toward the rear of the house, the rain lashing low under the front porch, soaking the lower half of his legs.

-33-

Dinner was over. Morgan gathered dishes to take to the kitchen. He'd changed out of his purple slacks, purple socks, purple shoes, into light green slacks, socks and shoes, but must have changed in a hurry, and not as fastidiously as usual, the light green clashed with his purple shirt and purple sweater. Stretching across the table for Karen's and Susan's plates to help Morgan clear up, Paul saw that Karen had cut up her steak and baked potatoes into small pieces, but toyed with them and hadn't eaten anything.

'You've not touched your dinner,' he accused.

'I'm not hungry,' she snapped, anxious to listen to Susan's ongoing conversation with Sam.

Paul hesitated, decided not to reply back and followed Morgan into the kitchen.

'She was her father's constant companion,' Susan was saying. Sam was seated next to her at the bottom end of table away from William Ryan's empty chair. A slight slur in Susan's voice suggested she'd had one cognac too many. 'The only time he would let her out of his sight was school.'

'And why not?' Sam replied. He gave Karen a flitting smile, letting her know he realized that Susan was a little drunk. 'Every man should have a daughter. I'm sure your father spoilt you, too. I know I spoiled mine something rotten–' he stopped mid-sentence, a catch in his voice.

'Yes, he did,' Susan continued, not noticing Sam's sudden change of mood. 'He and Karen's father were brothers, both were protective of us. Especially Karen's,' she confided, tipsily, 'to the point of being over possessive at times–'

'We were more like sisters than cousins,' Karen cut in before Susan went too far. 'Would you like to see some photos of us together?' she asked, not expecting Sam to accept.

Still brooding about Emma, Sam answered unthinkingly. 'Yes, I would.'

Bound by her offer, Karen pushed back her chair and made for the hall. Paul entered from the kitchen. 'Karen, you shouldn't be without your crutches.'

She paused in the doorway. 'I need them when *I* think I need them, Paul. And I soon won't be needing them at all.'

Warned off by her sharp tone, Paul picked up Sam's dishes and returned to the kitchen. Karen exited to the hall and into the sitting room.

Left alone in the room with Susan, Sam searched for something new to say. 'Do you read much, Susan? What are your favorite books?'

'Sure. I'm a romantic at heart,' Susan confided, her speech still slurred. 'My favorite is *Pride and Prejudice*. Especially Mr. Darcy. But at the moment, I'm reading *Gone with the Wind.*'

The wind gusted outside. Susan laughed at the coincidence, Sam fleetingly smiled back. Paul re-entered the room to the sound of Morgan still clearing up in the kitchen. At the same time Karen exited the sitting room into the hall, holding her photo album.

A man burst in through the front door. She screamed. He grabbed her to him. 'It's okay,' he soothed her. 'It's only me. Michael.' Feeling his familiar lean body against her, she responded, holding him tight as the shock of his sudden entrance seeped out of her. He closed the front door with his heel. 'Sorry, Karen. I should have knocked, but I need to see Sam.'

She moved away from Michael and brushed against a coat hanging up on a hook behind her. It was damp. She turned and saw it was Paul's black parka, and was puzzled why it was wet.

Sam exited from the dining room, followed by Paul.

'Hank's had a break-in,' Michael told Sam.

'When?' Sam asked.

'Couple of hours ago. I was thinking that maybe it was Paxton? Running out of food?'

Sam indicated the album in Karen's hand. 'You can show it me some other time.' He grabbed his jacket off a hook and put it on. 'Michael will stay until I get back.'

'Did you report the line down?' Paul asked Michael.

'I clean forgot,' Michael replied, making no apology for it.

Seeing Paul about to remonstrate with Michael, Sam said: 'I'll take care of it,' and opened the front door. 'Walk me to my car, Michael, and fill me in about Hank.'

He and Michael exited the house back into the storm, shutting the door behind them.

Still pondering about Paul's damp parka, Karen entered the dining room. Paul followed her. 'When will Sam be back?' Susan asked him.

'Could be he won't,' Paul replied, 'not if the break-in was Paxton. Michael's staying on.'

Karen threw the album down on the table. 'I'm going up to my room.'

'But it's only three o'clock,' Susan protested.

'My headache's got worse.'

Susan stood and gave her a hug. 'I hope it soon lifts. Come back down if it does.'

Karen turned for the door. 'No kiss for me?' Paul asked.

'What do you think?' Karen said.

'I'll bring your crutches up,' Paul persisted. 'I think you still need them.'

From the kitchen, amid the clatter of Morgan putting away dishes, the phone rang.

Shriiiiiiillll...

Sitting in his truck outside Clanryan, watching Sam speed off down the track, Michael rang out on the gold cellphone and got voice mail telling him the person he wanted to speak to was on the line to someone. He switched off the cell and called up IMAGES and looked again at Paxton's face, the cruel nature etched into every line of his visage, the cold, evil eyes...

He had to reach him – since seeing Julia's mutilated body, the last thing he wanted was for that to happen to Karen.

He redialed out and again got voice mail.

Morgan flung open the kitchen door, revealing the shrilling phone on the wall.

'The line's down!' Morgan looked panic-stricken. 'It shouldn't be ringing.'

'But it damn well is,' Paul snapped back at him.

'Should I answer it?' Morgan's voice quivered.

'Hold on,' Paul replied. He dashed to the sitting room and returned with the cordless landline.

'Together,' he instructed Morgan. Morgan crossed to the shrilling wall phone.

'Now!' Paul called out to him, switching on his phone.

Morgan picked up the kitchen receiver. 'Hello?' he queried, shakily.

As he listened to the voice on the other end of the line, Morgan's face registered revulsion at what he was hearing. Finally, he could take it no more. 'You're deranged, Paxton,' he blurted out. 'You should be locked up…' His voice broke off as he continued listening.

Susan extended a hand to Karen. She rejected it and moved away, her mind less on Paxton and more that with the phone working again, she could phone O'Hare once Paul, Morgan and Susan were asleep.

Pacing up and down the length of the receiver wire in the kitchen, Morgan was getting more and more agitated by what he was hearing.

In the dining room, Paul cut into the call. 'You're a sick bastard, Paxton,' he erupted, snarling into his phone. 'When I find you, I'll–'

Outside, a strong gust of wind howled along the deck. Something metal-sounding hit the window.

Paul looked almost disbelievingly across at Karen and Susan. 'The line's gone dead again.'

In the kitchen, Morgan let the receiver drop from his hand and dangle at the end of the corded wire down the wall. Dragging out a kitchen chair from under a working table, he collapsed into it.

Fuck, fuck, that means another night in this damn house with these three shits, and Sam or Michael outside, and Paxton watching it from God only knows where, waiting for his opportunity.

Karen stormed out of the room.

Paul caught her up at the foot of the stairs and clutched her arm. 'Karen–'

She flung off his arm. 'Fuck off, Paul.' And started struggling up the stairs without her crutches.

Paul watched her until she reached the top, entered her bedroom and slammed the door.

He returned to the dining room, crossed to Susan, opened his arms and she went into them.

Sam was parked alongside Ravens Pond trying to jog his memory as he looked at the rain-lashed pond, and the rows of black crows lining the branches of the trees, staring down at him with evil eyes, like Hitchcock's *The Birds* on their telephone wires.

Again, he could dimly recall Paul leap from his SUV, shout something and run for the pond.

Digging deep into the far recesses of his mind, he tried to recall what it was.

But all he could remember next was Paul diving into the pond.

Then Paul and Morgan in the water trying together to rescue Karen from her sinking car.

No matter how hard he tried, what happened in between was still locked away in his mind.

He gave up and drove off.

-34-

Karen crossed to her bedroom window and looked out. The storm was slowly abating, the rain had stopped, but the sky was still dark, with thin wisps of cloud scurrying under the dark mantle above as if symptomatic of how her thoughts about the extent to which she hated Paul and Susan were intruding on the darker thoughts of how she was going to kill them both, and then Morgan, and then Michael, and then Sam, and she wanted to dwell long on those much more than waste a single moment with just thoughts of hate.

Leaving the drapes open she crept back out on to the landing. The dining room door was open and she listened to Paul and Susan talking in low voices.

'Talk about having a short fuse,' Paul said, 'she doesn't even possess one. She just explodes.'

'Take her crutches up to her,' said Susan. 'Try giving her some love. And try showing her how concerned you are about her.'

Try giving me some love! Try showing me how concerned he is.

That's all it's been right from the start, Karen fumed, a pretense, a deception to get my money, and I fell for it, fool that I was, hook and line – but not sinker, on no, not sinker, and I will get my own back. Crouching low she peered through the banisters and watched Paul exit the dining room – hating the very sight of him – and enter the sitting room for her crutches.

Re-entering her room, she partly closed the door, sat on the bed, and switched on her bedside light.

The hall light switched on downstairs, followed by the stairs and landing lights, and Paul ran upstairs and entered her room.

'Fuck off back to Susan,' Karen said, 'and take the crutches with you.'

Paul placed them by her against the bed. 'I think you still need them.'

'Except I don't anymore. Nor do I need you.'

Paul tried another tack and made for the window. 'I'll just close the drapes for you.'

'I don't want them closed. I feel shut up enough in this house as it is.'

He crossed to her bedside table and picked up the phial. 'Try taking half a pill. A sleep might get rid of your headache.'

She snatched it out of his hand and slammed it back on the table. 'It will make it worse.'

He leant down to kiss her cheek. She turned her face away from him. 'For fuck's sake, go.'

He crossed the room and paused in the doorway, persevering with her. 'Tomorrow we'll talk about going somewhere safer. Maybe back to Italy, as you want.'

'Me – not we,' Karen returned.

'What do you mean by that?' he demanded.

Realizing her mistake, Karen screamed at him, 'I mean get out of my sight.'

He spun away, slamming the door behind him and ran down the stairs. The light filtering in under her door told her that he had turned off the landing and stair lights, but left the hall light on. She heard the dining room door close.

She exited her room on to the landing, but could now only hear the dim murmur of Paul's and Susan's voices talking low in the dining room. She went back into her room, closed the door, crossed to the window and looked out.

It had gone suddenly dark outside. Michael was in his truck, seemingly searching a cellphone screen, but hastily put it away in his glove compartment as Sam's car lights entered the dirt track leading to the house, and drove through the muddied pools of water and parked alongside him.

Sam crossed to Michael's truck, got in and sat beside him, and they talked together.

Staring out into the darkness, she continued to brood. One more night, that's all she had to get through, and tomorrow when the phone line was restored, she would phone O'Hare, and in hours she'd be the hell away from here…and away from them.

Paul…Morgan…Susan.

From downstairs, Susan laughed as if without a care in the world to something Paul said.

Laugh while you still can, bitch. The last laugh will be mine.

She looked down at Sam and Michael still talking together in Michael's truck.

You both, too. Just in case Paxton is in it with one of you.

Hiding in the shrubbery bordering the dirt track, he watched Sam exit Michael's truck and get into his car. Michael started his engine, switched on his headlights, cutting into the darkness, and drove off down the dirt track into the road and turned right for Ravensburg. His lights went around the corner and were swallowed up by the forest.

He turned his eyes to Karen standing in her window.

End it tonight?

Or give her one more night to suffer even more mental agony before he sliced her.

And sliced her. And sliced her. And sliced her.

Reducing that part of her body to bloodied strips.

He pulled out the carving knife and stroked its dried-gore-red blade, imagining it.

Sam opened his car window and shone his flashlight on the shrubbery.

Damn. In pulling out the knife, he must have disturbed the bush.

Sam got out of his car, holding his revolver.

He crept back into the deeper shrubbery.

Aiming his flashlight in front of him, Sam headed across the clearing.

Clutching the carving knife, he crept further back. He had to stay hidden. It would be fatal to come face to face with Sam now at this late stage.

Sam entered the shrubbery and probed about with his flashlight.

Then shone the light at the deeper shrubbery.

In the deeper shrubbery, he raised his knife.

If Sam came nearer he would have to kill him.

With but a thick bush between them he psyched himself up to kill Sam.

Standing in her bedroom window, Karen saw Sam's flashlight suddenly go out in the shrubbery.

Time seemed to stand still.

Sam exited the shrubbery, shaking his failed flashlight, and headed back to his car.

Closing her drapes, she got into bed fully dressed, wrapped the duvet around her and resumed brooding. Her dark imaginings and thoughts took over and she saw…

Paxton standing over her bed, carving knife held high and dripping with crow's blood, ready to plunge it into her.

The picture in her mind faded and became…

Paul and Susan making frenetic love, and Susan arching her back to meet him, and moaning with pleasure as Paul kept thrusting into her.

Banishing the scene, her dark thoughts turned to…

Morgan with his oh-so immaculate clothes, and his precise and sickening mannerisms.

Michael, as unforgiving now he was a hardened soldier as he was when he was an immature youth. Still bearing grudges.

Sam. It was her father who'd killed his daughter, why take his revenge on her? He should have sought her father out while he was alive, and killed him to exact it, not make her the scapegoat.

They would all get their due. All five.

Her head pounded. She felt she was going mad. She glanced at her bedside clock. It was still only late afternoon. There was no danger of Paxton getting to her at this hour. Stretching for the phial, she extracted a sleeping pill, broke it in half and swallowed it, and lay back on her pillow waiting for it to work and give her oblivion, if only for a few hours.

That was too close, he thought, from the deeper shrubbery as he watched Sam get into his car, but still brandishing his revolver in full sight through his window.

It was clear that Sam felt he was being watched, and was displaying his gun as a warning.

Maybe he should take it as a warning not to delay killing her any longer.

Maybe it would be best to end it tonight.

In the small hours when all in the house would be asleep.

And having killed her, there would be enough time to slice her, too.

Karen suddenly awoke. It was dark in the room. She switched on her bedside lamp and checked her clock. It was just gone 9.30 in the evening.

Lying in bed still dressed, she heard the sitting room door open and Morgan say "Goodnight" to Paul and Susan. He came upstairs and into his room and closed his door.

Karen threw her duvet aside, sat on the edge of the bed, undressed down to her underwear, got back into bed and pulled the duvet around her. Checking the Colt 45 under her pillow, she lay back, listening to the murmur of Paul's and Susan's voices coming from the sitting room.

Susan laughed at something Paul said, and Paul laughed with her.

Bitch! Bastard!

Tightening her grip on the revolver, she imagined emptying the chamber into them. Three into Paul, three for Susan. One between their legs. One into their chests. One between their shocked eyes.

Again she heard the sitting room door open, the landing light came on and Paul and Susan crept upstairs. Paul whispered something to Susan and she stifled her laughing response. Karen uncapped the phial, poured two pills out of it on to her bedside table, and laid the phial down on its side, cap open, and pretended to be fast asleep – but with her eyelids barely slit apart.

Her bedroom door quietly opened. Paul peered in. Seeing her seemingly asleep, he crept to her side, saw the upturned phial and the spilt pills, turned off her bedside lamp, and tiptoed out of the room, closing the door behind him. It cracked open.

She heard him whisper out on the landing to Susan, 'She's out to this world.'

They crept into Susan's bedroom and closed the door.

Karen gripped the Colt 45. 'And soon so will you both,' she swore.

Paul and Susan entered her bedroom. She crossed to the window to close the drapes and saw Sam sitting in his car looking up at her.

She stepped away from the window. 'Sam King's back.'

'Should I go?' Paul asked, hesitatingly.

Susan nodded, angry with herself. He exited, closing the door.

Switching on the light she returned to the window for Sam to see she was alone, that Paul was no longer with her. Taking hold of the drapes to close them, she waved Sam 'goodnight'.

Sam curtly nodded back and she realized he wasn't fooled by her gesture.

She savagely pulled the drapes together, sat on the edge of the bed, and looked at herself in the dressing table mirror. 'Idiot!' she scathed to herself. 'You, stupid, stupid, idiot.'

Karen heard Paul exit Susan's room and close the door, knock on Morgan's, open it and say, 'Goodnight again.'

From inside his room, Morgan replied, 'Goodnight.'

Paul closed Morgan's door, turned off the landing light, entered his own room and shut the door.

Lying in the darkness of her room, Karen brooded.

Three inside the house wanting her dead, one outside. No phone line – denying her access to the world outside. If only she had a cell, but it was too late to chastise herself again for that.

But tomorrow, once the landline had been restored, she would somehow phone O'Hare.

And start to work on her plans for revenge.

Sweet, sweet revenge.

Fully awake, she tossed and turned as she lived her thoughts, trying to think of ways to prolong each of their deaths and make them more and more agonizing, letting them know how she'd been on to each one of them from the start, and now it was their turn to suffer – until death itself would be a merciful relief to them. Eventually, she reached the point where even her very thoughts were too much for her, and was about to take another half pill to give herself relief from them, but she decided it was too risky. Laying her head back, exhausted, on the pillow, her eyes got heavier and heavier and she felt herself falling asleep.

A bedroom door quietly opened out on the landing.

A shadow slipped across the landing to Paul's room, entered it and gently closed the door.

My husband, bitch.

Karen tried to open her eyes, but blackness again descended on her.

Time passed…the house lay in silence.

Out on the landing, a shadow crept out of Paul's room and back to its own room.

Karen turned, disturbed again, and slept on.

Sam sat alone in his car watching the house. The rain had stopped, but the sky was still dark and hanging over the forest, and under it the air was heavy and threatening, and from above it came the rumblings of thunder, and the sense that a flash of lightning would suddenly cleave the night sky and one of its split forks would strike down to earth like the last lethal lash of a serpent's tail.

A crow cawed. Others join in.

Wolves howled in the distance.

Sam looked through his window at the darkness.

If Paxton was intending to kill her soon, tonight would be the ideal night.

-four-

-35-

She had escaped them and was the only passenger on the plane as it sped through the clear blue sky above the dark clouds on its way to Naples. She had earned a glass of champagne. She called the stewardess over. 'Yes, madam?' the stewardess questioned as she leant over to her. She had Susan's face. Her look was triumphant. Behind her, wearing an all purple uniform, was a male steward holding a tray. He smirked at her. He had Morgan's face. The pilot and co-pilot and the security guard joined them, and looked down at her with Paul's and Sam's and Michael's faces. Paul wore a scornful smile, Sam's expression was pitiless, the set of Michael's jaw was resolute. All five closed in on her, surrounding her. Behind them materialized a sixth figure. They parted to let him get to her. It was Paxton. She shrank back from him in her seat. He came nearer and loomed over her. His eyes fixed on her, the eyes of a crazed man. Morgan offered his tray to him. Paxton took something off it. It was a blood stained carving knife. He raised it over her…

A distant flash of lightning illuminated Karen's bedroom drapes, briefly silhouetting the figure of a man hanging from a wire around his neck outside her window, then came a roll of thunder. It disturbed Karen's sleep. She jerked awake, cringing into her pillow from the fall of Paxton's knife. Shivering with fear, she realized it had been another nightmare, pulled the duvet tight around her, peered at her bedside clock, and saw it was just after 9.30.

Flinging the duvet aside, she got out of bed and crossed to her window and opened the drapes, and stepped back in shock as she saw the man dangling outside her window. He turned his face and looked in at her, and she saw his logo inscribed cap and padded dark blue parka and realized he was a telephone repairman standing on the top rung of a ladder. He stared at her too long, she realized she was in her underwear and attempted to hide her body with her arms. 'Sorry,' he mouthed, and returned to securing a new wire to the connection box above her window.

Briefly aware it was still cloudy and dark outside but that the rain had stopped, and Michael was sitting below in his truck, she got dressed in yesterday's blue dress but didn't apply make-up, put on her flat shoes, decided to use her crutches, and exited the room on to the landing.

Paul's bedroom door was open, his bed tousled. Morgan's door was slightly ajar. Through it she could see that his bed was made up, immaculate. Susan's bedroom door was closed. *Sleeping it off after a night of fucking Paul, the slut.* From the study came sounds telling that Paul was in it, maybe working on his book. Sitting on the top stair, she descended them one riser at a time, taking her crutches with her. Reaching the hall, she stood up and crutched into the dining room.

Wearing tan clothes today, down to his moccasin shoes, Morgan was sipping what looked to be black coffee from his usual mug as he stood surveying his designs spread across the dining table. He looked around as Karen entered. 'Great God,' he said, tetchy, 'I'll never get my work done.'

'Don't mind me, Morgan,' Karen said, brusque. 'I'm going through to the kitchen.'

'I meant him, Karen, not you,' Morgan apologized, indicating the phone repairman who was now working on reconnecting a wire to the box over the dining room window, securing it with stapled hooks tapped into the external clapboard wall. 'I hope you slept well. Especially after yesterday's last horrid call from—'

'I don't want to talk about it,' she cut him off. 'Use my studio. I won't be needing it.'

'Are you sure?' Morgan questioned.

'I wouldn't have offered it otherwise,' she snapped back.

'But will you be all right on your own?' Morgan persisted.

She almost screamed it at him. 'The repairman's only outside.'

Morgan drained his coffee and placed the mug on the table. 'There's coffee in the percolator should you want some.' He waited for her to say thanks, she ignored him and made for the kitchen. Morgan gathered his designs in an evident huff and headed upstairs.

Karen entered the kitchen, took a mug from a cupboard, poured herself a black coffee, and sat at the kitchen table and brooded back to last night and her vague recollections of it.

A shadow crept across the landing to Paul's room.

She sipped her coffee, trying to recall it more clearly.

A shadow crept out of Paul's room and back to its own room.

Susan – the treacherous bitch.

I hope the wolves and the crows tear you to pieces and you feel every bite, you slut.

The back door opened and the repairman entered the kitchen and saw her sitting at the table. 'Sorry about earlier,' he said, 'I just want to make sure you're reconnected.'

Crossing to the wall mounted phone, he picked up the receiver, dialed three numbers, replaced the receiver and the phone rang and continued to ring.

'Okay,' he said, 'you're good.'

He picked up the receiver to stop it ringing and heard Paul's voice come from it. 'Hello?'

'It's the repairman testing the line, Mr. Archer,' the man replied. 'You're reconnected.'

'Thanks,' said Paul, and the repairman replaced the receiver.

Karen stared at him as the implication of it hit her. 'What did you just do?' she asked him.

'Checked the line.'

'By dialing three numbers?'

'It's our ring-back number to confirm you're reconnected,' the man said. 'Saves me calling the operator.

Karen could feel her heart pounding. 'Can you tell me it?'

'Sorry. It's confidential.'

Karen crossed to a cupboard, opened it, pulled two bills from a tin. 'Twenty?' she offered him.

He wavered.

She pulled two more bills. 'Forty?'

He pocketed the bills. 'One-Eight-Three. But you didn't get it from me,' he said and exited.

Karen looked at the wall phone, hesitated, picked up the receiver, dialed 183 and depressed a connection prong. The phone rang, then stopped. Gently releasing the prong, she cupped her hand over the mouthpiece and listened.

'Hello?' asked Paul's voice.

Karen held her breath.

'Hello?' Paul repeated.

In his study, Paul heard only silence coming down the line, not even a static background. He depressed his cradle bar and released it, cupped his hand over his mouthpiece and listened.

In the kitchen, Karen heard a click from Paul's extension. She put hers back on its wall mount.

In his study, Paul heard the click of a receiver being replaced in its cradle.

He replaced his own receiver and brooded.

It was Karen, he knew it.

Knowing her, she would even now be working out the significance of her discovery.

It was time to end it.

In his cabin, Sam extracted the print-photo of Julia's mutilated body from his pocket, unfolded it and placed it on the table and brooded over it.

Julia's death had been inhuman, barbaric.

Whatever his own need for revenge, Karen shouldn't suffer that same fate.

In the kitchen, Karen's mind roiled as she realized the implication of the ring-back number.

The reason why Paxton's calls weren't recorded was that they'd been made for him by someone in this very house.

Paul?

No. He was always in the room when the calls came in.

Morgan?

Her mind sped back to the many calls.

Morgan was never with them when they were made.

It had to be Morgan…

Which proved, without any doubt, that he was in this with Paul.

And now made it very clear it was Paul who'd hired Paxton to kill her.

And equally clear that neither Sam or Michael were involved.

Michael was out there now in his truck — he would protect her.

She crutched out on to the back deck and peered around the corner of the house, and saw Paul exit the front door and make for Michael.

She re-entered the kitchen, crutched through the dining room to the hall and checked outside.

Paul was talking to Michael through the truck's open window.

Sam. She could call him to speed back and get her away from here.

She looked upstairs realizing that Paul's study was empty.

Maybe he'd made a note of Sam's cell number?

Discarding her crutches on the hall floor, she climbed the stairs to the landing.

There was still no sound from Susan's bedroom.

She crept down the corridor.

Her studio door was closed but she could hear the sounds of Morgan moving about inside.

She entered Paul's study and silently shut the door.

-36-

Karen looked around the room. It was the tidiest she'd ever seen. The only thing on Paul's desk was a laptop, not a notepad or sheet of paper in sight. Unusual for a writer, surely, she thought? Shouldn't he have jotted down his thoughts and ideas as he typed up his novel? Her father had been meticulously neat with his paperwork, but even he'd had documents spread across the desk before filing them in folders on his bookshelves at the end of the day, together with his reference books. But with Paul, even the shelves were empty. It was as if he was taking inordinate care not to reveal anything about who or what he really was.

She opened the desk drawers, all empty except one, and that held only documents folded up together. She opened them, there were three. One was their marriage certificate, the other two were birth certificates, one was hers, the other Paul's. Wrapped with the marriage certificate as if he had them ready to claim her estate as soon as she was dead. She saw that he was born in Queens, New York. He'd told her Chicago. It was another lie he had made up about himself, the deceitful slimeball. Seeing her name on the marriage certificate, she recollected the day they'd wed and she had so excitedly signed it, and made her fume at herself for being so naïve. Tearing it into shreds she turned to his laptop. Everyone kept their details and their memos somewhere. It was likely to be where Paul stored his phone numbers.

She cracked open the study door and peered out. The doors to her studio and Susan's bedroom were still closed. The house silent. Paul must still be outside. She would chance it.

She returned to the desk, sat in Paul's chair and switched on the laptop. Its logo screen came up and she saw it was password locked – she should have expected it, naïve again, she thought. She racked her mind trying to think of words associated with himself he might use, realizing he could return any moment, and God only knew what he would do to her if he caught her with his laptop on…

Dismissing "karen" – hers would be last word he would use, as well as it being too obvious – she tried "newyork", where he was born. It failed. So did "queens", and so did "bigapple".

Her mind sped to his acting career, roles he'd told her he was proud to have been chosen to play – even though none of them were starring parts – and straightaway thought of Curley in *Of Mice and Men*, an obnoxious character she thought, having read Steinbeck's book, evil, a bully to his wife, yet constantly making a show of keeping his hand soft to caress her – yes, that was Paul, playing a role that must have suited him to a T.

She typed in "curley" – it failed.

Desperate now, she tried to think of another word, and heard Morgan exit her studio. With no time to turn off the laptop she moved to the door and flattened herself against the wall behind it.

Morgan called out, 'Paul', and opened the door against her. Reflected in the window opposite, she saw him pause when he saw the room was empty, then he crossed to the laptop and switched it off with a flick that said he was angry with Paul for leaving it on.

As he turned to leave, a large, moth-like insect landed on the window. He eased the window open and caught it in his hand and brought it in, slowly pulled off a wing, then the other, dragging out the pain for the moth, and from the expression on his face, savoring it, then each leg, then its feelers, threw its writhing body back outside, shut the window and left the room, closing the door behind him.

Fighting off her revulsion at his cruelty, she realized that Morgan was not as he seemed, that his fastidious exterior held a more complex character, certainly one without normal feelings. She'd underestimated him – well, no more.

Cracking the door open and hearing him go downstairs, she returned to the laptop, switched it back on and tried "morgan" as a password. It failed. She tried "morganhale". It, too, failed. Getting desperate now, she typed "mhale" and the screen showed the last thing Paul had been looking at.

It was the face of a young woman, Under it was: "Kim, Miami. Worth: $1,000,000?"

Karen clicked forward.

A film clip taken by a cellphone played on the screen: of a young woman's swim-suited body being lifted onto a wooden pier from a coastguard boat.

Then the words: "ACCIDENTAL DROWNING. Realization: $1,364,000" flashed up on screen.

Karen stared at it appalled as she realized what it meant.

She clicked forward.

Another young woman's face showed on screen, and "Helen. New York. Worth: $2,000,000?"

She clicked forward again.

Another film played on screen: of a woman's body falling from a top balcony of a brownstone apartment block onto the sidewalk. 'SUICIDE' flashed up on the body and "Realization: $1,938,000".

She quickly clicked on, and caught her breath as the screen showed Julia's face, and under it: "Julia. Los Angeles. Worth: $2,500,000?"

The accompanying film, taken from behind the killer – another person had been in the room – focused on a carving knife repeatedly stabbing Julia as she retreated from it, trying to shield herself with her arms, then she crumpled to the floor. A black-gloved hand raised the hem of her nightie, and the carving knife hacked at her genitalia.

She shut her eyes to the gruesomeness of it, then forced them open and saw Julia's body now lying in a pool of blood with "KILLED BY JEALOUS LOVER" over it. "NOTHING – NOTHING – NOTHING" angrily flashing over it in red.

She swiftly moved on and, as expected now, saw her own face on the screen, with the words:

"Karen, Ravensburg, Wisconsin: $3,000,000?", then on the screen flashed "MOTOR ACCIDENT", and "FAILED – FAILED – FAILED" angrily flashed over it in red.

As she went to turn off the laptop, the film of Julia being murdered suddenly reshowed on screen, and she froze as Julia's face dissolved, to be replaced by her own as she backed away from the hacking knife, crumbled to the floor and the carving knife mutilated her vulva, and "REVENGE KILLING – REVENGE KILLING" repeatedly flashed up across her bloodied body.

Horror stricken, she slammed the cover of the laptop shut.

With an effort, she controlled her shivering and the anger welling up inside her, and forced herself to brood over the significance of what she had seen.

Paul was clearly a serial killer, marrying wealthy women for their money and killing them in various ways for no suspicion to fall on him. And in diverse parts across the States to avoid a local pattern and make the police there suspicious.

Except – Karen continued to brood – although with Kim's death in Miami, he could have been acting alone, someone else had clearly taken the film of Helen falling to her death in New York.

The same with Julia's death in LA. Someone else had been in the room taking a film of Paul killing her. Could it have been Morgan? A minute ago, she'd never have thought him capable of filming such a gory act, but since seeing him so cold heartedly kill the moth, she no longer knew.

But there was a world of difference between killing an insect and filming a young woman's death.

So, could it have been Paxton?

Paul and he could have plotted Julia's murder together – maybe Morgan, too, he could have been in on the planning part of it – then when it was clear there was no money in Julia's estate for them to share, they had looked for their next victim – and somehow chosen her.

Paxton wasn't a wronged lover after all, seeking revenge for Julia's death, it was all a set-up.

And yet, was Paul, scheming, heartless, though he was, capable of such a vicious killing?

No, it must have been Paxton who killed her and Paul who'd filmed it.

And Kim in Miami, it would have been Paxton who drowned her.

And Helen, New York, it was surely Paxton who threw her to her death and Paul who filmed it.

Surely…

And after Helen they had chosen Julia as their next victim – only to find she wasn't wealthy in her own right, and had then moved on to her in Ravensburg, in lonely north Wisconsin, perfect for faking a car accident with no witnesses to it.

As for Morgan Hale, that he was here with Paul in Ravensburg, confirmed he was involved in her intended death – and almost certainly in with Paul and Paxton on the others too – his role in it all being to maybe search and find the right victims for Paul to marry, and Paxton to kill–

She heard Susan exit her bedroom. Crossing to the study door Karen cracked it open and saw her standing on the landing, listening. Hearing nothing, Susan knocked on Karen's bedroom door and looked in, then descended halfway downstairs, listened again, and came back upstairs and started up the corridor.

Karen glanced around the room for something to defend herself with, but saw nothing, then heard Susan call out, 'Paul!' Peering out again, she saw her turn back at getting no response and re-enter her bedroom and close her door.

Karen rebooted the laptop.

Susan?

Was there anything on it proving Susan's involvement in Paul's plan to kill her? Exactly how deep did she fit into it all? Susan had definitely set her up to meet Paul in Chicago, but maybe she was no more than a pawn seduced into it by him? – and being kept sexually happy by him, as the shadow creeping across the landing to his room last night clearly told.

Karen clicked to the next screen.

It showed what was patently a draft letter. The first paragraph read:

As we agreed, marriage is but part one of the plan. It doesn't affect, or lessen my love for you, My heart, my very soul, are yours. For eternity.

So Susan was involved, the scheming bitch. Karen read on:

*When it's finally over with Karen, we'll take a long vacation together.
Just you and I, alone as planned. And to plan our next–*

The letter stopped in mid-sentence, as if Paul had been interrupted, leaving Karen puzzled.

Next…

She could understand Susan being involved in her murder. But the word next implied she was in it much deeper than that. Was she party to all the others before her, too?

Kim – as far away as Miami?

Helen – New York?

Julia – LA?

Involved with Paul from the very beginning? No, she couldn't have been…

And yet…

Karen recalled the many weeks at a time that Susan had spent away from Ravensburg, saying she was driving to antique sales up and down the US, yet returning with hardly anything purchased.

What if she'd been going off to stay with Paul? To plot with Paul?

And taking it a step further, maybe it was Susan – jealous of her having inherited her father's money – who had suggested her as their next victim?

Looking away as she brooded, she saw Paul's cellphone, half hidden behind the laptop cover on the desk. Maybe there was a saved text from Susan on it? Grabbing it, she called up his Inbox – it was empty. So, too, was his Sentbox. She called up his Images and, no longer able to be shocked, saw the original cell photograph of Julia's body, with the words:

PAUL DID THIS TO JULIA
I WILL DO THE SAME TO KAREN

So, it was Paul who had sent it to Susan, even saying – in the first person – that it was *he* who had killed Julia, not Paxton. But there again it proved nothing, it could have been written that way just to further scare her out of her wits.

Well, think on, husband dear, she thought, recalling that she was here to find Sam's cellphone number for him to come and get her, and take her the hell away from here.

She returned to the laptop.

In his cabin, Sam picked up his ringing cellphone. 'Sam King.'

'It's Bert, Sam,' Quinlan's voice came down the line. 'I checked on Archer as you asked me. It turns out he was married twice before Julia. But that's not all…'

Sam listened as Bert read out the details. 'I've sent a couple of patrol cops to Paxton's place,' Bert said. 'I'll let you know if they find anything.'

Thanking Bert, Sam ended the call, pulled the print of Julia's mutilated body from his pocket and looked at it.

Horrified by the butchery, he sat, conflicted with himself.

Could he let himself do nothing to save Karen from the same gruesome fate?

In his truck outside Clanryan, Michael deliberated over his notebook. His own cellphone rang. He answered it, 'Michael Rossi.'

Sam's voice came over the line, urgent. 'Michael, I'm on the way. Get Karen out of there now.'

'Paxton's cellphone, Sam,' Michael cut across him, stretching to his glove compartment for the gold-cased cellphone. 'I've got it. I kept it, hoping it would give me a lead. For it to be me saving her from him—'

Michael broke off as a man's dark shape loomed alongside him. He hastily switched off his phone, stuffed the notebook out of sight under his thigh, and looked up.

He'd seen some battle-crazed eyes when he was in 'Ghan.

But these were the craziest eyes he'd ever looked into.

And in his hand, he held a bloodied carving knife.

-37-

Before she could start searching the laptop for Sam's cell number, Karen heard a door open along the landing, and Susan called out 'Paul?' again. If the bitch catches me in here, she thought, she'll yell for Paul. I'll just have to forego her being eaten alive by wolves and kill her now.

She opened a cupboard for something to use as a weapon and saw her father's old hunting rifle propped up against a corner wall, and on the floor a box of bullets. Mind racing, she looked at it. When she'd cleared her father's study after he died, she'd put the rifle away in the loft.

She looked out of the window at Susan's car still against the tree trunk – and knew where the shot that nearly killed her had come from. In her mind's eye, she envisaged it...

The lower half of the study window is open, the rifle's barrel rests on the sill.

Susan's car comes around the bend out of the forest.

The sights focus on her in the front seat beside Susan.

A finger squeezes the trigger – but her father's rifle always pulled to the right.

The bullet smashes the car's windscreen and passes between her and Susan.

The car slews across the road and skids into the tree.

Karen was brought back to now as Susan again called out, 'Paul?' – closer this time as she came up the corridor.

Grabbing the rifle, Karen held it by its barrel like a club and hid behind the door.

Susan opened the door, saw the laptop on and entered the room. Karen swung the rifle at her. The blow was slanted at an angle and slammed her across her shoulders and the back of her head. Susan crumpled to the floor.

Karen grabbed a handful of bullets from the box, put one into the rifle's breech, and the rest inside one of her blue dress pockets. She could keep Paul and Morgan at bay with the rifle until she reached Michael, and get him to drive her the hell away from here.

She limped out of the room.

Speeding in his car through the dark forest, flattening bends, Sam now heard only silence coming from Michael's cellphone. He had a bad feeling about it.

'Michael,' he yelled into his cell. Still no answer from Michael. Sam put his foot down on the throttle, brooding how Paul and Paxton had been in it together all along.

Having conspired in Julia's death – Paul marrying her and Paxton killing her, thinking to share her wealth once Paul inherited it – it had gone kibosh when they found it was all in trust.

And so they'd chosen Karen as their next victim. Paul doing the marrying again, and Paxton doing the killing. But their original plan had gone wrong.

First, at Carvers Gulch where Paxton had failed in his attempt to force her over the edge. Then at Ravens Pond, when Michael rescued her.

Not only that, but Paul hadn't reckoned on Sam arriving on the scene – nor on him being a cop – nor on him getting Hank to raise the truck within an hour or so of it going under – at which Paul must have realized it was only a matter of a short time before the truck would be identified – so, too, would Paxton as its owner, and their past association with Julia would be revealed.

Maybe panicking instead of thinking clearly, and deciding – there and then, or perhaps later – that the situation now thrust on them meant they had to find another way to kill Karen – they'd devised a supposed hatred between them…

Brooding along this line, Sam flattened another corner.

…And so they had invented the story of Paxton seeking revenge for Julia's death, "a life for a life", as he had threatened in his phone calls, and once he had killed Karen and Paul had inherited the estate her father left her – even bigger than Julia's – he and Paxton would share it – recompense for losing out on Julia's wealth.

And what about Morgan Hale? Sam thought, as yet another sharp corner sped up at him.

There was little doubt he was involved in it – and maybe in the deaths of Paul's other two wives, Kim and Helen, too – probably for a lesser share of the spoils. It was also more than likely that Paxton was in on *their* deaths, too – the three of them working together as a team.

Except…

Why didn't Paxton kill Karen the first night, when he got into her room, instead of dragging it out in order to make her suffer? A quick death would have been the thing to do, and be well on his way back to Chicago in the hours before her body was discovered.

The only explanation for it – *and* the Christ effigy painted to look like a whore hanging from a tree – *and* the carving knife in her pillow

– *and* the dead crow lying on it – was that Paxton was a raving psychopath – as was evident by the way he'd killed Julia – hacking her to pieces and ripping her genitalia – and his wanting to make Karen to suffer for what, in his mind, she had made him suffer, was genuine.

And as much as Sam wanted revenge for Emma's death, there was no way he could let Karen be killed in that horrific way.

Entering a short straight, he tried again to call Michael: 'Michael, come in. Come in.'

Still no answer – something was very wrong, Sam could feel it.

He switched off his cellphone. It immediately rang.

He answered it. 'Sam King.'

'Sam,' Quinlan's voice came from it, urgent. 'The patrol cops I sent to Paxton's cabin found it burnt to the ground and under the charred floorboards they found what was left of a body. It's Paxton. They identified him from a death head's ring it's said he wore on his left index finger–'

Sam cut the call, rang Michael again, and swore as he waited for Michael to pick it up.

Limping across the landing to the top of the stairs, Karen reached for the handrail and overbalanced.

Dropping the rifle, she grabbed at an upright. Her momentum carried her down two risers. Twisting her body she held on and stopped herself going any further, but felt her spine stretch and knew she had pulled it again. Sitting on a riser she slid down them to the hall, reached for her crutches and raised herself on to them and looked up at the rifle, its barrel overhanging the edge of the landing. *Damn! Damn! Damn!* Feeling panicky without it, but no time to climb back for it with her ricked spine, she hobbled to the front door and peered out. There was no sign of Paul or Morgan. Michael was alone in his truck. Could she risk getting to him and have him drive her to Sam?

And then, fuck you, Paul, she thought, once Sam has called the police it will all be over for you. With what they'll find on your laptop, Wisconsin should bring back the death penalty for you to fry in the chair, and flames coming out of your head. Still, you'll be spending the rest of your life rotting away in prison, getting older and older and older every day, every hour, every minute, every second, knowing you'll never be able to spend a cent of your ill-gotten money. A fitting end for you, husband shit.

She opened the door and waved a crutch at Michael to attract his attention, but he didn't turn his head. Angry with him, she risked going out on to the porch and tried again. He still didn't see her. She looked around again, there was yet no sign of either Paul or Morgan. In desperation, she decided to chance it. Painfully crutching down the steps, she hobbled to Michael's truck, getting angrier and angrier with him as he drowsed on, head on one side, his window open–

She stopped in horror.

Perched on Michael's left shoulder, pecking at his neck, was a crow with large rear feathers - the son of Midas. Michael was doing nothing to stop him. Then she saw he had two bloodied holes where his eyes had been pecked out, and the son of Midas was tearing at a gaping cut to his throat that had half decapitated him, ripping Michael's flesh off with his black beak, dribbling blood.

She swiped at the son of Midas with her crutch but missed, and the crutch hit against the truck door. Cawing in protest, it turned his head and saw her, and flew at her talons outstretched to claw her face. Furiously, she fought it off with her crutches, and it flew away, angrily cawing.

Turning away from the terrible sight of Michael, she saw a gold cellphone trampled into the muddy ground by her feet. She leant down to pick up. From inside the truck came the ringing of another cellphone.

Averting her gaze from Michael's gory neck, she looked into the truck and saw the cell on the seat alongside his thigh. Tucked further under it, she glimpsed his notebook. Fighting off a wave of revulsion, she stretched past Michael's body for the ringing phone.

A hand clamped on her shoulder. She opened her mouth to scream. The hand spun her around.

Paul. He stifled her scream with his other hand, let go her shoulder, reached for the cell, hurled it to the floor and stamped it into the mud.

Karen pulled her mouth free and screamed at him. 'Paxton's killed Michael—'

'Paxton?' Paul scorned. 'Not unless he's risen from the dead.'

Karen stared at him – it was like she'd been hit in the face.

He sneered at her, contemptuous. 'His body's where it will never be found, burnt beyond recognition - the cost of prying too much into Julia's death.'

Karen's mind raced as she took it in.

Paxton dead?

Then who had driven the truck that tried to run her off the road?

Paul?

No, it couldn't have been Paul, she'd phoned him here and he'd answered her.

Morgan?

No, he'd arrived at the pond with Paul and tried, alongside him, to save her.

Sam?

No, he'd been sitting in his car by the side of the road as she sped past him.

Then who had crept into her room and buried the carving knife into her pillow, and placed the dead crow alongside it?

Michael?

Being a soldier it would have been easy for him to get into the house, and then to her bedside without being heard. And Paul had now killed him – not only to shut him up in case he broke down and confessed to the police after she was dead – but also for Michael not to share in her money–

Paul pushed her toward the house, ending her conjecturing.

'But after I call Sam,' he prodded her in the back, forcing her to crutch faster through the mud, 'and he sees both you and Michael dead, it's Paxton he'll think killed you both – and it's Paxton the police will be looking for.'

They reached the house. He pushed her up the porch steps.

'Especially when they find you cut to pieces,' Paul said. 'Just like Julia.'

-38-

As she reached the top of the steps onto the porch, Karen turned and slammed Paul with a crutch. The force took it from her grasp. Reeling from the blow, Paul fell back down the steps.

Karen hobbled into the house on the other crutch, slammed the front door closed and locked it.

Paul stormed back up the steps and punched his fist through the glass top of the door. His hand cut and bleeding, he clawed for the key.

Karen rammed her remaining crutch down on his arm and impaled his wrist on a glass shard. Its sharp point tore through his flesh, blood spurting from the gash.

Mindless of the pain, Paul's eyes fixed on her with hate through the smashed panel. He began to slowly draw his wrist up off the shard.

Karen pulled the key out of the lock and hurled it away, dropped her crutch and turned to the stairs. Grabbing the rail, she started to climb them, her eyes on the rifle on the top riser. Nearing it she grabbed it and dragged herself up on to the landing.

Below her, Paul freed his bloodied wrist off the shard and kicked at the door.

She limped to her bedroom and heard the front door burst open. Entering her room, she closed and locked the door. Behind it, came the sound of Paul pounding up the stairs.

As Paul shook her door she calmly stepped back into the room, cocked the rifle bolt, faced the door and raised the barrel at it.

Kicking the door in, Paul remained filling the doorway to intimidate her, then saw the rifle pointed at him and advanced into the room, sneering. 'You don't have the guts—'

She shot him in the balls.

Paul staggered back, clutched at his crotch and dropped to his knees. He looked down almost unbelievingly at the blood seeping through his clenched fingers, then looked up her, pain reflected in his eyes, beseeching her not kill him.

She delved into her skirt pocket for another bullet, inserted it in the breech and pointed at his chest. 'Goodbye Paul,' she said and shot him, tearing a hole in him, and he collapsed on his face on the bedroom floor. She looked down at his bleeding body with dispassion.

Morgan burst from his room on to the landing screaming and brandishing a carving knife wet with Michael's blood, and hurled into her bedroom.

Dressed all in pink – sweater, slacks, moccasins, pink cravat tucked into his pink shirt – he was wearing lipstick, make-up, rouge, mascara, and bedecked with gold bracelets, a gold necklace, his gold Rolex on one wrist – and on the other was her gold Cartier watch.

Terrified by his appearance, his sudden entrance, she raised the rifle to use as a club. Morgan snatched it from her and threw it aside. Dropping the knife, he knelt by Paul's body and cradled his head, kissing his forehead, his empty staring eyes, his lips. Mascara running down his face, he looked up at her, vicious through his streaming tears and screamed at her, 'You've killed him, killed him, you whore, you whore!'

The truth hit Karen. 'You! You and Paul!'

Rocking Paul in his grief, Morgan cried out, 'Yes! Me! Me! Me! I'm the one he loved! Who did you think it was? That other whore, Susan?'

Lying paralyzed on the study floor, Susan heard Morgan's voice carry from Karen's bedroom.

'Yes! Me! Me! Me! I'm the one he loved!'

Mortification welled up inside her at how easily she'd let Paul dupe her, how easily she had succumbed to his seduction of her all those months back, with his protestations of love and their future life of wealth together somewhere exotic, far away from Ravensburg, once Karen's money was theirs.

She tried to move her head – a splitting pain shot through it. She waited for it to subside, then tried to raise her aching shoulders, but had no strength to lift them from the floor.

She lay there, inert, as Morgan's contemptuous voice came from Karen's bedroom.

'Who did you think it was? That other whore, Susan?'

Karen slowly edged away from Morgan toward the rifle. 'Paul's love letters? They were for *you?*'

Still kneeling, soothing Paul's face in his lap, 'Of course they were to me,' Morgan sobbed, saliva mixing with his tears and mascara, a ghastly sight. 'We met at a club in New York. It was love at first sight. We danced together. It was heaven.'

Recalling the music drifting up from the sitting room to her bedroom, she flittingly envisaged the scene that had been enacted nightly below her as she lay in bed listening to it. *Morgan, wearing garish makeup, and Paul, dancing, an arm around each other's neck and fondling each other with their free hands and kissing.*

She looked at the knife wet with Michael's blood, lying on the floor where Morgan had dropped it, recalling the film on Paul's laptop of Julia backing away from a carving knife as it hacked her, and she looked at Morgan, horror stricken. 'Julia! It was *you* who killed her.'

'And the two before her.' He stroked Paul's face. 'I couldn't fuck the whores. But Paul could. He married them. I killed them. Except Julia was insatiable. Demanding more and more and more from Paul. So I had to punish her. Desecrated her, the *whore*.' He glared at her with hate. 'And you were the same. Paul told me how you were with him in Italy, always wanting more, just like Julia. That's another reason you have to suffer.' His other hand stretched for the knife and a manic look came into his eyes. 'Before I desecrate you, too.'

Still edging to the rifle, she realized she had to keep him talking. 'And it was you who drove the truck that tried to kill me.'

'Of course it was me,' Morgan disdained. 'To see you plunge to your death down that gulch was to have been my reward.'

'And Susan's part in it all?'

'She was the wrong Ryan. When we realized, it was easy for Paul to persuade her to introduce him to you. And after you were dead, she would have died, too. *You two, pathetic, whores.*'

Listening to Morgan's sneering disdain, Susan tried again to raise herself off the study floor, but again failed. Sobbing with frustration, angry at herself for being so gullible, so easy for Paul to seduce with his honeyed words, his blandishments, she collapsed back to the floor.

Sam sped into Raven's Corner. Ahead of him a broken branch, torn off an oak tree by the storm, was blocking the road. He braked to a stop, looked at the pond, and at last he remembered what he saw that day in his rear mirror.

Paul leapt from his SUV and ran for the pond.

The name he was shouting was, 'Morgan! Morgan!'

He dived into the pond behind the slowly sinking BMW and under the surface.

Moments passed.

He resurfaced – with Morgan.

They embraced – like lovers.

Paul swam to Karen's door. Morgan peeled off black gloves and swam to the passenger door.

Pulling at the doors as if trying to open one, they rocked the car, sliding it further into the pond.

Stomping on the gas, Sam drove up the verge, around the fallen branch and sped down the road.

'Today I was going to kill you,' Morgan wept. 'I got dressed for Paul – for us to celebrate before calling Detective King.' He reached for the carving knife. 'But you're still going to die for killing Paul.' He wiped his tears and stared at her, his eyes now psychotic. '*You whore.*'

Karen grabbed for the rifle.

Morgan dived at her to stop her.

She got to it first and clubbed him with it.

Morgan collapsed on the floor.

Karen crawled past him.

Morgan snatched the rifle from her and grasped at her ankle.

She kicked his hand off and crawled out of the room.

Sam sped out of the dark forest into the last corner, and saw Clanryan ahead of him, standing grim against the still grey sky. He could see Michael's outline sitting in his truck – his head seemed to be tilted at an odd angle. Sam flattened his foot on the peddle.

Grabbing the handrail, Karen fled limping down the stairs.

Her foot slipped halfway down and she tumbled to the hall, ricking her spine again.

Lying there on her back she looked up at the landing, unable to move.

Morgan tore out her room and saw her stretched out and helpless below him.

He stood there at the top of the stairs holding the bloodied carving knife. Then he slowly descended, extending the moment.

Reaching the hall, he looked down at her, his eyes full of loathing.

Karen grabbed at her discarded crutch lying beside her.

Contemptuously, he took it from her and tossed it aside.

He straddled her, pinned her arms to the floor with his knees and raised the knife.

-39-

Morgan suspended the carving knife over Karen, Michael's fresh blood staining the blade, dragging it out, getting sadistic pleasure from the fear and the horror he could see in her eyes, that the sharp steel was about to enter her flesh, and after it would come the slicing of her pudendum.

Sam's car entered the dirt track and raced for the house.

'Detective King to the rescue,' Morgan sneered, 'but too late.'

He raised the knife higher to plunge it into her.

Susan hurled down the stairs and dived at Morgan, knocking him aside.

Snarling at her, he rose to his knees, still holding the carving knife.

Susan poleaxed him with the crutch and knelt alongside Karen and held her tight.

Outside, Sam's car screeched to a halt outside the house, and he leapt out of it.

Seeing crows tearing at Michael's throat, he pulled his revolver and ran for the front steps.

In the front hall, Morgan rose again and raised the knife over Susan's back.

From out on the deck, Sam fired.

Morgan flew backwards, hit in the shoulder and dropping the knife.

Sam entered, knelt beside Karen and Susan and held them both.

Morgan grabbed the knife. Holding it high, he came screaming at Sam.

Sam emptied his revolver at him.

An ambulance with Michael's, Paul's and Morgan's bodies drove down the dirt track away from Clanryan, followed by a police car. Turning left into the road, they disappeared around the corner into the forest.

Sam exited the house supporting Karen with his arm around her back. Susan followed. Sam gave her his free arm to hold. Reaching his car, he helped Karen into the back seat and opened the front door for Susan to sit beside him, then got into his driver's seat, said something to Susan and briefly smiled at her. She fleetingly smiled back and he headed away from Clanryan down the dirt track and into the road and turned right.

Sitting in the back seat, Karen got Michael's notebook out of her pocket and saw his entries.

SUSPECTS

killer: ~~unknown (loner/hitman??)~~
John Paxton (loner/hitman??) if hitman, hired by:
    Paul Archer (motive - money)
    Morgan Hale (motive - money)
    ~~Susan (motive - money)~~
    Sam (motive - revenge)

Poor Michael, she thought, all he was doing was trying to work out who was wanting to kill her, he wasn't involved in it himself after all. Ah, well, she shrugged him off...

She looked at Sam and Susan, seemingly getting on well in the front.

But not you two shits, she brooded.

You both wanted me dead, too.

And you've both yet to pay.

Paul and Morgan didn't die the way I planned for them, but you two will.

The wolves, the crows, are still waiting for you in the woods, cousin dear.

And you're still getting your head blown off in Positano, Sam King.

She gave a last look back at Clanryan. Sam's car rounded the corner into the forest and Clanryan went from her sight.

The son of Midas flew out of the oak tree and perched on Clanryan's chimney, and gave a sharp ko.

From the surrounding trees, crows filled the sky as they descended on the house. They settled on the roof, the windowsills, the porch, until the house was black with them. Together they cawed in chorus, a cacophony of sound.

The son of Midas gave another sharp ko, they all went silent.

Enthroned above them, he declared, 'My name is Midas.'

His voice was deep, gravelly.

William Ryan's spirit still ruled over Clanryan.

Richard Rees

Richard Rees is originally from Wrexham, North Wales, where he had an accountancy practice, but became a writer after the deaths of his young wife, Richenda, then his only daughter, Elisabeth, from ovarian cancer. He now lives a quiet life in the seaside town of Llandudno, at the foot of the Snowdonia National Park, doesn't drink or smoke, and so sounds a bit of a bore, but is gregarious, keeps fit, swims, drives fast and doesn't play golf.

For more information on Richard's books, including where to purchase them, or to contact Richard, go to

www.richardhrees.com

42253035R00200

Printed in Poland
by Amazon Fulfillment
Poland Sp. z o.o., Wrocław